ME SOLDIER

Bill Tainsh

Me Soldier
First published in Australia by Bill Tainsh 2023

*A catalogue record for this
book is available from the
National Library of Australia*

ISBN: 978-0-6486044-0-2 (pbk)
ISBN: 978-0-6486044-1-9 (ebk)

Typesetting and design by Publicious Book Publishing
Published with the assistance of Publicious Book Publishing
www.publicious.com.au

The author acknowledges the Traditional Custodians of country throughout Australia and their connections to lands, waters and communities. He pays respect to Elders past and present and extends that respect to all Aboriginal and Torres Strait Islander peoples today. He honours more than sixty thousand years of storytelling, art and culture.

For Christine

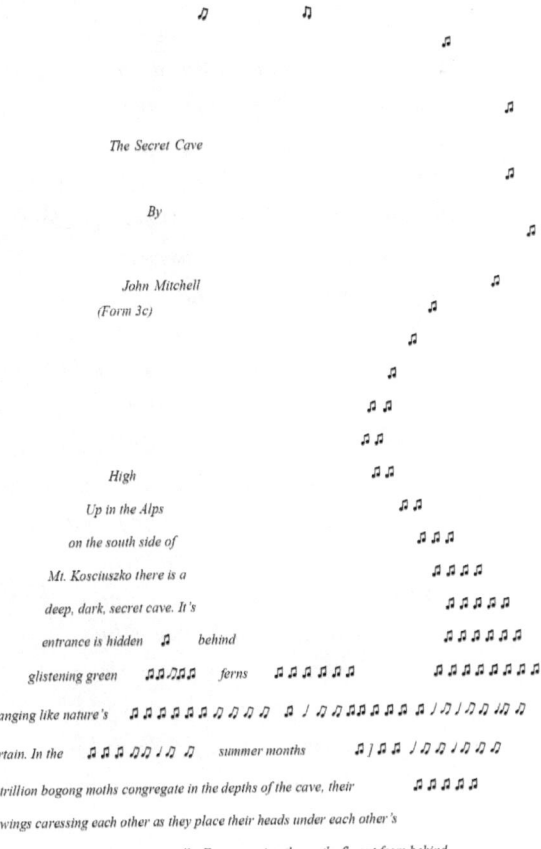

The Secret Cave

By

John Mitchell
(Form 3c)

High

Up in the Alps

on the south side of

Mt. Kosciuszko there is a

deep, dark, secret cave. It's

entrance is hidden   behind

glistening green   ferns

hanging like nature's

curtain. In the   summer months

a million, trillion bogong moths congregate in the depths of the cave, their

soft and downy wings caressing each other as they place their heads under each other's

wings so they can form layers on the damp cave walls. Every evening the moths fly out from behind

the ferns and spiral upwards into the night sky, moving through the mountain air like musical notes. There is

little food for them in the Alps and many don't survive the summer so when autumn comes around the survivors return   thankfully

to their birth places on the plains below to feed and procreate. The secret cave is left in peace until springtime.

The End

A soldier, a forward scout, a four-day war
veteran, feebly chopping his way through green,
green rainforest. Sweet, mouldy, foreign.
Pressure from behind to go faster, counter
pressure from entangling vines to go slower.
Fear, bravery, fatigue and warm rain dripping.
His right hand blistered and raw absorbing his
thoughts. Tape wrapped around the bastard impractical
machete handle might help … when they'd harboured
up … later … tonight … lots of it … maybe rags
under the tape. Armalite on his left shoulder.
When the first shot sounded it was muffled by the
rainforest, but it was the loudest noise he had ever heard.
It blew his senses apart.
Blood pumped in a microsecond to the
extremities of his body, his
fingernails, toenails, scalp.
Machete dropped, he dropped.
A cry of contact and return fire from behind him.
All his terrified focus on the jungle in front of him.
Then he saw it.
Movement.
A human form.
And he fired.
And the screaming was instantaneous.

Nine minutes later he was still in the
same spot, on his knees now,
face buried in the compost of the forest floor.
Shivering.
Shivering in the now icy rain. Penetrating
his greens, his milk white
skin, his non-fat layer, organs and bones.
His body as foreign as his surrounds,
not connected to his being.
Teeth bouncing together in crazy time,
cheeks shaking the boogaloo,
Coming away from their tendons,
shoulders heaving, feet and hands
spasming in the leaves beside him.

Chapter 1

He didn't want to open his eyes. Didn't want to know where he was, who was around him, what was around him.

But he wanted to break free from the screaming inside his head. The same screaming that echoed back through the years. Made in Vietnam. Packaged, exported to Australia but could never be unpackaged.

He allowed his lids to open into slits only to be blinded by starbursts of light. Quickly closing them he reached under his blanket for the bottle. It was empty.

A hard surface under him but not the concrete pavements he was used to, no clicking and clumping sounds from the heels of passers-by and none of their wafting perfumed body odours. Only a strong smell of mildew and the buzzing sound of his own ears, a minor torment among many. He wondered vaguely if he was safe. He remembered something about a barking savage dog and his right hand tightened around the neck of the bottle. Cold smooth and effective. He'd used a bottle before and he'd use one again on any man, woman or beast that menaced his addled world. He was beyond caring about consequences.

Rolling over, his senses surfacing one by one, John Mitchell realised he was up high in a dilapidated children's cubbyhouse. He pushed open a kid-sized door hanging precariously off one rusted hinge and saw a long backyard with timber and other building junk stacked down either side of a lawn with a house at the far end.

With no immediate threats to his well-being and the screaming inside his head having retired to its corner, John Mitchell felt overwhelmed by a weariness of mind and body. He squirmed to the back of the cubby, wrapped his lonely blanket tightly around his shoulders and, with the bottle-bludgeon lying on the floor within reach, drifted off.

Inside the house at the other end of the yard a lone woman was using her toilet. For Frankie her toilet cubicle was like a sanctuary. An inner sanctuary in the bigger sanctuary of her home. With the toilet door closed the four walls became an enclosing shield of titanium, keeping all things out, allowing her thoughts the freedom to flow undisturbed from their hidey-holes. She could examine them at will, unpressured by anything. For a precious few minutes, longer on weekends, her life would make sense. Or the day ahead, at least would make sense.

Today she sat contemplating what could be a tricky morning work session. A meeting with Abshir's mother, the tall Somalian woman she had seen leaving Amelia's office yesterday in tears. Poor thing.

Fearsome, Amelia had described her. Even you will struggle. Too intense for me. The refugees are your area.

Oh well. We'll see, Frankie thought to herself. At least I've got the afternoon off for once.

She flushed the toilet and left her little closet of calmness to face the bathroom mirror. Oh god, my eyes. Dark circles. That barking dog from next door. Why can't they keep it quiet at night?

Frankie tilted her head one way and then the other so that the overhead light caught both sides of her face, the mirror light not having worked for ages. Moisturiser first, concealer for my moon crater eyes and maybe rouge today. She sucked her cheeks in which accentuated her high cheekbones.

Something to be thankful for, she mused. They're like coat hangers keeping the wrinkles at bay. She smiled at herself and began working in the moisturiser. When she had finished she quickly ran a brush through her shoulder-length fair hair.

Done.

Her home had become her second oldest friend. Like most friendships, they didn't always get on, particularly on cleaning days, but they had shared the highs and lows of family life and could now reminisce together.

The old timber house spoke through every ding in the ornate dado rail, all the phonetically varying creaks in the floorboards that signalled the whereabouts of anyone moving around, the height marks of their daughter scratched onto the kitchen door architrave, and other more mysterious stains and odd marks from previous inhabitants.

She was making the long trek from the bathroom to her bedroom through the never used dining room when there was a dull thud on the dining room window.

She let out a small cry of angst, knowing full well the thud was yet another bird flying into the window.

Damn Asian mynahs, she cursed to herself. They were like a squadron of fighter planes ganging up on the locals and causing them to fly for cover and hit the glass. She peered out the window and sure enough, there was a bronzewing pigeon lying stunned on the grass outside the window. She restrained herself from rushing outside and helping the bird. Last time she did this the bird had become more stressed. Better to leave it. Sometimes they recovered, sometimes they didn't.

She unplugged her phone from the charger beside her bed and began checking messages, heading for the kitchen. She scrolled through them.

Work – work – ah … Angela. Grandbaby photos.

Before she could open the photos, the phone began ringing. Damn. Amelia.

No Amelia. Sorry, I can't put in a full day today.

Lighting the gas, kettle on.

Have faith Amelia. The new girl will be more than capable of managing. Everything will be fine.

Spooning her beloved Lady Grey hand-blended into the stained old teapot.

No, money's not the problem. You know that. Anyway, the budget is stretched to the max. I'm sorry.

As Frankie continued to fend off the imploring Amelia, she began cutting up fruit for her morning fruit salad. The knife was blunt: Knife sharpening had always been his job, she thought. Never mind, I'll just have to buy a new set of knives; I can afford them.

Ok. Fine, fine, she said brusquely to Amelia. I'll be in soon. Bye.

Now she could look at her daughter's latest baby photos, all the way from London.

What pleasure, what bliss. She looks so beautiful – and wearing one of the tops I sent her. The fit looks nearly perfect.

She made the tea and, still looking at the photos on her phone, went back to the dining room to see if the pigeon had recovered. It had. No sign, flown off.

Good.

She unlocked the rear door leading out into the backyard to pick a grapefruit for her fruit salad. Every morning she went through this. The slight feeling of dread before turning the door handle.

She steeled herself, opened the door and, as usual, felt that the whole backyard was staring at her. It was all him, an attack of sorts from every angle, trying to inveigle her emotions, rob them so she would have no resources left to tackle the day. She took a deep breath and stared back defiantly. She caste her eyes over his leftover building material, most of which she could itemise having helped him with his ordering.

Stockpiled aluminium windows, various timbers, four by twos, six by ones, treated hardwoods in the weather by the side fence, pine in the lean to.

He'd always said the backyard was his and the house hers. His territory, her territory. Well, I'm invading your territory, she said, looking at her rows of Chinese cabbage and heirloom tomatoes now stretching all the way from his rusting old ute to the back door. Having stared him down, she began walking up the strip of lawn in the middle of the yard.

The grapefruit tree was against the back fence between the bungalow and Angela's old cubbyhouse. But that was all him too, of course. He'd made the bungalow for his mother, now long gone, and the cubbyhouse was so typical of him, never quite finished. No stairs. Just the temporary ladder.

And it was then that she noticed it.

The ladder.

It was in place leaning against the now dilapidated deck that supported the small cubby about two metres above the ground.

She never left the ladder in place.

It was a habit that went back to the days when the Greek neighbours had toddlers who could climb and she was worried they would fall through the rotting deck.

She looked down at the spot where it usually lay in the grass under the cubby.

It had been there so long that the shape of the ladder was perfectly etched yellow in the green grass.

Frankie tried to peer up into the cubby, but her view was blocked by the surrounding deck.

She tentatively placed one foot and then the other on the bottom rung of the ladder. The ladder felt secure so she began climbing until she was head and shoulders above the mouldy deck floor timbers.

The first thing she saw was the empty wine bottle and then the filthy khaki blanket.

There was someone underneath it.

Frankie froze, the ladder suddenly felt wobbly and unsafe. If the intruder rushed at her she would be stuck on the ladder. She looked down and for a moment considered jumping backwards but she was up too high. Her attention returned fearfully to the intruder but there was still no movement from under the blanket.

She waited and watched.

Gradually her fear subsided and she began to feel annoyed. She decided to try and wake him.

She spoke in a small voice.

Excuse me.

There was no response.

She took a deep breath and tried again.

Excuse me. You're trespassing. This is private property.

Still no response.

I said excuse me! I'm going to call the police. This is a private backyard.

Again, there was no response. Frankie could just detect the rise and fall of someone breathing under the blanket. The uninvited guest was alive but out to it.

Frankie pulled herself up onto the deck so she could examine the intruder more closely.

He wore glasses. Comically large glasses on a small wrinkled face, fixed tight to his head with a knotted strip of elastic.

Frankie thought he looked too old and frail to have scaled the high corrugated iron rear fence. Behind it was a cobblestone alleyway which led down to a park where homeless people sometimes gathered. He may have come up this but entered from the neighbour's side which would explain their barking dog last night.

Deciding the sleeping form looked altogether too frail to represent a physical threat, Frankie leant through the doorway and, ever the cautious one, removed the bottle.

She wanted to try and shake him awake but was loath to touch him. His breath and clothing reeked of alcohol and stale sweat.

You're being ridiculous, she told herself. You've done this before, he won't bite.

Frankie placed the tips of her fingers on the blanket where it was stretched over his shoulder. It felt coarse and damp. She gave him a tentative shake that had no effect on his sleeping form but caused the blanket to fall away. She noticed a small tattoo on the back of his right hand, a heart pierced by a key.

I know that symbol.

She thought for a moment and then it came to her. Roc's old base drum from the band he'd been in before The Snoopies. Sure of it. Can't think of their name, but it'll come.

And under it another small tattoo, AB POS. A blood group, probably military.

That's enough for me, she thought. If I call the police or the Salvos it will mean waiting around and being late for work. No police, I'll leave him alone. Perhaps he'll be like the stunned pigeon and fly off when he's recovered.

The traffic in Bell Street was hell, only two o'clock and a parking lot already.

The driver behind Frankie was continually pushing closer to the rear of her car, refusing to let in other cars that were hopefully inching forward from side streets trying to join the vehicular dirge.

Frankie was more generous, leaving a gap when she could to let in other cars which she supposed would be infuriating the driver behind her.

Too bad.

She was thinking about her meeting that morning with Abshir's mother. The woman's English had been almost non-existent but there was no misinterpreting her anguish; it was palpable. Frankie had made a list of all the everyday problems the woman was contending with but the main one was accommodation. How was she supposed to send Abshir to school when she was in different temporary housing each week? Frankie decided she would make some calls from home this afternoon.

It started to rain, and the traffic slowed even more. Melbourne.

As soon as she entered the backyard, rain pelting off her umbrella, she knew he was still there.

A shape sitting upright in the cubby.

How would she handle this? Same as normal, she guessed. Press on. Up the ladder. Oh god, look at him. Sitting there like a little bird, peering at her from behind those ridiculous glasses.

Just speak your mind girl.

Hello, she said firmly. This is private property.

He spoke quickly. Instantly apologetic.

Oh yeah. Look I'm real sorry. I got sort of lost last night. Some dog mistook me for its bone.

He seemed to sense Frankie's eyes go to his bare, bony shins now protruding from under the blanket: connection drawn.

Can't blame it I s'pose, he added.

Was there a twinkle from behind those glasses?

Anyway, look, he said, I'll be gone as soon as this rain stops. Promise.

Can I give you a lift somewhere? The Salvos perhaps?

No, no. I'm right. Not keen on the clientele there.

I see. Ok then. Well … I'm getting wet here.

You get out of the rain, I'll be fine.

Sure?

Yeah, I'll be right. No worries.

Frankie was halfway across the backyard heading for the house when she faltered. What the heck, the cubby was leaking.

A minute later she was back with the key to the bungalow.

It took some time for him to make a shaky descent of the ladder, blanket still wrapped around his narrow shoulders.

She opened the bungalow door for him.

You can wait in here until the rain stops.

Aw, that'd be great. You've got no idea … this looks great. Real great.

But it's my space and I would like you to respect that.

I understand where you're coming from. Totally. If everyone respected everyone else's space … well we probably wouldn't even have wars, would we?

Perhaps not.

The bungalow smelt mouldy, so Frankie opened one of the windows.

I can heat you up some leftover dhal if you like?

There was definitely light behind the glasses now.

I couldn't say no to that. That would be so good. You've no idea.

Frankie, who was trying to maintain her 'gruff' face couldn't help smiling at the man's unfettered enthusiasm.

It's only dhal. Not very exciting I'm afraid.

Oh, it'd be great.

He didn't know what dahl was but anything that filled the aching hole in his guts would be heaven-sent. Maybe he'd found a pint-sized, temporary heaven.

Frankie gave the pot of dahl a final stir and turned off her stove. She poured it into a bowl and headed for the back door.

The rain had eased so there was no need for her brolly.

She knocked on the bungalow door and there he was. Big glasses dominating his face. Greying close-cropped hair, baggy old track suit pants and crumpled weatherproof jacket.

It occurred to her that he wasn't all that uncared for. He could obviously do with a shower but she had seen a lot worse.

You beauty. Thankyou. Thankyou. Taking the food and backing away into the bungalow.

Frankie stood poised in the doorway ready to leave but curious.

He gestured with the bowl toward a chair, already beginning to eat.

Your space. Go for it.

I hope you like dhal. I'm afraid I don't eat meat.

Frankie moved the chair slightly toward the still open door as she sat down.

Oh, you've no idea. This is great.

He was fairly shovelling the food into his mouth and he chewed in an unusual open-mouthed kind of way.

Frankie had never heard anyone eat with so much noise.

She repeated her earlier offer of a lift but after a moment of thought he shook his head.

Do you have somewhere to sleep tonight?

This time he just looked at her, mouth too full to speak, or perhaps unwilling to answer.

Frankie decided to move things along a little; after all, it was 'her space' and he was taking it up.

You spent last night in my daughter's old cubbyhouse. So how did you get there?

This caused a cessation of the vigorous mastication. There was a shrug followed by a childlike look of guilt.

Can't say I'm that sure to tell you the truth. I'd had a few.

Where have you been sleeping?

All over really. Lately, anyway.

And before? The Salvos? White knights?

Nah, steer clear of all that lot.

So?

I was at my cousin's old boyfriend's place. Besanko. Not that far from here.

So, you could walk home?

Not a chance, he's a weirdo. Never going back there.

He was now looking at Frankie. Agitated. Furrowed brow visible over the glasses.

Can't even tell you what I found out about him, and to think he was with my cuz. Makes me wanna throw up just to think about it.

Well, we had best not go there, then.

Frankie decided on a quick change of subject and indicated the tattoo on the back of his hand, she had remembered the band.

The Keystones.

This had the desired effect. Instant engagement, agitation forgotten.

You are *kidding* me.

A huge grin spread across his face, as big as the glasses.

How did you know that? Nobody recognises that tattoo.

I remember the heart and the key, they were on Roc's old base drum.

You know Roc?

Did. In a band with him and Dicko many moons ago but haven't heard from them for years.

Which band?

Frankie was wondering if she shouldn't be a little more reticent about sharing her life with this down and out baby booming relic from the past, but she was enjoying herself.

The Snoopies. Later I went solo, folk.

The Snoopies, wow. I remember Dicko being in absolute awe of your voice. Yeah, then solo, protest stuff. Comin' back to me now; The Station Hotel, that's where I seen you. Solo at the Station Hotel, not long after I got out of the army.

Frankie couldn't repress a fond smile. The Station Hotel. I loved playing that place.

Well I'll be buggered. What's your name?

Frankie Sanderson. I was Frankie Raye Jamieson back then.

She held out her hand and they shook formally.

John Mitchell. I was the bass player. Played bass.

You boys were good, such a pity you broke up. I remember Dicko saying one of you got called up to do National Service.

Yeah, that was me.

Vietnam?

He nodded.

Do you still play?

This caused some mirth.

Hell no. Don't even own a toothbrush let alone a guitar. Travel light these days.

There was a silence and he resumed eating. Frankie remembered the phone calls she needed to make for the Somalian woman and stood up.

Ok. Well, I'll let you eat in peace. Great to chat. Those days may have been a moment in time, but they were a really special moment in time. For me, anyway.

You can say that again.

Frankie was on her way out but, in two minds, she stopped in the doorway and turned to face him. He's trouble but we have connections, she was thinking.

He looked up at her hopefully. This was an all too common scenario for him.

The look tipped the scales his way.

Ok, she said, you can stay here for a bit but just remember one thing please.

The big smile returned.

I know, your space. And I will respect it and can manage a bit of rent if you want, you can rely on me.

Frankie looked down at him, perched on the edge of the bed, bowl gripped in both hands like a squirrel with its last nut.

Reliable? Highly unlikely, she thought. But she couldn't resist a smile as she walked back to the house.

Only three weeks later, but it seemed like a lifetime. Frankie waking for the third morning in a row to the screaming. John's screaming. Pitiful. Not crazy full throated, more a startled child. Short and sharp, then silence. Why did I not see this coming, why did I let him stay on, she thought to herself. Vietnam vet, alcoholic, derelict. With all my years of experience ....

John woke to someone vigorously shaking him. Total confusion, his mind still submerged in his nightmare. A female voice cutting through the confusion, a now vaguely familiar female voice, calling his name. Shooshing him. When he opened his eyes he could make out her form, blurry against the morning light. She was holding out something toward him, a cup of tea. She was now asking him a question. Not inclined to answer. Sitting up. Taking the cup of tea from her. Another question. Silence. Sipping the tea. Sweet, the infused tea aroma. More questions.

Was it Vietnam? Taboo subject, but this woman was turning out to be ok, a bit of alright, so he managed a reluctant grunted acknowledgment.

What happened? – You wouldn't want to know.

One incident or many? – You've got no idea.

Frankie watching while he continued to sip on the cup of tea, sensing he was beginning to return from wherever he had been with each sip. When he stole a look out the window to see that it was indeed a new day, she asked quietly. Where you in Vietnam for one or two tours of duty?

His response was surprisingly quick. No, no. No full tours of duty. Only went in late as a reinforcement. Me and a mate.

A mate?

Yeah, a bloke called Chub. West Australian. Came from a cattle station. He was everything I wasn't, but we got on strange enough. We knew half the platoon from back in infantry training. They all got posted to the battalion before it left Oz and me and Chubby were shoved in a reinforcing unit. We all finished up together anyway. But that's all water under the bridge. Yesterday's crap. You wouldn't want to know.

I do want to know. Talking about what happened is essential to peace of mind. Not just yours, but mine. I need my sleep and neighbours are complaining.

I'm makin' a racket, eh? Bloody nightmares.

So, Frankie asked. You saw action?

A bit here and there. They pulled us all out when the war was closing down. Back to ... he gave a vague 360-degree wave around the bungalow... this.

But something happened ... the nightmares?

A bit. There was one thing happened. Pretty bad.

Can you tell me about it? Like I said, it helps to talk about these things.

Not much to talk about. It was so long ago I can't even remember what really happened and what didn't really happen. Things stick, but over the years you lose trust in your own memory, if you know what I mean.

You could start by telling me the basics if you want? Were there many enemy? Was it a big battle?

Behind his glasses, John's eyes retreated a little. His face deadened.

There was no enemy. We were all mates. On both sides. Hedley's section and our section.

Frankie struggled to comprehend for a moment but the more she thought about what he had just said, the more sense it made. She had to be very careful about how she phrased her reply. She knew little about warfare, but one term came to mind.

Friendly fire?

John nodded grimly. His answer was obviously well worn.

Nothing very friendly about it, 'cept we were all friends.

Some of your friends were killed?

One and one injured.

One and one injured. Frankie repeated his words while she carefully thought through the structuring of her next sentence. She spoke softly.

John, did you kill one of your friends?

Anger flashed across his face. Brief, but it was the first time she had seen it in him.

Everyone opened up, no knowing any bloody thing.

But you all may be carrying the guilt.

Wouldn't know about that.

Frankie could see he was clamming up. She gave it one last try.

Can you tell me a little more about what specifically upsets you?

Too long ago, can't remember. Best left alone. He handed back the empty teacup and stood up. Sorry. Gotta go, indicating the toilet. When she heard the toilet door close and lock Frankie knew that was the end of their conversation. She might as well start readying herself for work.

Inside the toilet, John was sitting on the bowl, head in hands. He could remember what had happened and no matter how hard he begged his memory to let up and forget, it ignored him and kept churning out the same vision, the same sounds, the same crystal clear detail.

Chapter 2

The river paddock was flat, twenty miles across with not a single feature to break the horizon, southern half criss-crossed by a myriad of dry channels that formed part of the upper Murchison in Western Australia.

A flock of pink galahs was making the daily journey home from their feeding grounds in the open mulga country to their nest holes in the river gums that lined the channels. Sun low and shadows long. Only movement below a small mob of kangaroos unhurriedly exiting the path of two riders who were making their way across the open plains to the north.

Chubby Jackson's brain was in neutral, gaze hypnotically fixed on his horse's shadow gliding steadily over the ground. A succession of quartz, ironstone, tussocks of dried out Mitchell grass and stunted blood bush passing beneath.

Astronaut was a good walker if nothing else. Mouth on him like an old boot and slow into a gallop but he could walk along. Anyway, he was following. Chub's mind clicked into gear, turning by habit to his whereabouts. They were headed for the side gate into Paddy's but it was somewhere in the middle of a fifteen-mile run of fence. All looked the same. No stock pads to follow because there was no windmill at the gate.

A chubber at birth, hence the nickname, but merely solid now. Startling blue eyes in a cherubic face that could make a mother swoon. A year of swinging burning hot crowbars and scaling fifty-foot windmill towers since he had been home from Agricultural College had put paid to any leftover baby blubber. All sweated away into his wide brimmed Akubra and faded blue work shirts, rinsed into cattle troughs and melted into the baking hot red dirt. Fodder for the ants. Life a series of opening and closing gates leading he knew not where. Which way to go? What to do? Who to believe? But he was beginning to trust his instincts … just a little. One thing was for sure, his dad was holding the biggest, widest, most thorny gate open for him, succession of Eumarella, the family cattle station. All expectations lead through that one and he didn't mind the thought but wasn't in any rush

He turned in his saddle and squinted into the setting sun looking for the only signpost he knew, Mount Thomas, but everything was flat. Flat in all directions.

Ahead of him was the young Yamaji man, Hedley, Frank's nephew. Chub hardly knew him, his first day's mustering but he was leading the way. When they had yarded the cattle about an hour ago Hedley had been waiting, already mounted while Chub secured the gate, and off without a word. Chub had just followed.

Now he was musing about the situation. It was such a fine line. Dad always on his back about taking charge, setting the pace. We gotta make a quid. Stock numbers, labour costs. Let them do the blackfella stuff, they're good at all that, but you've gotta keep them going, kick their black arses.

Up ahead, Hedley leaned forward in his stirrups, his wild curly black hair tucked under a torn old hat that, along with a fearsome brow, shaded sensitive billy-tea eyes that could retreat in an instant. No one needed to kick his black arse, it was numb enough already from the cobbled together saddle the bossfella had meted out to him only days before. Copper studs that had been used in a last-ditch attempt to hold the saddle together were poking through the leather.

As Hedley rode his thoughts were not on the gate he was headed for, or the surrounding country, not even the boss's boy riding behind him. No, he was thinking about the red EH ute that belonged to the boy. Yurnanggu one, that one.

Several days earlier when he had first arrived on Eumarella it had been parked outside the machinery shed. He had put his head through the open driver's-side window and smelt the insides. The foreign smells of a near new car. Alluring intriguing smells that were still lingering.

He had never driven a car but had watched his uncle Frank shifting through gears in the station's old Bedford three tonner when he drove him out to the mustering camp. He could drive that red ute for warda. Waji jindiyimanha. Not stop … ever.

Two days later the mustering had moved from the river paddock to Paddy's, a smaller paddock closer to the homestead.

A brown calf with a large disorderly white splash on its rump peeked at Chub from behind a cottonbush. He turned Astronaut toward it.

Get you little bastard.

The calf turned and bolted, tail erect, up a sandy embankment to its mother. They both trotted briskly to the rear of the mob.

A line of tired ambling beasts twisted from where Chub was riding at the rear, down a dry riverbed and out of his vision around a bend. He watched absently as their dappled backs passed in and out of shadows cast by gnarled overhanging river gums.

A movement to his left caused him to twist around. More cattle. They were advancing at a trot, flashes of brown and white through the trees. Their bellowing floated ahead of them and was returned in kind by the cattle ahead of Chub.

Following the newcomers was Frank, his white mare conspicuous as he trotted her across the rear of the mob, standing in his stirrups. Whereas Chub slipped and slithered around in his saddle trying to follow his horse's movements, Frank, as thin and subtle as the end of a mulga branch, moved as one with his horse.

The first few cattle plunged into the waiting line of their fellows, starting little flurries of movement. As more and more cattle linked together the flurries became more pronounced until there was one big whirlpool of cattle churning around in the riverbed.

Frank rode down one side and Chub the other until the cattle started to move in the one direction.

The two horsemen met at the back of the mob. Sandy-haired white kid and black weatherworn senior statesman, Frank, Yamaji Elder.

Where did you find all them, Frank?

Big flat. With a jerk of the thumb. You know?

Chub nodded although he didn't know.

Where's the yard from here?
'Nother creek join this one down here. Go up him.
Far?
No.

The sun was setting by the time they reached the yards. Chub could just make out Frank through the dust haze, galloping across the other side of the packed milling cattle. Chub was guarding the end of a long wooden railed wing that led to the open yard gate. At the back of the yards in a separate pen were more cattle that Hedley had yarded earlier, single-handed.

Astronaut pranced and jerked at the bit, this was action time.

The cattle, under Frank's careful pressure, were ringing clockwise, forcing themselves further down the wing until they were packed against the yards. Leaders straining back against the weight of the others, eyes bulging with terror at the line of fire-breathing devils that only they could see, stretched across the open empty gateway.

Eventually several beasts were buffeted inside. Devils defeated, an avalanche of cattle followed them in.

Chub whooped with relief and momentarily let Astronaut move away from the end of the wing, allowing a cow and a steer to rush past him, headed for the open flat.

Instantly Frank swept his mare around the back of the mob, leaving a wide arc of hoof prints dark against the red reflecting plain.

He easily headed the two runaways and sent them scurrying back into the mob.

The cattle continued pouring into the yards until Frank and Chub were left alone in the gateway. They both dismounted and Chub limped, stiff-legged, to close the gate.

They leaned on the wooden rails staring at the heaving mass of hopelessly bellowing beasts, Frank doing a rough count.

'Bout four hundred. And maybe about fifty in Hedley's mob back there.

Not too bad. Should make the old man happy.

Chub's attempt at cheerful chat as usual never managed to get a foothold with Frank who stared over the cattle for a while then walked off toward the horses. Chub followed slowly.

It was nearly dark when Chub poured half a bucket of oats and chaff into one of the feed bins, an old forty-four cut in half. The horses were already hobbled. He was buckling a medium sized horse bell around Astronaut's neck when Frank sauntered over. Chub watched as Frank ran his fingers down one of the gelding's well-muscled front legs to the fetlock and felt gingerly around a raw patch under the leather hobble. Frank looked up at Chub from his stooped position.

Hobble sore. Might take 'em off. He won't go anywhere. Too buggered I reckon. Needs a spell.

Who will I ride tomorrow?

See in mornin'. Tucker time, now.

Frank's family, who travelled with the mustering camp, were grouped around a small cooking fire. Chub could see Hedley there beside big Jane, Frank's wife, who was hefting a cast iron boiler closer to the flames.

Kids darting about in the shadows. Jane exuded languid power, anyone looking into her beautiful broad features could tell she knew anything that was worth knowing in her world. But they could also tell she wasn't about to give up that knowledge, not unless you were special. Chub wasn't part of her world and he wasn't special.

Jane's attention was on the boiler, but she was aware of Chub's approach, walking a little behind Frank. Whitefellas either fell into the category of those who had the potential to make her suffer and those who didn't, but Chub floated uneasily in the middle ground. A harmless enough kid but he was the boss's son and that could take all forms of evil down the track.

Milyanji. Walybala? Frank asked her pointing at the boiler and then jerking a thumb toward Chub. She nodded reluctantly.

Frank beckoned Chub into the firelight.

Plenty stew.

Normally Chub kept to his own camp as instructed by his father but right now he was weary. The stew smelt good and he was starving hungry.

The fire had burned down to a small pile of glowing embers and stars sprinkled a sky that had been monotonously clear for over three months. Frank, Hedley and Chub were leaning against a log on one side of the fire, Jane squatting on the other side, all staring into the red and yellow coals as the acrid mulga smoke drifted around them, drawn to one side of the fire, then the other. Kids long asleep, tucked up in their shared swag roll some distance away. Despite a few attempts from Chub, conversation had been almost non-existent.

Chub was tired and close to retiring but this sharing a fire was new territory for him and he decided to give the chat one more try.

Put me name down for the call-up. You know, registered like yer s'posed to. He looked at Hedley who he figured was about his age. What about you, Hedley?

Bingo. A smile and a nod from Hedley.

You wanna get called up? Chub asked. Vietnam and all that?

Hedley nodded again. I'd like the shootin'.

You do a bit? Shootin'?

To Chub's surprise Frank butted in enthusiastically.

Sure does. We go huntin', he gets the three-O. Never misses. And want the army pay, don't ya. Buy one of them red utes.

Hedley smiled quietly again. Maybe.

And all that good tucker. Fatten you up.

Hedley's smile broadened some more.

Blimey, said Chub, might be on the same train to Perth if we both get called up. No rookie training in West Aus though. Be on a plane east for that. Been on a plane?

It was a stupid question; Hedley had no need to answer but Chub detected a tiny headshake.

No, me neither. Never been out of the state. Could be a bit of a hoot if it all happens.

The moon came up later that night close to full, dimming the stars into near extinction.

Hedley was lying on his back, arms wrapped around his chest, trying to recall the words of Chub, the Walybala boy. The talk of plane flights and leaving the state. He wanted to get out and liked the sound of the army. As long as he could remember, his childhood had just been a series of whitefella holding yards. Every time he'd become friends with another boy they'd be sent off in different directions or one of them would get crook and be packed off again to recover. Uncle had got him this job and he was keen to prove himself and stay on after the muster but uncle had warned him not to get his hopes up. He didn't want to go back to the town camp which he hated. No family in town, all dead or moved on after he had been taken away from them by the coppers. Only uncle and aunty left in his life.

Chapter 3

The moon was still up when Chub rolled over in his swag which was wet with dew. Hedley's lean form was standing over him, silhouetted against the moonlight.

Time get them horses. Uncle puttin' out feed.

Chub sat up as Hedley walked off into the dark. Still weary he shivered and, fumbling in the dark, wriggled into his manky fake leather jacket. He got to his feet, walked a few paces and relieved himself.

Hedley reappeared out of the dark with two bridles, thrusting one at Chub.

Tracks this way.

He started walking toward the morning star. Chub followed.

After ten minutes of stumbling over dead branches and rocks in his efforts to keep pace with the sure-footed Hedley, Chub found him waiting.

Listen.

They listened.

At first Chub could hear nothing except the shimmer of leaves in the breeze, but then a distant but distinct dong from a horse bell.

They headed towards the sound.

Fifteen minutes later Hedley stopped while Chub caught up again.

The bells where now cutting the heavy morning air with acute sharpness.

Hedley touched his shoulder.

Stay.

Hedley pointed at himself and made a flanking motion.

After he was gone Chub carefully felt his way forward until he could just make out the standing shapes of the horses. Two horses on the far side began moving towards the others, restricted by their hobbles.

He heard Hedley's soothing words and saw him slide between them, catching one and then the other.

The other horses leapt away, bounding along in their hobbles. Chub yelled and jumped in front of them bringing them to a resigned halt. Hedley walked up leading the two horses he had caught.

Put bridle on dis fella. He quiet one, I think.

In the broadening morning light, they caught and gingerly unhobbled each of the remaining horses.

Hedley leapt on his horse bareback and rode around them, keeping them tightly bunched together.

Chub gripped his reins short behind the horse's left ear, tensed himself and leapt.

The horse shuddered under his weight as he landed on its back but stood quietly.

The other horses had turned for the camp where they knew there was a feed waiting and were slowly walking away.

Hedley cantered around them, sticking gracefully to his horse's bare back. As if this was a sign to go, they all broke into a gallop. Chub's horse, determined not to be left behind, set off after them. He tried holding it back to a controllable canter but found that, without stirrups, he was sliding up over its withers. The cold morning air was blasting into his streaming eyes and the odd branch slapped at him wildly as his horse strained to catch up. Feeling a twinge of panic, Chub jerked at the reins but only succeeded in pulling himself onto the horse's neck.

The horse Chub was attempting to ride had put up with many a human enforced indignity over the years, but Chub's scissor hold around its throat was too much altogether.

It executed a neat baulk to the right and Chub continued forward and down, hitting the rock littered ground chest first, somehow protecting his face.

He lay flat on his stomach gasping for air that wouldn't come until Hedley appeared above him, still mounted.

You ok?

Chub didn't answer.

He tried rolling over and to his surprise found that he was capable of doing so. Slowly he got to his feet and limped around a little.

He looked up at Hedley.

Quiet one, eh?

Hedley chuckled. Better ride behind me.

When they arrived at camp Frank was waiting for them.

Chub slipped off from behind Hedley but his knees buckled as he hit the ground.

Frank helped him to his feet.

Take a tumble?

Nothin' serious.

Where you hurtin'?

I'll be right, just a bit stiff.

Frank was eyeing him like he would a bit of horse flesh. Due for a spell.

Maybe better we take day off. Plenty cattle already for branding.

Chub had no objections.

Later that morning Chub was over at the cattle yards making sure the windmill was turned into the wind and that there were no beasts down.

He took off his shirt and examined his now badly bruised ribs.

Lucky.

He was dousing them with cold trough water when he heard the distant sound of a vehicle.

Oh shit.

He knew his father never took kindly to anyone taking a day off in the middle of a muster.

Over in the camp he could see Jane standing and pointing to the little spec of dust growing out of the horizon. Frank was unmoved, sitting by the lunchtime fire, re-plaiting his worn old stockwhip.

Down in the creek-bed Jane and Frank's kids ceased their frolicking and stood in unaccustomed silence. Hedley was standing by Jane's side.

Chub quickly put his shirt back on and hobbled toward camp, hoping to intervene. But he was too late.

His father's Landrover came to a halt at the edge of camp.

Hugh Jackson wiped his ruddy face with a handkerchief, pushed his felt hat to the back of his balding head and wriggled out from behind the steering wheel. A small man with a big work ethic, so big it left little room for anything else. Mouth a grim dark line. He stood briefly to stretch then strode over to where Frank was still sitting plaiting his whip.

G'day Frank.

G'day boss.

What in the flamin' hell are you doing in camp at this time of day? You should be out cleaning the stragglers from the creek line back Windarrah way.

Frank remained seated in silence, still staring at the half-plaited raw hide strings in his hands. Hugh Jackson hovering over him.

I crossed plenty of fresh tracks down that way. There was a nasty tone in Jackson's voice now. No bloody horse tracks though.

Frank slowly raised his head until his eyes were holding Jackson's.

Day off, boss. We bin workin' hard. Muster all that flat country back to Paddy's hole.

Hugh Jackson's eyes narrowed.

Don't give me the running shits, Frank!

He was in full swing now.

I want you off your arse! Get your fuckin' no-hoper relative there, jerking his thumb at Hedley, and saddle up. Pronto. Turning to Hedley. And you are fuckin' gone when this muster's over. Gone!

Hedley's gaze never left Jackson, eyes beginning to blaze with anger as the enormity of Jackson's cutting aside settled inside his gut. Why me? He thought, why the fuck you sack me? But he said nothing.

Jackson felt pleased with himself. A neat little bit of theatrics to suit his needs. He'd intended to sack Hedley after the muster anyway so had used the occasion to justify this and give Frank a scare at the same time. Frank was too valuable to sack.

By now Chub had reached the Landrover but his father had still not seen him.

He stopped, overcome with embarrassment at what he was witnessing. He was embarrassed for himself, for Frank and Hedley, but mainly for his father.

And where's Chubby, anyway?

I'm here, dad.

Chub appeared from behind the Landrover.

Dad. It's not how it looks. We've got about four hundred and fifty head in the yards here. The horses are tired, we're tired …

Horses tired? Get another bloody horse son. Why do you think I sent you out with a dozen horses? It's not a bloody gymkhana for god's sake.

Already Hugh Jackson's tone was softening. His son looked close to tears.

He tried to approach Chub. Imploring. But Chub backed away.

Look son …

Hugh Jackson swept a frustrated look over the others.

He wasn't going to carry out family matters in front of them. That would be the last thing he would do.

Again, he tried to approach Chub but Chub continued to back away. He felt like running. Turning away and running as far as he could.

His father gave up in exasperation and turned back to Frank.

Clean up those stragglers for me, will you. I'll be back at sunrise tomorrow for branding. Make sure there's a fire going for the irons. Plenty of coals, ok?

Frank's nod was barely perceptible.

When the Landrover's dust had settled Chub looked at Frank, still seated. He didn't know what to say.

Frank looked back up at him.

Better get saddled up eh.

That evening, Hedley was squatting under a river gum not far from camp watching uncle and Chub filling feed bins, old familiar feelings of despair weighing him down. A week earlier when he'd been with uncle in the station Bedford they'd run out of petrol within site of the homestead. A short walk to fill up a jerrycan but shit had been pulled out of the bottom of the tank and gotten into the carby according to uncle. Hell of a business to get it going again. That's what's wrong with me, he thought. Shit in my carby, shit in my guts and shit in my head. He looked up into the upper branches of the rivergum above him, unconsciously looking for bird nests. Just the act of looking up there could lift his spirits and it did for a moment, but his thoughts quickly returned to the bossfella and his sacking that morning. Another dead end, nothing ever seemed to lead anywhere for him. He tried to think of the army, his only hope now. He relished the thought of the physical side of the army but he'd never learnt to read or write properly and filling out forms terrified him. What if he had to do written tests before they'd let him in?

He watched Chub now limping stiffly toward their camp. Uncle must've offered him tucker again and even aunty seemed a bit more open to the kid, showing him a spot by the fire where he could sit. Maybe he would try sounding Chub out about the army. He seemed to know a bit about it and, going by what had happened this morning, he may be on their side with the bossfella.

With a bellyful of stew that was left over from the previous night, mopped up with a gob of damper, Chub was beginning to feel a little better. As the day had worn on his whole body had stiffened up to the point he'd had to get off his horse and try walking it out, all to no avail. He'd felt no urge to engage the others in conversation as they sat around the fire for the second night in a row and was just glad of their company. He was about to force himself to his feet and retire for the night when Hedley spoke to him in a quiet murmur.

That army, you know, we gotta pass tests and all that?

Chub thought about this for a moment before replying.

Sort of, I s'pose. I know they make yer sit for a medical. Haven't really gone into it that much, chances of yer number coming up and actually getting called up aren't that high I don't reckon.

Hedley nodded resignedly. What about writing and sums and all that?

Dunno if they look into that side of things, Chub said. Why? How far did yer go at school?

Hedley's slim shoulders suggested a shrug and he looked down into the fire.

Did you go to school at Nanderra?

No.

Not from around here then?

Hedley looked to his uncle for help, this was getting too awkward for him.

Hedley from around here, said Frank. Long time ago. Taken from his mummy by them coppers when he was little. Taken down south away from us all. Bad business.

Chub wondered where Hedley might have been taken, he'd seen an imposing stone structure beside the road on the way to Perth. His father had said it was for black kids.

New Norcia? He asked Hedley. The stone building.

For a bit, other places too. Hedley then picked up a long stick and began pushing the fire together, turning his back on Chub in doing so. Chub sensed this was Hedley's way of ending any more talk about his past so he turned to Frank.

What about you Frank? You come from over Boreen way, don't you?

Yeah.

That's your country then? Where your mob's from?

Silence.

Jane's gaze had never left the fire throughout the whole conversation, broad smooth face, woollen beanie pulled down over both ears. Now Chub noticed her glance at Frank.

Eventually Frank answered.

No. This my country.

Here? Eumarella?

That right. This our country. All around here.

Now Jane was looking at Chub, gauging his reaction.

Chub puzzled over this revelation. There had never been any Yamajis actually living on the property. Frank and Jane had the run of the it when they wanted but mostly Yamajis were brought in at mustering time or whenever his father needed them, got paid off and went back to where they came from.

Must have been way way back? He ventured.

Frank nodded.

How far back? Chub asked.

My mother, her mother.

Chub was trying to calculate the years. He supposed it made sense. His family had settled the place several generations ago.

So how come your mob moved on then? How many in the mob?

Plenty. Big mob.

Chub had never heard any of this before.

So why? I mean why just up camp and move on? Must've caused a lot of crowding over Boreen way.

Frank rubbed thoughtfully at his white stubble and then looked up at the stars.

Chub was only a boy, but he was the bossfella's boy. Frank knew, they all knew, that the boss could take away their tucker. Kick them off the place. Their waterholes, their gorges, jump-ups, caves, their special places. Sacred places. Kick them off when he wanted. Anytime. Just like that. Some things were best left alone.

Jane was now rocking back and forward on her haunches quietly humming, fixated on the remains of the fire. Hedley the same. It was a unified silence.

Chub could sense there was a story to be told but the conversation was poised on a very wobbly bridge. He may have walked down this road a little too far, could be time for the swag. Anyway, old Mick would fill him in at rum time back at the homestead. He wouldn't ask his father.

Next morning, Chub was stationed at one of the big iron gates connecting the different sections of the yards. A mournful cow's face loomed out of the dust, head held low, horns ready. Chub pulled the gate open and Hedley, a slight figure darting in and out of Chub's view line among the hulking pounds of beef, slapped it on the rump. The cow lunged forward and past Chub. He slammed the gate shut after her and a huge following white bullock jerked to a dusty halt, staring at the gate rails in confusion.

When the last cow and calf had been drafted out, Frank slipped through the rails.

Look like plenty mickeys. Big lotta branding.

He grabbed the nearest calf by the tail.

Ridem' dis little fella.

Laughing, he straddled the animal's bony back and remained there for two convulsive twists before he let it bolt back into the seething mob of bawling calves and their mothers.

Hugh Jackson appeared at the side rails and all fun stopped in an instant. He clambered over the rails and jumped down into the finely churned red sand, all business.

Right. Don't stand there you blokes. Grab a leg rope each. Frank, front leg. Chub, rear leg. I'll toss 'em.

Yes boss.

Calling out to Hedley who was on the outside of the yards. You got those irons heated boy?

Frank answered for Hedley. They hot boss.

Can't he speak for himself?

He speak when he want. Bit shy.

That right? Here, get your leg ropes on the big mickey.

Thud. The first calf hit the dust, the weight of three men barely holding it down. Hedley launched the branding iron over the rails and Frank deftly caught the cool end.

The odour of burnt hair momentarily overpowered the smell of dust in Chub's nostrils. He kept his weight on the calf and watched as his father produced a little pen knife and in several quick strokes reduced the animal's testes sac to a gaping nothingness, neatly throwing the little white balls of flesh into a tin under the rails.

Frank crunched a pair of ear markers together, blood oozing from their imprint.

Release him! Ready, go.

Chub was last to release his leg rope and just managed to slip away from the pain-maddened calf as it careered back to its mother. The next calf was selected.

By day's end, all the calves were pressed dolefully against their mothers, ears dripping blood and rumps blackened. The testicle tin was full.

Frank was pouring sweat more freely than anyone Chub had ever seen. He looked at his own shirt and felt its patchy dampness.

Hugh Jackson picked up the testicle tin and offered it over the rails to Hedley.

Here. You fellas like these, don't you? Good tucker. Put hair on your chest.

Hedley took the tin with a nod and Jackson turned back to Frank and Chub.

Now that was a decent day's work. Credit were credit's due. You can let this lot go and head back to the homestead tomorrow. Leave the horses in the home paddock and give 'em a good feed. We'll get started on the open country next week. Ok, Frank?

Frank nodded. He looked awkwardly over at Hedley and then back at Jackson.

What about him, boss? Nephew.

What about him?

You know. What you said. Him finish up.

Yeah. I said when the muster's over. It ain't over till we've mustered the open country.

And with that he turned to go, stopping beside Chub and motioning with his head toward his Landrover and then briskly moving off with his familiar short sharp steps. Chub looked from his father's retreating back to Frank but Frank would not return the look, not his business. Chub followed his father.

When they were clear of the others Jackson turned to face Chub.

Generally quick with his words, he instead pursed his lips and gestured palms up with an exasperated shrug.

Look, about yesterday…

Chub was bracing himself for the usual tirade but when his father's words did come, they were spoken with a note of quiet reason.

You know full well that there's no taking time off in a muster, right? And what's more, you don't ever give the Blacks some slack or they'll be all over you.

Jackson was hoping Chub would agree and they could move on but Chub only stood in defiant silence.

Normally Jackson wouldn't tolerate defiance from anyone but he chose to interpret Chub's silence as weariness.

Look, I know you probably had the stuffing knocked out of you in the fall but you're tougher than that. Gotta set an example. The labour situation is a nightmare. Can't afford more ringers and still don't know if I'm gonna lose you to the bloody army or what. Meantime it's just you and me son, we've got to pull together, right?

Chub had heard all this before. He wanted to go.

Frank had now opened the gate separating the cows and calves from the rest, it was Chub's opportunity to take his leave.

Right Dad. Gotta go and help clear the yards.

Ok, but think about what I just said.

Chub nodded and began walking toward the yards.

Anyway, Jackson called after him, your mother's looking forward to seeing you. She's putting a roast on.

Chub acknowledged this with a backward wave.

Chapter 4

The native quarters, his mother liked to call them.
Frank and Jane's shack.

Dirt floor, bush poles, rusting corrugated iron walls and roof. All held together with fencing wire. Cooking fire pit to one side. The kid's mattresses arranged in the red dust along the lean-to veranda and a few more sheets of iron, propped up by three sticks, represented the guest quarters. Hole in the ground behind more sheets of iron the inconvenient convenience out the back.

What a grandiose spread it was.

Chub was parked out front, seated in the door-less cab of the old fifty-two Bedford station truck, contemplating the scene. Jane, Frank and Hedley were unloading their swags and blackened old cooking utensils from the back. Dogs and kids bouncing and streaking all around.

Come the day when his father eventually handed over the reins and he could set his own agenda, rebuilding this would be top of the list. He often played out this little scenario in his head.

What else would I do? What changes would I make?

Plenty. The list would be endless, but he'd have to sort something out with his brother though. Eric was still away at college and wanted to come home. They'd never be able to work together; Eric would want to be his own boss. Not room for everyone though and he, Chub, was the oldest. First dibs Sonny Jim.

Frank cut into his thoughts.

All done.

Right. Tomorrow at the yards, ok?

Piccaninny dawn.

He drove through the dry creek-bed that represented the Eumarella colour divide.

One creek bank for the Yamajis and the stock yards, the other bank for everything else.

The machinery shed was something he would never be able to improve on. Chub pulled into one side of the huge eight bay structure and switched off the motor.

The shed was corrugated iron, like all the buildings, but it was held together by a substantial steel frame, all neatly welded, a clean swept concrete floor featuring a six-yard grease pit for vehicle maintenance, generator, welder and an impressive array of tools. Every single one of them in its designated spot. Mess with the tools and you were in trouble.

Chub heaved his swag onto his shoulder and began walking toward the bizarrely incongruous bank of deep green citrus trees that hid the homestead. A green island in a red sea. Water and his mother's steely resolve could achieve miracles.

Chub had already made up his mind that he was going to move out of the homestead and into the single men's quarters. He'd had enough of his father. Breaking the news to his mother would create a fuss but he'd do it straight up. Get it over with.

Chub dumped his swag next to the Coolgardie safe on the wide front veranda and turned to face his mother.

'Lo, mum.

Connie Jackson had become a reflection of the country she lived in. Small black eyes cradled in nests of squint lines formed over twenty years of station life where even a glance out the homestead window demanded narrowing her eyes to slits. Hair cut short and shirt sleeves rolled up exposing strong brown arms. Always in jeans or jodhpurs, ready to jump on a horse if need be. If Hugh, or anyone else, thought she had lost some of her femininity then, bully for them. She didn't give a hoot.

Originally from Perth, she had met Hugh when she was in the Land Army after the Second World War and eventually taken to station life, now as involved in the property as Hugh.

She planted a light kiss on Chub's cheek and stood back to look at him.

What's this then? She gently brushed a scrape on his forehead that he hadn't even realised was there.

Bit of a tumble. Nothing to worry about.

You had difficulties out there with the men, I heard.

No difficulties there.

They made their way through the old timber home to the kitchen, a large Masonite-lined room, dominated by a huge slow combustion stove with a cast iron kettle over the heat and a teapot of freshly made tea to one side. Trevor opened a screen door that led out the back and looked around the yard. He turned back to his mother.

Where is he?

Your father's checking mills.

Mum. I'm moving down the men's quarters.

Connie looked at her eldest son. Fine, sandy-coloured hair. That was from her father, god bless him. But it was his face, the image of his face, that she carried deep inside her. No matter how manly he tried to be, Chub's face always projected a baby-like, round, rosy shine to her. At his very angriest, his brow would draw into a scowl, lips set in a hard, straight line. But his blue eyes always mutinied. They didn't know how to be angry.

She had been anticipating him moving out for some time. No fuss.

If that's what you want, darling.

She began pouring the tea.

Chub settled into one of the paint-worn wooden chairs at the family-sized kitchen table. This had always been his position, back to the stove, facing the screen door and the glimpse it provided of the dusty expanse beyond.

His mother had surprised him, as usual, by her acceptance of his moving out.

She must know why.

Mum. What's with dad? Why is he so down on everyone?

Connie finished pouring the tea and unconsciously slipped into her regular spot at the table, opposite Chub.

Sighing. He's carrying the weight of the world. Our world. I suppose we both are.

That still doesn't give him the right to yell at everyone. Frank works his backside off. We all do.

Darling, it just isn't that simple. I don't know what he tells you or what he keeps under that big hat, but ... look. We're going backwards. We can't afford to pay the new wages and support Frank's entire family at the same time.

They're just blackfella wages. Never broken the bank before.

That was before the referendum.

Chub nodded and sipped his tea, deep in thought.

Can't we just take the rations out of their wages, or something?

Not according to our accountant. Have a peek at Hugh's desk. It's piled high with bureaucratic this, bureaucratic that. It's a nightmare, darling.

Both mother and son sat in silence for a while. Chub digesting what he had just heard.

He began thinking about Frank's situation.

I s'pose we don't have to employ Frank full-time. But how do they pay for tucker when he's not working?

And there is the problem. Besides, cattle prices are still dropping. God knows where the bottom is.

I knew that.

Chub drained the last of his tea. He'd have to think all this through properly. Must be a way. Usually was. Mum, and especially dad, always got too tangled up in the negatives. What was that saying? Couldn't see the woods for the trees. That was them.

He stretched, smelling one of his armpits at the same time. Whoo! Better have a scrub up. Three weeks of washing in cattle troughs.

What about dinner? I was planning a lovely roast.

Chub was tempted but the thought of eating with his father was too much.

Thanks mum but I'm going to have to put up with old Mick's cooking from now on. That's the price of living in the men's quarters.

He rose and placed his chair neatly back under the table and gave his mother a quiet smile on the way out.

Jane and Mick were facing the setting sun gazing into its acres of red sky leaning against the corrugated iron wall of Mick's kitchen, backsides on a rough-hewn wooden bench. They smoked the last of their hand-rolled cigarettes.

The pair of them were a stark contrast in looks; Jane, smooth dark and broad featured, flowing across a good portion of the bench, Mick needing much less real estate for his scrawny bum. His thin wizened frame hunched into a tight question mark and narrow lined face brushed with a cook's pallor.

Jane's thick-soled bare feet were resting on the hessian bag of spuds Mick had just given her. She had a lot of time for Mick, her whole family did. Always good for a rollie and a chat and often snuck a few boiled lollies for the kids into their rations. He wore a quiet know-how like an old cardigan. There wasn't an egotistical bone in Mick's arthritic body. They hadn't spoken for a while, content to sit and enjoy the little stirring of a breeze that often wound its way up the dry watercourse at this time of the evening.

Mick blew out a faint stream of blue smoke through his nostrils without disturbing his fag-end which was hanging off his lower lip, barely alight. His bald bonce was patterned with large sun lesions and fringed with a thin remnant of white hair slicked down with some ancient concoction of Mick-made hair oil that gave off a faint eucalyptus smell. Pleasing to Jane.

Ran into your old aunty Meg in town last month, he said.

He spoke with a soft Irish lilt, nearly worn away by fifty years of nasal Aussie discourse.

Asking after you, she was.

Jane smiled. Better watch out old fella. She likes you, that one.

Well, she'd be wasting her time then, wouldn't she? No life left in this old dog.

This brought a chuckle from Jane.

Plenty o'life in Megsy. Always tryin'.

They both looked up as Chub appeared from around the corner, still wet from his shower. The boss's son: Jane was off. She stubbed out her fag end and stood up.

Thanks Mick.

She tossed her bag of spuds over one shoulder.

Right so, Janey.

Mick turned to Chub as Jane headed off. Did you leave any hot water in the donkey heater, lad?

A bit, but I stoked up the fire.

Good-oh. I'd better get your dinner on then. Earn my keep.

Mick disappeared inside his kitchen leaving Chub standing alone. He turned and watched Jane, now labouring across the creek bed toward the other bank with her bag of spuds. Back across the colour divide.

A little later, Mick returned with two chipped enamel mugs.

I never drink in front of the Yamajis. If your good father, in his wisdom, won't allow them one, then a man would be plain rude to drink in their presence.

True.

Single men aren't allowed to drink either, only me and the bosses.

How did you get the ok?

Special dispensation for bein' old and harmless.

So, are you going to give me one of those rums or drink them both yourself?

Dunno. Mick's pale rheumy eyes scrunched into well-worn humour lines. Depends on whether you're a single man now or the boss's son.

Definitely the boss's son. Give me a rum you old bugger.

They sat on the bench and raised the mugs in a silent toast.

Chub was quick to unload his thoughts.

Got a burning question for you.

Fire away. Font of knowledge, that's me.

Out on the muster, we got talking. You know, me and Frank. One night around the fire.

Mick nodded, sipping his rum slowly.

Frank reckons he came from this country. Said there were about fifty or more of his people living here. That right?

That's right.

Wouldn't tell me why they moved on. Went quiet when I asked. Any idea?

You should ask your father that one, lad. It's your family history.

Dad only tells me what he wants me to know, not what I want to know. Figured it was safer to ask you.

Not safer for me. I'm only here because of your father's good will, you know. Pension, tucker and digs in return for my cooking skills.

There was a certain irony in the reference to cooking skills that was not lost on Chub, but he was on a mission. Curiosity overload.

C'mon. Tell me about Frank's mob. He mentioned something about his mother's mother.

His mother's mother. That would be Rosie Yangaboora. Very fine woman, I'm told. Became a very respected elder in her time.

Well, why did she move on?

She didn't move on, lad. Not voluntarily anyway.

Mick sat in solemn silence. He turned to look at Chub.

Like I said. This is your family history. If you go back to your parents blurtin' all this back at them, they'll know where you got it from. Me. They keep quiet about it for a reason.

Ok. I get that, Chub said. I know there's always been the odd rumour floating around about killings in the very early times. I can remember a kid at primary school carrying on about some shooting but Dad said it was rubbish. Not connected, is it?

Mick was looking at the sunset.

Just tell me what happened Mick. I can keep things to myself. You know that.

Mick gave Chub a long look and then nodded.

You didn't hear this from me but, yeah, there was a shooting. Rosie was the only survivor.

The only survivor? Shit!

She was just a child. Lay under her mother's body and played dead, the story goes. Made it all the way to the Western Desert mob. They took her in.

Where did this happen?

Windahla waterhole. Every one of them shot. Men, women, kids.

Windahla? Who did the shooting?

Apparently, there was a party of them. Mostly from here. Old Paddy Jackson was the leader.

Bullshit. Old Paddy?

I warned you it was family history.

Chub found himself unable to speak for a moment. Paddy Jackson was a legend. Their legend. He'd been the one who overlanded the first cattle. He'd settled the place. He was in the history books.

Couldn't have been, not Paddy.

Lad, I've heard the story over and over through the years. Drovers, Aboriginals. Just because things aren't written doesn't mean they didn't happen.

Well, why? If there was a shooting of some sort, why?

Landgrab. Pure and simple, lad. Yamajis lived here; it was their country. Your lot wanted it.

But they didn't actually own it as such. They always came and went. You know, went walkabout.

Of course, they owned it! There was a fire in Mick now. You've worked with them long enough to know that. Who leads who around by the nose when you're mustering? They're part of the country.

Christ, Mick.

Mick had been telling stories to Chub and his brother Eric since they were toddlers. He could remember reading them the Digit Dick books and The Magic Pudding. Mick could recognize when they were floundering beyond their comprehension.

He patted Chub sympathetically on the shoulder and smiled.

I know lad. There's a lot to take in there. But you did ask the question.

Chub shook his head. Old Mick must have this one wrong.

Shall we retire to the dining room, lad? The vegies will be well-boiled.

Chub didn't feel like Mick's cooking right now. But he drained his rum and followed Mick inside his unlined corrugated iron kitchen.

Chapter 5

Next morning Hugh Jackson was helping Chub load the old Bedford in preparation for mustering the open country. He heaved the last of the feed bins up to Chub who was stacking them on the wooden tray.

Familiar prickles of pain in his chest caused him to lean back against the cab. Chub noticed but said nothing, he'd already been rebuked once that morning for expressing concern. The sound of a distant motor caught his attention.

Mail truck.

His father cocked a leathery ear.

Yeah. Going through Cogala Creek, judging by the revs. Be here in ten.

He passed Chub a bag of oats.

What time did the boys get going with the horses?

Not that long ago. At least a couple of them needed re-shoeing.

Hugh shook his head, not happy with the lateness of the hour. Every bloody thing took longer than it should.

They were tying down the load when the mail truck came into view. They watched as it lumbered closer slowing under a succession of gear changes and pulled up beside the hand pump bowser opposite the machinery shed. A twenty-year old Mack, all bull-bar and noise, reeking of diesel, tortured brake linings and hot engine. The driver opened his door with a loud creak and slid down from his perch. A thin man under a huge hat.

Hughey. How are ya?

Not bad, George. What have you got for us this week? Should be half a dozen fuel drums if I remember rightly.

Yeah. Groceries, mail. All the usual.

What's the road like from Nan?

Pretty good, mate. A bit of loose sand just before your boundary grid. Not too bad.

Chub finished cinching the tie-down ropes on the Bedford and joined them to lend a hand with unloading the fuel drums. He positioned an old truck tyre on the road beside the Mack to cushion the heavy steel drums as George flipped them off, somersaulting them so they didn't land on their sides and roll. They were burning hot to touch. Already the temperature was around a hundred and ten.

Chub was still struggling with the drums when George shouted his goodbyes and the Mack roared off on its three-day circular route through the neighbouring stations.

His father was standing over the grocery box that had been left in the dust, sorting through the mail.

One for you, Chub.

He looked at the envelope more closely.

Commonwealth of Australia. Department of Labour and National Service. This looks serious.

Chub felt a fizz of adrenalin. He left the drums and took his letter from Hugh, examining the familiar emu and kangaroo coat of arms on the envelope before he opened it. His father continued shuffling around letters that were spread out on the grocery box.

Another one the same. Hedley Yangaboora, care of here, Eumarella. Since when has he been a resident?

The comment didn't even register with Chub who was focused only on the envelope in his hands. Before he could open it, a small willy-willy came spinning around the corner of the shed sucking a plume of red dust from the road and scattering the other letters before careering in a drunken lurch toward the homestead and petering out in Connie's green oasis. While Hugh cursed and chased after the letters, Chub ripped open his envelope and unfolded the single page letter.

When a flustered Hugh returned with the windblown mail, he found his son standing, still fixated on the letter. Hugh knew his worst fears had been realised.

Don't fucken tell me… you haven't been, have you?

Chub looked up slowly.

Shit, dad. My number has come up. Report for a medical in two months. Geraldton.

Bugger, said Hugh grimly. There goes my workforce.

Bugger, all right. I might finish up in Vietnam. Anywhere. Chub was not showing it, but he could feel a little glow of excitement growing. Eric will be home in eighteen months or so and I might not have to go in for another six or nine. We'll get by.

Hugh grunted, hurdles springing up from everywhere in his mind, hand going involuntarily to his chest even though there had been no prickles of discomfort this time. His father's reaction was not lost on Chub.

Hugh scooped up the grocery box and thrust it at Chub. Anyway, he muttered, at least we can get the open country mustered. Put these groceries in the store, then you'd better be off. It'll be dark before you set up camp if you leave it any later.

As an after-thought he turned and held out Hedley's letter. Better pass this on. Looks like he's in the same boat.

Thin streaks of silver cloud were failing to curtain the setting sun as it touched down on the horizon drawing a stalagmite of earth up and into itself. Frank was breaking open haybales, setting them in different feed bins. The geldings trying to steal the mares' share as usual, but Frank was having none of it, cursing and waving the geldings away. Hedley and Chub were over at the truck. Chub reached into the wooden crate that served as a driver's seat and pulled out Hedley's letter as a nervous Hedley shifted his weight from one foot to the other. When Chub produced the letter Hedley couldn't take his eyes off it. He tried to wipe his hands clean on his red dust encrusted pants, nervous that he would stain the letter and somehow render it invalid, then he took it gently between one long forefinger and thumb. He had only received a few letters in his lifetime.

It's from the government, Chub volunteered.

Hedley knew this.

Open it up. It's either yay or nay.

Hedley began to tentatively pick at the envelope with his thumbnail until the flap began to peel back, careful not to tear it.

He could hear Frank in the background still cursing at the horses and Hedley felt that he should be helping.

When he extracted the letter and unfolded it, he was already confident of the outcome.

What does it say? Are you in?

Hedley just smiled.

Can you read it ok? Do you want me to read it for you?

I'm in. Hedley handed the letter to Chub who grinned as he read it.

You're in alright. You have to get through a medical in Geraldton, like me, but they want you down there later this month. I'm not until the following month.

New cause for concern. Hedley had never been to Geraldton.

How do I get there?

Chub quick to give him a reassuring pat on the shoulder, grinning.

Don't worry, I'll look after you. I have to buy a train ticket for myself, so I'll get yours at the same time. Army pays, not us.

Hedley's return grin was all white teeth. Guns, shooting, uniforms, good tucker and a red ute on the horizon.

When Hedley passed on his news to Jane she was subdued. Instead of sharing his felicity she turned away and yelled angrily at her kids, jindiyimanha bunthanyimanha! They were mock fighting with the firewood they were supposed to be stockpiling.

Hedley respected her unease and distrust of the whitefella's army, but his enthusiasm would not be dampened.

He left her to her kids and walked away on his own, mind ticking over.

He tried to focus on the challenges ahead. The training and combat he could do; it was only the whitefella customs and paperwork he feared. But he had help with that now. The boss's boy. Chub.

Not only was his red ute to be admired, but the boy himself was turning out to be ok too.

Chapter 6

The mid-morning sea breeze found its way through the window of Kruger's surgery, making the floor-length curtains billow like a pair of mini-sized spinnakers. He had already examined three potential conscripts that morning and had another dozen to get through before day's end. It was a process that bothered him, that went beyond mere medical assessments.

There was time for a quick ciggy and some contemplation before his next examination, so he opened a side door and pointed his long thin nose into the breeze, straight off the Indian Ocean, taking in the Geraldton briny.

It bothered him that the destiny of these young men was in his hands. His report could swing the army's view of an individual's suitability for the job in hand to the negative with a mere mention of a supposed mental deficiency or an attitude concern. He wasn't god, he wasn't even army. He'd taken to questioning each individual on their views toward conscription and allowing this to subtly influence the wording of his report. He sucked on his cigarette, inhaling the sea breeze at the same time as the nicotine. Maybe he was god.

Next patient ready when you are Doctor Kruger.

Last suck on the ciggy and then it was ploughed into an ashtray.

Send him in.

By the time Hedley tentatively opened the door, Kruger was back at his desk with Hedley's report open in front of him.

He saw a thin Aboriginal youth, medium height, deep brown skin, black curls, well-muscled with a straight posture. Probably three quarter or even full blood and probably from the back of beyond judging by his shy demeanour and worn clothing. At least he wasn't bare foot like one young man had been.

Come in and take a seat.

Hedley was obviously very nervous. He sat.

I'm Doctor Kruger and you are Hedley Yangaboora. Did I pronounce that correctly?

Hedley nodded. He was going to keep his words to a minimum so there would be less chance he would say the wrong thing.

Hedley, I'm going to give you a medical examination in a minute but first I'm going to have a bit of a chat. A few questions to fill in the blank spaces in your report here. First up, where are you from? It says here Eumarella. Where's that?

Up Nanderra way, sir.

Kruger noted that Hedley had a strong Yamaji accent.

I see, and your nearest relatives are Frank and Jane Yangaboora. Are they your parents?

No, sir.

There's no need to call me sir, Hedley. Believe me, I'm no sir. Doctor will do, or don't call me anything if you don't want to.

Hedley looked confused.

Now, what relationship are they to you?

Aunty and uncle

I see, and your parents? Their address?

Hedley shook his head and Kruger decided not to pursue the parenting question any further. Leave it to some bureaucrat. They had created the whole Aboriginal child removal mess, it was their problem.

Next question. Did you attain an intermediate certificate? You know, at school. Form three at high school?

Hedley shook his head.

Did you go to school?

This was an area Hedley was worried about, but Chub had told him to tell porkies, say anything. There wouldn't be any records of his schooling, or lack of it.

I went to school. Can read and all that. Do sums.

Kruger had been instructed to give anyone who hadn't passed Intermediate a psych test, but the questions were meaningless in cases like this. He decided to follow his instincts.

Look, Hedley, we don't have to go any further with this if you don't want to.

Hedley looked alarmed, he thought he was about to be rejected on the spot.

Why not?

Because you're Aboriginal. I can just write in your report that you're Aboriginal. Aboriginals don't have to serve if they don't want to.

But I do want to. I'm the same as everyone else.

So, you do want to serve then?

Too right I do. I can shoot straight. I'm not afraid. I want to be in the army.

Kruger smiled. That's good, Hedley. Some young fellows don't want to serve, that's all. I had to ask the question.

Hedley looked relieved.

Kruger went back to reading Hedley's report, which was very scant on information. Even his birth date only mentioned a year and a month.

I take it you volunteered for conscription judging by this?

Hedley nodded.

And there's no mention of a police record which is a bonus.

No police.

Well, I suppose you'd better get your shirt off then and I'll check you out.

Hedley couldn't restrain a grin. He knew he'd sail through this part. There was nothing wrong with him.

There wasn't. Hedley stepped out of the surgery and into sunshine and a blue sky. As Kruger had done earlier, he took a deep breath of sea breeze and decided to follow its scent. He had just passed his medical, a test that for him had held a raft of interwoven challenges from negotiating train timetables to filling out a patient form at the surgery reception. He felt a huge sense of achievement as he followed the sea breeze through Geraldton streets, heading for his next high, a look at the ocean for the first time. He crossed the main street and there it was, an impossibly blue, blue. Exhilarated, he began walking toward the beach, sand particles carried by the stiffening sea breeze already hitting his face. The water was a fascination of movement, white caps, colourful sails cutting back and forward and hulking ships over toward the docks. He was just about to descend a small set of stone steps down onto the white sand when a police car cruised to a halt behind him. Hedley's mood flipped in an instant. He knew what this meant. The driver, an overweight sergeant, beckoned him through the open passenger's window. He wasn't even bothered to get out of his seat.

New around here, aren't ya?

Hedley was careful not to touch the car or do anything that might upset the policeman as he bent to address him through the window.

Yes, officer.

Good boy. Ya know to call me officer, aye? Means you've been in trouble before.

Hedley felt a familiar sense of dread.

Anyway, I'm sergeant, not officer. Got it?

Hedley nodded.

So, what's ya name then?

Hedley.

And where might ya be stayin', Hedley?

Not staying. Catch train soon.

That right. And what's ya business here? What are ya doin' in Geraldton?

Doctor for army.

Conscript, aye? Got proof of that, then?

Hedley showed him his envelope of documents through the window. The sergeant reached out for them and Hedley reluctantly handed them over. They were his ticket to everywhere. He watched apprehensively as the sergeant began to read the main document, resting it on his belly. To Hedley's surprise the sergeant soon returned the document to its envelope and handed it back with a curt nod.

Ok by me. Best place for you lot. Vietnam. Makes my job easier.

As the police car pulled away and left Hedley beside the road with his envelope he began to ruminate on the encounter. Maybe this whole army thing was going to lift him up a notch or two, no policeman had ever let him go so quickly. Hedley had fully expected a grilling at the police station and being held for hours, missing his train. He wasn't even in the army but already he was getting some benefits.

Thoughts, thoughts and more thoughts. Chub loved it up here and he was now in complete relax mode. The task was done, he'd checked the oil level, replaced the rusted old gearbox cover and tightened the wing nut that was the highest point of the fifty-foot windmill tower. Chub had pulled the wind wheel with its eighteen lethal blades out of the wind and had it tied off to the tail with a scrap of fencing wire so it wouldn't turn in the slight breeze. He was now seated on the tail, one dusty boot hooked into the tower for support, enjoying the view over the homestead and trying to get his life into perspective.

Tomorrow he and Hedley were catching a ride on George's mail truck into Nanderra and then train down to Perth to report for army duty. He supposed it would be a break and he supposed that it would be fun, but two years was a long time. He looked down at the green-painted homestead roof surrounded by half a dozen round water tanks like encircling Daleks menacing the Tardis. The homestead building had travelled in time from the last century. Shifted in sections on camel wagons from a deserted mining town by his grandfather. Chub wondered if the legendary

Paddy Jackson had been around to help, he could've been alive then. This brought his thoughts back to the surrounding country. Who owned it? He looked down at Mick's kitchen, a small rusting box perched on the edge of the dry watercourse, and across to Frank and Jane's shack on the other bank. Mick had said that the Yamajis believed that the country owned them, not the reverse. Chub didn't feel that he owned it, strictly speaking his father's name was on the title anyway, but he did love the country. Did that make him some kind of an owner? An emotional owner. Or, again, was the reverse true? Did the country own his emotions? If the country had been ripped away from the Yamajis by Paddy Jackson a hundred years ago and those Yamajis were long dead and Paddy was long dead then, titles aside, who morally owned the place? Frank? The mining companies that were moon-scaping the country up north seemed to have the rights to do whatever they liked. Bloody hell. All Chub could conclude was that the property needed looking after and the Yamajis should be given all the access they wanted. He would look after it. No overstocking in dry times. He'd learnt a little at Ag school about stock rotation and leaving parts of the river country totally stock free to allow regeneration. His father thought it was a waste of their best feed country and totally rejected the idea but Chub would give it a go.

And then his mind jumped back to the army. Shit, two years was a long time. He would miss this place. Really miss it.

Reluctantly he eased himself off the windmill tail and down onto the little timber platform. He reached up to the tail again and released the scrap of wire that was holding the wind wheel. As soon as he released the ten-foot wheel it began slowly rotating and he had to climb down onto the safety of the tower ladder. He'd better start packing a kitbag and smile, smile smile. Goodbye Eumarella, goodbye Western Australia. He'd never been out of the state before. First time for everything, but.

Chapter 7

Six interviews and every one of them difficult. Not only had she dealt with the refugees but two teenage mothers, three school age kids in youth detention and, to top it off, she had to debrief a traumatised staff member.

Frankie pulled into her driveway and sat for a moment in her car, thoughts still churning.

What time was it?

Nearly six.

Oh god.

She had no energy for anything but she had to check on John. She'd lent him a guitar that morning in the hope it would give him some inspiration.

Car locked, brief case in hand, she walked around the side of the house and was immediately struck by the pleasant sounds of guitar playing. This was better than the little ping of sadness the backyard usually bestowed on her. She made a left turn toward the bungalow.

E A A E A F# A# E D E. John's plectrum was picking over The Apache riff. A roof over his head, a whole week without a single nightmare and now this, the loan of a guitar. He was happy, sitting on the edge of the single bed in Frankie's still mouldy-smelling bungalow. A knock on the door interrupted his reverie. It's only me, he heard Frankie call out.

C'min.

I heard the guitar playing. Apache, she smiled.

He played the riff again and Frankie mouthed the notes. De daah de de daah. Daah. De de daah daah.

He looked up at her grinning.

You know, that was the first piece I ever learnt. Just 'cause I wanted to impress Bernadette Hocking. She was a girl in form three.

Many a fine musician started with that piece, I'm sure.

Wow. Thanks a heap for this. Gently stroking the strings of the guitar. Yours? A spare?

No, it was his, Jack's, actually. My guitar's a Yamaha.

Jack?

My late and great. He was a builder as you can probably see by the state of the back yard. Spent time in Pentridge at age twenty for draft resisting, protesting against your Vietnam war, but it was mesothelioma that was his downfall. One of James Hardie's many victims.

Sorry to hear that.

Yes, poor Jack. He went well before his time.

Always the men, John was thinking as he began to play a few melancholy notes.

Ring any bells?

Sounds bluesy.

Delta blues. Blind Lemon Jefferson. I used to drive the guys crazy with all that. I was obsessed and all they wanted to play was Monkees.

Frankie gave him a quizzical look. I remember you guys playing some blues.

They moved my way a little, but not much. Hendrix, Cream and so on.

66

Frankie's phone began ringing and she fished it out of her handbag, retreating out the door as she answered it.

Angela, my daughter in London. Must go. Have fun. Indicating the guitar.

He gave her a thumbs up of appreciation and continued strumming after she closed the door.

Boy, he thought, have I fallen on my feet this time or what? Pity they're such wobbly feet, though.

He began picking over the Apache riff again. Memories. Bernadette bloody Hocking, he mumbled to himself. Bernadette ... that morning ... first day of the new term, it was. He remembered leaving for school that day, afraid. Closing the front gate, satchel swinging on his hip. That leather smell from the satchel. Tomato and cheese sandwich smells.

Behind the gate had been the Mitchell family home with all its layers of comforting familiarity and parental protection. Beyond the gate his school day beckoning to him, smiling toothily in treacherous invitation to front up for the terrifying ride that was the daily curriculum.

Being the first day back after the holidays had meant there would be extra challenges, such as new seating arrangements, which he had particularly hated. He was so shy back then, insular, no real friends. Not much has changed there, he thought wryly. But at least a full term sitting beside the same student allowed a miniscule amount of bonding gel to eventually set between them. Most of the class members had been quite indifferent to his presence, it was only when a teacher directed him a question that they even became aware of his existence.

He remembered having plucked a handful of ripe purple plums from the neighbour's over-hanging tree as he had walked up Lucille Street that morning, wondering how he would cope.

Sometimes you had to warm up to a big challenge like this by taking on smaller, more controllable challenges. He could choose numerous routes to school but that day he had let the traffic lights do the choosing. It was a game of chance that he had played before.

Lucille ran into Lacey which intersected with Mount Dandenong Road at the traffic lights, which he would be able to see when he rounded the corner from Lucille Street.

If the light in Lacey was showing green, he would walk to school down Lacey Street which was definitely the least challenging option and it meant that he would pass Susan Tuck's home. She had been his secret crush the year before and although she had faded in his pubescent heart and loins, a glimpse of her was still enough to brighten his morning.

An amber light meant caution, so if the light was showing amber he would take the Vernon Avenue route and run the gauntlet past the Humphrey brothers' house. This carried the potential for real physical pain or, at best, having his glasses stolen and the indignity of being chased by the younger brother who was half his size. He hated conflict or confrontation of any kind and the prospect of running into even a lone Humphrey brother filled him with dread.

So, what challenge befitted the possibility of a red light? He had mulled over this for a while as he walked down Lucille, plum juice now dripping on his school jumper.

The first day of term called for some steely resolve so if there was a red light he would walk on the railway tracks, including the bridge over Mount Dandenong Road. There was no escape if the Melbourne express appeared at the halfway point.

John was a fatalist.

John Mitchell. Now where are we going to put you this term?

John felt the eyes of the whole class on him as he stood, books in hand, waiting to be directed to a desk.

Miss Schneider the form teacher wore a midi skirt, not mini, not maxi. She liked to walk the middle ground.

We tend to lose you up the back. I think I'll try you next to Bernadette. Shocking Miss Hocking. She might make less noise and you might make more noise.

A ripple of laughter had greeted this comment. The back of John's ears so hot that he was sure the glow would be visible in the next classroom. He'd never even spoken to Bernadette Hocking before, she was as close to the top of the popularity stakes as he was to the bottom.

He shuffled self-consciously around the rows of desks and slid onto the wooden bench beside Bernadette, keeping the gap between them as wide as possible, but he was instantly aware that he was in rarefied air. Tiny orbiting particles of pure exotica buzzed around her in an orb that extended right to the end of the bench and beyond. He was in her gravitational pull. Musky perfume, mascara, hair dye, bare brown, female smooth arms and legs.

Fortunately the class's attention had now been diverted to Miss Schneider's next seating arrangement, so they did not witness his witless floundering in the Bernadette attraction zone.

She had flashed him a brief hullo smile and his response was a tight mouthed grimace, suddenly unsure if he'd brushed his teeth that morning. He wondered if she could see his red ears.

They didn't even speak for the first two days beyond a few obligatory greetings. She was always whisked away the moment classes ended by a huddle of girlfriends with the odd boy bobbing around the fringes, hoping for a look in.

It was not until morning recess on the third day, when Miss Schneider had insisted they all remain seated waiting for an announcement from the head, that Bernadette had turned to him, filling in time.

I read your English Expression story yesterday.

That Bernadette was talking to him was enough to send a bolt of panic through John, but the surety that she would have found his story stupidly incomprehensible compounded his panic.

You left it on your desk when the teacher called you up.

He nodded awkwardly. Her words and the breath that was floating them toward him were making him giddy.

I loved it. I didn't really understand it, but I just loved the way you described those bogong moths in their caves, all soft and downy and then when they flew out, you said they were like musical notes moving through the mountain air. It was really lyrical.

Yeah, said John, stretching his linguistic powers to their limit.

You could write songs with words like that. What bands do you get off on?

The Shadows.

Oh, cool. I was in love with Elvis, but that's all over. Now I just dream about Paul.

She pretended to play a few notes on an air guitar, bobbing her head back and forward, her long blonde hair swinging tantalizingly in front of John's eyes.

He immediately decided to find his Ivor Mairant's book of guitar chords as soon as he got home from school, resume his self-tutorage.

Chapter 8

John Mitchell's father, Lionel, had not been able to garage his cream coloured '64 Falcon sedan for two weeks.

The sight of his car out in the elements was an affront to his senses. His very sensitive senses. It may not have been the newest or most prestigious car in Lucille Street, but it was the most loved and cared for conveyance on the whole planet.

He had purchased a car cover to shield it from bird droppings and sap dripping from the neighbour's radiata pine, a disorderly array of branches and needles that intruded into his garden. Needles that wormed their way down through the slotted bonnet vent and into the engine bay. But now he was worried the cover was abrading the Falcon's duco.

He wanted his garage back.

It was Sunday. The dreaded band practice day. The day all the complaints had to be dealt with. The day of constantly tripping fuses and band members' cars, jalopies, parked higgledy-piggledy out the front.

Neighbours could see Lionel's long white socks, folded neatly just below his bare knobbly knees, scissoring back and forward on his green nature strip as he peered into the windows of the two jalopies that were parked on it. Lionel wore a perpetually dismayed expression on his pale saggy features that was now turning to perplexity. How could he mow his nature strip? They were on a break right now, in the house somewhere, probably scoffing his milk arrowroots with their coffee. He took the opportunity to peek inside his garage.

He cautiously opened the side door and was immediately assaulted by the odour of cigarette ash closely followed by the visual bombardment of chaos in his normally orderly work area. Speaker boxes and amplifiers linked by a profusion of electrical cords snaking back and forth across the concrete floor, junction boxes crammed with plugs way beyond their amperage-overload capacities, guitars propped here and there and the dreaded drum kit, the nucleus of most noise complaints, taking up the back corner. Somewhere at the rear of all this were his precious tools and immaculately clean work bench. One overflowing ashtray had been positioned dangerously close to the flammable egg cartons he had helped John line the walls and ceiling with in an attempt at sound insulation. He moved it, nose turned up in protest at the smell.

A family friend had asked him why he put up with all this noise and long hair and he'd replied lamely that he didn't know. All he knew was that his John, an only child, had finally broken through the barriers of his quietude. Something he, Lionel, had never managed to do. He was happy for him.

Rocco Pisano sat in the Mitchell's living room sipping black coffee, eyebrows two thick black lines across a face full of youthful Calabrian bravado. Very tentative bravado in his case. He was still trying to fathom the ways of the world outside his tight-knit family home and was taking in the lavender smell and austere surrounds of the Mitchell living room when his eyes went to the family photographs displayed along the opposite wall. The usual wedding shots were in the lower row, similar to the ones in his family home although without the overflow of relatives and friends that shared nearly every photo with his parents. Above these, more prominently placed, were two separate portraits of soldiers in their military uniforms. One was unmistakably John's dad in his youth and the other was from an older era. There were no military photos in his home. In fact, he wasn't even sure if his father had even fought in the Second World War or which side he may have been on.

Dicko, big loud and boisterous, was entertaining John's mum Amy with his banter as John, now wearing thick black rimmed glasses that made him look like a cross between Buddy Holly and Nana Mouskouri, listened quietly. John's hair was down past his collar and he had a face full of pimples.

Amy, a bird-like woman in a navy twinset and heavy makeup could listen to Dicko all day, he made her laugh and she enjoyed his irreverence. She welcomed this disruption to their Sundays.

Roc waited until she had bustled out of the room to refresh the teapot before pointing to the military photos behind John.

Your dad?

John twisted around to look at them, a little surprised Roc had shown an interest.

Yeah, that's him on the left. He fought in the Mediterranean. Tobruk. The Rats of Tobruk. And the other photo, that's granddad. Gallipoli and the Somme. That's in France. That's where he fought.

Roc sensed that John seemed to respect their achievements. He shrugged.

My father may have fought in the Mediterranean. He was there, of course, at home. Maybe he did.

Dicko found this amusing. He found most things amusing.

You heard what they say about the Italian tanks, haven't you? One gear forward, five in reverse.

Very funny, smart arse. I'll bet if it was you in the war, no one would see your arse for dust.

Dicko laughed. Too right. You won't ever see me fighting in any war.

What if you get conscripted? You registered, didn't you?

Uni, mate. If you're at uni they'll let you defer. 'Least that's what I heard from the student's union.

He turned to John.

That's right, eh? You're the same. You can defer if you get called up.

John shrugged. No idea.

Not that you've got anything to worry about, Dicko grinned. They'd never let you in the army, too soft for boy scouts. Couldn't kill a fly.

Rocco, who was observing this exchange with interest, was expecting another amiable shrug or similar response from John but was surprised when John glared at Dicko and gave him the finger.

John had ridden on his father's shoulders in the Anzac Day crowds as a toddler and never questioned the family tradition of serving king and country, no matter whose king that may be. He'd always assumed serving was something he could do if he had to, not that he'd really thought about it. He wasn't going to take that from Dicko.

Dicko laughed again at his glare. Oooh, touchy. Anyway, I'm deferring. The bloody Vietnam war can't go on for ever.

Five minutes later Roc's bass drum thumped a call of action and the two guitars followed in a half reasonable rendition of Under the Boardwalk.

Despite the egg cartons, neighbours swore, birds took flight from their perches on the garage roof and Lionel began washing his car on the front lawn, away from the pine tree. He was sure he could detect fine abrasion marks on the car roof where the cover had been flapping.

Finally. Finally Lionel had his garage back. Well almost. And probably only for a few weeks.

Summertime, and the Keystones were touring, the excitement levels vertiginous.

An old Commer van they'd bought cheap from the wreckers in Mount Dandenong Road had its rusty rear end backed up against the open garage doors and the boys were trying to make enough space for the last speaker box.

Lionel began rolling up one of the mike leads but John snatched it away, accusing him of getting it in a twist, scornful as only a son can be.

It's audio, dad. There's really fine wires in there.

They were booked for the entire south coast surf club circuit. If this was the big time, then they had made it.

It only took two hours of driving for the boredom to set in. Lionel had paid for the van so John was hogging the prized driver's seat. Dicko and Roc had been alternating between the passenger's seat and a tiny space in the back that consisted of a folded blanket atop one of the amp heads.

C'mon, man. Dicko, the tallest of the three, was wound up like a clock spring. Gimme a break back here. For Christ's sake four eyes, let me take the wheel!

I'm thinking about it. Maybe we could cut a deal here.

Dicko groaned. Don't tell me, more fuckin' blues in the repertoire.

Right on. I want to lose some Monkees songs, like Last Train To Clarkesville, and bring in another Animals song. Say, Boom, Boom, or House Of The Rising Sun.

Mate, pop equals fans which equals sex which is something you wouldn't know anything about.

John shifted down a gear in the gutless Commer. I know enough.

We're not losing Clarksville, the chicks go crazy. Agree Roc?

Roc nodded. He's right, we can't lose Clarksville.

Two weeks and three breakdowns later The Keystones were setting up in the Southview Surf Club for their big tour finale, New Year's Eve. The long thin column PA was in place, John's bass amp, the guitar amp, drums and mikes in stands. There were only two small coloured lights, their 'light show', to be set up, so John decided to go for a walk on the nearby beach. There was plenty of time.

He slipped off his shoes and meandered bare foot through the dunes. The sand was loose and hot so he picked up his pace until he reached the cooler, packed sand near the water. There was quite a crowd between the red and yellow lifesaving flags, the sea breeze carrying their distinctive sunscreen smell toward John. He felt a little self-conscious in his jeans, cool for musos but uncool for beachgoers, so he set off up the beach toward a less popular area.

Their first few surf gigs had been a learning curve, fun but punctuated by small mistakes and nervous starts. He was conscious of not quite being in Dicko's guitar playing league, but he was improving. He loved creating the music but found the crowds daunting and he always tried to set himself up as near to the back of the stage as possible. Dicko reckoned he was more suited to being a session muso, away from the frontline.

As he walked, he went over the various chords in his head. He didn't sing well but tonight he was going to try joining Roc in mouthing a few harmonies. It was more for the looks, Dicko had assured him. Don't fuck up the sound but try and make it look like you're joining in. We have to look like The Beatles, all singing, all doing something. That wasn't hard to do in a three piece. But the thought of singing was nerve wracking. What if he mistimed the harmony and his croaky voice was heard by all?

He needn't have worried, it was great. Roc in his silly striped trousers smashing cymbals and thumping his kick drum. Dicko, who'd been tippling away at a whisky flask all night was as loose as a goose, as he'd described himself. Paisley shirts, mod caps pulled down hard over their fringes and Carnaby street coats soon discarded in the summer heat. They were flying. As Dicko raced off into another riff, John came in at exactly the right spot mirroring his chords and adding his own variations. They exchanged knowing smiles in the mayhem of noise and flying arms and hair as the packed hall built up to midnight.

John was experiencing an exhilaration that threatened to transport him off into an unknown world; for the first time, he was actually enjoying the audience. He thought about putting the brakes on and refocusing on his plectrum work, but he was a fatalist after all. Stuff it. Just go with it.

All the standard rigmarole that New Year's Eve demanded had to be attended to at twelve. A shaky rendition of Auld Lang Syne, something of a chore for the boys, still managed to fire up the crowd.

One more encore was allowed after midnight, so a quick on-stage debate followed. John pleaded for Boom, Boom instead of Last Train to Clarkesville, their standard end of proceedings number. To his surprise, Roc nodded and Dicko gave a what the fuck shrug.

It was a hit but anything they played at that hour would have been greeted with youth-crazy adulation.

It would become the night that John lost his virginity.

Burley lifesavers and plenty of girls seemed to be the only other invitees to the surf club after-party. John allowed himself a can or two of bourbon and coke, but it took some time for him to unwind from the highs of being on stage. He wanted a musical analysis of their night's work, a team meeting, but the boys were obviously not interested.

Dicko was in full party mode, sculling whisky and throwing his arms around a succession of adoring girls. Roc, as usual, was playing it cool. The Italian stallion bullshit. A leggy beauty in a glittering mini skirt was running her hand inside his shirt, fascinated by the forest of hair within.

John retreated to a less crowded spot by a window. He was considering another walk on the beach when a dark-haired girl approached him.

At first, she didn't say anything and there was an odd silence between them. She took up a position in front of him, looking at him while she sipped at her drink through a straw. Square fringed and large breasted for someone so obviously young.

John nodded and smiled but she still said nothing and did not return his smile. She seemed to be regarding his face and John wondered if it was his Nana Mouskouri glasses that had drawn her attention. He'd begged his mother to buy the wire rimmed John Lennon look-alikes, but she had been paying so that was the end of the argument.

The girl moved quite close to him, still sucking on her straw. The top of her head only came to his chin, so he found himself looking down into her drink and beyond to the dark void of her cleavage. Her eyes were still looking up into his face and he could now smell her strong sweet perfume.

Finally, she relinquished her straw and spoke.

Hello.

Hi. Um. Did you enjoy the dance?

She didn't answer, still regarding him in the most disturbingly open way.

Did you like our version of Boom, Boom? John persisted.

She spoke again but it was not an answer to his question.

I normally only go for drummers.

John glanced over her head at Roc who was now embracing the glittering dressed girl.

I see.

Again, there was a long silence. She had very large, unblinking brown eyes that never released him from her detached appraisal.

He found himself staring back at her. She had full lips, accentuated by orange-coloured lipstick. He noticed her breasts rise slightly as if to greet him and her eyes softened, engaging his. This was enough to release a shower of tiny sparks through his senses.

There was a slight movement and he felt her hand, gently, but firmly, take his genitals. He had absolutely no control over their reaction to her grip.

A knowing smile came across her face.

Downstairs, in the bunk-room, she said. Which bunk is yours?

I don't have one. I mean we haven't sorted any of that out yet.

She wordlessly turned and, without relinquishing her grip, gently led him to a nearby door. They could have been any couple leaving hand in hand.

They descended a set of stairs and entered the bunk room. It was dark, but she led him to a bunk in a far corner and turned to face him, releasing the bulge in his jeans for the first time. Again, there was a stand-off between them. As his eyes adjusted to the dark he realised that she was once more staring into his face. She didn't move toward him and he thought that she must be waiting for him to take her in his arms, but he remained motionless, surprisingly calm. Whatever was going to happen would happen. He began to relax.

Eventually she moved toward him and began unbuckling his belt. He slipped off his glasses and placed them on the top bunk, he could see all he wanted to. It was not until they eased back onto the bottom bunk that they kissed and he tasted the fruity flavour of her lipstick, then the different cards of lovemaking fell in the order they should. Somewhere among the cards she produced a condom.

Next morning, he awoke to that condom, discarded on the mattress under his knee, cold and icky. She was still there, back to him, dark hair falling across her pillow, the silhouetted rollercoaster shape of her waist and hip under the sheet, gently rising and falling to her breathing.

He wanted to touch her, follow the rounds of her body, but he was afraid to wake her up. He'd never shared a bed with anyone before.

Without moving, he began to look around the other bunks in the morning half-light. He thought he could see Roc on the top bunk opposite him and hear Dicko's now familiar snoring somewhere on the far side of the room.

He returned his attention to the sleeping form beside him, now ever so gently running his fingertips over the shape of her hip.

It was then that the front door opened, letting in a blaze of light. One of the senior lifesavers barrelled into the room, looking around wildly.

Carol! Carol! Where are you?

His bed partner sat straight up, instantly awake. The lifesaver grabbed her roughly by the arm and jerked her out of the bunk.

Move! Your dad's in the bloody carpark already. I'll get you out the side door.

Without even a glance at John, she snatched up her clothes from the floor and allowed herself to be dragged across the room. As he was leaving, the lifesaver turned in the doorway and looked back at John.

Sorry son happens every week. Underage and her dad's a copper. You owe me one.

The door slammed shut and John was aware that everyone in the room was peering over and around bunks at him. Dicko, Roc, several clubbies and a few girls. He pulled the sheet over his head.

Chapter 9

The eleventh National Service ballot live on your TV, folks. Dicko was standing beside his old black and white television, speaking into an imaginary mike.

Sponsored by the good citizens of Australia.

Shut up man. Roc was nervously trying to adjust the television's rabbit-ears aerial. This is fuckin' serious.

John looked on from a bum-weary couch. Dicko's flat was an anthem to male muso mayhem. Used plates with days old food scraps, overflowing ashtrays, song sheets, randomly thrown clothes and instruments propped here and there. Dicko dropped down beside John on the couch.

Only serious for you guys. I'm next ballot and I'm deferring whatever happens.

Roc tentatively tweaked the aerial and a flickering black and white image of two balding public servant warriors in suits, flanking a hexagonal wooden barrel, appeared through the static.

Hold it man, Dicko barked. That's as good as it gets.

Roc took up a position behind the couch and they watched as the barrel was spun. A third man began producing numbered marbles from a trap door in the barrel as a uniformed army officer looked on. Dicko was leaning forward now, peering into the screen.

They're doing January. That's you Roc. What date?

I'm twenty ninth. What's he up to?

Dicko began counting the marbles. Looks like twenty second, twenty sixth, twenty eighth. Wait for it …

This was a moment in time that Rocco Pisano had been mentally sidestepping for months. Now it was on him he found himself closing his eyes. Without thinking about it he began praying, something he had not done since childhood.

Thirtieth! You're safe, man. We've still got a drummer.

Roc had been accused of being a drum beat behind at different times in the past but it was a good five or six beats before he finally opened his eyes.

That's it, I'm going to mass for the rest of my life. No army, no Vietnam. Thank god.

John had been quiet through all of this, sitting with folded arms, staring at the TV. He watched four dates fall in February and then they started on his month, March.

Dicko looked at him. Twenty first, right?

Yeah, my lucky number.

Dunno if that's a good thing.

Dicko began counting the marbles again as they were produced.

First, tenth, fifteenth.

The next numbered marble was pulled out and displayed and Dicko was politely silent.

It was twenty-one.

John sat, still staring at the tv, as the other two exchanged looks. Dicko spoke quietly.

Bad luck, mate.

John shrugged but did not answer.

You going to defer through uni?

It was a question that had been asked many times before, but John had always been non-committal. This time he gave a resolute head-shake, arms still folded.

No, I'm not. My number's come up so I'm going to do National Service.

Dicko was incredulous.

You can't! That's madness, mate. You're two years into uni with a career at the end and then there's us. What about us? We're just getting our shit together.

It was the most serious John had ever seen Dicko but he'd made up his mind and not even a serious Dicko was going to change it.

Sorry boys, my number has come up so it's like a signpost for me. I'll do Nasho, go to Vietnam and I might even apply for the SAS. If I'm in, then I'm gonna go the whole hog. Destiny and all that.

That's shit, mate, said Dicko. You're no soldier. You're a piss-weak muso like the rest of us. Accept it.

Nope. I'm going in the army.

John continued to sit, arms folded, eyes fixed on the tv again.

Dicko and Roc looked at each other with Roc giving a little head-shake.

In the Mitchell living room John's parents had been seated on their couch in front of the tv long before the marbles began spinning. Tray of biscuits and pot of tea with two cups at the ready on the small occasional table in front of them.

Amy began pouring the tea, it was a routine that she often used to paper over an array of emotions. Lionel used his neat, straight-backed demeanour to conjure a false appearance of control, Amy used the habitual solicitude of tea-making.

With the marble draw looming, Amy's tea pouring hand was trembling so much that she had to use her free hand to press down on the teapot lid to stop it rattling. Lionel began stroking her back and making vague reassuring noises that really didn't amount to anything more than a series of mumbles.

Our John. Strong inside. Be fine. War is … Not so … Be right.

Amy nodded and murmured agreeance, but she was struggling with two sets of emotions. Fear that her son would be conscripted and sent to war and fear for Lionel. Only she knew about Lionel's never ending war traumas. The Second World War battles he fought twenty-five years ago were still present in his dreams and often in his daylight hours. Anything could trigger a breakdown and it was always she who had to nurse him back to a point where he could cope with everyday life again. She was worried the marble draw could be such a trigger but there was nothing she could do about it so she tried to focus her thoughts on John. She had given birth to John four weeks before he was due and, in her mind, he had never quite caught up to the physicality of his age group. She had done her best to make him feel special throughout his childhood, every little treat that their meagre budget could afford had gone John's way. To her, he had always been like a leaf in a gale, a china cup in a shop full of bulls. But her most overwhelming emotion was that John was *her* son.

Her only son.

Her only child.

She was an only mother.

For him to be sent off to war would be simply unfair.

When the three wise men on the television screen began drawing out the marbles for March, Amy and Lionel linked arms in mutual support and leant forward, hunched together on the couch.

When twenty-one was drawn Amy felt a wave of nausea and she closed her eyes not wanting to believe what she had just seen and heard but she had no time to process her anguish because Lionel had collapsed to his knees and, in doing so, knocked over the occasional table, teapot and cups falling to the floor.

Amy rushed to his assistance, dragging the upturned table to one side and dropping to her knees beside him, trying to restrain his heaving and threshing body.

Lionel's guttural cries and moans were coming from a part of him that was shut off from everyday normality. A part of him that was bunkered behind armoured doors that were now flung open revealing body parts so sensitive that even the lightest touch of a feather would cause excruciating pain.

The only witnesses to the scene taking place on the Mitchell's living room floor were two uniformed Anzacs from two wars, staring down from their picture frames on the wall behind the couch. One being Lionel.

The Lionel in the photograph could see himself as he knew himself.

By the time John returned home the house was again in order. Lionel's breakdowns had been a regular occurrence in the immediate post-war years, but this was his first for some time and not as severe as some of his previous ones. The occasional table was now back in place, Amy in place, Lionel in place.

Lionel's greeting was stoic and supportive. John confirmed that he would not be deferring, and Lionel nodded and patted him on the shoulder.

As it should be, son. As it should be.

I could finish uni if I wanted. But …

Amy and Lionel waited for John to finish his sentence but there was only a protracted silence. Amy wanted to hold her son and squeeze him so tightly that every notion of the military would be forced out of his thin frame. She knew that Lionel had not been put together for war and that behind his and John's very different personalities they shared a common fragility. She watched Lionel give John another pat on the shoulder and thought how false this was. She knew Lionel was as terrified for John as she was.

It won't be easy, son. Lionel said stiffly.

Nothing's easy. John smiled wanly. You managed. I'll manage.

There was no malice or sarcasm intended in this statement, but it took Lionel a moment to realise this. His hands began fidgeting nervously and he had to sit down.

John turned his smile to his mother.

It's ok, mum. Duty calls. It's kind of like a message, being called up.

Now Amy hugged him as tightly as she could, tears forming as she pressed her face into his chest.

You don't have to go John.

But her words were muffled in the woolly jumper he was wearing. She waited until she felt more composed and looked up into his face, not releasing her hug.

There is no message, John. You must do everything in your power to get out of it. Defer. Do whatever you can.

Now John returned her hug and gently drew her face back into his jumper. She knew it was his way of silencing her. They held this position for some time as Lionel looked on, leaning back into the couch, still needing it's support. Eventually John released his mother and gave her a light kiss on the cheek.

It's ok, Mum.

He returned one of his father's shoulder pats and headed off to his room, closing the door behind him.

Was it ok? Would he be ok? He had no idea, but he did as he had always done and pushed his fears to one side, focusing on his predilection for accepting fate. The game was on; the tumbling marbles had spoken, and they were pointing the way. All he had to do was follow and accept.

The MCG loomed monolithically on the other side of the Yarra and morning trains rattled past on their raised line carrying commuters to city jobs. Those commuters may have wondered what was going on in the park below where there were several long, straggling lines of youths leading to the gates of the Swan Street army Depot. Surrounding them was a sea of angry agitators. Anti-war placard-carrying students, mothers waiving signs reading SOS or Save Our Sons and among these protestors were parents, girlfriends and wives sending off their loved ones. Behind the gates army order, outside the gates civilian disorder.

Lionel and Amy Mitchell were standing arm in arm on the freshly mown grass a little away from the throng.

Amy's head was resting gently on Lionel's shoulder. Her eyes were fixed on her son as he inched forward with the rest of the line closer and closer to the gates. He looked smaller and thinner than ever, bag in hand, hair now so long it reached halfway down his back, the wire-framed John Lennon glasses he'd bought himself ... in fact, she thought, he looked like John Lennon ... John Lennon standing in line with a row of heavyweight boxers, Sonny Listons, Cassius Clays and Floyd Pattersons. Tattooed, muscular, dangerous. She began to sob.

Lionel looked down at her and took a deep breath. He'll be fine, I'm sure.

Amy flashed a look at him. How can you say that? He's so slight, only a child compared to the others. He looks lost.

Lionel ran an eye over the line and shook his head.

He's no different to most of them. A lot of the other lads look bewildered to me. Just down from the farm, a few long hairs... granted, there are one or two thuggish looking fellows but overall, they're just a bunch of everyday twenty-year-olds disappearing into the army. Probably do them the world of good.

John had now reached the gates, where a soldier looked at his documents and pointed to somewhere inside the compound. John moved on and was quickly lost to view.

Amy dabbed her eyes with a white handkerchief and looked up at Lionel who was continuing to stare at the gate, now deep in thought.

Are you going to miss him? It was a provocative question, she knew the answer and was trying to needle some emotion from him.

He said nothing for a moment, still lost in thought. Then he took her arm and they began walking toward the train station.

Of course I'll miss him, he eventually replied.

You never show it to him.

Lionel's saggy features tightened a little. Just the way I am. The way I was brought up. My father.

That doesn't mean you have to be like your father forever. You're forty-five years old, for god's sake.

Maybe, Lionel said, looking ahead. But you can't be expected to understand. John's going to find out that showing emotion in the army is regarded as a weakness. Lionel looked down at his highly polished shoes, now covered in grass clippings. And I know the dangers of weakness better than anyone, he mumbled.

Amy gave his arm a little sympathetic squeeze, this was all she wanted from him. They continued to walk toward the train station, Lionel had to get to work.

I also know the dangers of war, he thought to himself, in all its many many forms. He willed himself to keep walking and not look back.

Chapter 10

Any parking spots today? Is that one? No, another driveway. Never mind, I'll park in Frankie's driveway if she's left any room.

Just enough room, I think.

No?

Yes.

Cindy Fong slipped her little Audi into park and switched off. She glanced at herself in the rear-view mirror and flicked at her fringe. She had always worn her hair long and, as the years had slipped by, her hair had lost little of its black gloss. She looked forward to this, her only constant. Double yoga with Frankie.

They had been locking hands, tugging against each other, twisting and stretching since childhood. Their sessions had become spasmodic through the busy Snoopies times and Frankie's child-rearing years, but since Jack's passing it had become a regular Saturday afternoon event.

A few minutes later they were locked in the Full Moon pose. She and Frankie. Balanced on their left legs, back-to-back, right legs extended horizontally, somehow gripping each other's feet.

They could never hold this one for long without giggling and they collapsed in a heap on Frankie's living room floor.

Frankie rolled over to a sitting position and flicked through a few pages in the time-worn folder that held the remnants of their sixties instruction handbook. Black and white photos and text preserved in separate plastic sleeves after they had come loose from the binding. She selected one of the pages and showed Cindy.

What about the Extended Hero? We managed the Hero last week.

How does that one go again?

Start with the Hero, palm on the floor, then reach up to touch hands above our heads. Remember?

Oh, yeah. That one.

As they stretched and reached, back-to-back again, Frankie randomly asked Cindy who her hero was these days.

I don't have a hero any more... Donald Trump.

Trump!

I'm being silly.

Just as well.

No, said Cindy, my grandfather was my hero and his hero was Robert Menzies. He became terribly disillusioned with all those weak leaders that followed. Sneddon, McMahon and so on. He thought Gorton was ok.

They pushed against each other, stretching right out.

We hated McMahon. Frankie felt her shoulder muscle spasm but she kept reaching for the ceiling, hand locked with Cindy's. I wrote a song about Silly Billy, Nixon's little willy ... or something like that. Very ribald.

They completed the stretch and Frankie gingerly rotated her shoulder. Cindy glanced at her phone.

Time for a quick strum before I go?

I loaned Jack's old guitar to John so I've only got my Yamaha.

You loaned him a guitar? My God Frankie, you're a soft touch.

I rarely use it and it keeps him happy.

The leopard never changes her spots. Cindy was shaking her head.

No, she doesn't, Frankie replied firmly, removing her guitar from its case.

How is he? Cindy asked. Still problematic?

Not too much of a problem. He keeps to himself but every now and again I find him wandering around, totally off his face.

Cindy shuddered. Don't know how you can put up with someone like that living so close. Right in your backyard. What if he has some kind of turn? Flips out and becomes violent.

No, he's harmless Cindy. I know the type. Very sad. I'm trying to draw him out and encourage him to talk about Vietnam and what troubles him. I think it's only the main trauma he really struggles with. But ... no success yet, I'm afraid.

Well, good luck with that. Better you than me.

Frankie began idly strumming.

Will we be ok with one guitar?

Fine, said Cindy. I'll sing along, you play.

Old or new?

You choose.

Would you mind if we do one of the protest songs from my uni days? Country Joe and the Fish. What're we fighting for. You know the one?

I do, said Cindy. But that was your fight, not mine. Your nightmare.

Sorry, said Frankie. Jack's birthday coming up. I've been a little obsessed. Going over the whole Police raid. All that waiting – if it wasn't for you…

Then we need to sing about it, Cindy interrupted with a bright smile. The positive was that you met Jack. So you play and sing; I'll follow. One two three.

Frankie began playing and their voices combined as they had for most of their lives.

What're we fighting for? Don't ask me…….

When Cindy had gone, Frankie continued to play different tunes from their early band days, her mind lazily meandering through childhood memories, instinctively trying to form the words of a new song… swimming through memories like swimming in a river, warm currents, cold currents, going on forever…

Chapter 11

Was the world a fair place? Frankie Raye Jamieson was lying on her back staring at the ceiling of her bedroom. Her father had lovingly painted dozens of tiny white stars on a background of powder blue, but she was not looking at his handiwork.

She was visualising a kaleidoscope of scenarios. Rich people, poor people. Lions preying on antelope. Countries at war – it was so unfair soldiers had to fight politician's wars like Vietnam. The giant gum tree outside her bedroom window and the way its fallen leaves never allowed the lawn to grow under its spread. The kids at school and their mean little groups, barbed words, twisted meanings, insincerity – she'd just used that word in an essay during the week and was still enjoying the way it played on her tongue when she said it out loud. In – sin – cerity.

What was fair in the world? Certainly not her share of the human anatomical gifts – she'd only just learned the word anatomical as well. Why did she have to stuff hankies down her bra? Why was she still waiting for her first period at age sixteen? Why couldn't she be like all the other girls, chatting about bra sizes, sex, period pains. She hadn't told any of her friends, not even Cindy. What a stupid, stupid secret. The world wasn't a fair place and something should be done about it. A word to god – but she didn't believe in religion. Her thoughts were beginning to mire in the complexities of religion when there was an urgent tapping on her bedroom window. A pale moon face was pressed to the foggy glass fringed with a droop of black hair. Cindy.

Cindy's tears flowed as soon as they made eye contact and Frankie moved quickly to open the sash. It stuck closed at first but then let go with a rush.

Cindy, what's wrong? Cindy was now sobbing loudly so Frankie took her arm and helped her through the window.

They hugged and Frankie could feel Cindy's tears running down her own neck and under the collar of her pyjamas. She had a strange feeling that she was actually absorbing Cindy's tears through her skin and with them her emotions. She had helped Cindy through numerous schoolyard "slanty eyes" and "ching chong" racist taunts but she sensed that this was something else again.

When she felt that Cindy had calmed enough to talk, Frankie asked her again what was wrong?

I allowed him xiè dú, Cindy finally whispered in Frankie's ear.

Frankie muttered an acknowledgement, but she didn't understand the Chinese words.

My very first time Frankie, my virginity – and now it's all over. Colin's left me.

Ok, Frankie thought, how do I deal with this? It was her difficult area. Cindy's numerous teenage romances had always stirred feelings of envy and inadequacy in Frankie thanks to her stupid secret.

Cindy attracted boys with her exotic looks and understated curves but they were attracted to Frankie as well, although she could never work out why. Cindy had said it was her blonde hair and tall willowy figure but that was nonsense to Frankie who considered herself to be too thin and shapeless.

While Cindy embraced each new encounter and allowed her emotions to run the full gamut, Frankie retreated from every advance. Her stupid secret ruled her emotions. How could she try and comfort Cindy when she had no experiences of her own to draw on?

Flowers, Cindy had said as she slumped onto Frankie's bed. Beautiful roses and talk of marriage. But that was before.

Did he use protection? Frankie asked, going straight to the nitty-gritty as was her way. A condom?

Nothing. In the back of his car after the dance. Then last night ... when I took Colin home to meet my family for the first time ... it all turned crazy. They thought he was unsuitable for me. Not Chinese, not studying to be a doctor ... you know how they are ... but I think it was more than that. Grandfather even called him a huāidan, a bad egg and he called grandfather an old chink. An old chink, Frankie! Can you believe it?

Frankie could. She had been wary of Colin from the start. Older and manipulative, in her eyes.

Colin was so angry Frankie. I couldn't calm him down. He drove away like a lunatic, so fast ... he never wants to see me again.

She had broken into sobbing once more and Frankie could only think that Cindy's grandfather had made the right call. She had always thought of him as a wise old owl. She knew Cindy would recover. She had her own way of coping with things: never confrontational, a strategic mental retreat that was in no way defeatist. She would advance in her own time. Frankie had seen it before.

Next Saturday morning they boarded the red rattler bound for the city and chose a seat beside the open door. Cindy was adamant that her life would go on as normal and this Saturday morning trip into the city was part of the norm.

A group of footy fans in black and white scarfs and beanies stood clutching the looped leather straps, swinging in rhythm with the train as it gathered speed.

Fifteen miles to Griffiths Bros Tea. The little blue sign flashed by.

Cindy's conversation had been in determinedly normal mode all week.

Remember when we stood down there with our parents and watched the Queen's train go by? She asked Frankie, making bright conversation rather than really reminiscing.

The train was passing near to their homes from which they'd traipsed half an hour to the railway station, a breezy two minutes for the train to retrace their traipsing.

How could I forget it? We must have been all of four. Standing in the blackberries.

She was on the rear balcony with The Duke, said Cindy. She waved to us. Did he wave too? Can you remember?

Frankie couldn't remember.

Cindy loved sewing and this Saturday trip into the centre of Melbourne and the Polish material shop at the top of Bourke Street had become something of a ritual.

The shop was like a dusty Aladdin's Cave with bolts and bolts of different coloured and patterned material stacked right up to the high ceiling. Cindy would choose something different each week and they would return to her grandfather's house in the afternoon where she would use her grandmother's old treadle machine to transform the material into a dress to be worn that night for a dance or a party or sometimes just for their own pretend concert performance. While Cindy was choosing her materials and later wandering around the department stores, Frankie had formed a habit of slipping down to St Vincent's soup kitchen and putting in an hour or two of voluntary work. She enjoyed the cheery banter of the other much older volunteers and the looks of appreciation she often received from the life-battered faces when they observed her youth, rare in these circles, as she doled out their soup.

The train pulled into Richmond Station, one stop from the city and what had become a press of footy fans spilled out onto the platform.

Cindy had been chatting feverishly nearly the whole way.

I want things to do, Frankie. Lots of things so I don't have time to, you know.

Frankie knew.

I want to form a proper band, said Cindy. Not just you and me, a proper band with lead, drums, bass and us singing.

They had often talked about this. They had been singing along to various records for years and their high school music teacher, friends, even their parents agreed they had something.

Sure. We could give it a go, said Frankie thinking only of all the organising that would have to be done.

We could take singing lessons, Frankie. It would make all the difference and sometimes those tutors have connections to managers and musos. I want to do it, Frankie. I really want to do it.

Ok. But lessons cost.

Grandfather.

He'd pay for singing lessons?

Cindy nodded. He's my grandfather, of course he would.

Frankie smiled.

Ok, then. I'll go check out Brashs Music Store before I go to St Vinnies. I'll see if they've got any tambourines I can afford. We have to start somewhere.

Frankie left Cindy in the material shop and stepped outside into the late winter sunshine. The Bourke Street crowds had a real chirp about them that morning as they shopped for pre-spring specials. Every clothing store seemed to be advertising a sale.

As Frankie made her way towards Brashs she began thinking about singing lessons and the band, if it ever evolved. She was beginning university the next year and her studies would surely be impacted. Ok for Cindy who only had plans to work in her parent's business – and then there was the music itself. She listened to Joan Baez and Bob Dylan while Cindy only had ears for pop. The boppier the better. Could she be bothered with pop or would Cindy brave the revolution?

Frankie shrugged the dilemma off. Cindy's thing. Let her run with it. She just hoped Cindy's period came that month. She hadn't been brave enough to ask Cindy about her period for fear Cindy might return the question. Ironic worrying about someone else's periods rather than her own lack of one. Would her hormones ever kick in? Would she ever feel all those things she longed to feel? Sexy, womanly. Have the courage to take on the advances of boys?

There was a large photo of slender supermodel Twiggy in the shop front she was walking past and Frankie looked from the photo to her own reflection in the window. She lifted her chest and straightened her back. If Twiggy could wow them then so could she.

Chapter 12

Cindy's eyes were everywhere as she and Frankie walked down Greville Street, Prahran for the first time. Nine months had passed since Cindy's boyfriend drama and, with no ensuing pregnancy and their singing lessons now complete, the girls were moving right along.

A bare-footed couple swung out of a rainbow-coloured doorway, laughing and embracing, nearly collecting Cindy before piling into an old van. They were followed by a bare-chested youth with an oversized bead necklace, calling loudly for the others to wait. He slammed the rainbow-coloured door behind him but not before it had released a pungent whiff of marijuana. On the other footpath, a waif of a girl was walking with a large Alsatian dog that she was leading with a tie-dyed scrap of chiffon. The narrow road surface and the old two-story buildings were grey, but the atmosphere was all colour. Further down the street, muffled rock music was coming from a corner pub. Frankie was trying to read street numbers but many of the buildings were numberless.

Number twenty-eight I think that says. An even number so we must be on the right side of the street.

They passed a traditional Hungarian restaurant, looking out of place among its neighbouring shops, most of which appeared to be closed up and used for living.

This must be it.

Frankie stood looking up at a sign above one of the shop fronts that read 'Alice in Vunderland'. The display window featured an ornate middle eastern hookah and various other smoking devices.

Cindy looked nervously at Frankie. You do the talking, ok?

Why should I?

Please?

Frankie rolled her eyes in mock grievance and led the way into the shop.

The interior was under-lit and under-stocked. In fact, there wasn't much for sale at all. Behind the counter was a gingery bearded rather puddingy fellow whose smile Frankie interpreted as an invitation to multiple layers of hedonism. He had black diamond eyes and a booming voice.

Good morning young ladies. What beautiful dresses.

Frankie felt a little like Red Riding Hood. They were both wearing rather frilly Cindy originals which were glaringly out of place in this frontier of hippiedom.

We're looking for Tim De Lucca, said Frankie. Have we got the right place?

You certainly have, and I know straight away what your business is. You two are the very pretty duo from the school of music looking for someone to put a band together for you. Bernardo has been singing your praises, excuse the pun.

Frankie excused his pun.

I'm Frankie Jamieson and this is Cindy Fong.

A pudgy, much beringed hand was extended over the counter.

Call me De Lucca. Everyone does.

He held Cindy's hand slightly longer than he held Frankie's. They had been open to taking on anyone who was willing to manage them but Frankie was opting for caution already.

You were one of a number of names Bernardo put forward.

Cindy glanced sideways at Frankie knowing that De Lucca's was the only name they had been given.

Well, first things first, said De Lucca. Come upstairs and meet Roc and Dicko, they've just lost their bass player to the army and I'm lining them up with another. They're all rock and bad habits but I'm sure they can play a couple of your tunes and I can listen to you sing.

He closed the shop door with a bang and locked it.

Upstairs, Dicko heard the door close below and looked at Roc.

Here we go. Ready to play fairy floss and candy music?

Roc picked up a pair of brushes and caressed the top of his snare drum with them.

We need the money, man. Just do what De Lucca says. You wanna keep working in the car wash? I don't.

De Lucca led the girls into the cramped room and introductions were made.

Frankie thrust her hand out to Dicko and smiled.

He shook her hand a little awkwardly, not used to girls who could look him in the eye straight up.

You look familiar, she said, we may have caught one of your gigs. Did you ever play the Dorset?

Dicko nodded. At least a couple of times.

Trio, said Frankie. Key something.

Keystones, Roc chipped in.

That's right, I remember now. You guys were great. Mix of rock and blues.

Dicko grinned at this. Blues influence always came from four eyes, our old bass player. Source of many an argument. Anyway, won't go down that road but thanks for the praise, always gets things off on the right foot.

Too true, said De Lucca stepping between them and turning to Frankie.

Let's run through your repertoire and we'll see what the boys can play.

Dicko quickly picked two songs and they were away. It was hard to feel nervous in this ultra laid-back environment and Frankie could sense an unspoken appreciation from Dicko and Roc as her and Cindy's voices soon filled the small space. De Lucca was focusing intently.

Pop-y. He said when they had finished. But that's great. That's where the money market is. You two balance each other really well. I'm impressed.

Cindy was now smiling, flushed with the moment. Even Frankie allowed herself a half-smile. The wolf seemed genuinely pleased with their mini performance but perhaps that was because he could see them becoming his next meal.

I'm sensing a genre, a look. You're both so natural. Give me a few more minutes and I'll even have a name for you.

He was getting excited now. Pudgy hands clasping and unclasping. Cindy seemed mesmerised by the blur of his rings.

To tell you the truth, your beautiful dresses looked a little out of place when you first came in the shop but now I'm not so sure. You've already got a certain sound and vibe. Kind of girly but cute as cute. Do you know Snoopy and the Red Baron? Novelty song, Royal Guardsmen.

Cindy nodded. We've never sung it, but I know it.

De Lucca ploughed on. I could see you covering that. Turning to Dicko, What do you think?

I'm sure the girls could cover whatever they liked with their vocal range. With a grin to Cindy, it's all practice.

But what about the whole look thing, man? De Lucca implored. The Little Pattie look? You know what I mean.

Dicko shook his head and laughed. I'm just the guitar player, Lucca. You're the king of crap. Your area, not mine.

But De Lucca wouldn't let go. He wanted this all sewn up as quickly as possible.

I'm onto something. I know I am. What about the name, Dicko? The name. Something to do with that Snoopy song. Baronets? Red something? Snoopies?

Dicko shrugged. Can't go past The Snoopies. What do you reckon, girls? It's your act.

This was happening way too quickly for Frankie but Cindy was right into it, even letting forth a quick handclap.

I like The Snoopies, she said. What do you think, Frankie? The Snoopies?

Frankie nodded. Ok, I suppose. Depends on where we want to go.

De Lucca could see a deal that needed crunching. He put his arms around both girls.

I know where we want to go. It's clear. The look, the sound, the name. Snoopies. We can get you girls off the ground in no time.

Frankie knew Cindy was sold and they hadn't even talked money: she would just have to strike the best deal she could. But one thing was for sure, she wasn't going to sign anything until her father had read it.

When the girls had gone, De Lucca locked the door again behind them and turned to Dicko and Roc who'd followed him downstairs.

What do think boys? I can get gigs for this, sure of it. You two interested?

Fuck man, said Dicko but a dark Calabrian glare from Roc cut him short.

De Lucca snatched up a notebook from behind the counter and waved it at Dicko.

Take it or leave it, I've got a book full of players here looking for gigs. I just need a backing band that does a job without throwing their egos around. You can still play your rock but my gigs come first, second and third!

De Lucca's black eyes were narrowed into two businesslike slits that swung from Dicko to Roc and Roc was quick to capitulate. We're in, he said, but what about a bass player?

Neil Baxter, best going round, but if you don't sign up for this show with the girls you don't get him. Simple. I keep him and get another guitarist and drummer. You in Dicko?

What the fuck, said Dicko resignedly. Do I get to sing in this circus?

Backing vocals only. You'll be playing a rhythm guitar and maybe the odd solo on lead and you, Roc, you'll have to pull your volume and play straight. No fancy stuff. Agree?

When they agreed they got a much firmer shake from De Lucca's pudgy mit than the girls had received. Dicko and Roc were locked in.

The Snoopies were born.

Chapter 13

Frankie could feel Cindy's nerves as they stood shoulder to shoulder, facing the huge studio cameras and blinding lights. Learning the song, Snoopy and the Red Baron, had been difficult. The song was stridently upbeat and it had been decided that she and Cindy would have to harmonise the whole song together to provide the necessary vocal oomph. There was a solo right at the start, the quirky little spiel in German. Neither of them knew any German so Frankie had been given the task of shouting out the word "achtung" and mumbling a few follow-up words in a German sounding accent which would hopefully be drowned out by the guitars. It was potentially messy.

A clapperboard snapped shut in front of the camera they were facing and Frankie moved forward to the mike on cue. The dozen or so studio audience that De Lucca had drummed up from somewhere began clapping on the same cue.

Frankie let rip with the best "achtung!" she could manage, and Dicko's guitar swept into the bouncy rhythm. Cindy stepped forward to her mike and Frankie quit her mumbled German and launched into the first verse with Cindy. They jigged and swayed in unison, their chiffon frocks floating up and down as they bent and straightened their knees together.

De Lucca was watching apprehensively from the wings with the studio producer. He felt a rush of adrenalin when the girls' voices sounded across the stage, past the cameras and out over the audience section of the studio. Boyo, they could sing, he thought to himself, and they looked great. He'd done it this time, really put something together.

The studio producer was nodding and smiling as she listened to the girls quickly move into the fourth verse. She was hearing their voices through her earphones.

> *In the nick of time, a hero rose*
> *A funny looking dog with a big black nose*
> *He flew into the sky to seek revenge*
> *But the Baron shot him down,*
> *"Curses, foiled again."* This was Frankie with
> another fake voice.
> *Ten, twenty, thirty, forty, fifty, or more*
> *The Bloody Red Baron was rollin' up the score*
> *Eighty men died trying to end that spree*
> *Of the Bloody Red Baron of Germany.*

At this point, the guitars and Roc's snare drum tried to mimic the sounds of planes and machine gun fire. It was corny but seemed to work.

Later, they were all sitting around a table in the studio canteen, De Lucca, the girls, band members and studio producer, a clear-faced young woman with thick sandy coloured hair.

Congrats one and all, she said. That went really well and the clip will be going to air next week.

De Lucca was pumped. We're playing Sebastion's on Friday and if management like us it could become a regular gig. I'm trying to get a look in at Berties as well. Both big city gigs.

Roc gave a little whoop. Bread. No more washing cars.

De Lucca managed a small smile behind his red beard. Wins all round. But you guys will have to improve your battle noises on the guitars. He turned to the producer, sitting next to him. What do you think?

The producer shrugged unconcernedly. I was thinking, she said, that I might add a few special effects on the tape before it goes to air. Something along the lines of The Royal Guardsmen's original version.

Frankie had been listening to all this with some reserve. She was still tingling with the buzz of having survived their first television studio ordeal, but thoughts of her tight university schedule were beginning to nag away at her. She had never considered the possibility of multiple weekly gigs and was now trying to digest De Lucca's grand scheduling announcements. Cindy, however, was smiling uncontrollably, small dark eyes darting from person to person, announcement to announcement. Her arm had been draped around Frankie's shoulder for some time and she gave her an excited hug. Frankie responded by reaching up and lightly taking Cindy's hand in her own and Cindy gave Frankie's hand an affectionate squeeze. Frankie knew Cindy was conveying a million thanks, but these things were not all one way. She had plenty to be thankful for as well.

The corner bar of The Prince Alfred, conveniently close to Melbourne University, was particularly busy for an early afternoon. Frankie was queued at the bar several deep, waiting her turn to be served. She shifted her weight from one foot to the other and back again, weary after another late night Snoopies gig. She looked back through the throng of student muddle at Cindy, seated at a table near the door, surrounded by the now semi-permanent circle of hangers-on. Cindy was happy. She had certainly achieved her goal of finding things to do.

Frankie counted six at the table and tried to remember the drinks order. Four beers, Cindy's Bacardi, a gin for the Janis Joplin looking girl and what would she have? Water would have to do, she had lectures. A barman took her order when she finally fronted the beer-soaked bar.

The Snoopies, right? A duffle coated guy beside her was staring in admiration. Frankie was getting tired of this. He spoke to her through a thin russet beard.

Can I help you carry all those drinks over?

I can manage with a tray, thanks anyway.

Did you catch the DRU meeting next door? The Draft Resisters Union.

Now he had Frankie's interest.

No.

That's why the pub's so jammed. It was cool. A draft dodger actually addressed the meeting but the cops got wind of it and they had to whisk him away. The pigs turned up but they were too late.

Wow. Sounds like high drama.

Two dollars sixty, love.

Frankie passed a note to the barman. Can I have a tray please?

Anyway, the duffle coated guy persisted, we hold fundraisers for the cause. Would The Snoopies be into a freebie? For the cause. You know?

Other drinkers were pressing closer to the bar so Frankie nodded toward a less crowded spot behind them. The duffle coated guy was quick to take Frankie's tray of drinks when it arrived and they wormed their way free of the crush, Frankie mulling over his request.

We have a manager. You can ask him but I don't fancy your chances. He's right into image and all that.

Not to worry, but there's always options. We have regular small music nights. Jams. Maybe you could appear yourself? Solo.

Frankie was interested. She had no idea how she could fit any more into her life, but she gave a half nod.

Drawing power zero, but I do have a few songs of my own that could be suited.

You would have drawing power. Once the word got around that one of the Snoopies was playing we would max out. Sure thing.

No posters or anything with The Snoopies on them. Ok? Verbal only.

Done deal.

They exchanged contact numbers. Frankie delivered the drinks tray to Cindy's table and said her goodbyes. She was now running late for her lecture.

Sing it! Everyone! Now! Well, it's one two three, what're we fighting for?
Don't ask me, I don't give a damn. The next stop is Vietnam.

Frankie wasn't sure if she had the words right but she was having fun. Two broken strings on her guitar, husky voice leading thirty or so charged dissidents in song, other random guitarists and tambourine players following along. They were crammed into one of the second-floor offices of Union House, Melbourne Uni.

And it's five six seven eight, open up the pearly gates. Well ain't no time to wonder why. Whoppee. We're all gonna die!

Frankie rounded off with another string-breaking crescendo and everyone broke out into whooping and hollering acclamation.

Country Joe And The Fish, everyone, she announced when the acclamation had died down. And that's me done I'm afraid. I'm just going to have to learn a few more songs. My songbook has just bottomed out. Thankyou.

There were cries of "more, more" but Frankie just smiled and waved, putting her guitar back in its case and easing her way out of the room and into a passage where she was immediately surrounded by students still caught up in a forcefield of bolshie fervour. After declining several after-party invitations she made it to open air and there was only one person between her and the exit. A solidly built, sun-browned fellow who had spoken to the room earlier. He greeted her with a nod and a relaxed smile.

Hullo. Enjoyed yer performance.

He had an earthy direct manner that set him apart from most of the uni students. She smiled back.

And I enjoyed your talk. As far as Frankie could make out from his speech, he was a draft resister who was being supported by his building union and the DRU.

Thanks, but I'm more at home with a hammer and nails than coming up with a whole lot of words.

Oh, I don't know, said Frankie. I thought you got your message across really well. I take it you are basically running from the law?

Yeah. Bastards could lock me up for the full two years if they catch me, more likely a fine though. I'm officially under investigation for violating the National Service Act.

That's crazy. It really is. We live in a supposedly free country and yet we can be jailed for refusing to fight in a war none of us agreed to. I feel for you. I honestly do.

Yeah, well that's it. After I got the call-up I just got to thinking, you know, having smoko with the boys and all that… how come we can be ripped out of our jobs, away from family, away from our lives to fight in some bloody war we know nothing about, like you said.

So you decided to become a draft resister. Surely you didn't make that decision on your own, did your union influence you?

He shook his head abstractedly. Wasn't in the union then. Just decided on my lonesome, really.

I admire that, said Frankie.

Anyway, he shrugged, I'm not copping it. We're planning a march soon, along with the SDS and Save Our Sons. It's gonna be huge. The Big Day out, we're calling it.

I'll be there.

Right on. Look, I can't ask you out for a drink or anything. The calm smile again. But you could come back to the little bolt hole they've given me here in the building if you like. There's always a bong going round if you're into that sort of thing.

Frankie returned his smile.

Tempting, but I can't. Exams in two days and I haven't even started to study yet. But we must keep in touch. I admire what you are doing. It's really brave.

Cool. I'm kind of incognito. Difficult to find, but if you ask the right people you'll find me. I can keep you updated on the march.

Who do I ask for?

Jack. Jack the Dodger. All the committee know who I am.

Ok then. Bye.

Frankie left him in the corridor and headed for the stairs, guitar case in hand and nurturing a little tingle as she thought about the young man she had just met. He was an earthy charmer all right but there was something else about him that appealed to her. She had picked up an intuitive sense of fairness, something she identified herself with.

When she was walking down Tin Alley toward Swanston the precinct was still alive with groups of students, even though it was now late evening. She was waylaid a couple of times by admirers of The Snoopies and this recognition was getting under her skin. Cindy enjoyed their success. For her, it was a kind of recompense for a childhood fraught with racist put-downs, but for Frankie, the best part of The Snoopies had been the early part. Setting up the band, singing lessons and watching Cindy blossom as the band blossomed. Now their manager, De Lucca, seemed equally intent on their income stream and Cindy's affections. Frankie climbed on a tram going down

Swanston and found a seat. She pulled out some change for the conductor, still thinking about The Snoopies. Another gig at Berties tomorrow night and then exams the next day. Something was going to have to go and it was not going to be uni.

Chapter 14

John picked up a pair of green, coarse-woolled army socks and placed them neatly on the left side of the middle shelf in his steel locker. His name was on the locker door, Private Mitchell. Next, he plucked his winter underwear from the pile he'd made in the middle of his bed where he'd upturned his kitbag. He folded the underwear and tucked it in cosily to the right of his socks. They had been given a written diagram eight weeks ago at the start of rookie training showing the correct way to lay out a locker. The diagram had been accompanied by a lot of 'in your face' shouted instructions that were repeated after every stuff-up. He now had it down pat.

He was on his own in the front cubicle of a long narrow, caterpillar shaped Nissen hut, ready to start infantry training at Singleton, NSW. The others would be here soon enough. He'd already checked the names on all the lockers and didn't know any of them from rookie training which was probably a good thing in his mind.

He finished unpacking and retired to his wire bed, hiding behind a book so he could avoid direct contact with them when they arrived.

Eventually they began to trickle in. Pairs, singles, small groups chatting loudly. Derisive, laughing, curious, swaggering, adolescent, lonely. Reading the name cards, trying to find their lockers. John noticed an Aboriginal man in one of the small groups, obviously popular, messing around with his mates. He'd seen the name Private Yangaboora on one of the lockers in the cubicle behind his and figured the name was Aboriginal.

Most ignored John but, without leaving his bed, he exchanged greetings with two of the three others who would share his cubicle. Voronski and Langer. Voronski had a bear-like physique that contrasted with a light easy smile and twinkling intelligent eyes. He made the effort to go over to John's bed and offer a polite handshake, forcing John to put down his book and sit up. John's guitar playing hand was lost in Voronski's giant paw. While Voronski was quiet and reserved in movement, Langer jibbered and jabbered his way up and down the hut, guffawing at nothing, cursing for the sake of it. Tiresome, John thought, wear anyone's patience out. But not Voronski's, he acted like he had a duty of care with Langer, had taken Langer under his wing some time ago and was going to look after him.

Langer immediately dubbed John a book worm, albeit with a cheery grin. But John knew how this went. An unspoken, 'you're not really one of us. Why can't you at least join in the usual shit? Strut whatever you've got. At least make an effort to be one of the boys.' But John didn't mind. He enjoyed the tiny space behind his book.

He'd just immersed himself in that tiny space again when a thick-set sandy-haired fellow threw his kitbag onto the fourth bed. Disarming and direct, he walked straight up to John with outstretched hand.

Chub, he said, Chub Jackson.

John felt obliged to get to his feet to return the handshake, so engaging was the fellow's manner.

John Mitchell, pleased to meet you.

Won't be pleased to meet 'im when the cow shit smell hits ya, Langer interrupted with his usual grin.

Fuck off Langer you dickhead, Chub shot back and, turning away from John, he gave Voronski a familiar wink and a slap on the arm.

Gonna find Hedley, he said and disappeared into the rear of the hut.

John had just resumed his position on the bed when he noticed a rough and ready looking fellow in his late twenties or early thirties appear quietly in the front doorway. John slipped his book to one side and adjusted his glasses. He sensed authority, although very casual looking authority. The man was dressed in a faded army tracksuit and thongs, mat of black hair and dark sunken eyes. He stood in the doorway for a moment observing all. John slipped nervously to his feet, still the only one to notice him.

Right, listen up! The man's bellowing voice could easily be heard right through the hut. All chatter stopped in an instant.

Not calling you up on parade, just an informal check-up. Corporal Davidson.

He moved into John's cubicle.

I want everyone standing beside your beds. Now!

The men moved quickly to their designated beds.

Right, head count. He began to move from cubicle to cubicle.

Four, eight, twelve, sixteen, twenty. Twenty fuckin' bozos all present and accounted for.

He looked each man up and down as he continued to stroll back and forward through the hut. His manner was menacing but weary, there was certainly none of the usual clipped military bearing the men were used to from their rookie training N.C.O.'s.

Twenty potential infantrymen. Twenty potential cot cases. We're calling you lot Three Platoon for want of a better handle. It's just for training purposes, I'll be your boss.

I'm not going to give you any big welcome speech. You probably don't deserve it and I don't get paid extra for overtime. Just to say I've done more tours of noggy land than you lot have had cuddles from mummy. The only cuddles I've had in recent years have been in Vung Tau which, as some of you will learn, is where all the nookie is. My job is to get you pricks ready for the big overseas trip. Cunt of a job. Believe me.

Davidson was now back at the entry doorway. He had a last look around at the four in John's cubicle. For some reason he gave Langer an extra-long look. Maybe he could sense trouble.

Good luck, the lot o' you.

A few days after arriving at Singleton, the platoon was out on the firing range. Hedley in his element, SLR at the ready, alone in the snapshot lane. He advanced slowly down the path, confident, tingling with anticipation. Whenever a target sprang up from behind a tussock of grass or sometimes up in a tree, to the left of him, to the right of him, anywhere, he was onto it before the target disappeared. Most soldiers fired from a standing position which was the quickest but least steady option. Hedley had worked out that there was just enough time, with his quick eye, to drop to a sitting position and get a shot off with his elbows supported on his knees. It worked for him and he never missed.

The D.S. overseeing the range greeted him with his score sheet at the end of the exercise. A perfect score. Best of the bunch.

Other members of the platoon quickly grouped around him and, for a moment, he was a hero. Chub was the first to congratulate him with a handshake and a slap on the back followed by Voronski and Langer. John was some distance away still mulling over his score sheet, trying to work out how he could improve his shooting.

Go Yanga-man, boomed Voronski. You're a legend, beer's on you tonight, buddy.

Hedley couldn't supress a grin.

Thought you blokes'd be buyin' the beer. I did the shootin'.

No way, said Langer. Winners lose. Shoulda' learnt that by now.

And Hedley did buy the first couple of rounds back at the wet canteen that night, he could afford it.

Chub was there as well, and he and Hedley shared a quiet beer amid the gathering storm of sculling and mystery shouts as the juvenile would-be soldiers let loose on the cheap alcohol.

What about that score of yours today, eh?

Hedley grinned. All that roo shootin' back home.

Voronski, now boisterous and half cut interrupted them to slap Hedley on the back and plonk another schooner of beer in front of him.

Hey, Yanga-man. You're a fuckin' legend. Get this into ya'. Then he turned to Chub. He's a fuckin' legend.

As Voronski weaved his way back to the bar, Chub grinned at Hedley.

Yanga-man? Where does that come from?

Dunno. They can't say Yangaboora I s'pose.

Doesn't bother you?

Hedley scoffed. Nah. What about some of the names other blokes got? Like that bloke from rookie training, Pelican Shit, 'member 'im? Big bloke, bit slow and not the smartest.

Yeah. Know what you mean, harmless enough, I s'pose.

Hedley took a swig from the fresh schooner.

Better than bein' called a boong or a coon. Names in the army are just blokes takin' the piss. Not like back home where they never let up. Always gettin' at yas.

They're just words, said Chub.

Yeah, but it's how people say 'em. Coppers and that. People round town, pub owners, storekeepers … That fuckin' Ronny the car mechanic bloke at the north end of town. He won't touch Yamaji cars. Reckons we don't deserve to own one.

It would be fair to say then, that you won't be taking your red ute there when you buy one.

No fuckin' way.

Later they found themselves at a table with Langer and Voronski who had just appeared back from the bar with his big hands wrapped around four schooners of a green concoction.

Mystery shout, he bellowed. Down the hatch, no fuckin' questions.

Aw, fuck man, said Langer taking his drink. Green and some red shit. Bet it's vermouth or muscat or somethin'.

Just scull it, stop lookin' at it. Veronski handed Chub and Hedley their drinks and swallowed his in one long gulp, banging his empty glass down in the middle of the table. Chub and Langer followed suit but Hedley cautiously took a sip and pulled a face of disgust.

Dunno 'bout this, he said. Feelin' crook already.

Drink it man, insisted Langer. What's good for the goose is good for the gander.

Hedley had no idea what Langer meant but he knew his own mind.

Nah. He shook his head. Stickin' to beer. Fuck this.

Fair enough, said Langer standing up and grabbing the back of his chair for support as his head began to spin.

Whoo, got the wobbles already. Anyway, my shout. This is gonna be a beauty.

Beer for me, Hedley reminded him.

Got it. Beer for Yanga-man.

They were the last group to leave the wet canteen and Chub felt the bite of cold night air as soon as he stepped outside. He still felt reasonably lucid but Voronski and Langer were having trouble holding each other up. Hedley had left some time before.

When they eventually made it back to the hut Langer and Voronski collapsed on their beds fully dressed while Chub stood unsteadily in the middle of the small cubicle, now beginning to feel the full effects of the alcohol. He could make out the chatter of other soldiers from further down the hut and he looked up at the lone light bulb on the ceiling directly above him. It seemed unbearably bright and was beginning to spin. He'd never drunk this much before, not even close. Chub, normally a placid and reasoned soul, was beginning to experience foreign feelings of mindless animosity, a negative energy that he couldn't fathom. He'd been taught how to box but had never used his fists outside the ring; now he wanted to use them and he found himself focused on Langer who was stretched out on his bed. He wanted to harm him. Why Langer? He didn't know or care. Nonsensically, he grabbed the nearside iron rail of Langer's bed and flipped it against the wall burying Langer under the bed and mattress. This created a chain reaction. Langer surfaced from under the wreck of his bed like a snarling animal, swinging wildly at Chub. Chub swung back and in the blur that followed he was conscious of Voronski between him and Langer and then they were on the floor. Others from further down the hut joined in and soon lockers were going over and it was general mayhem. Hedley had no desire to punch anyone and focused on trying to separate other soldiers in his section. John, who had been asleep, stayed in his bed and hoped no-one attacked him.

Just as quickly as the effects of the liquor had taken over Chub's senses, they mysteriously disappeared and he became aware of his situation, that he was under a mass of struggling bodies. In all the noise of yelling and cursing and crashing, he distinctly heard approaching whistles. He knew what that meant and, with self-preservation in mind, he fought his way out from under the maelstrom. He found his bed and rolled into a fake sleeping position, pulling the blankets over himself.

When the MPs burst into the hut, whistles in mouths and truncheons at the ready, only two soldiers were tucked up in bed, innocent John Mitchell, who'd never been near the wet canteen that night, and the perpetrator of all the fisticuffs, Chubby Jackson. Everyone else was charged and later punished with a confined to barracks rap.

Chapter 15

What's your name, soldier?

Corporal Davidson was glaring into Chub's badly bruised face. The platoon was standing to attention outside their hut at dawn.

Private Jackson, corporal.

Which section are you in?

One Section, corporal.

Up the front. I thought so. You were one of the two who were supposedly not involved in the incident. Is that right?

Chub was not sure how to answer this, so he stayed quiet.

Answer me! Were you on the charge sheet?

No, corporal.

Davidson smirked and prodded the bruise on Chub's face.

One thing you'll learn, that you'll all learn, is I hate smart arses. Smart arses that don't take the punishment with their mates. Jack men, shirkers. Where's the other soldier who was not on the charge sheet?

John was quick to pipe up.

Here, corporal. Private Mitchell.

Davidson checked over John's face.

No marks on you. Let's look at your hands.

John showed his hands.

No bruises on your knuckles so I'll give you the benefit of the doubt.

He began slowly walking down the ranks, eyes roving over cut cheekbones, still bloody noses and bleary bloodshot eyes. Their breath a combined miasma of stale alcohol fumes and vomit. He couldn't suppress a smirk.

What a sorry site. Look at youse.

When he reached the end of the line the smirk had gone and he wheeled around and moved quickly to the front of the group.

Right. I'll be brief and to the point. You're in the army. What happened last night was unacceptable.

He let this sink in for a moment.

So, we're going on a little march before breakfast. A forced march.

Again, he paused for effect. The men knew what this meant, and Davidson could see misery in their hungover, distressed faces.

Walk for five, jog for five. Full gear. Stay in your sections.

After an hour on the dusty Singleton roads, John was falling behind the other three despite having had an alcohol-free evening. He had a god-all-mighty stitch in his guts and his rifle was beginning to feel like it weighed twenty pounds instead of ten. He could hardly put one boot in front of the other.

When Davidson commanded the platoon break out into another cycle of jogging, John called out to Langer who was third in line behind the other two.

Going to have to drop out.

Langer didn't even bother to turn around, struggling to break into another jog himself.

John stopped, hands on knees, blowing hard. The next section behind them were past him in no time, including Hedley, then the next and the next. He could sense the looks of contempt or, even worse, pity from every passing soldier. Looking down at the gravel road surface, he felt a huge letdown. He shook his head in frustration at himself.

A firm pat on his shoulder caused him to jerk upright. It was Jackson from his section, who must have come back for him.

Give us your pack, mate. We can catch up.

Before John could object, the pack was being slid from his shoulders.

C'mon.

Look, you don't have to …

Just start jogging. You'll get a second wind.

John started jogging.

And for Christ's sake, let us know when you get that second wind because I'm not carrying this forever.

They jogged together, even passing a drop out from the section in front before the order to walk again rang out.

John turned to his saviour sucking in a big breath.

Phew! Thanks for that. I can take the pack back again now.

Sure?

Yeah, I'll be right.

John shimmied back into his pack and they walked in silence for a while, John still sucking in breath, until the next order to start jogging.

Again, John felt the weight of fatigue setting in but at least his gut stitch had eased off. By the time the next walk order was given, they had overtaken several more dropouts. John turned to Chub; he owed this man some conversation.

Where you from?

Oh, you wouldn't know it. Nobody does. Middle of nowhere.

Try me.

Place called Nanderra. Middle of WA. Desert country

Oh, sounds interesting said John diplomatically. And what do you do?

Stock work.

Stock work? You're a stockman?

Yeah, that's me. And other station work, of course.

Wow! A stockman. I've never met a stockman. I'm impressed.

Chub thought he looked impressed. Not taking the mickey. You? What do you do?

John shrugged. Nothing really. I study at uni and play a bit of music.

Music? In a band?

Yeah.

Groupies and all that.

This brought a shy smile and headshake.

Don't believe everything you hear.

An hour later, the sun was beginning to bite and John could feel himself beginning to flag again. Chub, who could sense this, turned to him.

How you travelling?

John nodded. Ok. Still going. Dunno how long for, but.

Chub smiled. Imagine there's one of your band molls waiting for you at the end. Legs open, big tits.

Fuck off.

You could always try mind over matter. Ever tried that?

Can't say I have.

This was the sort of thing that interested John. He wondered if Chub was serious.

It's my old man's big theory, Chub went on. Made me lift upright forty-four-gallon drums of fuel into the back of his Landrover with him. You can do it son, he'd say. Just get your hands under it, lean into me, use your legs and believe. Now he's got a fucked back and a wonky ticker, and I don't want to work with him anymore.

John chuckled. For real?

For real, but not for me. You could give it a go, though. Gotta put your mind to it. You know … my legs are fresh, energy to burn. All that bullshit.

When they started jogging again, John's mouth set in a firm line and he willed himself to pick up the pace. Chub jogged with him, amused by John's grim-faced exertion. Gradually, they overtook more and more frazzled and fatigued platoon members until they caught up with Voronski and Langer who were standing beside the road leaning on their rifles sucking in air.

Carn boys, Chub cajoled. Stick together and we can beat this mob back to the barracks.

Langer just shook his head, too exhausted to even talk.

Veronski straightened and waved them on. You blokes keep going if you want. We're fucked.

C'mon, Chub persisted. We're s'posed to stay in our section.

Fuck off. Veronski waved them on again. Chub could sense Veronski probably had the legs to keep going but he was not going to leave Langer.

Ok then. See you'se back there.

He and John broke back into a jog and left them.

A few miles later, Chub and John shared the last of their water. It wasn't just John who was feeling the pinch now, Chub was beginning to fade himself when the group turned down another road. At least half the platoon had dropped off the pace. Corporal Davidson was still driving them along, although his tone had moved more to one of encouragement, assuring them that they were nearly back at the barracks. Breakfast was only another mile away.

John was pleasantly surprised at himself that he still had some energy while so many others had fallen away. He managed a grim smile as Davidson called for another stint of jogging and Chub was slow to respond.

Want me to carry your pack?

Chub told him to fuck off and John smiled again.

Ever heard of mind over matter? It works really well.

Chub gave him the finger.

When the barracks were in site, Davidson asked them for one last jog. There was only John and Chub left, an athletic looking type called Turnbull, Hedley and two tattooed gorillas from New South Wales who, Chub suspected, had caused most of the damage during last night's brawl. One of them, whose nickname was Bones, had apparently won the interstate boxing championships at Rookie training.

Bones' tattooed mate soon came to an exhausted standstill and the others gritted it out until they were back on the parade ground.

Davidson ordered them to stand in line.

Ok fellas. Well battled out you five but it doesn't change anything. You're still a bunch of stupid dickheads. He singled Chub out again, pointing threateningly at him.

And you; I'm not impressed by you. You're a jack-man. You're on a charge with the rest of them. Got it?

Chub nodded shamefacedly.

Right, you're all dismissed, I'm off to mop up the rest of the silly buggers.

Bones and Turnbull immediately sloped off toward the Nissen hut leaving John, Chub and Hedley alone on the parade ground.

Chub turned to Hedley who he hadn't had a chance to talk to that morning. How'd you pull up after the blue? You ok?

Hedley answered with a tired nod.

Sorry, I s'pose I was the one who started it. Anyway, meet John from our section, we sorta got each other to the line, eh mate?

You got us to the line, I'd still be back there.

Anyway, John meet Hedley.

The pair shook hands and with fatigue surpassing the need for any more words, they headed for the shade of the Nissen hut.

Chapter 16

On the streets of Melbourne there was another very different type of march taking place. Frankie was walking down Bourke Street between the tram tracks surrounded by thousands of milling protesters.

Beside her was Jack the Dodger doing his best to keep a low profile, beanie pulled down over his ears and coat collar turned up.

The surrounding crowd was a cross section of everyone Frankie had ever seen or known. Old, young, political and non-political, straight and bent, white collar, blue collar. They had shown up, perhaps just to test the water, but now they were all drawn into a funnelling flow down Bourke Street. There was a huge END THE WAR NOW banner and smaller hand-held antiwar placards, people who were marching but could have been on a Sunday stroll, others chanting and screaming vitriolically. A man blocking his child's ears to protect her from the din.

Waves of exhilaration and wonderment were washing through Frankie's emotions, she had never experienced anything like this. Roads were meant for cars and trams, they were blocking the public thoroughfare. It was anarchy, glorious anarchy. It was a mass justification of her sense of right and wrong, fair and unfair. If all these other people had the conviction to walk down a public carriageway then her views were correct. Power in numbers. People power. She understood what it meant now.

Jack was taken by her animation as she completed a little twirl, blonde hair swinging in an arc catching the sunlight. He was equally caught up in it all but could only grin.

What are you thinking? He asked.

It's like some kind of giant performance, Frankie said. We are the players and the audience all rolled into one. There are so many people and so much energy.

Gets yer, doesn't it?

She threw her arms around him in a spontaneous hug and he hugged her back. They had met up a few times now to share a coffee or a bong and Frankie's attraction for him had been growing but this felt like a special moment to her, and they were sharing it. She felt like wrapping him up in her body, like a cocoon. Taking him inside her to keep there forever like an unopened present. She could only laugh at herself.

A 'stop the war' chant was gathering momentum around them and Frankie let her voice loose with the others. Jack hunched into his collar as a couple of policemen pushed past toward a performing group dressed in black and wearing red headbands, white make up and fake blood. They were forming a circle and beginning a rotational dance.

The atmosphere was continuing to build and the crowd pack together and slow its pace as they crossed Swanston Street and approached Elizabeth. Soon they were at a halt. Jack on his toes trying to peer over heads and see what was causing the stoppage.

It's my mob coming the other way. The boys. He grinned proudly at Frankie. Wharfies are there too. This is great. What a moment.

People began dropping to a sitting position on the roadway as a sign of solidarity so that soon only news crews and the non-committed were left standing. A half-pissed group of male youths began arguing with protesters behind where Jack and Frankie were seated.

Punch their bloody lights out if I didn't have to keep me head down, Jack mumbled to Frankie.

Jim Cairns, one of Jack's heroes, clambered on top of a vehicle and spoke in what Frankie thought were beautifully modulated tones, given the noise and the makeshift p.a. system he was speaking through. He thanked everyone for their attendance and talked about a way forward.

When the crowd began to disperse and police tried to open up the intersections again, Jack began to feel uneasy. He gently pulled Frankie closer to him and muttered in her ear.

Too many coppers now, better head back to the Uni. When Frankie nodded he drew her even closer and kissed her lightly on her lips. Frankie felt a little shiver. His calm grey eyes were looking into hers.

You could, you know…, he said awkwardly. Stay over tonight if you wanted. The little bolthole they've given me on the second floor.

Her words wouldn't come so she kissed him how she'd been wanting to kiss him for some time. No words needed.

The uni precinct was even more charged and crowded than normal and Jack was treated as some kind of heroic messiah as soon as they entered the Union

Building. He'd made it back from the march without being recognised and arrested, a cause for celebration. They were soon pressed into one of the upstairs offices with a fug of students seated on the floor, joints doing the circuit, everyone reliving the march. It wasn't long before Frankie received the inevitable requests to start playing. Her guitar was in Jack's room.

As soon as she was in his room, she wished that he was there with her. The guitar case was on his thin mattress which took up most of the floor space, his few clothes piled in a corner and a poster of Che Guevara the only decoration. As she removed her guitar from its case her thoughts were only on him. His aroma filled the room and, if forensically examined in the name of hygiene, would probably have laid to rest her thoughts of romance …. but it was having the opposite effect.

Her sex drive had finally kicked in and was making up for lost time, her concerns about ever feeling sexy and womanly long gone. She desired Jack, but her desire would have to wait. She had all night free for once with no gigs scheduled but back in the crowded offices they were waiting for her to do her thing. She gave the guitar a quick strum and decided it was near enough to being in tune for another doped out student musical free-for-all.

Frankie had only completed a few songs when, to her relief, Jack pushed through the crowd of now dancing students and asked if she'd had enough. She had.

When Jack finally led her out into the passage and back toward his room she felt her nerves begin their little eddying around the edges of her focus. Normally a new gig was her focus but this was a much bigger 'new'.

Her first time. Standing, facing Jack in the middle of his tiny space, mattress at their feet. She looked away from him to the Che Guevara poster for a moment, familiar little fears from the past were beginning to surface competing for attention in her emotions with her nervousness and her desire. What would his reaction be when she removed her clothes and he saw her body for the first time?

But her anxiety was dispelled in an instant when he reached out and drew her into a kiss. They continued to kiss as the clothes came off, the kissing becoming more intense with each shed garment, only ceasing when they were laying naked beside each other on the thin mattress. She was aware that he was erect and was expecting him to roll on top of her but he didn't. He moved closer until they were touching, laying on their sides facing each other. He seemed aware of her nerves and was in no rush, his hands began to gently touch and arouse. First her breasts and nipples, then her inner thighs. Slow movements, almost lazy, so light. She began to reciprocate, again no rush. When he finally prepared to enter her she was ready and when they pushed together the pain was less than she expected. Once inside he was content to remain motionless and she had time to adjust to his presence. She was able to move against him when she felt like it and their movements became controlled and rhythmic. A slow waltz.

Even the morning held no urgency. Frankie's first lecture was not until eleven so for the first time they were able to share a breakfast together. They chose a little eatery down Swanston Street and took a table at the very back beside a door that Jack knew led to an escape route.

Tell me, said Jack after they had ordered, what is it that you're studying? I mean, all I ever hear about from everyone is your band and the music you play.

Frankie laughed; funny you should say that... It drives me crazy. Anyway, I'm doing a degree of Community Services.

University jargon to Jack; he nodded with furrowed brow.

Social services, helping those in need. It's been a passion of mine since... early teens, I suppose.

So, where does that lead? I mean jobwise. You know.

It could lead anywhere, probably to some thankless position working in a charity for not much.

But it's what you want to do? I mean more than the music?

Frankie nodded. It is. I love playing but my studies come first. Playing here at the Uni is way more fun than the Snoopie gigs. They're just hard work. The Uni crowd are fun.

They are. I'm enjoying all the partying and that but, truth is, they're not really my type, you know? I miss the fellas at work and the physical side of work. Been holed up in that bolthole too long. Never even get to stretch me legs.

I was just thinking the same thing this morning when I woke up. You don't even have a window.

True, but... I'm there for a reason. Union blokes reckon it's the safest spot for me.

Surely that can't be right. They must have a house somewhere with a few comforts.

Who knows. Politics maybe, but one thing's for sure… he paused, looking into Frankie's eyes… Least I'm not in Vietnam shooting at some poor bastard I've got nothing against in a war that doesn't make a lick of sense.

She smiled and took his hand from across the table. She was about to reply when a waitress bustled into their space with coffees. They continued to hold hands and the waitress had to place the coffees in the little table space that was left.

Chapter 17

A few weeks into their infantry training Davidson had assembled his platoon in a building that doubled up as a gym and a lecture hall. The surrounding enclosure was jammed with decommissioned Studebaker six-wheel drive trucks from the Korean war era and Chub was more interested in these than the preamble they were receiving from Davidson. One of those trucks would be ideal on Eumarella. He'd have to see if they would be going out to auction sometime.

Davidson introduced another speaker, a Corporal Warner, who was going to be their other trainer. John, who was seated near Chub, was fascinated by the man's appearance. Warner was as thin as a snake. In fact, everything about him was thin right down to his face and long nose which was broken to the left and then changed direction back to the right. But it was his eyes that drew the most attention. Pallid pools of colourless nothing. Eyes that could be lining you up for a casual conversation or a bullet, there was no way of telling.

Some of you may see action one day, Warner began. I wouldn't know, I'm not a politician. The way I see it after a couple of tours is that we're fighting a whole lot of enemies. Not just the Nogs but people back home, too. Here. Some of them are politicians, some are enemy sympathisers, anti–war activists, draft dodgers, bludgers and bolshies.

He looked around the seated platoon for reactions.

John was surprised by this candid political swipe. It must have shown on his face because Warner seemed to fix him with a long stare.

The idea of this discussion is to open your eyes up. Some of you think you're tough. Glancing at Bones and his mate. You're not. You're babies. Babies who don't know nothing.

Chub's attention was already beginning to drift back out the window to the Studebakers, but John was mesmerised by the man's eyes. Hedley too was listening carefully, keen to learn everything he could.

I'm going to tell you a little story. Corporal Davidson can verify this one.

Davidson and Warner exchanged a look of affirmation.

Anyway, we were in Phuoc Tuy Province in '68 working out of a fire support base. Phuoc Tuy. Some of you may have heard of it, huh?

His eyes moved over the rows of listeners but there was no movement.

Ok, Phuoc Tuy is east of Saigon and where most of our operations are carried out. You'll be briefed on all that later if you're posted to a battalion that's assigned to Vietnam.

He glanced at Davidson who nodded.

All right, on with the story. We'd been tracking this slant-eye for twelve hours. He was a durable little cunt. Finally, my lead scout got a shot at him and down he went. We figured he was a messenger. Had to be.

And he was alive. The boys got to him first and did the usual disarming and frisking. When me and the sarge got there, he was laying on his side in the wet grass with his guts hanging out like a dog. Wouldn't talk for the interpreter so what do you think needed to be done? He was a messenger. He had info.

Again, there was no response from the listeners. When in doubt, be silent.

I'll tell you what we did. What the sergeant did. He was a tough guy, sarge. He put his boot in noggie's guts and gave them a little stir.

Warner zoned in on John.

You don't like this, do you?

All John could think of was, why did he pick on me? Was it my glasses? He said nothing. Warner kept at him.

Huh? I've been watching you. You don't like a word I've been saying, do you?

John could feel himself going red behind the ears. It was just like school. He shifted in his seat, not knowing how to respond.

You've gotta get used to this stuff, sonny. Just think how many lives could've been lost if we hadn't got that information, that an ambush had been laid. An ambush that your company, your buddies were walking into. And take it from me, sonny.

Warner's eyes were now boring into John. They were out of conversation mode and definitely in bullet mode.

There's nothing worse than seeing your best mate blown all over a rubber tree by a claymore. 'Specially when that claymore is one they stole from us. That's grinding it in.

Chub was taking in Warner's story with a little scepticism. He wasn't sure how the claymore bit tied in with the first part of the story, but it was obviously the part that cut deep into Warner.

Warner looked around the room again, long nose carving the benumbed atmosphere that he had created.

Anyway, enough of the waries for one lecture. The point I'm trying to make is that you're soldiers, and soldiers are expected to fight and it isn't a picnic. If you get a ticket over there, you'll learn quick enough that the only good nog is a dead one.

Chub was blocking out the words. Propaganda, brainwashing, call it what you like, he thought. He didn't know who these Vietnamese even were, but he was instinctively wary of the army's version.

Warner was finishing up.

How well you take in the things we're going to teach you in the next seven or eight weeks could have a bearing on whether you live or die. Every man I saw die, died because he made a mistake. Keep that in mind.

Chub was thinking that going to Vietnam was probably the first mistake they made, but John and Hedley were taking it all very seriously. Despite the unfair attention John had received, he had been trying to imagine himself in a similar situation. This was what he was going to have to face one day. He was sure of it. Vietnam was a war and he was going.

When asked where he bought the car Langer became vague. He mumbled something about Parramatta Road. He wasn't sure which yard. It was out there somewhere.

He was the only one who had a car and it was an incongruous little bucket of Japanese bolts. Incongruous for Langer that is. Incongruous because it was small and grey and conservative. If you believed Langer he was, at times, a homeless street kid who lived in the back-alleys of Sydney. Other times, he claimed a sophisticated high profile gambling life which Voronski, who was an inveterate gambler, scoffed at. And other times he alluded to a life as a bit actor who did some male modelling.

Whichever version of himself you believed, none really fitted the car. Voronski doubted he actually owned it but the bottom line was that none of them cared. It was a car and three platoon had been granted their first weekend of leave after their stint of being confined to barracks. They were off to Newcastle. Voronski in the front with Langer and John, Hedley and Chub in the back.

It seemed that every other soldier who was based at Singleton, and could jam into a motor vehicle, had the same idea. The road became a racetrack. Tin cans filled to overflowing with army haircuts and testosterone. Boys that were free from every shackle their young lives had ever seen. Particularly the army.

Newcastle was braced and ready for the invasion, a regular event. Pubs aplenty, doors wide open if they didn't mind a bit of trouble and entry barred to the invaders if they did.

The car was soon jettisoned at one end of Hunter Street and the expedition continued on foot. None of them had ever been to Newcastle but directions were unnecessary, it was a pub to pub reconnaissance. Objectives: beer, hamburgers, girls and music. Nobody had given much thought to accommodation.

It quickly became clear that the army haircuts were a dead giveaway and that the army was on the nose with locals. Whenever they entered another pub, civilians would turn their backs, particularly members of the opposite sex.

Turned backs didn't deter Langer. He had a reputation to live up to. A verbally self-perpetuated reputation that, combined with a very thick hide, made him a fearsome pest.

Check out these honeys, fellers.

They were playing pool in the corner of a saloon bar and three girls had just walked in and were ordering drinks.

Who's coming over with me this time? One of them's a bit of alright. She's mine. You guys can fight over the other two.

You're on your own, Langer, said Voronski who was working out his next pool shot. I'll come over after this game if they haven't sent you packing.

Ok. Your loss, my gain. Here goes nothing.

Langer picked up his drink and headed straight for the girls. When they saw him coming, they exchanged a few quick whispers and huddled closer together in a tortoise shell formation. The others watched as Langer took up a position beside the girls. Tortoise shells didn't deter him. He soon had them engaged in very one-sided conversation. The others continued their pool game, Voronski sank a couple of balls and left Chub with a snooker.

Jeeze, you've played this game before, Chub said. Where did you learn to play shots like those?

It pays to know your way around a pool table and a game of blackjack in my line of trade.

Which is?

Voronski was cagey. A bit of everything, really. But horses are my speciality area.

Mine too, and Hedley's. Only we ride them, you bet on them.

Voronski looked thoughtful. Can you blokes pick a decent bit of horseflesh?

Sure can, said Chub. Ridden in a few stockmen's races. We know what a decent horse looks like, eh Heds?

Hedley shrugged, never one to blow his trumpet.

You'll have to come with me to the track sometime. I work on systems and tips but occasionally I might bet on the look of a nag if I have to. We could form a team. Or at least have a bit of fun.

I'll be in that, said Chub. Not a particularly good pool player, he was now grappling with the geometry of trying to extricate himself from the snooker. John pointed to a spot on the cushion and told him to aim for that.

Langer soon returned after a fob-off from the girls and, after another game, all meandered off to fill up on hamburgers.

As the evening wore on they, along with most of the other army hordes, became more and more intoxicated wandering from pub to pub. Chub and John became separated from the others and eventually found themselves in a very crowded and smoke-filled back bar.

To the cheers of the onlookers a couple of drag queens were up on the bar putting on a show. Tit tassels swinging in a circular motion and other floppy body bits following the orbit. Buying drinks there took too long and everywhere else seemed to be closed.

What do you reckon? John asked. Any bright ideas where we might doss down?

Chub thought for a moment. Newcastle's a port, isn't it? Must be a beach somewhere. We'll just crash on the beach.

They blundered their way through dark streets until they found some sand dunes and a protected gully. The sand was dry and soft and they had a five-star view across the water to the lights of the docks.

You know, said John, I would never have thought of sleeping out like this. Guess I'm learning.

And moon above, too. Means no rain but there is a ring around it so could rain later.

They sat in silence listening to the crash of surf. Two dark silhouettes against a white moonlit dune.

So, what have you got planned after we get through this? Chub asked after a while. The army, I mean.

Dunno. Start playing in bands again and go back to uni, I spose. What about you?

Dad's handing the property over to me when I get out. So he says, anyway. His ticker's not so good anymore.

John had no conception of what even constituted "a property". The outback to him was a large expanse of nothing that lay somewhere to the west and he'd never had any interest in it. That was until now. Meeting Chub, who was far outside the circles he had previously mixed in, was opening up new vistas for him. A melting pot like the army could do this.

Wow. That must be a big responsibility. How many acres is it?

'Bout six hundred thousand.

That sounds like a lot. Can you look after all that on your own?

Have to. Can't afford an overseer on our budget. I'm gonna streamline the whole place. Get it running better. Improve the fences, the workers' quarters, sink more bores. Gonna be a showpiece by the time I'm finished with it.

Impressive, said John. He leant backwards until he was laying full length on the sand, looking up at the stars. As soon as he was horizontal drowsiness set in. He'd spent a few nights now sleeping in the one- man hootchies they were issued with on army exercises but the concept of sleeping with no shelter was new to him. You know, he yawned, I could get to like this life.

Chub, who had also taken up a reclining position, rolled on his side and wriggled into the sand, ready for sleep.

What we do for weeks when we're mustering, he said quietly. Ain't all bad if the weather holds.

The weather didn't hold and next morning they were woken by rain. They set off to find Langer and his car. They had to be back on duty at midday.

Chapter 18

Sunlight filtered through a canopy of black ash and red bloodwood as Hedley made his way from the ridge line down a steep tussocky slope littered with fallen branches. He stopped and waited for Voronski and Langer on a sandy shelf under a weathered sandstone outcrop, squatting and cradling his SLR across his knees. They had been randomly selected as part of a twelve-man squad tasked with playing the Viet Cong in a week-long exercise. 'Harassing the shit out of the rest of the bastards.' They had been dressed in black-dyed, caste-off old army gear, armed with blanks for ammunition and instructed to do their darndest. Hedley winced as the noisy descent of the other two drew closer. Once you were shot, you were out.

They eventually slid down onto the shelf.

Where the fuck are we, man? Langer had tied his army sweat rag around his head, bandana style.

Hedley motioned for him to be quiet. The three of them sat in silence for a while listening to the sounds of the bush. Currawongs calling, cicadas and the wind in the treetops back on the ridge line.

So, where are we? Voronski whispered.

Hedley pointed back up the gully and returned the whisper. Camp's back that way. You fellas go back. I'll be right.

On your own? You can't do that.

The Corp said split up if we want. I'll be ok.

Voronski looked quizzically at Hedley.

You sure, mate? On your own out there? They'll fry yer.

Gotta catch me first. See ya, fellers. Tell the Corp I'm gonna try and recce out their base. Don't come looking for me.

Hedley gave them a wave and continued on down the gully until they were out of sight.

For the first time in months Hedley was on his own and it felt good for a change. Their training focused on teamwork, which Hedley liked but this was different. They were supposed to be imitating a guerrilla force enemy.

He hadn't gone far when he picked up a movement higher up the slope. He dropped to his haunches and watched. It was a patrol moving along the ridge in what looked like a staggered formation. Hedley could see one of the scouts and guessed the other was on the far side of the ridge. The next soldier may have been the section commander or the 2IC, followed by the gunner and his offsider lugging the M60 and the ammo. He could make out a couple more riflemen and there would be a tail end Charlie back there somewhere. If he was going to open fire, he would pick off the gunner first and, if he was quick enough, the section commander. But this was just a game and no one would voluntarily drop dead when they heard his blanks. They would all turn on him like a pack of hounds. Better to try and work out where they had come from.

The going was too open up on the ridges, so Hedley wormed his way further down the slope towards the cover of tree ferns, cabbage-tree palms and lillypillys in the bottom of the gully. He took his time moving down the gully, observing another patrolling section on the opposite ridge before a pair of wallabies came thumping through the ferns toward him. Something had spooked them.

Hedley stopped and listened. Sure enough, he could detect the sounds of GP boots as they cracked twigs, stumbled over logs and set forth little rockslides. A patrol was coming up the gully toward him, bloody blokes everywhere. They weren't doing this exercise by halves.

He glanced around at where the wallabies had disappeared into a mess of broken sandstone rocks and decided to follow them. The further he went into the rocks, the more secure he felt, and the more crevices were opening up for him. They would have a hard time finding him, but he could hear and smell the patrol all around him now. He went a little further, wriggling around another corner and then he discovered a small cave opening. Perfect.

He wriggled inside and found that the opening broadened out into a larger cave. It was cold, dank and dark and reeked of wallaby urine but immediately he was overcome with a warm, cosy, womb-like feeling that plucked harmoniously at his body sinews. It had nothing to do with safety from the patrol outside, he didn't fear them, that was only a game. It was something else. He slowly got to his feet as his eyes adjusted to the dim light and took a few steps further into the cave. The walls were typical course, loose gritted sandstone, with ochre and grey shades giving way in blended layers to white on the back wall. As Hedley's eyes further adjusted to the light he could see there were ochre splotches on the white and realised they were very faded hand stencils. His people. One of the stencils had five fingers and a thumb. Shit; could be bugura. Not his country. Get the hell outa here. Heart still pumping, he waited in the cave entrance until the patrol had gone and then began making his way down the gully again.

An hour later he found the good guys' base camp. It was pretty obvious, stuck on a very open hill, rows of hootchies, a large tent in the centre that was probably their headquarters, the hum of a generator. They obviously had no need for secrecy. It was like a big bold fortress with encircling defence positions dug into the hillside. Attack me if you dare.

Hedley lay in cover, watching, as night fell. The perimeter defence was tight, no more than a few metres between sentry positions and lights had been set up that, when switched on, bathed the whole perimeter area in white light. Hedley was getting hungry, there would be ration packs a plenty in there. All he had to do was get in.

He could make out a rough road cut into the hill that followed the contours in a gentle curve and finished on the hilltop beside the HQ tent. A shallow table drain had been dug into the high side of the road at the base of a small roadside embankment. It was no more than a couple of feet high but it was creating a shadow, a dark arc that swept around the hill through the defences right into ration pack land. Trouble was sentries were positioned each side of the road. One right above the table drain. Anyway, Hedley reasoned, it was worth a go. Win or lose there would be a feed involved.

Hedley located the base of the table drain and started crawling up it, SLR held just above the ground in front of him. When he neared the lighted area, he slowed his crawling to a wriggle. Wriggle, freeze. Wriggle, freeze. It seemed like hours before he reached the guarded area. The guard on his side of the road was now just in front and above him, standing in the white light. The other guard was looking across the road in Hedley's direction. How could he not see him? Was he blind? Apparently so. Hedley wriggled some more and froze again. He was now level with the guards and neither had raised an alarm. Another painstakingly slow wriggle and he was past them. He might just be able to pull this off.

Thirty minutes later he was twenty yards further up the hill and out of the lighted area. There were a few soldiers walking around in the night doing he knew not what. They were mostly unrecognisable in the shadows so Hedley decided to get to his feet and walk. Incognito-like. Just one of the men. No one noticed his dark uniform, so he kept walking until the HQ tent was in front of him. There was a light coming from within, so he slipped his bayonet onto the end of his SLR and marched through the tent flap, bold as brass.

A long, thin fair headed fellow was seated at a desk tracing lines onto a map, open tin of golden syrup and half-eaten loaf of bread to one side. Hedley instantly recognised him as Second Lieutenant Ashmore, one of the 'big wigs' from back at the barracks, minus his pips. Ashmore looked up bleary-eyed, obviously expecting someone else, but was confronted by Hedley who proceeded to execute a neat mock thrust with his bayonet and then stood in front of him grinning.

Gotcha, sir.

Ashmore reeled back in shock and then sat confounded. His immediate thought the bollocking he was going to receive from his superior when this was reported.

Yes, you have got me. And you are Private …?

Yangaboora, sir.

Right. I remember you. The marksman.

Hedley eyed the bread and golden syrup, definitely not items found in his ration pack. He was too polite to grab them right away.

So, private … You're on your own?

Hedley wasn't sure if he should be disclosing anything tactical.

Ashmore snapped. I'm dead! We're having an informal discussion from the grave. My grave, unfortunately.

Yes sir.

So you're on your own?

Yes sir.

Ashmore softened.

You've excelled, private. Done really well. I'd like to know how you penetrated the defence positions without being detected.

Hedley shrugged. Crawled up the road, sir. Walked when I got in here.

Ashmore smiled in disbelief.

The road. I see.

Anyway, better get going, sir. Gotta get out of here now.

Well, like I said, you've excelled Private Yanga-boo …?

Yangaboora, sir.

Yangaboora. Well, private. You've got a real future in this army if that's what you'd like. Something you should think about, perhaps.

Hedley grinned. Thanks, sir. Mind if I take these? He pointed at the bread and golden syrup.

Spoils go to the victor. They're yours.

Hedley quickly pressed the lid back on the tin of golden syrup and snatched up the bread. He nodded and grinned again to Ashmore as he slipped out the tent flap and into the night.

Without really thinking about it he began retracing his steps. No one noticed him strolling through the camp and when he was sure no one was looking he pushed the can of syrup into one of his ammo pouches, the bread down his shirt and dropped to a crawling position. The exiting procedure was no less painstaking than it had been when he was entering but again, amazingly, the two sentries on the road failed to detect his presence.

When he was well clear of the encampment he devoured the bread and some of the sweet syrup, keeping the remainder of the tin as proof of his exploits. He elected to follow the more open ridges back to where he knew their own little base was.

As he walked through the night, alert to a possible ambush, he pondered the words of the second lieutenant.

The army seemed to like him and he liked the army. The army was barndi alright. He missed Frank and Jane and the country back home but he didn't miss the townships of Nanderra or Boreen. The constant put-downs. Moving from camp to camp. What *was* waiting for him after the army? He loved stock work, but he'd been sacked by the bossfella at Eumarella. Back to the town camp at Nanderra for the umpteenth time? Waji. No way.

The army was looking pretty good right now.

Chapter 19

Three Platoon were sitting on a footpath that skirted the parade ground, backs to a low block wall, enjoying a break from drill practice. Their rifles, fitted with bayonets, propped against the wall or lying on the footpath beside them. Some were smoking and chatting, others snoozing, giggle hats pulled over their eyes to keep out the droning flies.

Chub's palm rested flat on the sun-warmed cement as he watched an endless procession of ants disappearing down a crack, only half listening to John who was sitting beside him.

Got to talk with Turnbull last night, John was saying. He's the bloke in Hedley's section who finished with us in the forced march. He's going to apply for the SAS and I'm thinking of doing the same.

Why? Said Chub beginning to take an interest. I heard you gotta do a fifteen k endurance march carrying thirty kilos. Sounds like torture to me.

Part of the toughening process. I want to become tough. Become a tough guy.

This didn't make sense to Chub. He switched his attention from the ants to John.

Yeah? So what do you call a tough guy? That sergeant in Warner's story who put his boot into the wounded prisoner's guts?

John ignored this and barged on. You're tough, so is Hedley. Wrangling bulls and all that. You're readymade for the army, if you know what I mean. Me, I've got to become tough and don't worry, peering at Chub through his John Lennon specs, I will.

Chub held back a smile, John could be quite an intense little scarecrow.

It's all about fate, John persisted. Getting called up is like a direction. A message. Toughening up is part of that message.

At this point a one-eyed fox terrier appeared from behind a building and proceeded to trot aloofly down the line of resting feet, sidestepping the occasional attempt to grab him. It stopped in front of Langer and surveyed him, one ear pricked. This was enough to generate a few observations about the dog's attraction to Langer. Some of the platoon were still schoolboys; schoolboys in men's bodies.

The dog then turned his lone eye on John, sniffed his boot and was off. Little tail held self-assuredly erect as he passed down the line.

Chub had been thinking during the canine distraction. He nudged John who was still watching the departing pooch.

Ever done any boxing?

For a moment John feared that Chub might be about to throw down some sort of challenge. He shook his head warily. Why?

You wanna be tough. Could teach you a thing or two. Might help.

Yeah?

But there's a deal to be done.

A deal?

Too right. You've gotta set me up with a few of those groupies from your band days. Bet you've only gotta click your fingers and they'll come runnin'.

John smiled and shook his head. Wish that was true. I really do.

C'mon, mate. You're holding back on me. No girls where I come from. You need to get tough, I need to get laid.

John was slow in answering.

Well, the band I played with are backing a couple of girl singers now, poppy stuff. We're due some more leave in about four weeks but I think they're only performing in Melbourne. If they had a gig in Sydney we'd be a show of catching up but that would be a long shot.

Chub shrugged, long shot is better than none.

Infantry training rolled on. A process. A challenge for the trainees and a challenge for the trainers. The army tried to make all sizes fit one but some sizes would never fit – the soldier in front of Hedley moving forward with a pronounced limp as they queued to draw rifles for more drill exercises and Hedley wondering, not for the first time, how the little fellow had made it thus far. A promising jockey who'd had his leg broken in a fall at a country race meeting and an underqualified country doctor having set the broken leg incorrectly leaving him with one foot turned out almost at a right angle from the other. What was he doing in infantry? Foot sloggers, grunts. He couldn't even jog, let alone run.

When it was Hedley's turn to fill out the mandatory form before drawing a rifle he was confronted with the usual confusion of columns and headings. He'd done this before but still had trouble deciphering the jargon. He'd helped the jockey limp his way through the many miles they had to cover when on exercises in the bush and now the jockey helped him.

Date, the jockey said pointing to the first column. Copy what I wrote. Now the item – SLR – now tick the next bit and sign.

On the parade ground Hedley responded to the order of 'quick march' and swung into rhythm with the others. He hated marching. Proper mamany. But just what you have to do, he supposed. Don't make sense though.

In front of him the jockey began to square gait and the drill sergeant called them to a halt. At first Hedley thought the sergeant was going to go off again at the jockey when he strode over and put his face in the jockey's face. The drill sergeant pointed his nose up slightly so that he gave the illusion of looking down, a trick he didn't need to use on the jockey. Hedley had noticed that the sergeant often paused for effect before yelling at them but this time, after his customary pause, he spoke softly. He'd been through this with the jockey too many times, there was a rare tone of sympathy in his voice.

Private. He paused again. When we fall out I want you to come see me and have a little chat.

He strode back to the centre of the parade ground and spun around to face the troops.

On the command 'fall out', he bellowed. Fall out properly! Another immaculately timed pause.

Fall out!

Twenty boots lifted, twenty boots twisted, twenty boots slammed down and forty boots shuffled away.

Hedley never saw the jockey again.

The temperature was into the nineties and after a long stint of target practice on the baking hot rifle range, three platoon were marching their weary way back to base, carrying not only their rifles and ammunition but the targets as well. The targets were life-sized ply cut-outs of a silhouetted Asian figure, complete with a conical paddy hat and painted black. They were in single file and Chub was following John. It was to his great surprise that he heard John utter the words, *watch it*, in an aggressive tone to the soldier in front of him.

Chub's surprise came from not only hearing John use an aggressive tone – unheard of – but that the soldier in front of John was the no neck, hulking thug, Bones.

Bones swung around, ever prepared for a fight, but saw only John. He looked disappointed. John was glaring up at him through his sweat-marked glasses.

You bumped me with your target, said John.

So fuckin' what?

So I want to fight you. You did it on purpose.

Bones looked a little incredulous, perplexed even.

John persisted. In the toilets back at base. Sixteen hundred hours.

Bones look of perplexity was short lived. It was replaced by a mask of murderous intent.

Bring a second. You'll need one.

The line began moving again and John swung around to Chub.

Did you hear that?

Chub had heard it all right. He was nearly as dumbfounded as Bones had been. John was spoiling for trouble. Incubating a death wish.

The heat got to your head, or what? I've given you one half-arsed boxing lesson and you're challenging the bloke who won the championship at rookie training.

You be my second?

Jesus, mate. I hope you know what you're doing.

Sixteen hundred hours at the toilets and there was no sign of Bones and his offsider. Chub was warily pointing out to John that he would have to keep his fists up to protect his head. Bones, with his shaved head, piggy ears and scarred eyebrows knew how to throw a punch. He could inflict a lot of damage.

They were waiting in the more open urinal section of the toilets and Chub needed a slash, so he unbuttoned and prepared to do his business as John paced nervously behind him. Chub was mid pee when the entry door swung open and he caught a glimpse over his shoulder of pig dogs one and two bustling through the doorway, pig dog two with a white towel over his shoulder. Chub didn't have a towel, and this was obviously protocol for fight seconds. He heard a snarled, ya ready? from Bones and then the short, sharp thumping sound of rapid-fire fists on flesh. Before he could button up, Bones and offsider were on their way out, a blur of smugness, door slamming behind them.

Chub turned to find John lying on his back on the concrete floor, head propped up against one of the cubicle door jambs, glasses hooked by only one ear and skewed across his face.

He appeared to be only part conscious, but a broad smile came over his face when he realised it was Chub standing over him.

Wow. I've just had my first fight and it was against the toughest guy in the whole battalion.

Chub squatted beside him and put a hand on his shoulder.

Mate. You really are a tough guy. Tougher than the rest of us put together.

John's smile became even broader.

Chapter 20

University meetings usually bored Frankie, but not this one. It was Monday morning and she was packed into one of the rooms on the second floor of the Union Building with an army of dissentients: students, unionists and sympathisers.

Jack was part of a large assemblage of would-be speakers squeezed together out front. It was his turn to address the gathering but others were walking in front of him and the room was abuzz with uncontrolled chatter. Frankie felt a momentary wave of pity for him, his speechmaking experience was very limited compared to the union and uni members who surrounded him. He looked lost.

Look, he said. I've got something to say.

There was no P.A. so few noticed him trying to speak. Frankie felt like standing up and calling for quiet but it was not her place. Jack took matters into his own hands.

Look, he roared. If youse want cop bait, I'm it!

Now he had the floor.

I'm puttin' me hand up. Announcing to the world that I'm here. Fed up with layin' low. If the cops want me they'll have to bloody well come in and get me!

There was a huge roar of support and one of the students up front yelled that they'd have to arrest every member of The Draft Resisters Union first because they'd be blocking the foyer and the stairwell. This created more noisy support.

McMahon's as weak as piss, Jack went on. Makes the laws then doesn't enforce them in case the public wise up as to how many draft resisters there really are. Don't create a stir, don't give the press anything to feed on so all the mums and dads out there think everything's ok. It's ok for their sons to register and go off to Vietnam. Well it isn't ok! The public need to know we're here, we're resisting and we're waiting to be arrested. Radio Resistance is making sure the message gets out.

The mention of Radio Resistance was met with a big cheer. A student standing beside Jack pumped his fist in the air.

We're finally up and running, he announced. The aerial went up on the roof here last night. The cops will want to shut us down, so expect a raid anytime.

An agenda was set out. Stairwells to be packed with chairs, media releases, food, blankets and music. Protest songs. Frankie's area.

The atmosphere in the Union Building continued to build, everyone was having fun. Preparing for battle. Enjoying the drama. It was going somewhere. And for Frankie the best part of it all was that she was with Jack.

They didn't have much time to themselves, but that afternoon Jack took Frankie up on the roof to check out Radio Resistance. Another group of students was trying to mount a large siren to one of the parapets. Their faces lit up the moment they spotted Jack. Oh, man, one of them piped up, you're a tradie, this is your area.

Jack had to suppress a laugh when he surveyed their work; a mess of light tie wire twisted this way and that – the siren would've weighed around twenty kilos.

You blokes can manage it without me. You need a hammer drill, it's concrete. Hammer drill and dyna bolts. Half inch, I reckon.

He showed them where to put the bolts and told them to go to the storeroom in the next building. Ask old Curley, the maintenance bloke. Tell him Jack sent you.

He took Frankie over to the south-east corner where they could slip behind a stairwell wall, out of the cold breeze. They huddled together for warmth.

Jack pointed to an intersection just visible through other buildings.

That's Grattan and Swanston. Bike and scooter patrols are going to be cruising up and down those streets night and day. If the cops show up anywhere in numbers they'll send the word back here and this siren'll be cranked up. Be heard all over, I reckon.

What about you? Frankie asked. How are you going to get out?

No need to worry about me. Know this place like the back of my hand now. Plenty of escape routes.

I do worry. It's two years jail if you're caught, Jack.

They'll never get me. Jack be nimble, Jack be quick. That's me.

Jack tripped over the candlestick. That could be you.

Jack smiled. Are you calling me clumsy?

Frankie smiled back. No. I'm worried about what could happen, that's all. How soon do you think it'll be before the police actually react? I've got band practice tomorrow, then the usual Berties gig Wednesday night.

Jack shrugged. Dunno. More likely to raid at night if they're going to.

Then I might tell De Lucca tomorrow at practice that I won't make the Berties gig.

They may not take the bait and you'll be holed up here for no reason. Could drag on forever.

Oh well, said Frankie. More time with you.

Consolation prize. Can't win 'em all, Jack grinned.

Next day, band practice was being held in De Lucca's Greville Street shop. De Lucca and Cindy were waiting for Frankie downstairs while Neil, the bass player, Dicko and Roc were going through a few set pieces in one of the rooms above. A banging on the shop door announced Frankie's late arrival. De Lucca unlocked the door and she bustled in going straight to Cindy and giving her a hug.

Are you ever on time? De Lucca's black diamond eyes were fixed on Frankie.

Sorry, The uni has been hectic, I'm afraid.

The boys have a new song they want to try out at the Berties gig, he said testily. You've only got today to learn it so the pressure's on. They're upstairs waiting for you so you'd better get up there. De lucca was already mounting the stairs before he realised Frankie was not following him. He stopped and looked back down to find Frankie and Cindy in quiet conversation at the foot of the stairs. He read "problems" in their expressions.

What? He said warily.

Frankie looked up at him.

Um, Berties, she said. I can't play. Sorry, uni's just mental at the moment. Things I can't get out of. I'm sorry.

De Lucca's red walrus moustache began quivering in anger.

That's our bread and butter, he fumed. You're contracted to bloody well perform.

We can get by without Frankie for one night, Cindy reasoned.

How?

Easy, said Frankie. Dicko knows all the words to our songs. It's only a dance gig. It's not a big deal.

Not a big deal! De Lucca began to descend the stairs.

Not a big deal for you, he thundered. You don't have to organise every little goddam thing; like rehearsals, gigs, payments, every bloody thing. You just roll up to rehearsals and gigs when you bloody well feel like it! I spend most of my time trying to find out where you are. He stabbed a finger at Frankie, rings flashing. You are the big negative in all this. Always have been since day one.

De Lucca's anger took Frankie by surprise and she was slow to respond but not Cindy.

That is not fair, Tim! Frankie's voice is what makes The Snoopies! She writes our songs, she pushes us all at rehearsals to be better. You need to apologise.

Frankie had never seen Cindy react so quickly and strongly to anything in the past. It made her already fraught emotions run even higher. De Lucca quickly moved toward Cindy, pudgy hands fluttering in frantic calming motions.

Sorry love. Sorry, sorry. You're right, of course. He tried to take Cindy's hands but she pulled away from him sharply.

You need to apologise to Frankie, not me!

Of course, said De Lucca turning to Frankie. I was right out of order. I apologise Frankie. What I said was really stupid. I don't know… Strung out over trying to schedule things…

Frankie had been watching De Lucca's florid features and reading the insincerity behind them.

You can save your words, she said firmly.

Her mind had snapped shut, a decision made.

She turned to Cindy and hugged her whispering in Cindy's ear. I'm so sorry to do this to you. I can't go on anymore. I just can't. That's it for me with the band.

She tightened her hug, afraid of Cindy's reaction and hoping the hug would stifle whatever that reaction would be. She felt Cindy's tears, just as she had that morning when Cindy had appeared at her bedroom window.

See you when I can and we'll talk. She released the hug and they looked at each other in silence. Frankie had to leave in a hurry before she broke down. De Lucca didn't even get a backward look as she struggled with the lock on the door for a moment and then rushed out.

As soon as she was outside in the clear afternoon air, she felt a Vesuvian eruption on the way. There was a park across the street and she just made it to a bench seat before Mount Vesuvius erupted. A lava flow of tears. Tears of exhaustion, regret, relief and tears for Cindy. Alone with that bloated, parasitic De Lucca.

She had talked about splitting from The Snoopies many times with Cindy and Cindy had encouraged her to go if she wanted. But Frankie could only think that she'd deserted Cindy.

Two tram rides later, Frankie was back with her draft-resisting Romeo, arm in arm, walking through the safety of the Carlton cemetery, very light mizzle falling, making the concrete paths slippery underfoot.

The cemetery was just across the road from Jack's bolt-hole of safety in the Union Building at Melbourne uni and away from the eyes of cruising cops.

Jack had never seen Frankie teary before. Normally, she was unrelentingly positive about everything and her fresh tears were rattling his own emotions. They passed between the weather-stained headstones in the older part of the cemetery and stopped short of entering the rows of white marbled, faux-Roman monoliths of recent years.

He took Frankie in his arms and wiped a tear from her cheek with his thumb. It had been a while since he had handled a lump of timber but his thumb was still calloused and felt rough on Frankie's cheek. No matter, she loved his touch and smiled up into his face.

Sorry. You're facing the biggest week of your life, maybe even jail, and all I can do is blubber over my silly problems.

Jack didn't reply immediately. He stood, resting his chin on the top of her head, enjoying the press of her body and the aroma of her damp hair, looking down over the rows and rows of headstones to the cars and trams on Swanston Street and the distant Dandenong Ranges, barely visible through the grey mizzle.

The biggest week of my life, eh? S'pose I haven't had that big a life.

He tried to say that Frankie was the biggest thing in his life, but it didn't come out right. He mumbled something about her being big.

Frankie looked up at him, amusement surfacing through the tears in her eyes. She knew what he meant.

After days and nights of leading protest songs and chants, Frankie thought she had a good idea of who could sing and play an instrument. She had recruited a dozen or more tambourine players, several guitarists and even a sax player. Come Wednesday night she was exhausted but, like many others, was too on edge to sleep. Jack had been warned that the cops could raid at any hour. She spent the early hours spooned in behind him, mind churning, listening to the sounds of two hundred surrounding bedfellows. Finally she fell asleep.

A few minutes later she was awake again. Someone was violently shaking Jack's shoulder.

Wake up Jack. The pigs are only a block away. You know the drill. Move it!

Jack gave her a quick kiss and was gone.

Not long after, the siren on the rooftop sounded and everyone was ordered up to the third floor and told to sit down. Frankie snatched up a tambourine and her guitar and joined the queue up the stairs. The lower stairs were barricaded.

It took a while for befuddled, sleep-deprived student brains to function, but eventually most were seated. Frankie had been rehearsing this moment with her collection of minstrels and she was herding them to one side of the hall where they would be seen and heard by all when there was a loud crash downstairs as the Union Building's front doors were smashed down. Military-style shouted orders could be heard from the ground floor and more crashing as the chairs crammed into the first floor stairs were thrown around.

Some students were beginning to look alarmed so Frankie launched into John Lennon's Power To The People, clapping a tambourine above her head to encourage a rhythm. Her fellow musos joined in the chant and a dozen voices soon became fifty, a hundred and, before long, two hundred. Clapping, full-throated, stentorian, strident, rhythmic. The din in the confines of the packed third floor reached thunderous proportions. Frankie felt tears welling up but she continued to belt out a rhythm on the tambourine above her head. Just when it appeared the noise levels couldn't go up any higher, the sax player joined in and the place really went off. The Union building was vibrating and resonating from its footings to Radio Resistance, on the roof.

When the police finally threw the last of the chairs away and mounted the third floor stairs they were already defeated. A senior very exasperated custodian of the law tried announcing something through a megaphone, but he was a mouse in front of a roaring lion.

An hour later they were gone, leaving the students to clean up.

At lunchtime Frankie was walking out of yet another student meeting when one of the senior organisers pulled her aside. She knew him only as Jebs. The main man, Jack had dubbed him. She knew something was wrong straight away from his look of distress.

The pigs got him. They've got Jack.

Frankie had been dreading this. Stunned into silence, she couldn't ask any of the questions she wanted to.

We think they may make an example of him, Jebs went on. This may be more than a fine.

Frankie stared into Jebs's face as he talked, watching his lips move as he formed each word but not really listening to those words.

We don't even know where they've taken him. I'm trying to get our lawyer to see him but at this stage we're meeting a wall of silence from the police. That's why we're worried.

Frankie turned away for a moment, trying to think. She had little knowledge of legal matters, but she did have a childhood illogical faith in the bricks and mortar of a local police station.

She asked Jebs where the nearest one might be and was told Carlton. In his opinion she would be wasting her time, but she could try.

The blue-uniformed policewoman behind the front counter seemed preoccupied by many things. She appeared to have only half-heard Frankie's question.

What did you say his name was?

Sanderson. Jack Sanderson.

A blue paragon of disinterest, the policewoman began slowly thumbing through a clipboard of papers in front of her. A young Italian girl and her mother waited to be attended to behind Frankie, the girl nervously clutching a handful of forms.

Can't say I've seen the name on today's charge sheet, the policewoman said. Doesn't mean much though. What was he arrested for?

Draft resisting.

The policewoman focused on Frankie as if she was seeing her for the first time. She waited a couple of beats before answering.

Oh. One of those.

She nodded to a long wooden bench against one wall of the small room.

Better take a seat. He may have been sent anywhere. I'll make some inquiries for you in due course.

Frankie sat down and watched as the Italian mother and daughter began a pantomime of misunderstandings with the policewoman that involved much form shuffling, hand gesticulating from the mother and rolling of eyes from behind the front counter. It was an entertainment that went on for some time before the girl was whisked away for a driving licence test somewhere behind the police station.

She had been tested and failed before Frankie was attended to.

The front desk had been taken over by a male sergeant now, the policewoman gone on an overdue lunch break. He put the phone down and turned to Frankie.

You were inquiring after Jack Sanderson, love?

Frankie quickly rose from her seat and came over to the desk.

Yes, I was. Have you found out anything?

Not much. Seems like he's being held over at Pentridge. Can't tell you any more than that.

Frankie felt a stab of fear at the mention of Pentridge. Bluestone walls, hangings, breakouts.

Pentridge jail? Would I be able to see him?

This drew a rueful smile from the desk sergeant.

Need a booking to visit anyone in Pentridge. Difficult place to get into and a bloody site more difficult to get out of.

The man is being funny, Frankie told herself. She should probably smile but she could only feel despair and fear. What sort of country was this? Pentridge was where killers were sent. Jack *didn't* want to kill.

She spent the next ten minutes fruitlessly trying to organise a visit to Pentridge before she gave up and walked outside. She turned and looked back at the Police station, an old two-storey brick building with curved window arches and an incongruous little blue police sign. Another piece of her childhood faith in the world withering away.

She decided to visit Cindy.

I don't know, Cind. It's all shit. Everything is shit.

Frankie and Cindy had found a quiet corner table in The Prince of Wales Hotel where they could talk. Frankie's emotional spectrum was ricocheting back and forth. She was supposed to be the voice of reason, it was her role, but it was Cindy who reached across the table and took both of Frankie's hands in her own. Cindy's hands were fine and her touch as light as a feather. Her calm was contagious and transcended the need for words. They sat like this for some time until Cindy broke the silence.

Do you know where it was that I lost my virginity? That night after the dance in Colin's car. Do you know where it happened?

Frankie took a moment to comprehend. Yes … the park, wasn't it?

Fong Park. The park that my grandfather donated to the community when his pear orchards were cut up and sold. The park was named after him.

Frankie waited for Cindy to continue, not sure where she might be headed with this.

That park was special to him. I'm special to him and what we've done with the band was special to him. My grandfather died three weeks ago.

Frankie felt a wave of love and loss. She remembered his stooped thin frame, his brown, wrinkled, kindly features. He had been Cindy's lantern all through her childhood and they had whiled away more hours in his sage-like company than they had with either set of parents.

I'm so sorry, she said.

You don't need to be sorry, Frankie. He died thinking good thoughts about me. That time we first performed on TV. He saw that and was so proud of us, of me. The band has been good, but it has run its course.

And what about you? De Lucca, the relationship?

I'm fine. I ended it with Tim last night.

Frankie felt relief. And the band?

Dicko, Roc and Neil left after you pulled out, they've scored a rock gig in Kings Cross, but Tim has put together some session guitarists and a pianist. We're going upmarket, cabaret. Tim's amazing the way he can totally switch things and pull it off. He's not all bad, so see? You're wrong. Everything is not shit and your man will be out of jail soon. And anyway, he's only doing what he believes is right. That's good. It's all good, Frankie.

But it wasn't all good. Frankie had heard from Jebs that their suspicions were right. Jack was being made an example of. A scapegoat to bolster public opinion of the government. They were throwing the book at him.

She watched Cindy's slim back weaving between drinkers as she made her way to the bar, long vee of black hair and pale shoulders disappearing into the crowd.

She recalled her teenage thoughts that morning when Cindy had tapped on her bedroom window. Some things were just not fair. She could only imagine the bluestone archaic cells of Pentridge. The dark, and her Jack.

Chapter 21

Dark threatening storm clouds were snuffing out the upper stories of Sydney's CBD one by one as John and Chub traipsed down the long William Street hill from Hyde Park towards The Cross, their second stint of leave having finally come around. John had only heard days before that the Keystones had reformed and were performing at a bar in Darlinghurst Road, he was keen to catch up. Chub had taken no persuading to tag along. For Chub, Kings Cross represented everything he'd never experienced and ached to experience while John could only think about reuniting with the Keystones.

Reckon we might get a bit wet, Chub was looking back at the advancing black clouds.

John grunted an answer, mind on the reunion. He was actually feeling a little apprehensive about meeting up with Dicko and Roc again. Would he get the off-handed, yesterday's bass-player treatment? Or would they have some time for him? A little friendship. Affection, perhaps? Anyway, their bloody Commer van was still registered in his name and no-one had reimbursed him for the rego money. They'd better have some time for him.

When they were almost at the corner of Darlinghurst Road, a wall of rain swept across the intersection, hammering cars and pedestrians alike.

The boys ran for the shelter of an awning that wrapped around the corner.

Told yer it was looking dodgy. Chub wiped his now dripping sandy hair with an equally wet sleeve.

John was trying to dry his glasses. You don't say. Ever considered a career with the weather bureau?

But Chub was now engrossed with the sight of a large, heavily made-up woman with a huge pile of white hair stacked up on her head like a block of sun-bleached units. She was sheltering in a nearby doorway smoking a cheroot, several shopping bags at her feet.

Did ya get an eyeball on her? Neighbour's prize ram back home'd be interested. Could be good breeding stock.

John made sure he didn't look at her, embarrassed by Chub's ogling.

Behave, man. You're not in the boondocks now. Anyway, she's probably a he.

Bloody hell. Now that would confuse the poor old ram.

John ignored him, eyes on a billboard.

Easybeats. Wow. Playing right here, tonight. I'd love to catch them.

Chub smiled amiably. You're the section leader. You choose the route, I'm tail-end Charlie.

John fished out a scrap of paper from his back pocket with directions on it.

Ok. So, this is the strip. They're playing in a bar down here somewhere on the right. The Groovy Room.

They came to the end of the awning and had to make a dash through the rain across an intersecting street. Any scrap of shelter was now becoming crowded with smartly dressed GIs and circling mini-skirted women, business types on their lunchbreak, hippies, mutton-chopped spruikers, idlers, leaners, walkers. Chub's eyes were all over. There was colour around but right now the Cross was getting a right old hosing down from mother nature. More than an underarm daub with a damp washer.

John spotted a flashing Groovy Room sign on the opposite side of the road.

Follow me.

He set off into the rain again, Chub a couple of paces behind, dodging traffic.

The Groovy Room entrance was an uninspiring set of well-worn concrete stairs descending into the gloom. John could recognise the sound of Dicko's guitar straight away, echoing up from below. A beer-bellied spruiker with a slicked-back rocker hairstyle greeted them from his spot, leaning back against a tiled wall beside the stairs. Arms folded, tatts on show.

G'day, fellas. Cheap drinks today. Music. Lots of girls due in soon. Free entry.

He had Chub's attention. Girls, eh?

Not a lot now, mate. But you just settle in down there and enjoy a few drinks. They'll come.

John was already on his way down the stairs, so Chub followed.

The Groovy Room had two main attractions that didn't strike John as being particularly groovy at four o'clock in the afternoon.

A long bar to the right, empty except for two girls chatting to a barman, and a stage to the left with Dicko, Roc, and John's replacement on bass, strumming and tapping their way through a well-worn instrumental. They were flanked by a pair of empty dancing platforms made up to look like bird cages. There was a lot of pungent beer-soaked carpet between the stage and bar and no dancers on the dance floor.

When Dicko caught sight of John, he beamed and managed a mock salute, while continuing to play. Roc pointed a drumstick at him and then flicked at his long hair with the stick, obviously amused by John's army haircut.

A mumbled announcement by Dicko to their almost non-existent audience quickly followed. Time for a break, folks.

Dicko jumped down from the stage and grabbed John's hand, slapping him on the back.

Oh, man. Are we glad to see you! Mate, we are fucking arse-busted broke. The bastards haven't paid us since we've been here, we are literally starving.

John nodded and smiled, but he knew what this meant.

Roc joined them and pumped John's hand, even giving him an Italian style pinch on both cheeks.

Love your buzz-cut, buddy. Suits ya. Laughing.

The third band member joined them and Dicko theatrically gestured in his direction.

And this is our new bass player …

The bass player went down on one knee and John thought he must have dropped something for a moment. Dicko repeated. And this is …

The bass player? John ventured with a smile.

Fuck you're slow, four eyes. What's the man doing?

John twigged and smiled. Kneeling. His name's Neil.

Finally. Neil's our resident wit.

Thought that was your role.

John shook hands when the man had regained his feet and introduced Chub who'd been watching all this with quiet amusement. Dicko was quick to return to his topic of choice.

Arse-busted broke, we are. You wouldn't believe the string of blood-sucking arseholes we're supporting. How many fucking agents and managers have we got, Roc?

One in every state.

Yeah, fucking De Lucca in Melbourne got us this gig when we split from The Snoopies but all he does is sub us through this Sydney agency who have an office way out in Parramatta Road. We have to go out there to be paid, only to be told ... What was the latest bullshit, Roc?

Rent. They couldn't pay us anything because it had all gone on paying our rent.

Why did you split from The Snoopies? Thought you guys were hitting the big time.

Girls were great, said Dicko, but not our scene. De Lucca set up The Snoopies to line his pockets, not ours. When Frankie left to do her own thing we were outta there. Never going to be the same without her, she had the voice from hell, eh Roc?

Roc nodded, sing anything.

So anyway mate, Dicko looked imploringly at John, we're bloody starving. Couldn't lend us some dough, could ya?

John turned away for a moment, adjusting his glasses. Something he did when trying to buy some time.

Fuck, Dicko, he said quietly. You haven't even fixed me up for the rego on the van.

Dicko looked a question to Roc. Roc shook his head and Dicko turned back to John.

Jeeze, sorry, man. I forgot about that.

John shrugged despairingly. Never mind … we'll sort something out. You could start by fixing us up with somewhere to crash for tonight. Have to get back tomorrow.

Again, Dicko looked at Roc who had no answer.

Dicko was choosing his words carefully now, reluctant to insult his creditor.

Unfortunately our flat is a shithole. I mean we're sleeping on what floor space there is and it's across the bridge out at Manly.

Roc had a thought. Neen will know of somewhere. She's a local. Calling out to one of the girls talking to the barman. Hey, Neen. Crash pad for the guys here. Just tonight. Any idea?

One of the girls swivelled around on her barstool, sucking on her cigarette. Her black hair was swept up high and held with a wide band.

Could try Lo Lo, she called back. On the right, halfway down the hill in Victoria Street. There's a sign out the front, Lo Lo's Lodgings. Can't miss it. Tell her I sent youse and she'll give you a special rate.

There you go, said Roc, not far at all.

Dicko swivelled round as a group of four sailors came down the stairs.

Shit. We'll have to start playing again. Tell you what Johnno, we're on twelve to five, six to midnight. Sort your pad out and come back. This place goes off later and then we'll show you the town when we knock off tonight.

When John and Chub came back that night, turning the corner from Victoria Street into the strip, they found the half-drowned old girl of a precinct they had paddled through that day had been given chest massage, mouth to mouth resuscitation, heart-thumping CPR. She had a pulse now. A fluoro pulse. Competing shades of pink and violet and red. Flashing, strobing, blinking. Twisting serpent-like into multiple words and messages. Pussy, pink, crazy, Venus, show, gaiety, open, girls, girls and more girls. Boys didn't get to feature too much up on the signage, but they were everywhere on the ground. The sidewalks were now heaving with dudes, military and otherwise. Mostly in groups, mostly on the hunt. Door to door. Bright light to bright light. The signage was doing its job.

Chub only had eyes for the girls who were there as well, in parties of two or three, sometimes linked in with the marauding males, who were mainly escapees from the Vietnam war. The girls mainly escapees from the western suburbs.

Down in the bowels of The Groovy Room, things were looking a whole lot groovier. Now packed with drinkers, two tassel-breasted go-go dancers in the bird cages doing the Monkey, dance floor full and the Keystones in full swing. John felt a rush of adrenalin. An urge to be up there with the boys. He turned to Chub, having to shout over the racket.

I introduced that song to the band. Jump blues. Good Golly Miss Molly.

Chub was taking in the vista.

Seems to be going down all right, he shouted back. Want a beer?

Yeah, I'll get it. There's a trick to these joints. You have to know someone or they'll serve you watered down piss and charge a motza. That girl today, Neen, who put us onto the lodgings, she'll be one of the staff here. Paid to chat to the GIs and con them into buying drinks. Keep your wits about you, Chub.

John pushed his way to the bar.

Two schooners of Toohey's, thanks mate.

When the barman returned with the beers and demanded eighty-five cents, John announced proudly that he was mates with the band.

So?

John handed over the money and skulked off with his beers.

As soon as the boys stopped for a break, John was waiting for them behind the stage. Dicko greeted him with a grin. You want to play, don't you? Think you can handle this?

He pushed a guitar case across the stage floor to John. My old Maton rhythm. We've been talking about adding another guitarist. You know most of the songs, so this'd be a good chance for us to get a handle on what the three guitars would sound like. Gonna be a lot fatter, I reckon.

John unclipped the case and felt the strings, his spirits soaring. This was going to be more than a one song guest pick and flick. The boys genuinely wanted him back up on stage.

Dicko handed him a flat plectrum. Here, you'll need this. It's in tune, you'll only need to give it a tweak when we get you hooked up.

Chub found himself a position at the bar where he could see the stage and ordered himself another beer. He'd been too young when he was at Ag college in Perth to be allowed into any of the rock venues, but he'd caught what bands he could and even bought a couple of Mamas and Papas singles. He may not know the finer points, but he could see that John was fitting right in with the band. He looked relaxed, exchanging looks with the others, nods of appreciation. John could obviously play. He was what he said he was, a musician. So many blokes in the army were full of bullshit.

The band had a fan in the fellow beside Chub at the bar. Eyes closed, swinging rhythmically from side to side on his bar stool, hands lazily following the drum beat on his knees.

Whooo. He opened his eyes and turned to Chub. Sure can play for white boys. No offence intended, brother.

None taken, said Chub. He felt underdressed in his well-worn jeans and plain shirt beside this fellow.

Afro-American, with a slick widely-lapelled black leather jacket and crisp white shirt. When he smiled at Chub, a pencil-thin moustache stretched across his top lip.

You're Aussie, huh? Thought you may've been one of us.

Yeah. I'm Aussie.

But you're military, ain't you?

That obvious, is it?

Military want us all to look the same. Where you from, brother? You city boy or country?

S'pose you'd have to say I was from the country.

The man's face lit up. No shit? Rural, like me.

Chub had always been fascinated by the American westerns. He'd often taken a front row deck chair at the old Nanderra open air cinema, just to study the cowboys' riding styles. Bizarre though it sounded.

Rural? Like in the wild west? Chub asked.

The man laughed. That's all shit, brother. No. Crop country. Sellin' great big motor cars to big fat farmers. That's me. Nothin' wild about that. Anyways, what's yer name? I'm Calvin.

Chub.

They shook hands.

What yer drinkin' there, Chub?

Chub thought about this. He'd heard the GIs had money to splash around and he didn't want to get into a shout he couldn't afford.

Thanks, Calvin, but I've got my beer. I'll be right.

Bullshit, man. I'm getting you a beer. Matter of fact, I'm getting you a bourbon like what I'm havin'. We're all brothers here aren't we?

We're brothers but … Calvin had already spun around and was yelling out the drinks order.

So, he said handing Chub his drink, what line o' work you in? I mean, before the military.

Chub was trying to explain station work to him when Neen, the girl who had lined up their lodgings, stopped in front of him. Her companion had the blondest hair and the shortest mini-skirt Chub had ever seen.

Neen pushed up to Chub.

Your friend's going for it with the band. He really makes a difference to the sound.

Neen's companion squeezed in-between Calvin and Neen.

Chub nodded enthusiastically. Great, isn't he? Never heard him play before.

Calvin interrupted. You're buddies with the band? You didn't say. They're a good band.

Chub grinned. For white fellers.

Calvin laughed and slapped Chub on the back. You got it, brother. Anyway, who's your friends, here? Holding out his hand to Neem. I'm Calvin.

Oh, sorry. Chub said. This is Neem and …?

Carol. The blonde one filled in for him, taking Calvin's handshake for an inordinately long time while she fixed him with a smile.

Ok, then, Neem and Carol. Drinks are on me, Calvin announced. What are you having?

While Calvin was ordering the drinks, cocktails Chub had never heard of, he thought he noticed a look pass from Carol to the barman, behind Calvin's back.

John was disappointed when midnight came around and Dicko had to announce an end to the night's entertainment. Last drinks were being taken at the bar and he could see Chub there, still in company with the two girls and the black guy. He unplugged the Maton and was returning it to its case when the rest of the band joined him at the back of the stage. Dicko actually embraced him and the other two were full of the moment.

Fabulous, mate. Dicko said. The sound was so much better with the four of us. You know where to come when you're through with that army shit.

How much longer? Roc asked. I mean, in the army?

John could only shake his head. Dunno. Forever. Anything could happen.

Oh, well. Anyway, it was just like old times. The Keystones on fire. Speaking of which … Roc looked a question at Dicko. The tattoos. We were gonna all get a Keystones tattoo to set us in ink forever if you know what I mean. Tattoos. That's what you do in The Cross, isn't it?

Trouble is, Dicko interjected, no dosh. Can't afford them unless ... I mean we could all get them, and we'd have to pay you back.

John glanced across at Neil and then Roc. They were obviously into it. John acquiesced with his quiet smile.

Ok, he said. Where do we get these tattoos done? Nothing too over the top, I hope.

Roc beamed. No. Just the stone with the key through it, like on my bass drum. We were going to get them done at Painless Chaters, down in Paddington. Tomorrow morning suit you?

John nodded. Have to be done by eleven. Our ride back to base leaves from the city at twelve. In the shit big time if we miss that.

They all finished up at Sweethearts café, not far from The Groovy Room. John, Chub, the band, Calvin, Neem and Carol. Carol's rear end was placed squarely on Calvin's thighs and she had one arm firmly around his shoulders. No doubt where that was headed. Chub was sitting hopefully beside Neem.

Calvin's bonhomie knew no end but Chub had politely declined, he could only accept so much. Not so, the band. They were dining out on Calvin's U.S. dollars like starved coyotes.

John was still amped. It was too late to catch The Easybeats now but that didn't matter anymore, he had experienced his own musical nirvana.

He asked Roc if there was any grass floating round. He could do with a joint.

Roc took a break from his voracious food shovelling and shook his head.

We don't have any, but I could get you some. The yank's been asking, too.

What about the girl with Chub? Neem. Has he got any chance?

Tell him to just ask her for a fuck. Better get in quick or someone else will.

John leant across to Chub, who was sitting on the other side of him, and gave him a subtle nudge in the ribs.

Chub took his advice with a worried look. I can't ask her that, he whispered back. Bit rude.

He said someone else would if you didn't. Quick and the dead, mate.

Chub thought about this for a moment. Neem was pulling out another one of her Alpines, so he whipped out a cigarette lighter. He didn't smoke but had been given the good oil by Voronski. Always carry a lighter for the ladies.

She accepted his light without ceremony. She was an earthy type. Almost one of the boys, Chub thought. But she certainly wasn't a boy, hair up, tits up, hemline up. He knew she was paid to socialise with the Groovy Room customers but wasn't sure about anything else. He tentatively began to stammer a question.

Would you like to, um … come back to our pad with me? Lolo's?

She fixed him with a matter of fact look.

Depends what for. You boys got a stash? Weed? Hash? Hammer?

This was a long way from Chub's sphere. Drugs were something he knew nothing about.

No, no. Nothing like that. I mean … you know. He looked around, then took in a big breath and spoke very softly. Sex?

Neem's expression remained so-so.

You want that?

Yeah.

I don't do tricks for free, soldier.

Right.

Heavy balls, heavy wallet. Light balls, light wallet.

Right ... How light?

Neem took a long drag on her cigarette while she considered this.

You're pretty cute darlin' and you're with the boys and all that ... Say, thirty for you.

Right. Chub's mind was spinning one way, his balls the other. A week's pay for a root. John and his mates would think he was a goose ... but he was always going to roll with his balls, the bourbon had made sure of that.

When Neen and Chub had left, Roc winked at John. Hope your friend doesn't skimp with the frangers. He'll need them with that one.

Painless Chater wasn't painless. Far from it, John thought. In fact, he seemed to be pushing the tattoo gun into the back of John's hand with unnecessary force. John was reminded of his first haircut as a four-year-old. The barber had been an old boy, like the tattooist, with brylcreemed hair parted down the middle and bulging tattooed forearms like Popeye the Sailor Man, attacking him with a fearsome instrument in front of a shop full of customers waiting their turn. Chub interrupted his reverie.

Know yer blood group, mate? Chub had left the long waiting bench where The Keystones were still seated and was standing beside him.

Blood group? Yeah, why?

Get it tattooed somewhere they can find easy. You know, like Davidson and all the regs. For the meds if your dog tags get lost in action.

This made sense to John. He nodded and turned to the tattooist.

AB positive. Put it on my wrist under the key and stone.

Chub then began scoping the walls of designs for something that might take his fancy. There were plenty of military originals, including one of a slouch hat wearing combatant jabbing a bayonet into the rear end of a Viet Cong who was jumping comically, conical hat flying off, oversize drops of red blood spurting out behind him.

Lovely, Chub thought. One to show mum.

He chose a small dragon design for three dollars, about all he could afford after the previous night's outlay. It could go on his forearm along with his blood group.

John had not had much time to mull over the weekend's happenings but, sitting in the back of the old Commer van as they neared their drop off point in Pitt Street, he was very subdued. The others were chiacking and ribbing Chub about his night with Neen but John was wondering if he'd made the right call about not deferring his call up. Playing with the band again had been a revelation and the thought of more guard duty that night not so enticing. He hated "no-man's land", craved direction. He clenched his fists and squeezed them between his knees hoping the pressure would somehow clear his brain. It was a routine that had helped him in the past and it helped again. He couldn't lose sight of his destiny, he thought, and his destiny had been decided by the spinning balls that had come up with his number. The army and everything that came with it was his destiny. Dicko pulled the van over to the kerb in Pitt Street near to where John and Chub would be meeting their lift back to Singleton and they all bundled out onto the footpath. Dicko threw his arms around John in an unexpected hug.

Missed you four eyes. When you're done with all that army shit, look us up.

Roc also gave him a hug and Neil a warm handshake.

Loved that fat sound of the third guitar, said Roc. Why don't you go awol or something, we'd look after ya.

Roc, you lot can't even look after yourselves, John chipped back, smiling.

Too right, Dicko laughed. Late for our midday gig, gotta go.

The Keystones piled back into their van and headed back to the Groovy Room in a blue haze of exhaust fumes leaving Chub and John on the windswept Sunday-empty Pitt Street footpath. Chub hoping they hadn't missed their lift, John wondering if he'd ever play another note with the Keystones.

A week later Chub was slumping his way up a set of concrete steps at the rear of the mess hall on his way back to the platoon hut when he became aware there was a group of guards being marched down the road in his direction.

If there was one thing that gave Chub the shits more than anything it was having to stand at attention for dumb-arses, and here was a prime candidate for dumb-arse of the year marching the guards along. Chub didn't know who the dumb-arse was but he had to be a dumb-arse or he wouldn't be taking his task so seriously. Young face a mask of military intensity, anyone would think he was marching them into The Battle of Waterloo rather than a stint of boredom guarding the Singleton perimeter fence. Bugger it, he wasn't going to stand at attention for this dickhead. He spun around and tried to slip around the back of the kitchen to avoid the road but nearly bumped into a big-bellied cook coming out the kitchen rear door.

What the fuck are you doin' here, soldier?

The cook had a set of sergeant's stripes and plenty of tattoos to proclaim his authority.

Oh, wrong way. Sorry, sergeant.

Chub climbed the stairs again as slowly as he could, hoping the contingent would pass before he reached the road, but there was no escaping it, they were still approaching. He waited for them at the top of the stairs and came to attention when they reached him, looking the part, except for his mess tin mug hanging from his little finger.

When they had passed he continued on his way, taking his time, enjoying the chilled evening air. Training had been fairly hectic and there never seemed to be any time to ponder what they were doing or where they were going. He supposed the army did this on purpose. They were into their last week of infantry training and were waiting on deployment instructions. He reached into his back pocket and pulled out a crumpled letter that he'd received the day before from his mother and had already read several times. It took a lot of digesting. His father had suffered a stroke and was on light duties. Chub was now missing Eumarella and only wanted to be back there taking the reins from his father.

Most of the platoon were out the front of their hut when he got back. It looked like they had just been dismissed from an unscheduled parade ground assembly and there was an air of excitement. Hedley was the first to greet him, grinning broadly.

Deployment, mate. Just been told where we're all going. I'm off to Vietnam. Same battalion as Voronski and Langer.

Is that what you want? Said Chub cautiously.

Bloody oath. A bit of action.

But I'm not in the same battalion, I take it?

No, you're in some reinforcement unit I think. Same as John.

Chub shrugged. Suits me.

He found John inside, sitting on his bed, head in hands. He looked up when Chub entered then put his head back in his hands.

What do yer know? Chub asked. Heard we're in some reinforcing unit.

Wouldn't believe it, John mumbled through his hands. Missed the S.A.S. and now the only battalion going to Vietnam.

Chub opened his locker and put away his mess gear.

Reinforcements can happen, can't they?

Long shot at best.

Chub flopped down on his bed. So where is this place we're going?

Ingleburn. Near Sydney.

The Cross.

Forget it. They'll be getting us battle-ready. Can't imagine it'll be any picnic. Just a matter of whether we'll ever see any battle.

Chub stretched himself out on his bed and focused on the ceiling.

Battle or boredom. Sounds like nothin' but fun.

Which would you prefer? We may be given a choice, you know.

Chub continued to examine the ceiling while he mulled over this conundrum.

Dunno. Boredom sounds like the safe option but at the end of the day someone's going to have to cover your arse. S'pose that will have to be me.

John smiled despite himself and Chub rolled over toward the wall and closed his eyes.

Chapter 22

Second Lieutenant Doug Ashmore had been monitoring Hedley's progress since Hedley's single-handed invasion of his HQ.

Ashmore was now a platoon commander and Hedley one of his charges. His platoon was now as settled as possible with Canungra out of the way, all the Mount Spec exercises complete and only another few weeks of live firing and orientation work to do around their base at Townsville in tropical far north Queensland. Then they were boarding a troop ship for Vietnam. Couldn't come quickly enough for him. But he was worried about the section Hedley was in, the section leader was a veteran and first in line for a promotion if there was a problem higher up in the ranks which was a very real possibility. This would leave a gaping hole in the section. Hedley was the only other section member with any initiative, but he was struggling with his map reading. The kid seemed to have an uncanny sense of direction but give him a compass bearing and he couldn't make head nor tail of it.

The platoon was straggling into Lavarack barracks after a particularly gruelling twenty-kilometre trek back from the operation area, expiring in the cling wrap tropical humidity. Ashmore watched Hedley working with Voronski and Langer, the two section slackers, to get them over the line in some sort of order. It wasn't his job, but they were his mates. The kid reminded him of his father's border collie rounding up sheep back on the farm. Something in the effortless way he moved, urging Langer along, then back on Voronski's case, back to Langer. Endless patience and endurance, always grinning, the only thing he lacked was the border collie's red tongue, lolling out the side of his grin. Hang it. He decided on the spot, he would present Hedley with a stripe. Promote him to lance corporal. The kid had promise and he would just have to give Hedley extra training with the orienteering.

A couple of evenings later, Langer and Hedley were on kitchen cleaning duty in the huge canteen building. Langer was inside one of the egg-shaped stainless steel vats, scraping out fat and passing it to Hedley who was binning it. They were stripped down to their army green singlets and shorts in the stifling heat and Langer was giving Hedley a hard time over his new tattoo, etched high on his right arm.

Ya can't even hardly see it, mate. You're too black. What is it, anyway?

Get your eyes tested, dickhead. Hedley flexed his bicep in Langer's direction. Donald Duck. See?

But Langer's eyes went to the rear door. Lookout. It's Ashmore.

Ashmore pointed at Hedley from the doorway and gave him a curt 'follow me' motion. Hedley, never at ease with any form of authority, looked at Langer.

Wonder what I've done wrong?

Piss off, Yanga. Teacher's pet. Don't worry about me, I'll be right. I don't mind cleaning out another ton or two of this shit on my own.

Hedley grinned and wiped his greasy hands across Langer's back. Bit more for ya, mate. See, ya.

Ashmore took him to a room behind the officer's mess where he had a large map of Australia laid out flat on a table. The map was shaded from red to green. Red for the desert country and a strip of green for the vegetated area up the east coast.

Right, Corporal Yangaboora. What's this?

Hedley hadn't been presented with his stripe yet and was feeling decidedly uncomfortable with the promotion. Proud of himself, but uncomfortable. He was also a little phased by this one on one with an officer. He looked at the map. It was a map, what did he want him to say?

Where do you come from, Hedley? Point to it on the map.

This was easy. Hedley pointed to Nanderra, surrounded by the familiar red desert colour.

Ok, said Ashmore. Now imagine you're there, right where your finger is. You're in your country. Now, what's to your north?

Hedley thought about this, unsure where Ashmore was leading him.

The road, sir. The road up to Tulla.

And south?

Road down to Coorum.

East?

Road to Boreen.

West?

No towns out that way, sir. Just that Murchison river country.

Right, said Ashmore thoughtfully. So, you know your north, south, east, west. All we have to do is teach you the degrees. How far can you count, Hedley?

This was embarrassing. He'd only just started to get the hang of basic numbers. 'Bout twenty, sir, he said, watching as Ashmore produced a compass and placed it on the map, centred on Nanderra, and orientated to the north.

That's ok, that may be all we need. Now, can you read the number on the compass where north is? The inside number, not the outside, we'll worry about them later. The little number on the compass right at the top under the N.

Hedley felt a familiar confusion coming on. Dunno, sir. Numbers.

Correct. But don't think of them as one number like twelve or twenty but as individual numbers. Read them out, one at a time.

Three, six, nothing.

Ashmore beamed. Well done. You just gave me a compass bearing. Only it's not nothing, it's zero. Three, six, zero. If we're on patrol and I give you an order over the radio to take your section on a bearing of three, six, zero degrees, you head north up to Tulla. Nine, zero degrees, Boreen, and everywhere in between has its own number. So, say we want to go here, Ashmore stabbed his finger on the map. What bearing is that from Nanderra?

For the first time, the deeply perplexed plough furrows in Hedley's overhanging brow began to relax. He read slowly from the compass. Two, five, zero, sir.

Two, five, zero degrees. Well done.

Hedley felt another of life's many mysteries beginning to make sense. There was some logic to all this after all.

Ashmore began rolling up the map.

I'm going to give you this compass and map and I want you to work out every single degree on the compass and what it points to around Nanderra. You need to be familiar with where those degrees are on the compass face. Later, after more lessons, you'll be able to relay directions where the enemy is, where you are, where the firepower must be directed. A few short weeks and we'll be in a war zone. Ok?

Hedley nodded. He was already thinking of the waterholes and homesteads back home in map terms instead of just instinctive terms. His confidence on the march.

The ocean off Townsville was calm except for a small wind chop. Hedley had never been on a boat before and now he was jammed shoulder to shoulder with Langer and Voronski in one of half a dozen landing craft that were ferrying the battalion out to the 'Sydney', an aircraft carrier that had been converted to a troop ship.

The boys were trying to peer over the side as they rounded Magnetic Island, Langer babbling on about a day trip he'd taken out there.

… Tree had a pair of tits on it like you wouldn't believe and a bikini painted on. Red polka dots, like the song. Got a photo of me with me face buried between 'em.

But Hedley's attention was on the 'Sydney', now visible, lying at anchor further out to sea. It was huge, looming out of the misty tropical showers like a grey behemoth. Voronski, who carried a worldly nonchalance with him at all times, sensed Hedley's awe.

Ever been on a ship? He asked Hedley.

Never even seen one, mate. Not this big anyway.

Voronski thought about this for a moment. It was hard for him to comprehend that Hedley had never seen a large ship. He had spent many weeks at sea as a small boy coming out to Australia from Russia, something he rarely talked about.

Nervous?

Before Hedley could answer, Langer butted in. A cruise. We're off on a luxury Pacific cruise. He started wiggling his hips. Hula girls! Cocktails. Gonna be great.

Next day, with the ship well underway, it was shooting drills, firing from the rear of the ship at balloons; Hedley, as usual, topped the scoring. That evening, while the others were scoffing their beer ration, Ashcroft found time to continue Hedley's orienteering tuition. It was near impossible on the crowded ship to find anywhere quiet, but Ashmore had asked the ship's chaplain if they could use his cabin. When Hedley was ushered into the chaplain's cabin he found that the map of Australia had now been replaced with a map of Phouc Tuy Province, the area they would be patrolling in Vietnam. Ashmore spent about half an hour going over the map with Hedley and reinforcing all the things he had taught him. He finished up by giving Hedley a set of co-ordinands for a village and telling him to find and name it on the map. Hedley was quick to find the spot but faltered when he tried to name the village.

Can't read it, sir. B… something.

Binh Ba. Never mind, everyone struggles with the Vietnamese names. You'll manage by spelling them out in your communications… You'll have to, anyway.

This was said with some finality and Hedley felt confused; communicating place names and co-ordinates was not his job.

Ashmore could see the confusion and grinned.

I'm promoting you again. Section 2.I.C. First in line to be promoted to section leader if there's a reshuffle down the track.

Hedley was taken aback. What about Murphy, sir? He's been to Vietnam before. Knows all there is to know.

Yeah, true. But Murphy doesn't want any form of responsibility. He went through enough on his last tour.

I wouldn't feel right tryin' to tell Murph what to do, sir.

Don't worry, I've spoken to him. I put Murphy in your section for a reason. You can lean on him when the shit starts flying. Anyway, for now, you're only the 2.I.C. Just learn as much as you can from your section leader and be prepared for the possibility he might be promoted, and you might have to replace him.

Chapter 23

Frankie tried to organise her thoughts as she sat on a north-bound Sydney Road tram that was clanking and dinging its way through a congestion of cars. What would she say to him? To Jack. Pentridge jail was only a few stops ahead on the corner of Bell Street and he'd been in there for over three months now with no clear date for release. She was worried that the visits were becoming more and more awkward with each passing week. He was so reserved, no doubt wanting to spare her from the grim machinations of prison life and she, in turn, found herself yabbering. Trying to fill in the visit with prattle that he, surely, couldn't be interested in. Her music, her uni exams. Their relationship had always been woven around Jack's attempts at avoiding incarceration, now it revolved around his incarceration.

Pentridge loomed out of the muddle of two story shops like a misplaced medieval relic. Gloomy, castle-like and threatening amid the suburban bustle of cars and pedestrians.

Frankie alighted from the tram and crossed the road toward the ridiculous stone-arched entry. All it needed was a moat and drawbridge. She was wearing a knee length skirt and sleeved blouse, mindful of her first attempt at visiting where she had been refused entry for wearing a mini.

She joined the line of visitors, mainly women, a few kids and the odd besuited lawyer. These people were paying a visit to criminals. Inmates who had committed real crimes. What had Jack done? More to the point, what hadn't he done? He hadn't registered for National Service, refused to take up arms, refused to kill Vietnamese in their own country because Australian politicians followed the direction taken by the U.S. She was fed up with thinking about it.

After the now familiar routine of security checks, she was allowed through to the visiting room and there he was. His look launched across the room and went straight to her heart, *that* look. His, but it was for her. She owned it. He did love her. He did want to hear her prattle. They weren't allowed to touch so they embraced without embracing, made love in an instant. Hells bells, she thought, it didn't matter what they said. Just wallow in every precious minute.

They didn't say much at all for a while then Frankie asked him how his week had been. Jack looked away for a moment as if to gather his thoughts and Frankie immediately thought the worst.

Did something happen?

No, no. Nothing I couldn't handle, anyway.

You must tell me, Jack. Did you get into trouble with the guards? Other prisoners?

Nothing like that. Don't worry about it.

Jack. Tell me.

Nothing happened, ok? Just starting to go a bit spare in the head, that's all. Nothing to do.

Frankie nodded, unconvinced by his answer, but accepting.

Have you thought about trying to continue with your apprenticeship? she asked.

How? No carpentry tools allowed in here.

No, but what about the other side? Theory. You could be getting on with your studies.

He considered this for a moment and then nodded slowly.

Worth thinking about.

I could contact your union. They might be able to organise it.

Possibly. The union boys do seem to have a few connections in here. He looked at her, beginning to smile. How come you always have the bright ideas? I should've thought of that.

Frankie smiled back and shrugged. I'll ring the union tomorrow.

Jack glanced surreptitiously around at the guards. None of them was looking directly at him so he touched Frankie on the back of her right hand where he knew she had splashed her au de cologne. It was a lightning quick, subtle movement and he got away with it undetected. She would feel that touch for days and he would carry her scent on his fingertip, treating himself to regular sniffs for as long as her perfume lingered.

When Frankie left at the end of visiting hours, she turned around in the doorway hoping to catch another of his looks, but the guards were already bustling him into a line with the other prisoners.

Chapter 24

Hedley's first week in Vietnam was dominated by his arse and his nose. Like most of the section, he had a bout of dysentery; but he found the myriad of new smells overwhelming. He had always used his acute sense of smell to source water in a dry landscape. Roos had their special scent which he could pick up on a slight breeze from half a mile and cattle, much further again. Here, in Vietnam, there were so many strong smells that he was hard put to pick up the milder ones. Apart from the latrine stench, most of the smells were chemical. The kerosene smell from the avtur that fuelled the whirling choppers, the cocktail of fumes left after the various explosions they witnessed on their first shakedown operation when the centurion tanks put on a show of fire power for them. The smoke grenades they carried had their own burning smell and then the subtler, creeping toxic chemical odour that wafted up from the defoliated ground they were walking over. When they patrolled through a Vietnamese village, not too far from their base, there were pig smells and rotting vegetation smells, ripening fruit and the smell of the villagers themselves. The Aussie soldiers smelt of repellent, soap and sweat that oozed their diet of army tucker. The villagers had a totally different smell that reflected their environment. It was quite exotic to Hedley and he wouldn't forget that smell when there were enemy around. But picking who were enemy and who weren't was a nightmare according to Murphy. Murphy was a few years older than the rest of them and war-weary, kicking himself for signing up to a second tour of duty. He was sitting between Hedley and Voronski on the edge of a hard-trodden, red clay pathway, backs to a clump of bamboo, eating from their ration packs. Others were on watch while the platoon took a break on the outskirts of the village they had just patrolled through.

Murphy had a head on him like a second grade potato; oblong shaped and plenty of blemishes, more hair growing from his ears and nose than the top of his nut and tiny black eyes like those in a spud. Hedley liked him but Voronski was wary.

This is pretty safe here, Murphy was saying. We're close to base, but you blokes just wait till we're a bit further out. These villages have been here forever. French, Yanks, Cong, us … seen 'em all. They don't give a shit. All they want is to be left alone. When we're here, they're all smiles and kids bottin' sweets. When Charlie sneak in, they're all sympathisers. Those kids bottin' sweets'd just as likely give yer a burst of AK47 fire if it was in their interests. They don't give a fuck about us. They know we'll go home and they'll still be here.

Voronski was following this with interest. Can't blame them, I s'pose, he ventured. We'd feel the same if the boot was on the other foot and they were in Oz.

Murphy gave Voronski a sharp look. Don't start thinkin' like that, moron. The idea is to get outta here alive and in one piece. Any of those cunts back there in that village could kill yer. Yer just don't know which one.

Their first real operation came a week later. There were at least a dozen helicopters lined up on the airfield, all noise, flying rotors and fumes. Ashmore and the platoon sergeant were sorting the boys into a boarding order. Hedley stuffed his hat down into his shirt so it wouldn't be blown off and checked his Armalite for the umpteenth time that morning. He had ten mags of ammo in his pouches, two grenades and a smoke grenade. Even knew the co-ordinands for the patch of jungle they were going to be offloaded into. He had developed a confidence in the system and everyone around him; he just did as he was told. Everything in the army seemed to unroll in front of him like a comfy carpet, maybe not physically comfy, but there was a comfort in knowing that he was part of a long chain of order. There were a lot of people above him doing their share of the thinking, all he had to deal with was his little area. They were all as trained as they could be. Was he apprehensive? Yes. Scared? No. But Langer looked terrified. Murphy had to shove him from behind to get him up into the chopper.

C'mon sunshine. Up you get.

Voronski, who was already in the chopper, reached down and hauled Langer into the machine. Hedley followed. Soon they were banking over rice paddies, morning sun reflecting off the water. There were no doors, but they'd been told numerous times that they couldn't fall out, even though they were looking straight down at the paddies and bomb craters below. The chopper soon levelled out and it wasn't long before they were making a descent into a jungle clearing. As soon as the chopper touched down Hedley was out and running under the rotor downdraught. He remembered his training: get clear of the Huey, drop to the ground, wait for the chopper to lift off, then run for the nearest cover and take up a defensive position. Easy. He only had to follow the section leader, anyway. One day, that might be him.

The section had been in their defensive position for about ten minutes when the section leader returned after a quick briefing from Ashmore.

Search and clear, he barked. Single file, stopping every kilometre so I can take a locstat reading. You all know the drill. Keep yer eyes peeled for booby traps and be on the alert for any possible ambush.

The section leader then took the lead scout aside for further briefing leaving the others in a group for a moment. Langer was wild-eyed with fear.

Gonna be behind you Murph, this place's givin' me the heebie-jeebies already.

Bullshit, Murphy snapped. Take up your usual position and keep yer safety on. Not takin' a bullet up the arse from the likes of you. Anyway, should be pretty ho-hum if you ask me so take a chill pill. Everyone be alert but chilled.

It was slow going through thick rainforest and all the new boys were on edge, even Voronski was seeing movement in the jungle where there was none and trap wires that only turned out to be vines.

By 1600 hours the message came through from Ashcroft to cease patrolling. Everyone was to clean their weapons and have a feed while it was still daylight. He wanted them all in a circular harbour formation with machine guns and sentries in place before nightfall. He ordered a row of claymores be set up along a trail about thirty metres from their position.

One day of patrolling in the damp jungle and oppressive humidity and they were exhausted. It was Hedley's job as 2 I.C., to draw up a gun picket roster for the night. He gave each man a two hour stint and saved the dreaded midnight shift for himself. Most of the men had complained about wanting to fall asleep but Hedley had no trouble staying awake. There was nothing to see except the occasional firefly flickering and fluttering randomly across his vision, but he was enjoying listening to the sounds of the night. Bird calls – what gagi that? A slight breeze in the treetops which must have been fifty feet high and the drone of insects which he wasn't enjoying. Bloody nyumis, he cursed to himself as he rubbed at his numerous bites.

After an hour of staring into the blackness he thought he could hear some faint sounds of movement coming from the direction of the trail where they had set the claymores. He strained to listen, wondering if he should wake the section leader. Then he smelt the same odour he had detected in the villages.

Shit, would anyone take him seriously? A smell in the night? Stuff it, he had to get the message out. He quickly alerted the section leader who passed the message on to Ashmore. Ashmore obviously had faith in Hedley's intuition because he ordered the platoon to stand to and joined Hedley at his post.

Can you still hear them?

Not now, sir. But I could a moment ago.

Right. We'll detonate the claymores.

But what if they're just villagers, sir?

Villagers wouldn't be out on some fuckin' midnight stroll. Detonate the fuckin' things!

The claymores were detonated and when the shock waves had stopped reverberating, both Ashmore and Hedley detected the sound of movement and voices. Someone was withdrawing in a hurry. Ashmore made the decision to hold their position until morning and everyone was put on high alert.

At first light, Ashmore led a recce party. They advanced cautiously down to the track and waited till the forward scout called the all clear before inspecting the damage. No bodies but plenty of blood and drag marks.

When the site had been cleaned up Ashmore pulled Hedley aside.

Good work, corporal. I should've picked up on it more quickly. Still, reckon we might have taken out at least one enemy judging by the drag marks.

Ashmore was about to move off when he turned back to Hedley.

Oh, and by the way … you're losing your section leader next week and you know what that means.

Hedley felt a twinge of panic. He knew what it meant and didn't feel ready. Ashmore held his hand out.

Congratulations, corporal. You will be the section leader on our next op.

He shook Hedley's hand and gave him a pat on the back. Hedley didn't know what to say. He wondered if he would still be one of the blokes.

After another week of patrolling and harbouring up each night, the platoon was beginning to run out of rations. There had been no more contact with the enemy but the late afternoon downpours, heavy rain-soaked gear and being on a constant state of alert, were beginning to take a toll. Voronski had developed a body rash that was driving him crazy and most of the men were either constipated or had the runs. There seemed to be no inbetween. A resupply was called for and a smoke grenade let off to mark their position for the chopper pilot, who dropped a bundle of ration packs, dry clothes and even a few letters.

Hedley knew he wouldn't be getting any mail so he busied himself distributing the gear while the lucky ones opened their letters. Langer had been going over his letter for some time when Hedley walked over and gave him his share of ration packs and dry clothes.

All ok back home, Lang?

Langer looked up at him. Yeah. Letter from mum. Apparently, the newspapers are full of all the protests. S'posed to be some sort of a withdrawal in the wind. Makes you wonder why we're here dragging our arses through this leech infested hell hole.

Hedley had no answer. He knew nothing about politics and didn't care. He was playing his part and getting the most satisfaction out of anything he'd ever done. The whole platoon was in the same boat, they had a job to do and they were doing it. He left Langer to his letter and went on with his task.

Five days later they were back in the base camp at Nui Dat having survived their first stint of patrolling in a war zone. No real action to brag about but now they weren't total newbies. Their bodies were starting to adjust, psyches a little less fearful, but they all shared a growing awareness that this was going to be a very long nine or ten months.

Voronski and Hedley were sitting at a table in the wet canteen, Voronski writing bets into an exercise book. A race broadcast from back in Australia was coming through the radio system and a group of soldiers at the bar were listening intently, their betting money with Voronski who was now running a book.

An outsider won the race and there was general grumbling from the group at the bar, Voronski ruled a line through the bets he had taken.

Do yer ever lose? Hedley grinned.

Course I do, said Voronski matter-of-factly. But not at the end of the day. Anyway, who gives a shit about money around here? What's to save for? Houses, jobs, cars… all that stuff don't matter here. Know what I mean?

Hedley nodded.

Even family, Voronski went on. They're another world away, might as well be on Mars.

But we can get letters, said Hedley.

True. Thought you didn't get letters.

No, but I can write one. Gonna give it a crack, anyway. Hedley pointed to Voronski's exercise book.

Can I have a page?

Yep, have a couple and I've got an envelope here too. Voronski ripped out some pages from the back of his exercise book and passed his pen to Hedley.

Need some help?

Nah, should be right. Me first letter, but.

Hedley carefully wrote across the envelope; Frank and Jane Yangaboora, Nanderra. He remembered how to spell Nanderra from the map Ashmore had given to him.

Chapter 25

Australia post had somehow done its job and that letter was now in Jane's hand as she followed Frank across the dry creek bed toward Jack's kitchen. With Chub gone, Frank had to make the crossing over the colour divide from their shack to the homestead at least twice every day for new work orders.

It was nearly time for Mick's evening rum and he was sitting on his kitchen veranda, smoking a durry and watching their progress across the hot red sand in the creek bed.

Frank eased himself down on the wooden bench beside Mick without a word and proceeded to pull off one of his worn elastic sided boots and empty sand out of it. Mick offered his packet of tobacco and papers to Frank as Jane flopped splay-legged beside him, tucking bits and pieces of herself back into an undersized, very faded floral print dress.

Such was the ease and familiarity of the three, that Frank and Jane had both rolled and lit up one of Mick's durries before anyone spoke.

Mick's inevitable question more a statement of the obvious.

Letter?

Jane nodded and offered the letter to Mick. Think it's from nephew.

Mick examined the details on the back of the envelope.

Yep. From Vietnam. Yer know what that means, don't yer?

Jane wasn't familiar with the word Vietnam, but she nodded. She knew her nephew was in a war somewhere, he'd been in her dreams.

Hedley's over there fightin', Mick went on. Fightin' at the behest of our foreign masters. Same old story, if it ain't the bloody Brits, it's the bloody Yanks.

Frank had now emptied the sand out of his other boot and sucked in enough nicotine to satisfy his immediate yearnings.

You open the letter old man. Read it for us.

Yes sir. Three bags full, sir. Haven't you heard the word, please?

Frank acknowledged Mick with a half smile. C'mon. What does it say?

Mick gave Frank a mock pissed-off look and pretended to reluctantly open the letter, but he was just as keen as they were to read it.

His face registered surprise when he realised it was Hedley's handwriting.

Where did he learn to write?

Frank was getting impatient. What does it say?

Hold yer horses. His writing's not that easy to understand.

Mick produced a set of reading glasses from a plastic pouch clipped in his shirt pocket and began reading aloud.

Dear aunty and uncle. Hope you are good. The army made me a corporal with 2 stripes and a ... think that says something leader. Section. Yeah, section leader. The blokes in my section are good blokes. Can do sums. I think I will sign on. Hedley.

Mick looked over his specs at Frank. What do you think of that, eh? A bloody corporal. Frank was nodding proudly.

That's some promotion, said Mick. Means he's one of the bosses. Last I heard, young Chub was cooling his rear end in some reinforcing unit. Still a private.

Frank continued to nod as he digested the news at his own rate.

Nephew a good young fella, he said thoughtfully. Try to tell boss that but he won't listen. Can do sums, eh? Smart fella.

Smart, all right, said Mick. He turned to Jane. What do you reckon about your nephew? The lad's done alright, eh?

There was a note of disgruntlement in Jane's reply.

Nephew, 'e's always done orrite, that one. Doesn't need to be in that army, he can be orrite anywhere.

Frank took the letter from Mick and looked at Hedley's writing before handing it back with a nod of satisfaction. He took a final toke on his durry and stubbed out the morsel that was left on the wooden bench beside him and stood up slowly, stretching.

Gotta go see the boss. He be waitin'. Cranky fella now he's crook.

Mick grunted. Yer can say that again. Needs to put on at least one more man. You can't keep doin' all the work on your lonesome.

Frank made his way around the kitchen and up to the homestead with its wide, wrap-around verandas. He was about to step up onto the veranda and knock on the kitchen door when he heard raised voices from within. He did an about turn and retreated to the shade of a tree about twenty yards away, too polite to interrupt. He'd wait until things cooled down and then some.

Inside, Hugh was lying on his back on a day bed set up beside his work desk. Connie was sitting at the desk with Hugh's latest medical report in front of her.

Hugh, you can be as pig headed as you like but Doctor Kahl couldn't be clearer. It says here – in bold! **NO WORK!** None! You simply can't afford to have another stroke, it'll be your last. Is that fair on me? Is it fair on the boys? No husband, no father.

Hugh had irritable bowel syndrome, a result of his stroke medication. Otherwise, he was just plain irritable.

Someone's got to do the bloody work! Can't afford to employ. Overdraft's at breaking point. It's either pull Eric out of his final year or … let the place go down the gurgler like them next door.

I can take over all the windmill runs and fence checks, Connie said. We've been through this again and again. Eric must be allowed to graduate. That Ag certificate is the difference between him landing an overseers job or becoming a station manager. You know that. We can't cut him short, Hugh.

Perhaps there's another way out. Hugh looked up at Connie. She shook her head. She knew what he was thinking.

No. No, you can't do that. You promised the property to Chub. It's not his fault things are the way they are. You made a promise to him. He's the eldest.

He's the eldest, but he's locked up in the damn army. Sometimes you've just got to break with tradition. Do what you have to.

No!

Hugh closed his eyes in frustration. Look, it's one thing you checking the mills but another thing expecting Frank to keep fixing them on his own. I'm going to have to get off my backside and pitch in. There's no other way.

There is another way, Connie said. Hugh opened his eyes.

And what would that be, pray tell?

I'll help Frank fix them. I can winch him down into the wells and pass down the tools. I've done it for you, heaven forbid. I can do it for Frank.

Hugh set his jaw and glared at the masonite ceiling.

Connie, darling. His voice low and hard. Sweetheart. You are *not* going to be working with blackfellas. Got it? I'm going back to work at the end of next week. Doctor or no doctor.

Outside, Frank had heard no sign of the raised voices for some time. He reluctantly left the shade of his tree and moved toward the kitchen door. The sooner he received his orders, the sooner he could start loading the truck for tomorrows tasks and the sooner he could knock off for the day. Hopefully, he wouldn't be finishing in the dark again. He'd started at dawn.

Chapter 26

Four months in, and the whole company was on a search and destroy mission in a new area. Hedley could tell something was up when Ashmore summoned the section leaders in for an urgent confab. They'd had plenty of meetings before, but nothing described as urgent.

Right, listen up. Ashmore motioned for the men to move in closer. They were standing in a small jungle clearing.

Joey Dixon's platoon has found a whole bunch of cut off tree stumps that have been covered in clay. Fresh clay. Means there'll be new bunker systems close by. Logs are used to roof over the systems before they are covered with soil and camouflaged. Ashmore looked around the three section leaders to make sure they were taking this in. Hedley was the furthest from him and looking down but Ashmore knew he would be listening carefully.

We're going to be on high alert for the next twenty-four hours and you'll be working with tanks for the first time. Because of the large number of gooks in the area we're moving as a company. We're going to be bringing up the rear but that could change anytime.

It was slow going and not much chance of a rear attack so some of the boys were becoming bored, but not Hedley. He was trying to keep an eye on his section. Two scouts, who were in front of him, the gunners and Murphy behind him, Voronski and Langer bringing up the tail. He noticed the last two were bunching up and sent back a hand signal, two displays of five fingers, to remind them they were supposed to be ten metres apart.

Then heavy firing broke out somewhere to the front. Hedley gave the signal to drop to the ground and hold their position until orders came through. He could recognize the different sounds made by the various weapons now. It sounded like mainly small arms fire, AK47s and their own SLRs and Armalites. Murphy joined him. Hedley's relaxed manner belied his subsurface tremors, a skitter of nerve ends dancing to the tune of the gunfire.

What do you reckon, Murph?

One of the forward platoons must've hit a bunker system. Sounds like Charlie's not holding back on the ammo.

Must be a pretty fair dinkum system, then?

I reckon. Tanks'll be called up for sure. Good thing we're back here at the blunt end.

They were still holding their position when approaching tanks could be heard in the thick jungle behind them, intimidatingly noisy, engines roaring, smashing through the jungle. Ashmore dropped in beside Hedley and Murphy, his manner direct and purposeful.

There is a tank coming up behind us now, he said to Hedley while Murphy listened in. Your section will be moving forward on it's right flank. You're to work together with the tank crew. Move ahead of the tank, stop, let it draw level, then move ahead again. Keep repeating the manoeuvre.

Hedley nodded. Right, sir. Got it.

But for fucks sake, Hedley, make sure the men stay down flat on the ground. We don't want casualties! This one's yours, Ashmore pointed to a tank that was now breaking into view through the thick understory. Other tanks were now also appearing further to the left of Hedley's tank.

Ashmore hurried off toward the next section and Murphy looked at Hedley, grim faced.

Blunt end to pointy end. This won't be fun, Yanga.

The sound of firing up front was getting heavier. When they began crawling beside the huge Centurion tank, its steel tracks grinding through the forest-floor litter, Hedley was more worried about being run over by the tank than the bullets that were beginning to hit the trees above them. How would the driver be able to see them lying on the ground when he was surrounded by all that armour plating? Hedley led the way, wriggling forward with his Armalite cradled in front of him. The roar of the tank engines and heavy firing made verbal directions to the men impossible, so Hedley relied on hand signals. They had only advanced a dozen metres when the enemy started firing rocket propelled grenades into the trees above them, raining down branches and shrapnel. It was the first time they had been under fire and Hedley felt adrenalin that had been pumping around his body in a fast idle, suddenly become supercharged. Ngurlu. The bullets flying just over their heads were making a high pitched snapping sound followed by the muffled weapon noise. Head down, keep wriggling. The gunners were keeping abreast of him to the right and, to his surprise, Voronski was up level with him on his left. Good on him.

It was pointless firing their weapons as they couldn't see into the thick rainforest and every time the tank drew level with them it would let off its main twenty pound gun at the bunker system. All they could do was block their ears and wriggle forward again. There was much yelling on the other side of the tank and Hedley could only surmise that somebody had been hit by the shrapnel that was coming down on them. An enemy machine gun opened up from somewhere very close in front and the bullets where ricocheting off the tank. One hit a log right between Hedley and Voronski and they exchanged a look. Voronski looked calm and Hedley caught a flicker of a smile. You just couldn't tell with some blokes. The tank responded by firing a twenty pounder and then one of its cannister shells that blasted away the jungle in front of them and they had their first clear view of one of the bunkers. Hedley and the gunners with their M60 opened fire immediately, as did the tank's machine gun from its elevated position. There was no return fire from the bunker, which had taken the full blast of the twenty pound shell. On cue, Hedley scrambled forward and hurled a grenade into the bunker opening.

They continued forward like this, gradually clearing bunker after bunker until the company commander called a halt to proceedings. Hedley spread his section out in a holding position, still lying flat on the ground, and waited for Ashmore to give them some more orders. The tanks were using their weight to cave in some of the bunkers so Hedley assumed they must have successfully taken this particular system. It wasn't until he had been laying still like this for a few minutes that he realised he was beginning to shake. What was happening to him? Childhood memories of savage beatings by institutional "carers" flashed and were gone. He tried gripping his rifle more tightly but it only made the shaking worse. He was glad no one could see him.

When his shaking eased, he was hit with a stabbing reminder: check your men. They're in your care; forget yourself. He quickly set off in a crouching shuffle, aware snipers could still be in the area. He moved from man to man, a brief pat on the shoulder and a few words for each one. Some were still on a kind of high and full of slightly manic chatter, others stunned and withdrawn. He found Voronski with his arm around Langer who was a complete mess. Blubbing uncontrollably. Langer looked up at Hedley, his face a smear of black camouflage grease and mud. Underneath were his tears and contorted features.

You ok, mate? Hedley asked. No injuries?

All Langer could manage at first was, Oh, mate. He said this several times through his wracked sobbing. Trying to gulp in air.

He ok? Hedley said to Voronski, who nodded, his big square face full of sympathy and embarrassment for Langer.

Oh, mate, said Langer again. Right near us, on the other side of the tank. I saw it. One of the blokes in two section. He got his back ripped open. It was …

Again he dissolved into blubbering.

Hedley reached out and put a comforting hand on Langer's shoulder. Don't worry mate. He's probably in a dust-off chopper right now headed back to the arms of all those nurses in Vungers. He'll be right.

Langer continued to suck in mouthfuls of air.

You did great, Lang. We all did. Hedley was looking at Voronski when he said this and Voronski acknowledged his compliment with a slight nod.

Hedley could see Ashmore approaching so he gave Langer another pat on the back. Great, Lang. You did great. He told Voronski to make him a brew. Safe enough now.

Hedley quickly rose to meet Ashmore before he caught site of Langer, not wanting Langer to be marked down in any way.

Ashmore called the section in.

Right, He said to Hedley. All present and accounted for?

Yes sir.

Injuries?

None, sir.

Good. Well done. Now, I need a volunteer from this section to go down into the bunker behind us to search the bodies for documents.

Hedley looked around at his charges, all eyes were on the ground. No takers. He gave Ashmore a reluctant nod.

Good man, said Ashmore.

Where are the sappers or assault pioneers? Murphy wanted to know. Why should we have to do this shit?

No time to wait for the sappers, Ashmore snapped. Assault pioneers are flat out and company command want the bunkers destroyed while the tanks are here.

Ashmore took Hedley over to the bunker and gave him a torch.

Be extra careful when handling the bodies. Sometimes they've been booby trapped, although I doubt this lot would've had time.

Hedley steeled himself and began to squeeze gingerly through the small opening.

Won't be pretty down there, corporal. Quite a few grenades went in.

Hedley switched on the torch and froze when he was wholly inside the bunker. It felt wet underfoot and still reeked of explosive. He played the torch around carefully looking for trip wires or any sign of life. As soon as he saw the bodies he was overcome with nausea. His shakes returned and all he wanted to do was get back out into the daylight. He lay still for a while and he heard Ashmore's booming voice call out.

All ok in there?

This seemed to kick start Hedley's response system again. He managed a feeble, yes, sir.

He inched toward the nearest mutilated body, a female, and tried to feel inside her front shirt pocket with his right hand while avoiding looking into her face. But he couldn't avoid it. She had acne pockmarked cheeks and her dark eyes were wide open and looking straight at Hedley. Hedley's right hand was now shaking violently. He tried to will it to behave itself and reach into the dead woman's pocket, but it wouldn't obey. He was starting to see spots and felt like puking. He had to get out, there was nothing else for it. Ashmore was looking down at Hedley as he emerged from the bunker feet first. He could see a soldier in distress.

Too much, eh? Never mind. How many bodies?

Three, sir.

Ok. Well done. I'll find someone else to go in. You go back to your men and tell them to harbour up for the night. Sort your positioning out with the other section leaders and put the sentries on high alert. I'll have more orders for you in the morning.

At daybreak Hedley's section were ready to move out but were still waiting for their orders. Voronski was making a still shaky Langer another brew, watched by a concerned Hedley, when Ashmore appeared from the jungle moving at an urgent clip. He strode up to Hedley, ignoring the rest of the section.

Corporal, need a word! Over here. He led Hedley away from the others. Problems, he said to Hedley when they were out of earshot. Manpower problems in the platoon. Both other sections are down a man with shrapnel wounds but that's not the worst of it, I'm afraid. Change of Government policy, their cutting nasho down from two years to eighteen months.

Does that mean me, sir?

All of you, said Ashmore. Means all Nashos who were in the call up before yours will be sent home sometime in the next month. That's both your gunners and another half dozen from the other two sections.

But not me?

No, but your service will be cut back by six months unless you sign on.

Then I'm signing on, sir. Soon as I can.

Good decision corporal but doesn't affect our manpower problems short term. Going to be a real topsy-turvy month or two ahead. I suppose they'll be sending reinforcements, but God knows when and how well they'll be trained. In the meantime, we'll have to get by with the men we've got.

Chapter 27

Jack Sanderson felt like a drowning man. Drowning in a stale toxicity, trapped between the multiple damp stone walls of Pentridge Prison.

In an effort to fight this feeling of mentally drowning he tried to recall the time he had almost physically drowned, anything to take his mind from the present. Swept out to sea as a young teenager with dozens of other swimmers when a sandbank collapsed at Portsea back-beach. The helpless feeling he'd felt when he rose with a wave and saw that the beach was a far distant strip of white. Cries for help all around, his arms and legs turning to jelly as he took mouthfuls of salt water from pummelling ten-foot waves. Each mouthful going straight down to his guts, sending ever increasing surges of debilitating panic through his body. An overworked lifesaver had appeared in front of him, a flash of red and yellow cap in the blur of cascading green turbulence. He'd helped Jack stay afloat until the panic had subsided. Other less able swimmers were floundering nearby and needed the lifesaver's help so, after a few words of encouragement, he had kicked off into the waves leaving Jack to cope for himself.

Now, visiting hours over, his lifesaver, Frankie, a human-sized field of positive energy, had left him yet again. She always left him with a gift parcel of that positivity, but it had evaporated, replaced with little clumps of hopelessness. He picked up the four hardbound volumes of 'The Australian Carpenter & Joiner' that she had left with him and felt their weight, some of her presence still lingering in their mass.

She had finally managed to organise with his union and employers that he be allowed to continue the theory side of his carpentry apprenticeship while serving his jail term. He was a strong young man, as he had been a strong young teenager. He had survived drowning at Portsea back-beach despite taking in a lot of seawater, but he didn't know if he could survive Pentridge. It was getting to him. Claustrophobic melancholy closing in around him, damp tendrils of despondency worming their way inside him, wrapping around the remains of Frankie's gift parcel and strangling the life from it.

He sat on his bed and opened one of the volumes at a random page. Bricklaying, not his trade but associated. Stretcher bond, all the perps lined up neatly in the illustration. He looked at the bluestone wall in front of him as he had done countless times before, every square inch of that wall was imprinted in his brain like a photograph. He knew that the perp on the fifth row was an inch out of plumb and it bothered him. It bothered him that the mortar under the eighth row, seventh stone from the left, had been scratched out by a former inmate. Most prisoners would be thinking of ways they could scratch out more mortar, escape in mind, but not Jack. He wanted to replace the mortar neatly and even re-lay the entire wall, stone by stone. He was going nuts.

He looked at the trade books again and thought of his workmates on the tools, joking their way through the day's labour. Which pub would they be going to after work? Who was taking out which girl? Smoko. Sausage rolls 'n sauce. Footy. Drop in and see me, he'd written to one of them, I'm always home. But that workmate never had dropped in.

He could be with them, but he wasn't. He could be with Frankie, but he wasn't. Why? Principles. The fucking stupid Vietnam war. Fucking stupid National Service. The bare bald naked wrongness of it all. The American politicians, Nixon and all them, were out and out lying power-obsessed cunts. The Australian politicians were cunts and so were the Australian people who elected them. These thoughts made him feel better. Jack against the world, Jack against the bluestone walls, Jack against the tendrils of depression. How long did he have to keep this up for? The Draft Resister guys had told him he had only about three months to run on his sentence, but anything could happen in the meantime. Shit, he wished anything *would* happen. The drowning feeling was there again. Could he last another three months? He needed his lifesaver at his side all the time. Sharing his life. He looked at the four volumes of 'The Australian Carpenter & Joiner' and heard Frankie's voice. Her father's oft quoted words. 'There's a positive in every negative.' Use the time inside to finish your theory.

Jack opened the first volume at page one. Timber and it's Uses. His studies were way more advanced than this, but he had plenty of time for revision.

Chapter 28

Every now and again the Thai Airforce, 'Baby Herc' lost altitude and then climbed again. Probably a manoeuvre to avoid possible enemy ground fire, John hoped. He was strapped in beside Chub and the other reinforcements along one side of the drummy fuselage, conversation impossible above the roaring engines.

Somewhere, deep inside, John had known he would finish up in Vietnam. Even when he'd been posted to the reinforcing unit back in Australia he had not lost hope, but now that he was here the road he'd imagined for himself came to a foggy dead end. All his life he had recognised and followed the signals when they had popped up before him from the schoolboy traffic light game to the rolling marbles of the conscription draw. He'd survived so far, even crossing the railway bridge as a boy, no matter how stupidly stubborn that action had been. Thank god his mother had never known. But now he was in unknown territory. Did he really want to be here? For the first time in his life he was beginning to question his blind acceptance of fate. He'd had choices.

The engine revs eased and John could feel the old plane diving quite steeply until he glimpsed rolls of barbed wire and defence positions followed by a violent lurch as they made contact with the airstrip at Nui Dat.

The first familiar face they ran into was Langer, on his way to the latrines.

Lang, yer goose! Chub called out. Langer took a moment to recognise them, but when he did, they were not greeted by his usual silly grin, he was uncharacteristically subdued. They all exchanged handshakes.

So, what's it like? John asked, taking his specs off and wiping them.

Fuckin' hell hole. Never stops rainin', fuckin' jungle all round, pressin' in on ya. Those glasses of yours, mate, they'll cause ya no end of grief, foggin' up in the rain and humidity.

Noticed that, said John putting them back on.

Just want outer 'ere.

Seen any action then? John asked.

Fuckin' action, said Langer. Too much. Seen one bloke in two section get his back ripped open.

Everyone ok? Chub asked. Voronski and Hedley?

Yeah, but fuckin' miracle with what we've been through. Anyway, on the way to the shitter and gotta go in a hurry. Another joy waitin' for ya. Dysentery. The shits.

Hedley was cleaning his Armalite when Chub and John appeared around the sandbag wall that protected the front of his tent.

Well, I'll be buggered, he said, laying his weapon down carefully. You blokes made it after all.

A smiling Chub pushed past the tent flap, hand extended, and they shook warmly.

What's this, then? Chub gave Hedley's shirt sleeve with the two stripes a good-natured pinch and a shake.

Nothin' much. Blokes got promoted so some mug had to fill in. You know how it is.

Well, who would've thought … Well done. Old Frank know? He'd be tickled pink, wouldn't he?

Dunno. I wrote, but the old bugger can't read.

Wrote a letter yourself?

Hedley nodded.

Jeeze, good on you. He jerked a thumb toward John. Remember this bloke?

'Course I do.

John stepped forward and shook Hedley's hand.

Congrats on the stripes, mate.

Hedley just smiled.

So, what's it like here? John asked. We ran into Langer and he said you've all been to hell and back.

Not that bad. Lang's strugglin' a bit, but you know old Lang.

You've seen action, though?

Yeah. Some.

What about us? Do you reckon we'll see action?

Hedley smiled and shrugged.

John persisted. No idea, eh?

Hedley began to assemble his weapon. You never know what the brass're thinkin'. Been a bit goin' on though. You blokes know which platoon you're going into?

Fourth, two section, said Chub.

Hedley smiled wryly. Old Greeny. On his third tour. Cranky old prick.

There was a short silence as Hedley continued assembling the Armalite.

You off duty, Heds? Chub asked. Up for a drink?

Yeah, no worries. Boozer's pretty cheap here. Just give me a sec to finish this.

Just as they were leaving for the boozer, Ashmore appeared with two more reinforcements.

Corporal, a couple of fresh faces for your section. Privates Rigalo and Freeman.

Rigalo was small and swarthy while Freeman looked nervous and distracted. Hedley shook hands with them both.

Better get acquainted pronto, said Ashmore. We'll be out on another search and clear operation tomorrow and there's been a lot of activity reported in the area. Would have preferred a couple of shakedown ops to ease in the reinforcements, but it's not to be. Go easy on the turps tonight fellas and I want you new blokes to double-check your gear. Hedley will sort you out.

An hour later after Hedley had shown the two new reinforcements their tent and had made sure their gear was in order, he caught up with Chub at the boozer. John, having taken Ashmore's advice, was staying away from the booze and was back at his tent. Chub, who'd been drinking with Veronski while he waited for Hedley, was now sitting at a table on his own while Hedley brought their beers. Chub watched Hedley at the bar peeling off notes and passing them over to Voronski as he made a bet. Hedley had changed since Chub had last seen him. He carried a confident ready grin now, something he'd never had before the army. Chub wondered why and supposed that Hedley had never had much to grin about back home. He could hardly suppress a grin himself at the sight of Hedley up there at the bar with his two stripes, exchanging a joke with the urbane Voronski.

When Hedley returned with the beers they compared tattoos, Chub with his small dragon and Hedley with his barely discernible Donald Duck. Soon they were chatting about home. Chub pointed out that, with the government shortening National Service by six months, they'd be discharged ahead of time.

Got a place for you back at Eumarella if you want it, he said. The old man has been crook and I'll be taking over sooner rather than later. Want to build you blokes proper quarters among other things.

Hedley nodded his appreciation, but he liked the army. Probably gonna sign on, he said. Ashmore reckons he's got plans for me. More promotion. Been teaching me maps. Can even read a bit now and do a few sums. Add stuff up. All that.

Good for you, said Chub, but not so good for me. Was looking forward to working with you back home.

Well, ya never know. Uncle's still got a few more miles in 'im yet.

Chub smiled. A few. Anyway, he raised his glass, here's to you coming back one day 'cause all that stuff you've learnt can be put to good work on Eumarella. Not just the army.

Three days of patrolling later, John was on hands and knees in half light and torrential rain. His Armalite was partly disassembled on his poncho in front of him under the protection of his hootchie. He was fumbling with the bolt carrier as his section leader, Corporal Green, towered over him.

Fuck soldier, Green bellowed, yer should've had the thing back together five minutes ago! Didn't they teach you cunts anything?

John was trying unsuccessfully to slip the bolt carrier into the upper receiver. His fogged-up glasses weren't helping.

When did yer last clean the fuckin' thing.

Last night Corporal.

Bullshit! Told yer to clean it at least twice a day in this rain. This thing jambs it's a matter of life and death, dickhead! My fuckin' life! Haven't arsed me way through two fuckin' tours to be brought down by some green cunt when I'm nearly through me third!

John finally managed to slide the bolt carrier in and put the two main sections of the weapon together.

You're scouting again tomorrow and there'll be shitloads of nogs in the area so pick yer game up, Buddy!

John nodded.

Rostered you for watch at midnight so get some sleep.

When Green had gone John finished assembling his weapon and tightened the stays on his hootchie. Soaked through to his underwear, he crawled into its meagre shelter. As soon as he was horizontal he felt a cold rivulet running down the small of his back and into his arse crack. Exhausted, his blisters from wielding his machete red raw, he scooped his pile of webbing under his head as a pillow and tugged his Armalite in closer to make sure it was out of the rain. Every bit of his body ached.

So much for my bloody fate, he thought. Kicked me right up the arse.

He tried to sleep but his mind would not let go of the day. The constant fear of walking the patrol into an ambush and the overwhelming sense of constantly being on trial, of not being good enough. Green made him feel like the worst soldier in the whole army. A liability. Eventually he did sleep but it was very broken. He slipped in and out of a kaleidoscope of dreams as the rain pitter-patted down on his hootchie ...

> *Trying to cock his weapon when it wouldn't cock. Trying again and again. Moisture in the weapon. Pressure all around. Corporal Green screaming abuse at him. What's wrong with me? Why can't I cock the thing? Everyone else can. Useless! Fucking useless!* ... Another dream. A separate dream. ... *School. The class laughing at him, Bernadette Hocking shaking her head in scorn ... Wings. A pair of white feathered wings. Hovering, unattached, independent of each other, yet moving in unison. A feeling of being closed in on all sides but open space above, the wings still there ... Calling? Was someone calling? A female. Now wailing ... His mother, Amy. Arms outstretched toward him, weeping for her son.*

At exactly the same time in Western Australia, Frank stumbling out of his tin humpy at Eumarella into the dark, hands pressed hard to his ears.

Jane inside, wailing, screaming ... Banagee. Banagee ...

Hedley, harboured up in the rain with his section only ten kilometres from John's platoon, turned in his sleep, following his aunty's voice. My maraji.

1100 hours next morning, a dust-off chopper was hovering fifty feet above the ground, winching a litter up through the rainforest canopy. Strapped into the litter was a wounded soldier, his whole upper body wrapped in white bandages.

Hedley could only remember the sound of the bullet hitting him. It had been an explosion of noise as it tore through his webbing and into his flesh.

Every movement in the litter brought on waves of agony. He couldn't see down as he was strapped in on his back, only straight above through tree branches to the floor of the chopper, with the winch arm and machine gun protruding from one side. The winch jerked him higher and he could see that he was going to be swung into one of the tree branches. He tensed himself and when the litter hit the branch, the pain was even more excruciating. He passed out again.

The scene below was chaotic. In the middle of the chaos lay a body covered by a poncho. Langer.

An acrid gunpowder smell still lingered in the rain-soaked foliage as Corporal Green yelled at Murphy to take control while he reported to the brass.

Voronski, big and angry, not far from tears, lunged at Chub and hurled him into the base of a tree before turning on John.

Which one of you was it? Everyone else has had the I.D. exercise rammed down their throats! Identify your target before you fucking shoot!

Chub was back on his feet in an instant and coming at Voronski.

You blokes fired on us first! He screamed at Voronski.

Murphy stuck his spud head between them and pushed them apart, just as angry but holding his emotions in check.

Cool down, the lotta youse! Not one man here is to blame. The platoons shouldn't have been in the same area. All blame lies with the platoon commanders. I fired, we all fired. We were just doin' what we're s'posed to fuckin' do.

Voronski looked instantly chastened and released John. He let out a loud, frustrated FUCK and kicked the ground savagely. Murphy looked around the circle of stunned men, most now sitting, holding their heads.

The platoon commanders and sergeants are being quizzed now, he said, then it'll be our turn. Friendly fuckin' fire. Nothin' we can do but say a prayer for Langer and hope to fuck Yanga pulls through. They didn't deserve this.

There were murmurs of agreement and Chub slumped back against the tree Voronski had tossed him into earlier. The incessant rain was starting up again and his mind was a mess. He clenched his eyes shut and willed himself to another place; his precious Eumarella, riding Astronaut through sparsely clumped mulga, tailing cattle. God, what was he doing here and why? Why were they fucking here?

John, the lead scout, the four-day war veteran, sagged to the sodden ground and put his head between his knees. When he vomited, it was almost as if someone else was vomiting and he was watching their vomit as it settled into the leaf matter, instantly attracting a stream of tiny green and red forest bugs, like minute ladybirds. What would he say when it was his turn to be questioned? He'd shut up, say nothing to nobody. He had no answers. No answers to anything. He just wanted this day to end but he feared that it would never end.

Hedley regained consciousness for the second time when he was being transferred to a trolley under the downwash of the chopper rotors. He recognised his name being called out, followed by his rank, but they said corporal. He was a …? Next thing he knew, someone was cutting off his boots and then he passed out again.

Chapter 29

2nd Lieutenant Doug Ashmore entered the stiflingly hot ward at 1st Australian Field Hospital, Vung Tau. Two rows of beds, one each side, stretched out before him with most of the occupants lying on their backs. His senses were hit with a mix of hospital smells, iodoform, chlorine and bleach. One patient was strolling down the aisle toward him, dressed only in pyjama bottoms. He looked around for Hedley and then realised with shock that the man walking down the aisle toward him was Hedley.

He only had one arm. His right arm was severed just under the shoulder and the skin stretched and tied at the bottom of the stump. Where the skin was stretched, it was white and Hedley's Donald Duck tattoo, now highly visible against the white skin, was stretched grotesquely with it. Donald's yellow beak drawn up in a boomerang shape and white stubby tail now long and pulled down into the knotted skin under the stump.

Ashmore was rarely lost for words but he had no idea what to say. Neither man spoke until Hedley managed a smile.

Can't really salute, sir.

No. No, of course not. Ashmore felt like a dill. He wondered for a split second if he should shake Hedley's hand, but that would be really stupid. He had to manage some words, for Christ's sake.

How are you feeling, corporal? He heard himself say. Even that sounded stupid.

Hedley seemed unaware of Ashmore's discomfort.

Not too bad, sir. Feels like it's still there. Bit painful.

Phantom pain. Think that's what they call it when you have a missing body part and you ... you know? Can still feel ... something.

Ashmore was regretting going down this road. Everything he said sounded whacky and off key. Plain wrong. He tried a fresh tack.

How are things otherwise?

Can't complain. Tucker's good here.

And the staff? How are they treating you?

Great. Nurses are great.

Ashmore suddenly became aware half the ward were listening in on their conversation. He looked around.

Anywhere we could sit down for a private chat?

Hedley led him to a spot outside the ward but there were more wounded diggers there smoking and chatting. They eventually found a couple of chairs away from the others.

So, how are the boys? Hedley asked. How are they handling losing Lang? Can't stop thinking about it.

Voronski's the worst hit, said Ashmore gravely. But he's managing. I'm keeping an extra eye on him.

Poor bloody Lang, never hurt nobody.

No, said Ashmore. He didn't. No justice in any of this.

So who's running the section without me? Hedley asked. Who's doing my job?

This was more comfortable ground for Ashmore. Murphy is filling in for you. He had no choice. He said to say ... they all said to say ... that they hoped you were ok. Recovering well.

Hedley didn't answer.

Everyone was very concerned for your welfare; we didn't know if you would pull through. I mean, the arm … it's a terrible loss but at least you pulled through.

Yeah, the arm, sir. Will I be able to serve out in the sticks again? The doc said something about a false arm. He wasn't sure.

Ashmore knew the answer to this but, if he was to be truthful, it was akin to telling someone their loved one had passed on. It wasn't his job but he felt a responsibility to Hedley. He chose his words carefully.

Prosthetics are very good these days, I believe. But even if they can fit one I'm afraid it wouldn't render you fit for duty, Hedley.

What do you mean? Hedley was suspicious of Ashmore's change of tone. Suddenly aware of his unease.

The army has some pretty set policies on this sort of thing. I mean, I don't necessarily agree with them myself.

Hedley was perplexed.

So, what do you mean, sir? What sort of duties would they put me on? You said I should sign on and I'm gonna. I like the army.

Ashmore pursed his lips and looked away before turning back to Hedley.

This is not my area but I don't think that's possible, Hedley. The army is a robust organisation and, with the exception of office staff, there aren't any positions for disabled soldiers.

Hedley was mortified. Ashmore could read the disbelief in Hedley's eyes. A disbelief that was turning to anger.

He continued to speak, hoping Hedley wouldn't have time to let loose.

Compensation. There is compensation, of course. Every disabled soldier is entitled to a disability pension and it's not an amount to be sneezed at.

Hedley was never going to let loose. He was now looking toward the horizon of jungle and plantation patched hills, brow jutting out and jaw set firmly.

Ashmore kept talking, not sure if Hedley was taking in a word.

I'm going to make a special case for you Hedley. I promise you that I will help you through the whole compensation process after you're discharged.

Hedley turned to look at Ashmore. Discharge? They gonna discharge me?

This was now rock bottom for Ashmore. He kept talking.

Not just yet. I'm sure there are many more medical procedures to go through. Rehabilitation and so on. But it will happen, unfortunately.

Hedley could feel the same nausea that he had experienced down in the bunker beginning to grip his guts. The army had been something else. Everything had been laid out for him in the army and now it was about to stop. Just like that. He had really felt that the army valued him. He was useful; more than useful. Now he'd lost an arm doing all the things they wanted him to do, and they were getting rid of him. His gaze was again fixed on the horizon. Familiar dark clouds of despair were rolling in, obliterating his senses. Obliterating the man sitting beside him.

Their tent back at Nui Dat had collected even more black mildew. Every time they returned from patrol it was the same and there never seemed enough time between patrols to clean off the black gunge.

Just back from a ten-day operation, Chub was unlacing his mud caked g.p. boots. John, in shorts and thongs, ready for a shower, rummaging through his pack looking for a towel.

Fuck, Chub said. Never seen so much claret. How good were the medics, eh? Dunno how they can face that sort of thing every day.

Miracle workers, John murmured absently.

Didya see what was left of the detonating device?

John shook his head.

Just powered by a coupla torch batteries, Green reckons. Chub was now pulling off one of his damp socks revealing a milk-white foot and a set of rotting toenails. Made from one of our artillery rounds. Two torch batteries: seven blokes out of action. Glad it wasn't our platoon or Voronski's lot. Losing Langer and Heds was enough.

John nodded agreement finally producing a towel from his pack and smelling it, pulling a face of disgust.

Rancid, eh?

Putrid but it'll have to do.

Chub was now free of his footwear and unbuckling his webbing belt.

Helping the medics made me think of Hedley and what happened that morning, he said. Still can't figure out how he copped it. We know Langer copped a burst from the M60 but Hed's is a mystery. Could've been someone from his own platoon, there were that many bullets flying round.

Could've, said John. But his mind was saying something entirely different – *I know how he copped it. It was me, my bullet, I saw the movement, I fired, I heard the scream straight up.*

Where do you reckon the bullet came from? Chub asked. You were up front; closer than me. 'Cause I fired, y'know. Keep thinking it coulda been me.

Dunno, said John. Thinking – *my actions, my bullet. Now he doesn't have an arm. My doing. Useless, useless fucking useless. Gotta tell Chub, anyone. But I can't.*

All I know, said Chub, is I want outta here. Need to be back home runnin' the place with Dad crook. Eumarella needs me and I need Eumarella. My safe place, if you know what I mean. Gets me through every day sloggin' away in that fuckin' jungle. Just keep thinking of riding across the open country. Flat open plains. Not a tree in site.

He looked at John. You got a safe place in yer head?

John looked defeated. 'Fraid not. Nothing safe in my head.

You need some place to go. Chub was regarding him with sympathy, he'd been worried about John for weeks now. They were interrupted by one of the section members who was doing the letter delivery round.

Letters for ya's. One each.

He handed John two letters and was gone.

John pocketed his letter and passed the other to Chub.

From Dad, said Chub looking at the envelope as he sat on the edge of his bed. Bit odd, usually Mum who writes.

Leave you to read it in peace. John slung his towel over one shoulder and left. When he was clear of the tent, John opened his letter and skimmed through it as he walked. It was upbeat as usual but questioning.

Why hadn't he written? Was everything alright? Did he need anything? How long did he have to go?

Not long, thought John grimly, but it seemed like a lifetime. Or it could be the end of a life.

When John returned, fresh from his shower, Chub was still sitting on his bed staring mutely at one of the many pages of his letter.

When Chub looked up his eyes were shimmering with blue emotion, normally cheerful features racked in despair.

John felt awkward, not sure what to say. It was not until Chub looked back down at his letter that John felt he could say something. Bad news? He asked softly.

Chub nodded, still looking at his letter.

He can shove it, he mumbled. Not workin' with Eric.

John had noticed that Chub sometimes had a habit of widening his eyes to accentuate a point. Now, when Chub looked up again, his eyes were veritably bulging.

Fuckin' dad. He's given the whole show over to my brother. Brother's sacked Frank already and using contractors to do everything. Wants me to work with him. Well, he can get fucked!

Shit, mate. John felt awkward offering sympathy to the normally infallible Chub. The property was yours, wasn't it?

Was. Chub scattered the pages of his letter contemptuously on the bed. Can't believe dad would do that … and mum. They sat in silence for a moment as Chub struggled with the enormity of his news, different aspects of it playing with different parts of his mind.

Frank was Hedley's uncle, he finally muttered. Worked on the place all his life in shit conditions. Gave his all and knew the place like the back of his hand. Why put him off?

This wasn't really a question to John, so he didn't answer.

Chub was on his feet now, pacing the tent.

Could only be Eric cutting his own territory, putting his own stamp on things to stick it up me. Fuckin' little prick. Well. he won't get me back there, that's for sure.

What will you do then?

Fucked if I know.

Chub's pacing slowed until he was standing motionless, eyes fixed on the discarded pages of his letter.

Fucked if I know.

Don't really have any idea what I'm going to do after the army, John said quietly, but you're always welcome to stay with me back in Melbourne until you can get sorted.

Christ … Chub flopped back down on the side of his bed and put his head in his hands, burying his face, then slowly lifting his head to look at John. Just can't figure out how they could do that to me.

The offer stands if you're stuck, John said.

Thanks, mate. I can't even think at the moment, but yeah. Sounds good. He put his head back in his hands, talking to himself. That's it. My place… My safe place. Gone.

Walking wounded you are, mate, Hedley had been told. No stretcher for you. Seated against the webbing on one side of the noisy Hercules medivac headed back to Australia, he ran his eyes down the line of stretchers on the opposite wall that carried many of the men wounded by the booby trap and other longer-term casualties. There were a variety of different bandaging techniques on display covering a variety of body parts. Body parts that would never again function as they had.

Young men whose lives were now open books with open endings, the chapters on their youth closed.

One soldier was fitted with a bundle of tubes that led to a gas bottle strapped to the side of the plane. Hedley watched as the nurses checked and rechecked the apparatus while the digger lay unmoving, face hidden behind a swath of white bandage, blood seeping through in two small patches.

The noise on board made idle chat impossible so each man was left to his thoughts. Hedley thought about Murphy, the two-time veteran leading his section for him. He wanted to be Murphy. He ached to be back with the boys, working through the daily challenges with them. Lumping resupplies through creeks, changing the shifts around to nurse the strugglers. Some blokes went through periods when they were down, like Langer, and he'd been quick to recognise this and lighten their workload. There had been an unsaid appreciation, the boys had liked him and he missed them, missed that appreciation.

He tried to focus on his future. He didn't even know where the plane was taking him, only that he would eventually be back in Nanderra. Chub had paid him a visit in hospital and given him the news about Frank and Jane. Kicked off the property. Didn't surprise him. Nothing whitefellas did back home surprised him. Yamajis just got booted around and that was that. He didn't have to go back but it was his country, it was where he wanted to be. Towns were trouble though, it was all the shit that went on in town that he had to avoid. Wirrgiriny, he thought to himself. He'd enjoyed a few in the army but he wouldn't allow himself to get caught up in the drinking back home. Working with Chub at Eumarella had been ruled out and anyway, what use was he with one arm? Hedley felt the hard end of his stump where they had tied the skin up. He was beginning to get used to it, doing everything with his left arm, but it was weird. He couldn't cut his fingernails, so he bit them down. It worked. He thought about the fingernails on his missing arm, were they still growing? Where was his arm? Burnt? Buried somewhere? Floating in the ocean? Weird. Gotta stop these thoughts. For fucks sake, I'm goin' mamanyimanha.

Ashmore had said something about compensation. Dough. Sounded like nothing but trouble. As soon as the word was out, he'd be the town muni-man. Fridges, cars, TVs, booze, paying off fines, parole. Where's that feller Hedley with all the muni? They could have it if they wanted, but all the bickering over who got what would be one long hassle. He could buy that red ute he'd always wanted but changing gear and steering would be a bugger. Hedley thought about it. He could probably press down on the wheel with his stump to hold it straight while he changed with his left. Or get an automatic. That'd be easy. He began to feel better within himself, the ute was something to look forward to.

Hedley turned his attention back to the nurses fussing around the poor bastard with the tubes and gas bottle. He was fucked.

Hedley gave his stump an impulsive whack with his left fist. Tender, but not too painful. What was an arm in the overall scheme of things? Barndi.

Chapter 30

0900 hours, Watsonia Barracks Melbourne. Voronski, John and Chub ready for discharge, ready to sign whatever they have to sign to get out the front gate as quickly as possible. Voronski and John had been inducted in Melbourne and so were being discharged in Melbourne, but Chub, who had been inducted in Perth, had managed to wangle a Melbourne discharge on the grounds that he never wanted to return to West Australia ever again. He was sticking with his mate John.

The duty sergeant, a jowly lifer with prickly grey hair, was in no hurry to complete the discharge procedure and was punctiliously dwelling on each form. It wasn't long before Chub's patience ran out.

C'mon, sarge. We've got places to go and people to see. Eighteen months is long enough, you don't have to drag it out any longer.

The sergeant looked up from his desk at Chub standing in front of him.

Back off, sonny. You're officially in the army until midnight tonight, so until then you're under my command. Got it?

Chub was well past adhering to army protocol.

In that case, I'll fuckin' well discharge meself. He turned and headed for the door.

Stop right there, soldier! The duty sergeant was on his feet. One more step and I'll have the guards on you!

Chub spun around ready for a scrap but John was quick to put a firm hand on his shoulder and give him a 'cool it' look.

Half an hour later, their discharge papers were signed and handed over without a modicum of ceremony.

So that's it? Voronski asked. We're out of the army?

You're out, said the duty sergeant. You've completed National Service, done your bit, and now, looking squarely at Chub, you can fuck off.

The five o'clock throng of city office workers was pouring into Flinders Street Railway Station when the three ex gladiators walked into the corner bar of Young and Jacksons across the road. They were still in their army uniforms with kitbags over their shoulders.

They stopped just inside the doorway and turned to look back on the sea of worker bees swarming over the intersection, homeward bound, briefcases and handbags swinging by their sides. Only days before the three had been in a foreign country, armed and locked in a constant struggle of kill or be killed. Were they looking at reality? Or was Vietnam reality?

S'cuse me, fellas. You're blocking the doorway.

A couple of drinkers pushed past them from inside the bar and headed toward the railway station. The boys continued to stand and stare over the busy intersection.

They've got no idea, murmured John. Voronski and Chub knew exactly what he meant.

Reckon they appreciate us saving them from the yellow peril? Voronski mused.

Mate, said Chub, I don't reckon they even know or care where 'Nam is. What a' yas drinkin'?

They found a spot at the bar and ordered beers. Some of their fellow drinkers asked polite army related questions but others gave them a wide berth. Especially when the beers had been going down in quick succession and they were becoming loud. Maybe they were oversensitive to anti-war vibes or a general indifference toward what they had been through, but the uniforms were going to cause trouble and they were up for it. Trouble wasn't long coming.

A group of half cut youths in shirts and ties were making their way into an adjoining bar and Voronski thought he heard the muffled words "baby killers" come from their midst among general laughter. He was amongst them in a flash, pinning two of them to the bar, one bear-like paw on each youthful chest.

Who said that? Which one of you little smart-asses made that comment about baby killers?

Neither youth opened his mouth to respond and none of their friends showed any inclination to get involved so Voronski held them for a moment until he felt that his point had been made and then reluctantly released them.

The barman beckoned to Voronski from behind the bar. You're lucky I picked up what that little shit said buddy, or I would've called the bouncer. But a word of warning; take it easy, all right?

The boys continued drinking. Chub eventually posed the question they had all been ignoring. Where we gonna crash tonight, fellas?

This was the sort of question they hadn't had to ask in the army. The army told them where to sleep, where to eat and where to shit.

Races tomorrow at Flemington, said Voronski. Stay in the city and head out to Flemington in the morning. I'll give you blokes some tips if you wanna come.

Sounds good to me, said Chub.

John shrugged. Never been to the races but first time for everything. Parents want me home but I'm in no hurry. Certainly not tonight anyway.

Voronski nodded. I'm the same. Folks can wait until I'm ready to see them.

And my folks are on the other side of the bloody country, Chub put in. Anyway, they're arseholes and I don't wanna see them.

So, said Voronski, plenty of cheap dives down the bottom end of the city or … we could live it up and book into the Southern Cross. Only get an honourable discharge from the army once.

Where the Beatles stayed, said John. Could be expensive but what the fuck.

They looked at Chub for a response.

Don't fuckin' care, he said. Not my city. You're the home town boys, I'm tail end fuckin' Charlie as usual. Go anywhere, do anything.

Frankie was admiring Cindy from the wings. She had always been beautiful, slim-hipped, immaculately proportioned in body and countenance. Could wear anything.

Now she looked elegant. Standing out front on her own, centre stage, in a shimmering black evening gown. Frankie knew that Cindy had made it herself and she knew that the material had come from the Polish drapery shop at the top of Bourke Street. Backing Cindy were two guitarists and a pianist. They wore tuxedos. The Snoopies had morphed into a cabaret band.

The event was huge, rows and rows of white-clothed tables, waiters and the upturned pale faces of the invited guests, all fixed on Cindy.

Frankie, who was not invited, could just make out De Lucca seated at a table near the front with the Lord Mayor and other dignitaries.

Fresh meat for the wolf, she thought with a wry smile.

Cindy was into her last number, voice filling the vast auditorium and then softening to a murmur for the last few notes.

The audience broke out into loud applause and an encore was in order.

Less than an hour later, Frankie and Cindy were weaving through the night traffic up Swanston Street in Cindy's new green Mini Cooper, with its racy speed stripe.

Cindy's gown replaced by jeans and denim jacket. They were headed for their old haunt, The Prince Alfred.

You're holding your notes for so much longer Cind, Frankie was exclaiming, and your range has expanded. Love the little wind down at the end; my old trick.

Cindy smiled, pleased with herself, but ambivalent. Thankyou. Extra training. But I still can't generate the energy you can.

Diners don't want energy. They might choke on their hors d'oeuvres. I think you've really sussed out that scene and you've put together a complete, finely tuned act. You were always so good at detail and goddamn it Cind, you work so hard.

Tim helped me with all that. I know he's not your favourite, but he knows the industry.

Is he still taking fifty percent?

Yes, but he creates the gigs and the opportunities.

And you create the music. Anyway, I'm so glad you ended the relationship with him. He's a user, that man.

Cindy accelerated away from a set of lights, leaving a carload of leering hoons in her wake.

I'm dating a new guy, Giovanni. I met him when I was investing grandfather's money. Specializes in property.

A new guy? Frankie smiled. You've been keeping him quiet.

I wanted to make sure he was right for me before I announced him to the world.

I'm not the world Cindy.

No, but you're always so critical of my boyfriends. I can never get it right according to you.

Well, you keep going back to the same type of man. We had a component at uni about this. I think they called it tension based attraction.

This is starting to sound like a sermon.

No, it's true, explained a smiling Frankie. Bad boys. Your guys are always big on the words but short on the things that matter. Love, caring, respect.

Thank you for that gem. Little Miss Perfect.

Frankie looked at Cindy, now braking behind a tram, instantly remorseful.

Sorry Cind. You're right, of course – my love life's not exactly perfect right now.

Cindy felt for Frankie's forearm and gave her a light squeeze. I know. I didn't mean it like that.

Neither spoke for a moment, both thinking about Jack.

The tram moved off and Cindy was able to slip past it on the inside.

Have you heard any more about his release date? She asked Frankie.

No, I haven't. Everyone who should know, doesn't know. The government keeps playing with the legislation. Just wish there was a resolution in site, Jack can't last in there much longer.

I worry about you and Jack every day, Frankie, but things will be ok in time. I'm sure they will be.

Cindy indicated a left turn into a small parking area. The car parked, they walked arm in arm to the pub.

Chapter 31

John tried to keep up with Voronski and Chub who were pushing through the Flemington Racecourse crowd ahead of him. He had no hope. Voronski was light on his feet for a big man and in his element. Alive, like a ballerina on stage, pirouetting hither and thither, looking around for connections in the crowd while monitoring the changing odds and checking his form guide notes. Chub on his heels, also in the moment but his attention like a windsock in a willy-willy, swinging from mini-skirted women in long white boots to inviting rows of beer taps and back to Voronski who was giving him a running discourse on the finer points of picking winners.

Voronski came to a halt under the board displaying the latest odds, finger pressed firmly on his form guide under the name of his chosen nag while watching the fluctuating odds above. Chub joined him and Voronski cast his eyes around for John like an impatient tour guide standing in front of the Mona Lisa, waiting for the rest of his tour party to assemble. Voronski could detect a Mona Lisa smile sneaking across the odds board.

See that? he said to John when he arrived. Fifth horse down. Tambourine. Just came in from twos to six to four. Big drop and he's the one I've been putting research time into. Needed the run last start, underweighted according to my calculations and now the smart money's coming in. My bet for the day but we've got to move quickly. Try and get him at six to four before he drops any more. Ok?

John felt for his wallet.

How much? How much do I put on? And where do I go?

Half your betting kitty, said Voronski firmly. Never go beyond half, like I told you before. Anyway, follow me.

Voronski moved through the crowd with a practiced weave while John and Chub found themselves having to force their way through. They found him in the bookies ring, standing on his toes, surveying the offered odds.

Bloke down the end, he barked. Quick, he's got Tambourine at seven to four.

When Chub and John joined him, Voronski was already passing the bookie a fat wad of twenties. Far more than they had.

I'll wack a bet on for you, mate, Chub offered. I'm putting down twenty, what about you?

Ten is about all I can afford. John handed over a note and Chub slipped in behind Veronski who was taking his betting ticket from the bookie.

Thirty on the nose, Chub called out. Tambourine.

As soon as the bookie had stuffed Chub's notes in his bag and scribbled out a ticket, he glanced at the surrounding bookies and flicked Tambourine's odds in a notch.

Voronski shepherded his little tour group away from the throng of punters in the bookies ring.

Well done boys. Quick and the dead in this game.

Watch it from the bar, eh? said Chub.

Not me. Voronski was flicking pages in his guide book. Got more fish to fry. I'm heading over to the interstate bookies. Like the look of something at Morphettville, then that's it for me. Might back Nutshall in the fifth here if he shapes up ok but not much else of value today.

We'll see you at the bar up the back here. Chub jerked his thumb at the stand towering behind them.

No worries. Voronski disappeared into the crowd again.

Chub and John, drinks in hand, watched the race from a packed bar, peering over and around other drinkers as the horses came thundering down the iconic Flemington straight. Chub had a beer and John one of the neat rums he had taken to drinking of late, seeking the quick hit.

What number we got? John had to yell over the crowd noise.

Chub peered at the scribble on their ticket. Can't read this. Five, wasn't it?

The crowd was roaring now and the fellow beside John was driving his horse home with a rolled up form guide, whacking his own backside. John could only see a blur of horses as they approached the finishing line, then a huge roar went up as they crossed. Chub seemed unsure of who had won, straining to hear the race call over the PA so John turned to the fellow beside him.

Who won?

Ah, that bloody Tambourine. The favourite. Shoulda picked it.

John let forth his first grin in weeks. He raised his fist to Chub who responded in kind.

You beauty! Chub promptly sculled the rest of his beer.

How much did we win? John wanted to know. Chub again peered at the ticket but couldn't interpret the crayon marking.

Not sure. Seven bucks for every four we put on, whatever that is. Another drink, eh? Then we'll pick up our winnings. Have to wait for them to call correct weight and all that.

Later they put a bet on Voronski's next tip, Nutshall, but it was ridden upside down according to Voronski and they were now behind on the day.

Almost out of drinking money, Chub decided he would go down to the mounting yard where the horses in the next race where being led around. See if he could use his horse sense to pick a winner.

Crazy. Voronski passed judgment. A maiden. No form line to get a handle on.

Chub wouldn't be put off. He and John headed down to the mounting yard while Voronski went to pick up his winnings on the Morphettville bet which had come in for him. He was done for the day and not lending anyone a cent, his racetrack rules.

When he caught up with the others at the mounting yard, Chub was surveying the circling horseflesh.

Nice horses, he said. Thoroughbreds. No good for stockwork, but. Snap a leg before they got out of the home paddock.

You don't say? Voronski clapped Chub on the back, full of sarcasm.

Chub grinned. Give us a chance.

What about this one? John pointed to a horse being led past them. It looks keen.

Nah. No way. Lather of sweat. Too nervous. Run its race already.

Chub settled on a roan with a nice easy gait and pricked ears. Relaxed but focused. Gonna dump the rest o' me stakes on it.

Chub's pick came second last and the boys decided to head for Prahran and the Station Hotel on John's advice. Voronski had a mate who lived in the area and they were ok to spend a few nights on his living room floor.

John had suggested The Station Hotel so they could catch some good music, but they were stuck in the corner bar and the bands were in another section of the pub. Voronski had his head buried in yet another form guide, spouting doubles and trebles, while Chub, his apprentice punter, darted from horse talk to girl talk to beer talk.

John heard a band strike up. The previous band had been pumping out some pretty average rock, but this new band sounded good. Folky stuff led by a very powerful female voice. The other two weren't showing any inclination to move from the front bar so John left them and followed the sound.

As soon as he pushed through the intersecting door, he was struck even more by the power and quality of the singer's voice. She was standing up to her mike at the front of the stage playing a dobro, striking in her presence and intensity. Behind her were two other guitarists and a drummer and they were working their way through an old Joan Baez number that John recognised. He leaned against the back wall and listened. The packed room, minutes before jumping around to rock, seemed mesmerised by her. Eyes closed, she was barely whispering into the mike, sotto, when suddenly she exploded into sound and movement. Eyes opening wide, strumming the Dobro in double time, milking one of the Joan Baez lines for all it was worth. It was a crescendo and when she had finished, John quickly turned to a girl standing nearby and asked who the performer was?

Frankie Raye Jamieson. She used to be in The Snoopies. Gas, isn't she?

John could only agree. His mind drawing the connection with Roc and Dicko. She must have been the girl Dicko was talking about who left when they were still playing in The Snoopies.

After the Joan Baez number, Frankie announced in a husky, overworked voice that her next song was written by a friend of hers, Reid Stevens, back from Vietnam a few years now. The song was called Martian on the Moon.

Chub and Voronski wandered in to listen and joined John, leaning against the back wall, beers in hand.

The drummer sat out and the other two guitars followed quietly as Frankie's fingers picked over the chords in a slow melancholy lope. When her voice cut in she held each note with a clear, steady pitch that contrasted with the deeply resonating Dobro, barely altering the pace:

> *I used to walk around in my home town*
> *Like a Martian o-on the moon*
> *If I found an old familiar place*
> *I couldn't leave too so-o-n*
> *Well I knew I'd change, but I never knew*
> *how mu-uch*
> *My eyes could see, but I could not feel to tou-uch*
> *I always ended up, on my own*
> *In my self-imposed cocoon*

The drummer cut in at this point, a background beat but lifting the tempo a little.

> *I used to lie awake till the break of day*
> *And wonder wha-at was wrong*
> *I never thought that I could feel this way*
> *Used to be so stro-ong*
> *Was I still afraid, that I might hurt someone?*
> *'Cause some feelings stayed when they took awa-ay my gun*
> *Caught up in the eye of a silent storm*
> *That raged inside so lo-ong*

Frankie's Dobro took over in a controlled riff. The other guitars and drums followed and her voice lifted into the chorus.

> *Fe-eelin' like, a Martian on the moon*
> *A Martian o-on, the mo-oon*
> *Fe-eelin' like, a Martian on the mo-oon*
> *A Ma-artian o-on, the moon*

By the time she was singing the last verse, voice a shade louder, holding the notes a little longer, John had the gist of it. An empathy.

> *I didn't know it then, but now I understa-and*
> *And I no longer look, for bloodstains on my ha-and*
> *But it took me five long years on a lonely road*
> *To make it home, from Vietnam.*
> *Yes, it took me five long years on a lonely road*
> *To make it home, from Vietnam*

The song finished with another of Frankie's Dobro riffs, winding down to the final resonating note.

John joined in the applause and turned to Chub. Voronski had already meandered off into the crowd.

That was something else! Did you get the words? What did you think?

Chub took a swig from his beer before shaking his head.

Bloody protest shit. How would she know what it was like over there?

You didn't even listen. Did you?

John felt so exasperated he had to walk away. Tomorrow he would make the journey out to his parent's place. Chub would be fine with Voronski for a few days.

Chapter 32

After the gig, Frankie packed up in a hurry. She only had an hour to get all the way over town to make the Pentridge visiting hours.

When she arrived, flustered by her multi-tram-hopping journey, she had a few moments waiting in line at the gate.

Slow yourself down, she thought to herself. Frantic gig and travel time to jail time. She looked up at the bluestone walls above where she was standing and thought of Jack enclosed behind those walls, away from the sounds of trams, delivery trucks and the general hum of life. Usually this looking up had a sobering effect on her but this evening she only felt frustration.

When she entered the visiting room he was there with his usual beatific smile, arms folded, waiting for her. She knew his calmness was a sham, that he was hopelessly stubborn about revealing the day to day goings on inside the jail. As if she needed protecting … what a load of phooey.

She noticed the guard standing behind and to one side of Jack seemed to be harbouring his own little smirk that evening. Perhaps Jack's smile had gone viral, she thought.

Jack reached out and took both her hands in his as soon as she eased onto the hard wooden chair opposite him. They were allowed to make contact now; Jack's security status had been relaxed.

Sorry I'm late, none of the trams were in synch, she flustered, trying to will herself to relax.

Doesn't matter. You're here, that's all that matters, he said, smile never wavering.

I'm here …you're here, she said, but you shouldn't be. Sorry, but it's all I could think of on the way over. Month after month. How much longer?

Jack nodded, still smiling despite Frankie's show of angst. His reply almost amiable.

Troops have mostly been brought home and good luck to them. Not us though.

Frankie felt annoyed at herself. The last thing Jack needed was her unloading on him. He was behaving like he'd swallowed a magic zen pill. Respect his mood.

I'm sorry, she said, trying to imitate his smile. Have you finished the next lot of trade papers yet? I dropped the last component back to your tech. Roof framing, or whatever it was.

Oh, thanks. I'd be totally lost without you. You know that, don't you?

I'm sure you'd be fine, she said, trying to manage another one of his smiles. So? Not finished?

Not quite.

Have you heard from any of the DRU lawyers?

Jebs was in here the other day. Because the Nashos had their time cut to eighteen months he reckons our terms should be the same. Could be out soon, but it's still up in the air.

God I hope so. I don't know how you've coped this long.

Normally after a few minutes of visiting time, Jack's cheerful front would be cracking, but not on this day.

Got a question for you, he said. Sick of stuffin' round.

And what's that?

Frankie could sense something going on. Jack was looking at the guard who appeared to glance around the visiting room before giving Jack a barely discernible wink.

Jack released one of Frankie's hands and reached into his shirt pocket. He produced something but shielded it from Frankie's view, smile back again.

Then his smile disappeared, and he became awkward. Frankie felt his hand tighten on hers.

Been thinkin', he said looking more at her hands than up into her face. Look, I fully expect you to tell me to rack off. Get knotted …you know. I'm just a dickhead chippy and you're …well, pretty famous I suppose.

Frankie was filled with curiosity. This is not like Jack, she thought. She made a concerted effort to push aside all the fluster of her day and clear her mind so she could comprehend what was taking place before her. Realise what was *actually* going on. And then it hit her and she was overcome by a rush of tenderness, pity, appreciation and love.

Jack finally looked up into her face.

Made this for you. Pretty stupid really. Just balsa wood. All they'd allow.

He showed her the object he had taken from his pocket. A carved ring painted gold.

Wow, Frankie exclaimed. You made that? It's so tiny, so gorgeous.

She took the ring from him and examined it more closely. There's writing on it, so small I can't read it.

Our names. Did it with a hot needle and a magnifying glass.

Frankie slipped the ring on her ring finger and rotated it back and forward a couple of times.

Bugger me, Jack exclaimed. The bloody thing fits. Who would've thought?

Who would've thought. Frankie repeated his words as she continued to examine the ring. It's gorgeous. You're gorgeous.

He was looking down again. Navel gazing.

Frankie waited. Silent. The stage was his.

He looked up, pursing his lips, then spoke quickly.

Like I said. I'm just a dickhead, but … what do you reckon? Marriage. You know? Would you come at marrying me?

Frankie had been anticipating this but when Jack's words came tumbling out they were like tiny keys opening up treasure boxes inside her that were filled with her most precious and closely guarded emotions. Tears welled up but she fought them back and remained calm on the outside.

Jack. I decided that I would say yes to any kind of a relationship you wanted to have with me a long time ago. That day when we were marching together in the moratorium. If you want to marry, then we'll marry.

Fuck, said Jack, sagging with relief. If only I'd known. Could've saved meself a gutful of wishin'.

They held hands, not permitted to kiss, but not needing to. Eyes locked together.

They sat like this for some time before Frankie's shoulders began to move. At first Jack thought she was going to begin weeping, but her hand went to cover her mouth, suppressing the makings of a laugh. Jack looked amused but bemused.

What's so funny?

You.

Me?

And him. Frankie rolled her eyes in the direction of the guard who had been watching them, still smirking.

He's in on it, said Jack.

I know that, silly. Do you think I'm blind?

Jack surreptitiously showed a raised thumb to the guard who immediately responded with a little silent clap. No one else in the visiting room seemed to be aware of the proceedings.

Do you want to be married in here? Frankie asked. It might make the time go faster.

No way known. Soon as I'm out. A proper wedding or the registry office. Whatever you want.

A registry office would be fine. We could have a small get together after. You know, family and friends, that sort of thing. Nothing big.

Wow. This is really happening then.

All we need is a date, said Frankie.

It'll come. All things come eventually.

Chapter 33

John began to relax a little. Sitting in the train on the way out to his parents' place, watching the familiar stations come and go.

Dressed in a comfortable old pair of jeans and brown canvas jacket, uniform forgotten, he felt a degree of separation from the army, but one degree was not much. He still sported the severe haircut and his internals were still aligned to army time, army speak and army thinking. These would all take some growing out. The small comforts he was getting from the familiar eastern suburbs sights were outweighed by the realisation that everything from his past life now looked ridiculous. Unreachable. The train was an express, not stopping at all stations and his past life was like one of those stations the train was whistling through. Gone. Behind him. And the train wasn't going to turn around.

As he walked up Louise Street past the neighbour's overhanging plum tree, he let his kitbag slip to the ground and picked a handful of plums. They tasted a little sour and he wondered for a moment how he could have spent all day at school thinking about them. He supposed his pallet had matured.

A few steps more and there was home. Driveway up the side, garage doors open and a new car inside. Same brand, same colour, new model. Good on you dad, don't break the mould, John thought. But a new car was something, he only upgraded every one hundred thousand miles, or kilometres it would be now, John mused to himself. All the new cars would be metric. Still, it was a gauge of how long he'd been away.

John stood in the gateway and took in a big breath. This wasn't going to be easy. For some reason he felt an illogical annoyance toward his parents. Annoyance that they would be expecting him to be full of achievement and upbeat. Why should he have to share the joy they would have at his homecoming? He didn't feel any joy, it was another pressure.

He walked slowly up the path and knocked on the front door, something he had never done before.

His mother opened the old Edwardian door with its familiar stained glass panel and looked up at him. A confusion caused her mouth to open into a red lip-sticked O and then she promptly burst into tears, almost like a cartoon character, Olive Oil or Betty Boop. Tears seeming to shoot out, away from her face and into the space between them.

Her familiar eau-de-cologne citrus, her unchanged hairstyle and sad, powdered features overwhelmed him. He leant forward and took her tenderly in his arms, giving her a gentle loving hug rather than the exuberant, traditional homecoming hug that he felt was probably expected of him.

He would have held the hug for as long as she wanted but she broke away after a moment or two and became Mrs Mitchell again. Dabbing at her eyes with a white cotton handkerchief conjured from the cuff of her cardigan. Eau-de-cologne citrus again.

You look thin dear, were her first words. Lionel! Look who's come home, were her next words.

Lionel soon appeared behind her in the narrow front passageway, reaching around for a handshake.

Welcome home digger. Come in spinner and all that.

John knew what he meant. Blokey, ex-soldier stuff.

How are you dad? You look well. You too, mum.

Good as can be expected, son. His father said. And you look well yourself, for a young man returning from the trenches.

No trenches over there, dad.

Figure of speech.

I'll put the kettle on, said Amy. Come through, your room's all set up for you just as it was.

Let me. Lionel reached down for John's kitbag which was lying on the front doorstep where he had dropped it to hug Amy. John let him pick it up and he let his mother usher him into the living room while his father closed the front door.

You sit yourself down dear. I'll make a pot of tea and Lionel will take the bag into your room for you, won't you Lionel?

For a moment John was left alone. He sat on the old couch that had been there for as long as he could remember.

The room, the house, his parents and the occasion were tossing his emotions around like an angry ocean. None of it felt right.

Something made him turn and look at the wall behind him. A framed photo of himself in uniform was up there, right beside Lionel and his grandfather. An early photo from rookie graduation.

His guts churned, anger welling up inside him. Without thinking, he jumped to his feet and ripped the photo off the wall. He was going to fling it at the fireplace but stopped himself and was caught mid action by Lionel returning from the bedroom. Lionel could see his intent and was instantly distraught.

John! What are you doing?

Amy appeared in the kitchen doorway, hearing the tone in Lionel's voice.

That's your photo, implored Lionel. We put it up there because that's where you belong. You know our tradition.

John looked at his father, trying to calm himself.

Dad, I don't want to be up there.

He handed the photo respectfully back to his father. Don't put this back up, alright? I'll just take it down again.

He turned to Amy, still standing, stunned, in the kitchen doorway. I'll have a cuppa later, thanks mum.

John made his way up the corridor to his bedroom, pulled the door closed and collapsed face down on the bed. He tried to fight back his tears but they quickly overwhelmed him and he became that soldier again, face down in the compost of the jungle floor, spasming uncontrollably.

The ringing phone woke John after another scratchy night's sleep, eyelids glued shut with crust from an eye infection he had been carrying since Vietnam. He could hear his mother's muffled voice in the hallway answering the phone.

Christ. She was talking to aunty Meg. Sounded like she was organising a family barbecue. They were putting him on display. Home from the war, alive and well. Sounded like the whole circus was coming.

John managed to hide in his room for as long as possible under the pretext that he had an army discharge report to fill out. What a load of rubbish. He'd found one of his favourite books and was re-reading it, listening to family members walking back and forward through the house. His name being bandied around.

Eventually he had to succumb to his mother's wishes and join the family.

Greetings, hugs and handshakes. They were warm, and he should have been thankful for the interaction with familiar faces, but he wanted to run away. Be on his own. He steeled himself for the inevitable questions and they came thick and fast.

How was it over there? What did you do? Was it as bad as they say in the newspapers?

He played a straight bat. It was ok. We didn't do a great deal, patrolled mostly within our area of operations, Phouc Tuy Province. I've no idea what they said in the newspapers back here.

Lionel passed him a sausage wrapped in white bread and John took it thankfully, glad for a diversion from the questioning.

One of his little cousins asked if he could see John's uniform. John hesitated for a moment and then asked, why?

The boy, all of seven or eight, swivelled back and forward shyly on one foot, eyes glued to the pavers that lined the barbecue area. He looked up at John. I like playing army games.

Would you like to play with the uniform?

The boy smiled. I'd like to try on the hat. Is it one with the side turned up?

Tell you what young man. How would you like to have the uniform? The whole lot. Boots and all.

The boy nodded enthusiastically. John led him inside and told him to wait in the corridor. When he came out of his bedroom, he had every item of army clothing he could find stuffed into a couple of boxes. He asked the boy where his parents' car was parked.

Dumping the uniforms in the car boot made him feel a little better. Back in his bedroom he poured himself a neat rum from a bottle he'd had stashed in his kit bag and sculled it. The fluid went down his gullet and hit the sweet spot, letting loose a strange flutter of apprehension. He'd never been much of a drinker but that was changing fast. Had to keep a lid on it in this company. He poured another shot of rum into the glass, shoved the bottle back in his kitbag and returned to the barbecue.

Old aunty Meg, his mother's sister, approached him. His parents had always referred to her as a bit of an odd bod. Ten years older than Amy, single with her grey hair clipped unfashionably short. She had always been direct of manner, something John had appreciated in the past but was now a little wary of. Sure enough, after some catch up chat, she asked him if he had heard anything over in Vietnam about the massacres that were showing up in the press. Mai Lai.

John felt a resurgence of the annoyance he'd experienced the day before when coming through the front gate. Why did he have to answer these questions?

He didn't know anything about any massacres, he assured her. Didn't know anything about anything except cutting his way through jungle in pouring rain. Day after day. That's all there was to tell.

Aunty Meg looked a little rebuked, hurt even, maybe he'd been too forceful in his answer. He was beginning to feel overwhelmed. He finished his rum in one gulp and asked about Meg's health, sure to soak up a few minutes. Meg's health was too good and before long she wanted to know what effects the protests were having on the morale of the soldiers?

He gruffly pointed out that the war was as good as over, so it didn't matter.

It was then that the same little cousin whom he had given his uniform, buzzing from the joy of receiving the rare gift, shyness forgotten, pushed in front of aunty Meg and asked him straight out if he'd shot anyone?

The boy may as well have shot John. The question was like a bullet.

John reeled for a moment, aware those clustered around the barbeque had heard the question and seemed curious as to whether he would give the boy a straight answer. John fought down a rising feeling of nausea and mustered up every skerrick of self-control he had left. His legs felt weak and for a moment it took all his focus just to stay upright. Eventually he managed a grim smile and ruffled the boy's hair before heading wordlessly inside to the sanctity of his bedroom.

Later that evening, when the guests had departed, John lay on his bed staring at the cut-outs he'd pasted on the walls as a teenager. Bands, footy players.

He tried to focus on the memories each cut out conjured up but, as always when on his own, his thoughts were drawn kicking and screaming to the Hedley shot. He still hadn't talked to anyone about it, not even Chub. He was becoming fearful of the bubble that was building up in his head. Fearful it could even send him mad, not that he knew what madness was.

As he lay there, trying to focus on the cut-outs, they began to move. This weirdness was happening more and more frequently to him. He tried willing the cut-outs to behave and remain stationary like inanimate objects are supposed to do, but they kept moving. It terrified him. The walls began to advance on him, then move away. In his mind he had dubbed this the near and fars. Maybe it really was the walls of the room that were moving.

He sat up, scared to look at the walls anymore, and buried his face in his hands.

Dad. He thought. Maybe I could tell dad.

It was a thought he'd had before but rejected because his father had never shown a shred of insight into anything he'd ever done. But he was desperate. He needed to confide in somebody now. Right now. Anyway, his dad had always backed him, supported the band, helped with his homework. Also, he'd been to war. He had the photo on the living room wall to prove it.

John found Lionel out in the yard on his own in the fading evening light, cleaning the barbeque with his usual fastidiousness.

John lurched toward his father, wanting to unload while there was no one else around. Suddenly it was a matter of extreme urgency, nothing else mattered.

His words tumbled out of their own accord like a mouthful of bad fruit, all timing and steadiness having deserted him.

Dad – in Vietnam – I shot one of our own men – Hedley – an accident – but I shot him.

John hadn't given any thought as to how his father might react, his priority had been getting the words out. Probably his father would respond as they did in the movies and take him in his arms, at least give him one of his back pats.

But his father spun away from him and gripped the barbeque for support, not even attempting to look back at his son.

John stood looking at his father's turned back. The diamond pattern on his conservative woollen vest, the nape of his neck, neatly clipped grey hair. John had never felt so alone in all his life.

Neither man uttered a sound.

John waited for his father to recover.

When Lionel turned around he appeared to be shaking. He looked at his son and spoke stiffly.

Were you court-martialled?

No, said John and walked back inside. He hurriedly packed his kitbag and left by the side door.

Hair of the dog?

Nah, mate. Voronski pushed away Chub's proffered can of VB.

His eyes were on a line of factory workers filing through a security gate on the opposite side of the street.

They were sitting on the front step of a rundown Victorian terrace. Chub flicked his empty beer can into the weed-choked front garden and cracked the one he had offered to Voronski.

Lucky last.

The factory workers were all women and Voronski was trying to work out which nationality they may have been. Headscarves. They had a look that was familiar to him, not Russian, not enough of us to form a factory queue, he thought. Eastern European most likely.

He noticed a forlorn figure coming up the hill beside the security fence stooped under a kit bag. He grinned.

Here's trouble.

Chub looked up.

Johnno.

Chub waived until John spotted them and they watched him slowly cross the street. He looked how they felt.

Found you. John dropped his kitbag and flopped down beside them on the step. Chub shoved his beer toward John.

Here, mate. Look like you need it more than me.

John finished it in a few gulps.

Thought you were stayin' with your olds? Voronski queried.

Was. Left last night.

So, where did you sleep?

Dunno. Couldn't find this place so … John waved vaguely back in the direction he had come from. It was late, so I found a nice hard bench.

He looked at Chub. Learnt that from you. Remember Newcastle?

Sure do, might all be on a bench tonight. Done our dash here. Kicked out.

And with good cause, too. Voronski added. Can't piss on all night, the rest of the world have jobs to go to. He looked back across the road at the workers, still filtering through the factory gate. There was a pause before he spoke again, still looking at the factory workers. I'm going out tonight with an old girlfriend. If I don't get lucky then I'm off to my sis's place.

Sister, eh? Chub perked. Keeping quiet on us?

No way, Jackson. Married with kids. I'll be on the sofa. You guys need to do some thinking.

Chub and John looked at each other. Where would they go now?

There's that music festival I told you about, said John. Mulwala. S'posed to be like Woodstock. Steven Stills, Canned Heat. Camp out for the week.

Where's Mulwala?

Not sure. Up near Yarrawonga somewhere.

No wheels, mate.

Train it to Yarrawonga and hitch.

Chub shrugged. Sounds a bit like hippy-heaven but I'll be in anything.

John turned to Voronski. What about you?

Voronski shook his head. Not me. Got an honest living to make. Mid-week races coming up.

Chapter 34

Frankie couldn't help noticing that Cynthia Perkins had problems with her feet. Hardly surprising considering the number of times they'd hurried back and forward down the long corridor from admin to Cynthia's office, where they were now. The business end, Cynthia called it.

Cynthia was direct of manner, no time for fools or small talk, thick red hair pulled back into an untidy ponytail and she never stopped moving, even when seated at her desk. Frankie could see one of her stockinged feet vigorously rubbing against the other while she talked on the phone. She pressed a button on her desktop intercom to end the call and pressed another beside a red light that had been nagging away for some time.

Yes? Ok, ok, send him in.

Cynthia rolled her eyes toward Frankie as she put down the phone.

Troubled Tobias, one of my favourites. Harmless kid but he did half kill his uncle. Typical sexual abuse case; he reached a tipping point. Now, we can only do our job, prepare him for the outside world.

When is he due for release?

Only two weeks.

Frankie felt a little shiver. Jack was due for release in two weeks.

I hope you have the energy and endurance of a marathon runner and the hide of an elephant, Frankie, because you'll need all of that and more in this game. Oh, and a husband who earns a good wage because my wage barely covers the grocery bill.

Frankie noticed Cynthia slip her feet back into her shoes as she fished out Tobias's report.

Tobias is very sensitive to anything that is outside his routine, so he may be overwhelmed by you sitting in on the interview. No coping mechanism. Are you familiar with walk and talk?

Yes, said Frankie. We've been taught that at uni. A calming technique.

Good. You'll know what's happening then if I have to take Tobias away. Just make yourself a coffee or something.

Tobias reminded Frankie of Bambi, the fragile cartoon deer, only he was six foot and tattooed. He approached Cynthia's desk in a crab-like fashion, keeping his back slightly turned to Frankie.

Good afternoon Tobias. Cynthia smiled warmly and beckoned him to take a seat. Don't mind Frankie, she's here on work experience and I've just been telling her how well you are doing.

Frankie didn't know if she should say anything. She opted for a quick, Hi.

Tobias acknowledged Frankie's presence with a tiny nod, eyes still averted from her.

Cynthia began to chat her way through Tobias's report for the week, but his responses were minimal. It wasn't long before Cynthia suggested they should take a stroll.

With a nod to Frankie, Cynthia escorted Tobias out into the garden.

Frankie wondered how Tobias could possibly cope for himself outside the detention centre in two weeks' time.

She found an electric jug and a jar of instant coffee. As she waited for the jug to boil, she thought about Jack, his release would be in stark contrast to Tobias's. A job to go back to, a marriage – their marriage. Her thought pattern trailed on to the unknowns... A house? A devoted housewife to come home to every night? Children?

She dug a teaspoon into the crusty coffee.

I love him and I want to be with him, she thought, but I don't even know him. Not really. Not on a day in, day out basis.

Frankie poured boiling water over the coagulated lumps of Nescafé.

They had never had time to talk about how either of them saw the future, so overwhelmed were they by the here and now.

His jail term. What if he's so scarred he goes all conservative on me? Understandable given what he's been through. How to deal with that? I said yes to marriage but not to snuffing out all the other things in my life. I want to keep performing. And I'm certainly not giving up this. Cynthia may be underpaid and run off her feet, but the work matters. Sugar? Where do they keep the sugar?

Frankie found it in a cupboard and stirred in a teaspoonful.

She took her coffee over to the window and looked out at Cynthia and Tobias walking side by side along a concrete path, the wind blowing Cynthia's ponytail and making her cardigan billow. It looked cold out there.

Beyond the path Frankie could see a Cyclone wire fence topped with barbed wire and beyond that, the straw-coloured roly-poly weeds that she had only ever seen in these western regions of Melbourne.

Tough territory. They had been warned right through uni that social work would be tough. Not for the faint-hearted, was the oft-repeated mantra.

Tough. Frankie rolled the word around in her head. Well, Jack's tough. Surely he won't want to retreat into his shell and he always seems to care about me. He can't have changed that much in prison.

She watched Cynthia, animated, smiling gesticulating as she walked beside the hunched Tobias. When he did occasionally speak Cynthia would listen intently, drawing more words from him with her practised magnetic pull. They were coming back toward the office. Frankie turned away from the window, afraid of being caught spectating.

Married in two weeks. Her mind wouldn't let go. There is no backing out now and ... hell, I don't want to back out. It will all be ok. And if it isn't ... it isn't. You'll work it out girl. Jack is a beautiful man.

John had never seen so many speaker boxes. They were stacked up on the giant Mulwala stage like condominiums. Roadies rushing from amp to amp, running cables, sound tests.

Chub stood beside him, hands in pockets, gawking at long haired youths and girls, barefooted and many openly toking on cone-shaped joints. Everyone seemed to know everyone although nobody knew anybody, an open vibe that included all except them. John and Chub. It was more than the army haircuts, their clothes. What was it they were carrying that everyone could see? John seemed oblivious to it as he stood staring at the speakers, but Chub thought he seemed oblivious to most things lately.

Steven Stills brought John to life for a while. Thin, wispy haired figure in the middle of that huge stage, putting out a sound that upset the milking timetables of dairy cows on surrounding farms. The whole festival paddock jumping and jiving, a mat of flying hair. Mulwala, the first of the Aussie music festival biggies.

That evening the rain started and Chub had to share his hootchie with John who had given his away with the rest of his army gear.

Remind you of anything? He asked from the dark as they huddled together under the tiny nylon sheet.

Yeah, wet through in Vietnam, said John. Being cold at the same time is something new, though. At least it was warm over there.

Bloody Vietnam, Chub muttered.

They were quiet for a while, alone with their thoughts. Then Chub said something unexpected, something he didn't intend to say. But he said it anyway.

Who do you reckon shot Hedley?

There was a silence before John answered.

Does it matter?

S'pose not.

Another pause.

Wonder how he is? said Chub. Prob'ly back in civvy street by now. Wonder if he went back to WA?

John shook his head in the dark and curled himself up into a ball. A sign he wanted to end the discussion and try for some sleep.

The tactic seemed to have worked. John could hear fractured shards of conversation from surrounding tents but only steady breathing from Chub.

A minute passed and John tried to focus his thoughts on Steven Still's performance; anything but Hedley. He was beginning to have some success when Chub's voice sounded in a whisper, barely discernible above the rain falling on the hootchie.

I still can't help thinking that it may have been me that shot Hedley. I let off three rounds into the jungle in the general direction. Could have been one of those rounds that blew his arm off. Buggered him for good. Can't stop thinking about it.

In a reflex action, John pulled himself into a tighter ball.

Had to speak. Couldn't open his lungs to suck in enough air to speak. Back to Chub. Must face him.

Lay there like a frozen slug, curled up in the dark, three inches from Chub but three light years.

The Yarrawonga train let them off at Spencer Street. They'd had a few on the train and weren't in a mood to stop so, after a series of pub hops, they found themselves back in Young and Jacksons.

When last drinks were called they shuffled out into Flinders Street with the last of the other drinkers. A blast of cold southerly wind caught a pile of autumn leaves that had been heaped up by a street sweeper and sprayed them across the intersection, glistening wet under the street lights.

Where now? Chub managed a little drunken jig, trying to stay warm.

John looked back down Flinders Street, then up in the other direction.

The park. Up past Exhibition there's a park.

A park? Jeeze, you're keen. Are we that broke?

I am.

Jeeze. Chub was still jigging around, hands in pockets, trying to stay warm. S'pose we've got the hootchie. Camping out in the big city. First time for everything.

They set off up Flinders Street, blustery wind to their backs. Two more hunched up figures with nowhere to call home.

Chapter 35

Already the party had split up into tribes. Not warring tribes but different collections of the species that viewed the same glass of everyday life from different angles.

Jack's workmates standing around a blue and white esky under an oak tree drinking cans of Fosters. Frankie's parents and Jack's parents sharing a picnic rug, cautiously feeling out each other's company for the first time, avoiding all the conversational traps of politics, religion and footy teams. Frankie's band, loose, long haired and smoking, chatting with Cindy while Cindy's new real estate-developing boyfriend stood to one side, looking like he wanted to be somewhere else. Jebs and a few friends from the Draft Resisters Union passing around a flagon of riesling.

Where are the happy couple? someone asked.

The party was being held in the Treasury Gardens, the same gardens John and Chub had bivouacked in the previous night. The newlyweds were in the adjoining Fitzroy Gardens having their photo taken at Cooks' Cottage. Married in a registry office and free to be together. Handsome couple. Clickety click. Jack in flared black pants, white shirt with a big collar and waistcoat. Frankie's white silk flowing kaftan, casual-chic. Clickety click.

When they re-joined the party, Jack went to the parent tribe and Frankie to the band tribe. She wanted some music and was quickly accommodated. Two acoustic guitars appeared from their cases and the band were into it. Low key stuff.

Cindy took Frankie's arm and drew her into a hug.

You look beautiful, Frankie. You know you are my most favourite person in the whole wide world, don't you?

You too, said Frankie returning Cindy's hug, aware that Cindy's boyfriend had shuffled away from them. Cindy retrieved him from the outer and slipped her arm around his waist. He had a sulky Sicilian demeanour emanating from a Hollywood gangster face.

Giovanni and I are moving in together next week.

Really? Good for you two.

Toorak, if you don't mind.

Worst house in the best street, said Giovanni, allowing his mouth to relax a little, suggesting a smile. Only picked it up last week. Needs a lot of fixing up.

What about Jack? said Cindy. He's a carpenter. He could fix it up.

Sorry, pet. Booked in Angelo and the boys already.

He turned to Frankie, apologetically. Could be a job for him with Ang if he doesn't mind working with mad Italians.

No thanks. He's starting on a new site in Collingwood, which reminds me. Jack wants to buy somewhere over that way. His decision, not mine. A mortgage – yuck! But I guess my little bedsit is at bursting point.

We've got plenty of listings around the inner north. Come and see me at the agency, I'll find you something special.

Frankie's band struck up a mock version of Here Comes the Bride and Jack made a big show of walking Frankie along an imaginary aisle.

Frankie stopped him. Dad's supposed to be doing this.

She dragged her father to his feet and the tribes came together at Cindy's urging, forming two lines for Frankie and her father to walk between. Jack's mother took on the role of celebrant and they carried out a spontaneous re-enactment ceremony.

That night in Frankie's bedsit, Jack was sitting naked on the end of her bed while she made a pot of green tea. He accepted his cup of brew with some trepidation.

And you drink this every night?

Sure do. Try it. Guarantees a good night's sleep.

He tasted it and handed the cup straight back to Frankie.

Uhh. Sorry. Not for me.

Frankie emptied his cup down the kitchen sink and sat beside him on the bed, sipping her tea. Jack put his arm around her.

Big day, he said.

Frankie nodded. Happy?

Yes. His tone was strangely sombre. Today has been the happiest day I have ever had. It may be the happiest day I ever have.

Frankie looked at him quizzically. What did he mean? She thought.

She decided to keep her thought to herself. Jack seemed of no mind to explain himself.

She sipped her green tea while he sat, arm still draped over her shoulders, staring thoughtfully at nothing.

These wharfies could drink. John hunkered down on his bar stool and glanced up at the old clock over his head. Seven o'clock in the morning and they were pouring into the early opener. Blue overalls and some red, maybe railway workers. A few Gas and Fuel boys getting a couple in before work.

John examined the rum he'd been tippling at. He couldn't afford to buy another shout but not keen to leave the warmth of the bar.

Beside him Chub's empty stool and half-drunk beer. John was aware of Chub's dwindling patience, that things were getting strained. He knew it was not only their moolah that was running low. Just didn't have the mental energy to take on the octopus inside his head and Chub was part of that octopus, one of the many entangled arms pulling him to pieces. Guilt. Fear. That night in the hootchie at the music festival Chub had tried to talk about Hedley but it had terrified him. Why? … what was this insane fear of everything?

John put his head in his hands, elbows on the bar, and pressed hard. But the octopus wouldn't come out.

When Chub returned from the gents after an inordinately long time, he slapped a copy of The Weekly Times down on the bar.

See these?

He ran a finger over the rural vacancies page.

Jobs in Queensland. My cup of tea. Station hands, fencers, cooks – you can cook a bit, can't yer?

John shook his head. Sorry, mate. Not for me. You're on your own.

Chub looked at him, exasperated. He didn't know what to say.

The pair of them sat in silence. John staring into his rum, Chub casting an eye around the workers.

He needed to find work. Do something; all this filling in time was wearing thin. Since Voronski had moved in with his old girlfriend they had seen nothing of him. Always quick on his feet, he'd moved on.

John had become an omnipresent mood that moved around with him, on his shoulder, beside him, behind him, always around somewhere. He didn't need to look at him to know where he was.

How would John cope if he, Chub, took off? How would he, Chub, cope with John if he didn't take off? All a bit of a conundrum. Too much to think about at this hour of the morning.

He finished his beer and plonked the empty glass down. Where was the barmaid? Chiacking with a wharfie on the other side of the bar. She looked like a cheerier version of Connie, his mother. Fiftyish, similar thin features and that same weary look around her eyes. He thought about his mother.

He could understand his granite-headed father handing Eumarella over to Eric but what part did his mother play? It was something he hadn't been able to get out of his head. He wanted to ring her but couldn't face the possibility that Eric or his father would answer. Anyway, she'd still be asleep, two hours behind over there. Should let her know where he was, though. Maybe a letter.

But Connie was awake, walking among her citrus trees looking at the first red glow of light on the flat horizon. She was reading Chub's thoughts, mind racked with despair. If only he knew it had not been her, she had nothing to do with it. She had begged Hugh but he had overridden her and now she was trying to cope with the fallout. She thought about her situation as she did most mornings when she had a little time to herself. Nursing Hugh while doing her best to help Eric with the books. Eric had his theories on how to grow the property and Hugh had backed him. The overdraft was mounting at an alarming pace but Eric assured them that they had to get with the times, subcontract like everyone else. Wages were a thing of the past. She knew they were headed for a financial cliff but didn't know what she could do about it. Outvoted every time. Chubby's vote would even the ledger but she had no idea how to contact him. The army had not been able to provide her with an address of any kind. What was she to do?

Later in the day she decided to visit old Mick in his kitchen. Eric had been trying to replace him with a younger cook who could keep up with the voracious appetites of the new fencing contractors.

She found him sitting in the middle of the kitchen on an old sea chest, smoking one of his rollies. Every possession packed away, ready to go.

Connie stood in the doorway, looking around the near empty kitchen shelves as the realisation set in. Mick was as much a part of Eumarella as the windmills and paddocks.

Not you too, Mick.

She felt like weeping.

Mick blew out a stream of smoke through his nose before looking up at her angrily.

Sure, your boy has turned into a right eedjit.

You have a home here forever. You know that.

Frank's old humpy aint no home. You call tryin' to dump me in there a nice thing to do?

In the native quarters? Eric asked you to move there?

He did, and the answer is no. Movin' into town where I'll be welcome somewhere, I'm sure.

Connie sagged slowly onto one of the kitchen chairs.

Mick. I'm so sorry. I feel useless in all of this.

I know, said Mick. Watched it all unfold, I have. Some voices get heard and some don't. Young Eric's only listening to one voice. His own. Don't know where Hugh fits into all this.

Hugh has always hated change, Connie said despairingly. I can't believe he has consented to all this. I think he's given up, Mick. I really do.

Mick sucked in the last of his rollie, holding the butt in tip of forefinger and thumb.

Chub had the right idea. Always had a real feeling for the place.

He did. He does. Connie wanted to cry. Blasted army. Damn and blast their conscription.

Not comin' back, eh?

I don't know, Mick. I wish he would.

A boot to the ribs and a blinding light in his eyes woke Chub. His first instinct was to cover his head, then grope for his SLR which wasn't there.

Next to him, John grunted as he too copped a boot. Chub instinctively lunged for the boot that had kicked him and pulled his attacker to the ground, scrambling into the top position and going for the throat. He had a good hold and was squeezing as hard as he could when he heard the cry, police! And was hit from behind with something heavy.

Three minutes later, he regained consciousness and found himself in the back of a paddy wagon with John and a heinous headache. He felt the back of his neck and his fingers came away sticky with blood.

You ok? He heard John say.

Dunno. Where the fuck are we?

Headed for a night in the South Melbourne lock-up by the sound of it.

Fuck.

In the morning he and John were visited by a desk sergeant. They were in luck. He had a nephew just returned from Vietnam, he explained. A bit of sympathy for them.

Not gonna put youse up in front of a magistrate boys but count this as a first and last. Ok? Assaulting a police officer is a big one. A very big one. Fortunately, the constable concerned is alright save a bit of bruising.

The sergeant waited for a response but neither John nor Chub were forthcoming.

Is that clear, you two knuckleheads? A first and last.

John nodded. Chub was still simmering over the whole incident. Kicked awake and then bashed.

Now, I've gotta ask, for your own good, why you're only out a short time and on the streets?

Neither John nor Chub had an answer for this, even if they were of a mind to answer.

On the piss, eh?

Again, no answer.

Well, if you're gonna keep up this sort of behaviour, we'll be draggin' you in every night and I don't want that, and you don't want that. I'm gonna furnish you two with some addresses. Help groups, soup kitchens. St Vinnies and so on. I'm only lettin' youse back on the streets with the proviso you follow up by gettin' some help. That's if you can't help yourselves. Ok?

When they were outside the police station, kitbags over their shoulders, Chub turned to stand in front of John, blocking the footpath.

They stood face to face. Chub's voice was grim. He spoke slowly and purposefully.

What now, John?

What do you mean?

I mean what are you gonna do now?

John didn't have an answer.

They stood like this for a long moment before Chub shook his head in frustration.

Sorry, mate. I'm off. Gotta go while I can still afford a fare to Queensland.

He held out his hand and they shook. John looked so forlorn that Chub felt like dropping his kitbag and giving him a hug. But he didn't.

Without another word, Chub turned and walked away.

Chapter 36

The train to Nanderra clanked and rumbled its way past a long-redundant siding in an expanse of flat, red stony plains. The concrete platform edge and a dilapidated open weatherboard shed all that remained of the siding.

Hedley recognised the faded yellow lettering on what was left of the shed as he looked out the open window.

Doonan.

On the trip down to Perth nearly two years ago he'd assumed the sign said Doonan, but now he could actually read that the sign said Doonan.

He felt an unexpected little glow of pleasure. He was back in his country, he could read to save himself and he was in uniform.

The uniform bit was a worry, though. It would draw attention as soon as he stepped off the train. Did he want that? He'd always kept his head down in the past, making himself a small target. Another black kid, one of the mob. If he stayed out of trouble and didn't cross any of the invisible barriers that criss-crossed the towns wide dusty streets like concealed trip wires, he was safe.

But he was proud of the uniform and proud of what he had achieved in it.

When the diesel loco pulled into Nanderra, the end of the line, Hedley was one of only half a dozen passengers to alight into the heat. A gang of workers were lounging at the end of the platform ready to start unloading the string of goods wagons that made up most of the train and one of them recognised Hedley.

Hey, mate!

He was one of the Wongal brothers. Charlie, the young one who could *really* play footy. Probably why he had the job. He bounded up to Hedley, grinning, until he noticed the right sleeve of Hedley's polyester army shirt pinned back on itself.

Shit, mate. Heard you was comin' back but ... What happened?

Hedley knew he was going to have to get used to this.

Lost an arm, that's all.

In battle, y' mean?

Yep.

Jeeze, no good.

What happens when bullets are flyin' round.

S'pose so.

Do you know where uncle 'n aunt are stayin'? Hedley asked.

In the res. Right down the back in me brother's old place. Just for now, 'cos he's back from the mines soon.

Right. Thought I might check into the top pub for a couple of days first. Gotta see this bloke tomorrow about rehab. Army stuff.

Young Charlie Wongal raised his eyebrows at this.

The top pub, eh? Then he grinned. You come back a cheeky feller.

Nothin' cheeky about that.

Don't reckon?

They both held each other's gaze for a moment.

Anyway, Charlie looked back at the other workers who were now opening up the first of the goods wagons. Gotta go. See ya round, mate.

See ya.

Hedley picked up his kitbag and made his way out of the station.

There were only two drinkers at the top pub public bar when Hedley walked in. Old blokes staring into their beers.

Bogger Branigan, publican, barman and general all round authority on any subject matter that might arise within the paint peeled cluttered walls of his bar, was seated on a stool behind the taps, head in a newspaper.

He looked up when Hedley's silhouetted figure appeared in the doorway and sauntered over to the bar. The sinews in Branigan's weather beaten face were like raw strips of brisket and they tightened when he saw that Hedley was Aboriginal. Normally anyone in uniform was ok by him but the sight of an Aboriginal in uniform left him with a severe case of conflict. He decided to open up with a little bar chatter while he sussed things out.

G'day, young feller. Returning or still in?

Returning, said Hedley.

Good on yer, said Branigan. And a full corporal, too. Vietnam?

Hedley nodded.

Good to see a young bloke doin' his duty. He turned to one of the old drinkers. Agree, Ted?

Ted agreed, eyes never leaving his beer. He knew what was coming and wanted none of it. Hedley knew what was coming as well, Branigan still hadn't offered to serve him.

So, said Branigan to Hedley, you're from around here?

Sort of.

And somewhere to go, then?

Hedley had waited long enough.

I have, but I'd like a room for the night and a beer, thanks. Emu Bitter.

Branigan slipped off his stool and fronted Hedley across the bar.

The room I can help you with, no worries. The drink though … Sorry, son. You're across the road.

Hedley had been anticipating this reaction, but it still jarred. He looked into Branigan's face, the tensed grey stubbled jaw and hollowed cheeks. His reply was more a gritty challenge than a question.

What do you mean, across the road?

The Railway Hotel. If you're from around here, you'll know that's where you can be served.

Many things were racing through Hedley's mind from sharing beers with Voronski and Langer, unchallenged by colour, to attacking the bunker system in Vietnam. He wanted to attack Branigan.

You don't think I'm good enough to drink your beer? Is that what it is? Good enough to serve in Vietnam but not good enough to drink your beer.

Normally Branigan went into action at the first sign of trouble but this time he hung back. He was dealing with an Aboriginal, but he was in uniform and only had one arm. He needed to keep his cool, even felt a bit sorry for him, but there were rules.

Mate, Branigan said firmly. I appreciate that you've served and all that, but ... look, you deserve a beer and, bugger it, I'm gonna give you one on the house. But only one. Is that clear?

Hedley stood at the bar for a moment and looked around at the other drinkers, still studiously studying the contents of their beer glasses. The top pub was just the first bunker in a system that made up the whole of Nanderra. There were other ways to win this battle and keeping his cool was step one. He turned back to Branigan.

You can stick your beer and your room.

He strolled out of the bar, composed on the outside, fuming on the inside. He'd walk down to the res and find Frank and Jane.

As soon as he was out of the pub Hedley wanted to be out of the town, off the streets and in the wilds. He slipped up a side street keeping to the shade of a high rusty corrugated iron fence that ran up the side of the pub. Soon he was clear of the houses and climbing an old mullock heap. He found a shady spot under a mulga tree and squatted at its base, looking back over the town with its shambling grid of hot bare streets and beyond to the flat shimmering horizon.

Now he didn't even feel like walking out to the res and all the attention he'd receive out there. He wanted somewhere to disappear to, somewhere to lie low for a while until he could sort himself out. But he had this army meeting tomorrow, first step to getting the compo Ashmore had been on about. Couldn't miss it.

He decided to wait until after dark before walking out to the res.

Frank looked older. Squatting beside Hedley, firelight reflecting off his white hair and beard. Maybe it was the new beard that did it, Hedley thought. But Frank was at a loose end, alright.

The bossfella's almost ngaya, he said. The missus' trying to nurse him and the youngfella's takin' on all these walybala mustering and fencing contractors. No room for us. Our country and we're not welcome no more. Old Mick's in 'ere and reckons 'e wants out of town, but nowhere to go.

Nowhere for us neither, Jane said from the other side of the fire. She began to explain in Wadjarri how she didn't want her kids growing up on the res with all the drinking when, right on cue, there was the sound of breaking glass and a violent exchange from the neighbouring tin shack. Jane screeched back at the top of her voice. *Leave 'er alone! Ya bloody bajabaja.*

When Hedley rolled himself up in a borrowed swag on the dirt floor of the shack, jammed between the kids and the back wall, he could still hear the odd screech and curse from next door and the sounds of drink fuelled arguing from further afield. Gotta get outer here, he mouthed into his kitbag which he was using as a pillow. The lot of us. Just a matter of where.

Next morning when Hedley fronted up at the shire offices for his meeting, he was aware that his uniform was now very grubby by army standards and his armpits had developed a life of their own. Jane and Frank's rainwater tank had been one rung off empty, so washing had not been an option.

The girl at reception was Yamaji, slim and pretty. He knew her from somewhere. Her hair was pulled back in a bun and she was all smiling white teeth and huge, dancing brown eyes. Her smile vaporised to concern the moment she spotted his tell-tale folded shirt sleeve. He brought her smile back with one of his own.

'Ullo there, he said. Seen you round. I'm Hedley Yangaboora. Come here to meet some fella about the army pension.

Hullo, she said. He's waiting for you in the back office. I'll take you down.

What's your name, then? Hedley asked as he followed her easy walk down a carpeted passageway.

Delli, she flashed him another smile over her shoulder.

Delli, eh. Delli with a belly. He grinned at her look of mock indignation.

Just kiddin' ya. No belly on you. Could be Miss Australia if you wanted. At least Miss Nanderra.

This time she laughed and waggled an admonishing finger at him. You keep them comments to yourself, Mr Hedley. You're here now.

She stopped outside a glossily painted white door and knocked lightly.

C'min, said a deep male voice.

Delli opened the door and put her head in. Mr Yangaboora's here, Mr Nisbett.

Oky-doky.

Hedley was confronted by a large pot-gutted man with a thick moustache that tailed down the sides of his mouth, sitting behind a paper strewn desk. He smelt of aftershave and looked like he'd been fitted out in an

R.M. Williams shop, right down to the Stetson hanging behind him. He rose to his feet and reached an island sized right palm across the desk for a handshake. Hedley inverted his left hand and they completed a cack-handed, arse-about version of a shake. Pleased to meet you, Hedley. Name's Graham Nisbett but I've been Tex for longer than I can remember. Sit down.

They sat.

Sorry about the back office here but it's all I could muster up. I also do a bit of sales work for Elders and they normally let me use their office. Not today, but.

No worries.

Just to put you in the picture, I'm here on a voluntary basis, alright?

Hedley nodded.

Nothing official about me except I'm on the exec of the local R.S.L. Ex-serviceman meself. Korea. We're a long way from the big smoke here and I got fed up with watching every returned serviceman from these parts get bamboozled by bureaucratic pen pushers in Perth, so I put me hand up to help youse out where I can. With me?

Hedley nodded again.

Tex picked up a handful of the papers that covered his desk and dropped them theatrically.

More clauses in all this than you'd find in a Santa shop. All these pension and compo cases are as complicated and convoluted as the they can make them but yours shouldn't be too bad. You're a veteran, which for the record, he began reading from one of the documents in front of him, is a person taken to have rendered eligible war service of an operational or a non-operational nature.

He looked up at Hedley. Means you're eligible for basic benefits, ok?

Right, said Hedley, but what about the compo? My Platoon Commander said I'd get compo.

And he'd be spot on. Tex flicked over another page of the document and began reading.

Disability compensation benefits. A disability pension or allowance is a benefit paid to Australian veterans – that's you, he said glancing up at Hedley – as compensation for injury or death that has been determined …

Hedley let him read on for a while until he'd finished the document. Tex looked up at Hedley.

Are you with me so far?

Not really. All I want to know is do I get compo and how much?

Nisbett pushed the paperwork to one side and clasped his big hands together on the desk like a schoolkid who has just come under the eye of a teacher.

Fair enough. Look, I could read you out the various acts that have been passed by governments over the years but it would drive you silly. Basically, you were incapacitated while serving your country in a war zone. You're eligible for a disability pension, but how much and how it is paid, is pretty complex. I can't tell you how much you're going to get, that's up to them down in Perth and they're supposedly working on your case right now. So much for a leg, an arm, that sort of thing. But, as Johnny on the spot, I can try and interpret their decisions for you and provide them with an address to send your cheques. All that. Have you got an address yet?

Hedley shook his head.

Anything coming up?

Again, Hedley shook his head.

Hmm. Tex smoothed down his moustache, thinking.

Says here you're a station worker, eh?

Was.

Yeah, bit hard doing station work with one wing, I agree. But … look, as I said, I flog a bit of stuff for Elders. Salesman. With the arse fallen out of the cattle market there's a hell of a lot of smaller properties for sale right now. There's one I know of needs babysitting if you know what I mean? Owner up and walked off. Needs a caretaker while it's on the market. No pay, but free rent. Interested?

Hedley sparked up. Could be. Where is it?

Place called Happy Valley. Out in the jump-up country.

I know it, said Hedley. Billy goat country.

Yeah. Hard one to sell. Can't see it going tomorrow. So?

Need a car to get out there.

Might be able to help you out there, too. Tex began flicking through the papers again. Clause here somewhere about a vehicle assistance scheme for disabled veterans.

And would I be able to put up uncle and aunty?

I don't know about that one. Owner might crack up if I let too many folk on.

Just the two of them and their kids, said Hedley. Uncle's a head stockman and I'll need a hand round the place. Can't do much with one arm if things go wrong.

Tex thought about this for a moment and then nodded.

Ok. Makes sense, but keep a lid on visitors, ok? Remember, you're supposed to be looking after the place.

When Hedley was on the way out through reception he asked Delli if she would like to go to the movies with him that Saturday night. She was too coy to give him a straight yes or no, but the smile she gave him was enough for Hedley. There was hope.

Chapter 37

Happy Valley wasn't a valley and, as far as Hedley could see, there was nothing particularly happy looking about the place. He guided his ute along a pair of twin stony ruts and pulled up on a little rise so he, Frank and Jane could take in the overall picture. The ute was immediately invaded by bush flies, quick to zone in on eyes, noses and ears.

An old asbestos cottage with a front veranda and a noticeable lean seemed to be the only real building. Nearby was a shed consisting of several grey mulga posts rising from the red dust at contrary angles, labouring under the weight of a mess of rusty corrugated iron. Further down the track, they could just make out a windmill and some ramshackle yards with another shed to one side. The place stank of goat's urine and was littered with their droppings. Any trees seemed to have been stripped bare by them.

Jane and Frank's kids, who had been asleep among the swag rolls in the back of the ute, were now awake and energised. They bailed out over the side of the ute and, followed by the dogs, sprinted toward the cottage calling and laughing to each other.

Hedley's ute fell a long way short of the one he had dreamed about buying. Not red, not new. A battered FJ that he'd picked up from Charlie Wongal's brother when he'd come home from the mines. It was all that had been available around town at the time.

Bin overstocked, was Frank's only comment as he looked around the bare creek flats.

Goats aren't helping, neither, said Hedley looking up at the escarpment that rose behind the homestead. A line of motley-coloured feral goats dotted the upper slope.

Only Jane was smiling. Her eyes fixed on the escarpment with its contrasting hues of deep red washing into lighter reds and creams, almost purple in the shadows. The sun was hitting an outcrop of white quartz running along the ridgeline and just above the goats was a large cave entrance.

Old ones up there, said Jane. Jin.ga.

She climbed out of the ute and stretched, eyes never leaving the escarpment. Frank and Hedley watched from the ute as Jane ambled up the slope in the direction of the cave, bare feet picking their way around stunted mulga and yellow bundi shrubs until she reached a small outcrop of quartz. She hauled herself up onto the outcrop and stood, balancing on top, facing the cave. Bringing both hands to her cheeks like a megaphone, she began calling out in Wadjarri, her voice echoing back from the escarpment. When she returned to the ute and climbed in beside Frank and Hedley, she was smiling again.

We all welcome 'ere. Like this place.

There was a silent acceptance of this. Maybe the whitefellas had got the name right after all.

Hedley put the ute in gear and followed the wheel ruts to the cottage.

Jane opened the unlocked front door and went inside, but soon emerged, broad nose screwed up disdainfully.

Wathi. Not livin' in there. Shed'll do.

And that was that. They unloaded their gear in the shed.

Jane and the kids began collecting firewood while Frank and Hedley wandered off to look at the water situation. A small two hundred gallon rainwater tank around the back of the cottage was full and the water drinkable. They headed for the windmill.

Pumpin' ok, said Frank, pointing to where the sun was reflecting off a thin intermittent spurt of water coming from the windmills outlet pipe and dropping into an ancient corrugated iron tank. Frank hoisted himself up the side of the tank and peered in.

Bin concreted inside. Few cracks but holdin'.

Hedley was looking at the ground around the trough.

Cattle tracks and at least a couple of horses. Plenty of goats.

Good, said Frank. Might pull this mill out of the wind. Shut off trough. See how friendly them horses are in the mornin' when they're hangin' round for drink.

Those goats'll be comin' down for a drink tonight, too, said Hedley looking up at the escarpment. Might try and pick off a nice fat one.

Ok, but not close to mill. Don't wanna scare off everythin' else.

Easy.

Frank looked quizzically at Hedley as he joined him at the trough.

You ok to shoot? How you gonna hold that gun?

Hedley grinned. Don't worry about me, old fella.

Frank didn't look convinced so Hedley dropped to a sitting position and, pretending to hold a rifle in his left hand, cocked his right knee up for a support.

Piece a piss, old fella. Pow. Pow. Two goats down.

Only need one.

Must have a hangin' room around here somewhere we can keep meat for a few days.

Didn't see one.

Then we'll have to make one. Next trip into town, buy some flywire. Enough junk round here to build the rest.

They walked over to the small enclosed shed near the yards.

Stables I reckon, said Frank.

He dragged opened a corrugated iron door that was more reliant on the dirt floor for support than its hinges. He peered into the gloom.

Yeah. Few old saddles, bridles, shoeing stuff. Catch them horses in mornin' eh? Have ourselves a look around.

After a look over the yards, they ambled back to the main shed where Jane had selected a cooking area and had a fire going.

Alfie, Frank and Jane's eldest came running to meet them, proudly swinging a freshly clubbed goanna round his head.

Bangara. Bangara, daddy. Caught it down the flat.

Frank nodded approval. Good fat one. Give it here.

Frank took the bangara over to a dead stump. He pulled out a sharp pocket knife and deftly cut around the bangara's ring to free its guts. Alfie found him a small forked twig and Frank shoved it into the reptile's mouth and twisted until its tongue was firmly wrapped around the stick. He then pulled the guts out through its mouth with the stick. Alfie took the carcass over to Jane's fire and tossed it onto some hot coals.

Hedley collected Frank's old 303 with a full magazine and began walking up the side of the escarpment. He soon found the main goat pad and set himself up under a low mulga bush about fifty yards away. This would be the first time he'd fired a rifle since losing his arm and he wasn't as confidant as he'd made out to Frank. The three-o had a hell of a kick and if he missed, he'd have to work the bolt action. How was he going to do that with one bloody arm? He figured out that if he was in a sitting position and gripped the thing between his knees, he could work the bolt with his left hand. It would be slow, but he could do it. He began practising.

At sunset the first goats began to cautiously make their way down the slope. Hedley waited until several had passed and then selected a younger looking goat that was in reasonable condition. He followed it with the sites for about ten yards and then tensed his left shoulder and squeezed the trigger as gently as he could. It felt strange, but he got the shot off. Not perfect, but a hit. The goat jumped and took off across the hill, bleating loudly. All the other goats scattered. Hedley fumbled with the bolt action and, by the time he'd put another round up the spout, the goat was nearly out of sight. He fired in hope and missed, but the goat eventually dropped anyway.

Hedley slung the rifle and started walking after the goat. He'd have to improve or wear out a lot of boot leather retrieving the things.

Next morning there were about thirty head of cattle in very poor condition camped in the shade of some rivergums about fifty yards back from the windmill. They were waiting for someone to fill the empty trough. Four equally bony hangdog stock horses stood drooping beside the trough.

Frank and Hedley had little trouble approaching them with a pair of bridles and, while Hedley held them, Frank ran a finger and thumb over their backs and fetlocks. He selected the two in best condition and inspected their hooves.

Better shoe 'em. Stony country.

Hedley helped Frank find some shoes and nails in the stables, but when it came to the actual shoeing he felt like a bump on a log. No way he could hang onto a hoof and drive a nail in at the same time. He had to content himself with handing Frank the pliers, pincers or whatever else he required. He couldn't even reshape the shoes on the anvil, although he tried. All that he succeeded in doing was belting himself with the hammer when he tried holding one of the shoes against the anvil with his knee. The army doctors had measured him up for a prosthetic arm but he would have to travel down to Perth to have it fitted. Hedley had been indifferent to the idea of a false arm but now he was beginning to change his mind. Anything had to be better than this.

The sun was high in the cloudless sky by the time they were riding up the escarpment. Hedley found mounting and riding easy enough and soon he forgot his frustrations and began taking in the vista. They reined in at the top and surveyed the landscape.

What do you reckon? Hedley asked.

Frank eased back in his saddle and hooked one leg across the pommel. He looked back at the creek flats and then scanned the rugged country in front of them.

Dry enough. S'posed to be rock holes in some of them gullies between the jump-ups.

How many cattle could it run?

Cattle? Dunno. Pretty bony. Even in a good season wouldn't be much feed.

So? How many head could ya run here?

Dunno. Think this place goes all the way out to Mount Trelour.

Sixty thousand acres, it is. Tex told me. It's for sale, cheap.

Frank was focused on the horizon, trying to work out where the boundary might be, mind still on cattle numbers.

Maybe I could buy it with the army money, said Hedley.

Frank swivelled around in his saddle and looked intensely at Hedley.

What for?

Well … I dunno. Hedley was a little taken aback by Frank's response. Place of our own.

This Djujima country. Can't buy. Whitefella talk.

Frank spat into the dust.

Hedley didn't have an answer to this at first, but he thought about it.

I could buy it from the whitefellas and then let the Djujima mob live here if they wanted. We could still run cattle.

Frank shook his head and didn't reply.

What's wrong with that? Open the place to all our mob.

Frank remained impassive, but he was beginning to listen. Wheels turning. He respected Hedley.

Get some of those kids away from all the trouble in town. You and aunty don't want young Alfie gettin' mixed up in that shit.

Frank gave a tiny thoughtful nod, only detectable by a slight movement in the brim of his battered old Akubra.

Worth thinking about if I could pull it off.

Frank looked at Hedley, puzzled.

How? How you buy this place off white fellas?

Like I said. army money. Dunno if it's enough, but I could find out.

Frank nodded again.

So, what do ya reckon uncle? Make a go of it?

Frank looked back at the creek flats and the small mob of cattle still hanging around the windmill.

Bin overstocked but light on now. Maybe a few in the gullies. Fences gone. No water out the jump-up country 'cept a few rock holes, but they not for cattle. Special places.

Cattle prob'ly messed 'em anyway.

Frank unhooked his leg from the pommel and slipped his foot into the stirrup. He gave his horse a light kick into action.

'Ave a look, eh?

Hedley followed Frank down the steep incline.

Maybe we could fence off the rock holes, he called out to Frank's retreating back. Keep the cattle out but sink bores nearby. Gotta be water nearby.

Frank kept riding, not bothering to answer.

Chapter 38

It was in Tex Nisbett's interest to sell Happy Valley to Hedley. No one else was interested in the god-forsaken wreck of a property, that was for sure. But there were many complications, conflict of interest being the one sitting uncomfortably at the back of Tex's grey matter.

Hedley was sitting on the opposite side of his desk again – third visit in a week – a mess of paperwork between them.

Hedley's brow creased in concentration as he pored over a jumble of notes the pair of them had put together on the last visit.

So, the place is for sale at twenty thousand, right?

Sure is, said Tex. They had been through this many times by now.

So, if I could get onto some cull cows, really poor quality stock, at fifty bucks a head, and I bought a hundred of them, I'd be up for another five thousand dollars.

Correct.

Plus another five thousand for fencing and bores.

And that would total thirty thousand dollars.

Right, said Hedley. Thirty thousand dollars. So, how much is my compo?

Let me put my other hat on. Tex made a show of picking up his cowboy hat.

Sorry. He tossed his hat back on the desk. I know this is serious and I'm doing my best to sort it out, but I'm only a go-between.

Tex scooped up a sheaf of documents from the pile in front of him.

Look, they've given you a pretty generous pension in my book, but a pension is not going to cut it as far as a sale goes. As I've explained before, you're going to have to apply for a lump sum advance payment, if I've got this right.

He read from the leading document.

If receiving a pension and you require additional funds you might be able to get some of your pension paid in advance.

But I want the whole lot in one hit, said Hedley, frustration beginning to show. I won't ask the army for another cent. No more pension. Ever. Just tell them I want thirty thousand.

Tex gave an exaggerated shrug.

If only it was that simple.

Hedley thought it was simple.

Tex could sense Hedley's frustration. The young bloke was determined. He admired that.

Ok, Hedley, we can only give it a go. We'll fill out an application. The board in Perth will consider that application and if they agree to an advancement then they will set an amount based on your pension. We can't demand a certain figure. It's up to them.

What if they knock us back?

Then you can appeal that decision. Won't happen overnight, though

When they had filled out the application, Hedley insisted on adding a personal note nominating the magical figure of thirty thousand. Tex was insistent he not mention the particular property he wanted to buy.

As Hedley was leaving, Tex handed him two letters. One, a regulation newsletter from the army and the other from 2nd Lieutenant Doug Ashmore. He slipped them in his back pocket and nodded goodbye to Tex.

Half an hour later, Hedley ordered two milkshakes from the milk bar across the road. One was for Delli, on her lunchbreak, waiting for him at one of the Laminex sheeted booths that ran the full length of the building.

Jane had warned him that Delli was out of bounds. Wrong skin. Jane could set him up anytime with a number of girls who were right. All he had to do was ask.

Hedley respected this but, hell, he could still share a milkshake and a chat. He liked Delli.

He had to make two trips with the large, fluted aluminium milkshake containers, each one a handful. When he was seated opposite, he asked her about Tex Nisbett. What was the word around town? Was he someone to be trusted?

Delli was unsure. He seemed ok, but she had heard one of the clerks talking.

I think he said something about property deals. Delli was trying to spear her floating dollop of icecream with a straw as she talked. Mr Nisbett does a lot of deals. Finger in everything, I think.

That right? Maybe I'd better watch 'im more closely.

Hedley reached across the table with his left hand and speared her icecream with his straw, pretending to steal it. She laughed and smiled. It was her smile Hedley liked.

Next time Hedley caught up with Tex Nisbett, the news wasn't good. His application had been rejected. Tex reached across his desk and showed Hedley the documented response from the review board, but Hedley didn't need to read it.

Tex hadn't been sure how Hedley would react but, given his lack of education, he assumed that Hedley would find the complexity of it all too much. Surely the young bloke would throw in the towel.

Not so.

The young bloke produced Ashmore's letter. The one Tex had given him on his last visit. He brandished it in front of Tex.

I want you to write to this feller for me please, Mr Nisbett. Want you to tell him I got knocked back and I want you to tell him that I wanna buy this block of dirt for twenty thousand dollar and fence it and put down the bores and …

Tex cut him off.

Hang-on. I take it you want to appeal.

Yeah. That's the word. Appeal. But I want this feller Ashmore to be in on it. He knows me and what I did in Vietnam. He might make a difference.

Fair enough. Better show me that letter and I'll jot down some details.

Tex took the letter from Hedley and began writing.

There were many things swirling around in Tex's head as he wrote, not the least being conflict of interest. He had to structure the letter so his name would not be associated with the property sale. Perhaps this Ashmore would decide to deal directly with the board. Bypass him altogether. That'd be handy.

As he concentrated on the wording, Hedley's voice bored into him from the other side of the desk.

Tell him the amount I need, Mr Nisbett. Has to be thirty thousand. Don't need any more. The army can keep what's left over.

Tex stopped writing, his train of thought broken. He looked up at Hedley. The young bloke was like a dog at a bone, you had to hand it to him.

Thirty thousand, said Hedley again.

Yeah. I think I got that, said Tex.

As Hedley climbed into his ute, he thought about stopping off at the Railway Hotel and buying a box of tallies to take back to Happy Valley.

Maybe not. He'd have to run the gauntlet of afternoon drinkers on the bot and anyway, Frank wanted to keep alcohol off the place. A habit he'd picked up out at Eumarella. Leave the drinking for town visits.

But he did pick up groceries, some insect mesh to knock up a meat hanging room, new leathers for the bore pump and some ammo for the three-o. Goats were getting a hammering.

Just out of town the bitumen dropped off into a sea of gravel corrugations. Hedley gunned his ute down the bitumen, imagining he was a fighter pilot taking off from an aircraft carrier deck. For a moment his ute answered the call and became airborne before crashing down into the corrugations. A bit of a sideways skip and Hedley had the ute trimmed and on course for Happy Valley.

His mind turned to the aircraft carrier that had shipped them over to Vietnam. Shooting target balloons from the flight deck.

Less than a year ago, he thought.

What a year. Seemed like it had gone on longer than his entire life.

Started off the best year, then finished up the worst year.

Gone the army career, corporal stripes, mates and arm. Now they were splitting hairs about his compo.

He floored the accelerator until his ute began skimming over the corrugations.

Bastards. Ashmore'll fix 'em. Said he would, anyway. Said he'd help out with anything. We'll see.

Chapter 39

Alfie's ten-year-old face screwed up in effort as he strained to hang onto a six-inch adjustable spanner, pushing against Hedley and his spanner as they struggled to undo a stubborn connector nut.

He'd do anything for his big cuz, Hedley. Nobody was like cousin, cousin made stuff happen. Cousin told them a different war story every night around the fire and last night, he'd let him touch his stump. The fascinating stump, the mysterious stump that was never mentioned in any of the war stories. The stump that had been hidden behind pinned-back shirt sleeves for a while but now was on constant display. Alfie had felt the knobbly bit at the end and traced the Donald Duck tattoo with his finger, all stretched and weird.

The nut they were trying to undo was part of the bore pump which Hedley was disassembling on a workbench he'd set up on the shaded side of the old cottage.

Alfie gave the spanner an extra hard shove and without warning it slipped on the connector nut and his knuckles hit the workbench with a thud. Painful. He clenched his eyes tight shut, determined not to cry, not in front of cousin.

Nyuwil? Hedley had a sympathetic grin. Alfie shook his head vehemently, eyes still screwed up tight.

Gotta keep the spanner wound up tight like I told yer, Hedley explained. Now you've burred the nut … and always pull the spanner. That way, if it slips yer don't hurt yerself. Ok?

Alfie nodded, still ringing his hand.

Anyway, you're going great guns and I think I can hear your daddy coming back from town, so you can take a break.

I wanna keep helping.

Ok, then. You can help unload the ute.

They watched as the ute morphed from its dust cloud, driven by Frank. Jane appeared from the shed and they waited for the ute to pull up.

There was an unexpected passenger.

Jane let out a cry of glee and went to the passenger's door. She pulled it open and old Mick, the Eumarella cook, came spiralling out, landing in the dust. He lay there helplessly on his rounded back, arms and legs flailing uselessly like an upturned turtle.

Bin on a bender, Frank explained from the driver's seat. Found him like that so thought I'd bring 'im 'ome.

Jane scooped Mick up to his feet where he tottered back and forward until she supported him again.

What you bin up to, old feller? Bin missin' ya, she said.

Sure. Missin' me smokes, more like. Mick's watery eyes were having trouble focusing, but he spotted the cottage.

Bejayzus. Not feeling well. Wouldn't have a spare bed in there, would yer Janey?

Jane laughed. Old feller, that whole house yours, you want it.

As soon as Mick reached the shade of the front veranda, he collapsed in a chair.

This'll do. Too early for bed.

He looked around at the others, now grouped about him, Alfie included.

So, you're serious, then? The lotta you.

No one answered.

You own this place?

Hope to, said Hedley.

Right so. Hope to, eh?

Depends if the army come good with me compo.

Mick caught site of Hedley's stump and he shook his head sadly.

Heard about that, son. Sorry business but that's what happens when all the power is in the hands of eedjits. The likes of us cop it, not them.

Mick turned unsteadily in his chair and peered into the dim interior of the cottage. He looked back at Frank.

Can help, you know. Earn me keep.

I know that, old feller. Maybe plenty mouths to feed.

Not thinkin' of taking on contractors, are youse? Know where that leads.

Young Yamaji kids from town, said Hedley. Give 'em somethin' to do.

Mick gave Hedley a long look as if seeing him for the first time. Hedley thought Mick was just struggling with alcohol impaired vision but Mick was assessing him.

Frank always said you was a bright one. Like the sound o' that. I'll cook for the kids if you pull all this off. Don't expect me to create wonders out of nothin', though.

Don't worry. Frank put a reassuring hand on Mick's shoulder. You just take it easy old fella.

To the surprise of all, Mick's face crumpled and his head dropped. Frank was quick to put a comforting arm around him muttering, you'll be right old fella, you'll be right. Been one helluva year.

Hedley thought he could detect the sunlight reflecting off a tiny rivelet of moisture running down Mick's cheek, but it was soon absorbed in his crusty maze of wrinkles.

This was some achievement. Tex double checked the documents and slipped them into a briefcase. He put the briefcase on the front seat of his Landrover and did a u-turn in Main Street, heading out toward Happy Valley. Ok, he'd managed to facilitate the lump sum thing – thanks to the Lieutenant – and somehow avoid any accusations of impropriety when he claimed commission for selling the property. That was a feat. But it was the young bloke. The young bloke was a real goer, the first blackfella he'd ever heard of buying a run in these parts. It was a major. Did he get a good deal for the kid? Probably not. Place's a dump. Vendor would've come down more if he'd been pushed. Should've stepped in there and given the young bloke a heads up, but a sale is a sale.

Tex accelerated his Landrover off the end of the bitumen as Hedley had done a month earlier only he wasn't thinking of aircraft carriers, he could only think of the Landrovers suspension as it recoiled at the corrugations.

Two hours later, he pulled up at the homestead and was immediately surrounded by dogs. The kids weren't far behind.

G'day mister. G'day mister.

Are the dogs gonna take me leg off?

Dog's ok, mister.

Won't 'urt ya, mister.

Tex gingerly opened the door and placed one elastic-sided boot in the dust. Immediately one of the mutts jumped up and left red paw prints on his clean white moleskins.

He could see Jane in the open shed chopping up cuts of meat but no sign of Hedley.

Tell me, you young 'uns. Where can I find Hedley? Got a very important present for him.

Buildin' the new hangin' room, mister, said Alfie. Down there. He pointed toward the yards.

Tex could just make out Hedley's ute through the heat haze where the kid was pointing.

Might drive down.

We ride, mister?

Yeah, s'pose so. No dogs though.

The kids bundled into the back seat and he stopped to offer Jane a lift but she waved him on, intent on her meat chopping.

Hedley greeted him with a big grin, he'd been waiting for Tex. Frank kept working away on the half-built meat hanging room.

Congratulations young feller. Tex slipped out of his Landrover and extended a hand. Hedley pocketed the fencing pliers he was holding and they managed one of their cack-handed shakes.

Vendor's signed, said Tex. Only need your signature and the property's yours.

Hedley's broad grin said all.

Uncle, Hedley called. Come over and meet Mr Nisbett.

Call me Tex. Told you that a million times.

After he'd shaken hands with Frank, Tex produced a sheaf of documents and a pen from his brief case and laid them out on the bonnet.

Frank and the kids watched on as Hedley completed his best left-handed signature and the deal was done.

So, said Tex. Just happen to have a few beers in the back. Warm, but they won't kill us. Celebrate the deal.

To his surprise, Hedley declined the offer.

Nah. Need to talk about the stock while we got yer. Come over in the shade. You too uncle, need yer in on this.

The three of them squatted in the shade of the old stables.

We already done a round up, Hedley said, and we reckon we got ninety head on the place.

He scratched a nine and a zero in the dust with a stick.

You might have had a win there, Tex pushed his Stetson to the back of his head. Contract said fifty head but I won't say anything if you don't. He winked.

Hedley ignored him, too focused on his calculations.

Ninety head, but uncle reckons that by the time we get rid of the goats we can run another fifty, building up to three hundred when the country comes good. Right, uncle?

Frank nodded. Sink them bores first. He held up four fingers.

Yeah. Four bores. Need to sink a couple now and buy some of them cull calves you talked about while the market's down. Say fifty.

Hedley scratched a five and a zero under the ninety.

Well, you've got your ten thousand secure in the bank, said Tex. Can get cull cows for fifty dollars a head.

Twenty, said Frank firmly.

Tex looked at him and nodded. Possible, but you'll be able to play a nice tune on their ribs. Looney tunes I reckon. Probably keel over on you tryin' to get them out here.

I'll get 'em 'ere, said Frank.

Right, said Tex.

As the discussions meandered on, young Alfie inched his way into the circle of men and adopted their squatting pose. He listened and watched. When they nodded, he nodded and when there was some head shaking, he shook his head. He even managed to look thoughtful when they did. Nothing to it.

When Hedley had finally worked through the improvements he wanted to make, Tex stiffly rose from his haunches and stomped some blood back into his legs. Hedley and Frank had no such trouble getting to their feet.

Feel like you've picked my brains to shreds, Hedley. Not that there's much to pick.

You'll make a bit more of your commission if we buy stock and fencing gear through you.

Fair enough, said Tex. You're learning.

He looked up at the distant sound of approaching vehicles. The others had been aware of them for some minutes.

Djujima mob, said Hedley. Their country out the back here. Said they can camp there.

Driving out of the homestead, Tex had to pull over for three old cars, not a registration plate among them, spewing dust and loaded up to the gunnels. Swags and bric a brac roped to every spare inch of car body.

Bloody blackfellas, he said to himself. Place'll be back on the market before you know it. Non payment of rates, most likely. Still, a bit more commission in the pipeline for me. Young bloke's onto it though and good luck to him, he'll need it.

Chapter 40

A northerly had been blowing for two days and Melbourne was dusty and hot. Cindy and Frankie were rolling up their yoga mats in Frankie's living room after their usual Saturday morning session, both sweaty and flushed, both feeling every one of their sixty two years.

Coffee time? Cindy asked.

Best idea you've had all morning.

After some fuss over the settings on Frankie's coffee machine, a recent gift from Cindy, they sat at the kitchen table with its view over the backyard. Cindy with her half shot of beans, quarter teaspoon of honey and thick crème and Frankie with her flat white.

I need to buy an air conditioner, Frankie sighed. I've opened every window that isn't seized up and the place is still like an oven.

We could always do yoga at mine when the weather is like this. I nearly expired this morning.

You and me both, girl, said Frankie. But we can't break with tradition, I've been meaning to buy an aircon for ages. The whole place needs modernising and cleaning up, starting with all that junk in the back yard.

The sight of the leftover building material still lining the yard jogged Cindy's memory.

Oh, yeah. I met a guy who may be interested in buying all that old stuff from you. Would it be ok if I brought him around tomorrow?

Tomorrow's fine. Tell him, whoever he is, that he can have the stuff; take it all. Who is he?

Cindy smiled and dismissed the question with a wave of her hand.

Frankie looked at her knowingly. I see. Another one of those. A new one?

Just the one meeting, said Cindy. A builder. He seems nice.

They all seem nice at first. Where did you meet him?

Same dating site.

Pics? C'mon. Show me.

Cindy produced her phone and brought up the site.

Why don't you join? It's about time, Frankie.

I get enough entertainment watching you. Is that him? Frankie pointed to a photo of a lycra-clad cyclist that had come up on Cindy's phone as she scrolled through. Phil from Oakleigh.

No, no. He was someone I was texting. Eighty percent match rating, but I didn't follow him up.

What about this one? Frankie stabbed her finger at another passing photo. He looks uber-handsome in his hiking get-up.

Don't! Cindy tried to shield the phone from Frankie, laughing. You touched the like button. My profile will turn up on his feed, you idiot.

He's sexy. I might have done you a favour.

Yeah, and half my age. Right on, Frankie.

She found the photo she was looking for and showed Frankie.

Frankie peered at the image.

You say he's a builder?

Uhuh.

Then why is he so soft looking? I don't think he's ever been out of an office. And all that bling ... honestly Cindy.

Cindy closed the site with an exaggerated flourish.

I know what you're thinking, Frankie Sanderson. History repeats. She always goes for the same type. Shallow fly-by-nights.

You forgot to add the word, user.

Yeah, that too.

They smiled at each other.

At this point, John appeared from his bungalow and, unaware they were watching, began to shuffle stiffly toward the side gate.

So, that's it! Cindy clicked her fingers in a mock light-bulb moment. Now I know why you're not interested in going on the dating site.

Frankie's head was shaking even before Cindy had finished the sentence.

That is not funny, Cindy. Don't go there.

He's kinda cute in a beat up sort of way.

Enough, or you'll never be welcome here again.

Ok. Ok.

They watched as John skirted Frankie's vegetable patch and disappeared from view.

Cindy finished her coffee and glanced at her phone. Time to go.

So, what hour of the sabbath can I expect you and your new lothario?

Cindy gathered up her bag and phone from the kitchen table.

I think Daniel was talking morning sometime. He had a car rally or something on in the afternoon. Does that suit you?

Morning's fine.

Frankie smiled. Daniel. Car rallies. What's his match rating?

Very high. Thank you for asking.

Next morning, Frankie was watching them with some amusement. Cindy in one of her short black numbers looking very out of place, tiptoeing in her shiny red sandals through the building detritus. Daniel in front of her rummaging through various coloured window frames, roll-a-doors and random timbers. Occasionally he would ask her to hold one end of this or that while he examined the underside.

Got to watch out for rats. Frankie heard him warn Cindy.

Cindy quickly dropped the length of timber she was holding for him and returned to Frankie's side.

They watched him together as he fossicked around, wearing only a tight-fitting singlet in the hot morning sun, gym-toned body on show, gold chain flashing occasionally as it caught the odd ray of sunshine.

Does he know what he wants, Cind? He can have the whole lot, like I said. For nothing.

Cindy shrugged absently. He's having fun. Let him do his thing.

Daniel let a length of stair stringer go and it crashed back to earth with a thud that caused Frankie to wince and glance apprehensively at John's nearby bungalow.

Can you ask him to keep the noise down, Cind?

Cindy called out his name and he looked up. She pantomimed a downward motion with her hands and put a forefinger to her lips. He acknowledged her with a cheery smile and dismissive wave. A stack of blue coloured roof sheeting leaning against the front of the bungalow had caught his eye and he began peeling them back, one by one, counting their number.

Something penetrated John's universe. Voices that sounded like they were coming through rain drenched jungle. Somewhere close. Eyes glued shut but explosions were detonating right in front of him. Flashes inside his closed eyes. A scraping metal sound right next to his hootchie, tearing at his guts. Bayonets. They were driving bayonets through the thin fabric of his hootchie, rolling him up in it. Then a huge crash. No time to shoot. No glasses, doesn't matter. Crawl, run.

He crawled and ran. Vomiting as he burst out of the hootchie into blinding light and straight into one of the enemy. Pushing, falling, blinded and terrified, unaware he was pissing himself and unaware he was naked except for a now urine-sodden pair of Y fronts.

Cindy recoiled, using Frankie as support as she just managed to pull herself clear of the plunging near-naked man who proceeded to nose-dive into one of the piles of 4 x 2's at their feet.

She screamed. Daniel screamed. His scream, a high-pitched *fuck*, as he picked himself up from among the roof sheets he had accidently dropped just before the deranged old rat-man had come bursting out of his rats' nest.

Frankie grimaced as she saw blood spurt from John's forehead like the Trevi fountain after a wine for water transformation.

John felt his brain exploding inside his skull, everything around him spinning uncontrollably. Blinded, but enemy forms all around. Crawling, then running to break free of their encircling malevolent intent. Clear of them, don't stop.

Frankie held Cindy, still rocked to her red sandal foundations.

Is your friend alright? Frankie asked. I must go after John. Sorry about this.

Frankie! Don't be crazy. Let him go for god's sake.

Can't. He's bleeding.

Frankie gave Cindy a final apologetic look and bolted for the side gate where she had last seen her scantily clad headache disappearing into an unsuspecting world.

She only had to follow the blood trail along the concrete footpath and she soon found him cowering under a neighbour's hydrangea bush. He seemed to be coming to his senses. At least partly focused on her as she approached cautiously.

John. It's only me, Frankie.

He tried retreating further under the bush, bare feet failing to gain purchase in the leaf matter, Y fronts now scrunched into the full wedgie, hiding little.

Frankie didn't know whether she should advance, retreat or hold her ground. He looked terrified and hopelessly confused. Hopelessly pissed, she guessed.

She held her ground.

John. Take it easy, it's me, Frankie. Let me take you back to the bungalow. You want to go back there, don't you? Safety. Your own little safe place.

She thought about trying to stem the flow of blood from his head wound but that would mean using her nice white tracksuit top. It appeared to be coagulating anyway.

John looked at her blurry, silhouetted figure, heard her now familiar voice and felt a slight realigning of his senses.

She was advancing and he made a half-hearted attempt to wriggle backwards but gave up. Everything began spinning again and he felt her take his arm and draw him out from under the bush. An eternity passed before he could stand upright and then he was being led. One shuffle after another on feet that seemed a fog away from the rest of him. Everything was a fog.

Frankie kicked several empty wine bottles out of the way and laid him on his bed. He quickly rolled over and closed his eyes.

She straightened and stretched her back, aching after the interminable trip back with him. Ok for Simpson's donkey. At least Simpson didn't have to fend off a parade of 'concerned' passers-by, who were wondering why she was half-carrying a near-naked man down a suburban footpath on Sunday morning. The joke about returning Jesus from a crucifixion rehearsal for next year's Easter pageant had only been met with strange looks.

His head wound needed dressing and she thought about calling a help group and being done with him once and for all. But no. She couldn't do that. She would spend the rest of her Sunday cleaning him up.

She wondered where Cindy and her friend had gone. Scarpered to the nearest slow eatery for a steadying glass or two of Cullen's Cab Merlot, no doubt. Who could blame them.

She went back to the house and fetched her first aid kit.

Chapter 41

Two days later she had been about to sit down for dinner when she heard his voice in the back yard. She switched on the back light and went to investigate. He was in a fit of the horrors, rolling in her freshly composted heirloom tomatoes, muttering incomprehensively. Shaking and twitching, letting out an anguished muffled yell followed by more gibberish. She stood there looking down at him wondering what could possibly be going through his head and then he yelled again, loudly and forcibly. A half scream. What must the neighbours think?

He was watching a bullet in slow motion, spiralling toward Hedley's shoulder, ripping into real motion, tearing into tendons, bone, through tatters of army green fabric and flying away into the surrounding jungle with a mess of body parts and fluids. Unseen by eye but seen by brain. Frankie was forced to sedate him with a large dose of Valium.

Next day after work Frankie found him lying in his bed, fully conscious and contrite. Predictable, she thought.

Sorry. I'm a bloody idiot, I know.

He tried to lift himself onto one elbow, grimacing.

What are we going to do with you, John?

I know. You don't have to tell me. Hopeless. Bloody hopeless, I am.

They looked at each other, John waiting for her to speak but she didn't. He filled the void.

I dunno what I did, but it was bad, wasn't it? You want to kick me out. A pause while John waited for Frankie to respond. No luck there, so he continued blabbing. Just when things are good, I stuff them up. Right? Hopeless, I am. Hopeless.

Frankie spoke when she was sure he had run out of words. She wanted him to listen.

John. You simply can't keep going on like this. Whatever happened, happened over forty years ago. You need to talk about it.

I have talked about it. All I can remember anyway. Look, stuff happened but I can't talk about things I can't remember. It's a ... nothing.

She knew this was baloney.

I know I've asked this before but is there anyone else who might remember?

John shook his head. Haven't seen any of the blokes. Went our separate ways.

What about military reunions?

Never been to any. Not keen on all that Anzac stuff. Remembrance Day. Didn't do dad any good.

Your dad was an Anzac?

Was. Dead now.

Frankie thought about this.

Did you admire your dad? The Anzacs?

Wouldn't say that. I guess I wanted to be like dad and Grandad. He was an Anzac. Gallipoli and all that.

But … nothing worth remembering about my Gallipoli. Whole Anzac thing backfired on me. You've no idea.

So, there is no one you can think of who might remember what happened?

Like I said, they all went their own way years ago.

You mentioned a Chub once before.

Yeah. Chub. My mate.

What happened to him?

No idea. Went off to look for work up north somewhere. Wanted me to go, but no. Not for me up there.

Can you remember his surname?

John looked up at her quizzically through his oversized glasses and she thought he may have been about to smile.

You don't give up, do you?

She smiled for him. No, I don't.

He looked down again, thinking.

Jackson. Private Jackson.

Frankie nodded and shrugged.

Common enough name, unfortunately. But I can try and look it up. You never know.

Probably wouldn't want to know me, even if you did find him. Nobody wants to know me and that's fine.

Not necessarily true. Nothing stays the same John. Can you remember his Christian name? I assume Chub was a nickname.

John thought for a moment and nodded.

Trevor. Private Trevor Chubby Jackson. That was him.

Good. Frankie felt tired. Must go, I'll drop you in something to eat later.

She left and John felt under his bed in the hope there may have been another bottle under there. No luck.

After cooking up a meal of stir fried vegies, serving John and eating her own, Frankie tapped her P.C. into life. She opened and played a ten second video from Angela in London. Baby Jordie crawling through a sea of first birthday presents and wrappings. She should be over there sharing her grandson's birthday. Why couldn't she be there? Work and this new predicament she'd brought on herself. John. Could he be left alone? Absolutely. He could drink himself to death for all she cared. But she did care, that was the trouble. Only herself to blame.

Frankie played the video again and again before weariness began to tug at her ten seconds of grandmotherly buzz.

Time for bed but why else was she here at the damn computer? Oh, yes. John's war friend. Trevor Chub Jackson.

She typed the name into her search engine and endless pages of performers came up. It irked her that her own performing career always came up with never a mention of her real work. The work that really mattered in her eyes.

She tried typing in the name with the words, Australian farmer. After a few pages of scrolling, she started to draw a few strings together and began a list of possibles. This was going to take some time.

The next evening, she showed John her printed list of possibles.

Lot here, he grunted.

Which state did he hail from? Try and narrow it down.

Western Australia, John remembered. But when he left Melbourne, he was headed for Queensland. Could be anywhere and he may never have brought property. We drank our army money pretty quick.

Frankie helped him go through the pages of Queensland connections without success. Nothing rang a bell so they started on the Western Australian listings.

A website that specialised in obscure historical narratives in Western Australia caught John's eye. Frankie had included it because it mentioned the family name Jackson.

Eumarella, John read. Think that was the name of his family property. Name like that, anyway.

No mention of your friend?

Not that I can see, just history. Something about a Paddy Jackson who pioneered the property. Seem to remember Chub mentioning the station had always been in his family. It was a big deal to him.

Are there any contact details for the property?

No, but he wouldn't be there anyway. Brother inherited the property and Chub swore he'd have nothin' to do with him. Big family split. Why he wanted to be discharged with me in Melbourne.

The family may know where he is, though. Time can heal.

Possibly. He was pretty pissed off as I remember it.

As John continued to read through her print out, Frankie tapped the property name into her phone and it came up with a mailbox number in Nanderra, W.A.

She would write.

A couple of weeks later, in the back yard, John picked his way around the blue roof sheets – yes, they were still leaning against his bungalow – and found a sunny corner out of the cold southerly. He'd thought about offering to tidy up the yard for Frankie but he found even the thought overwhelming.

Instead, he settled his backside on a stack of convenient timbers and leant back on the fence, sun warming his bones. Soon he was dozing.

Frankie's voice, calling him from her back door, cut into his slumber.

John! Phone call. Where are you?

Phone call? Nobody called him. Had to be trouble. He reluctantly answered her and Frankie came over, thrusting her mobile at him.

Someone wants to speak to you, she smiled.

John was wary of people smiling when there was nothing obvious to smile about. Trickery of some sort. He accepted the phone like it was an unexploded bomb and looked at it, not sure what to do next.

Speak into it, said Frankie.

He tentatively raised the device to his ear, holding it the wrong way around. Frankie impatiently flipped the phone in his hand.

Talk into it, she said.

Hullo? he said.

Is that you, mate? said the phone. John?

Yeah, said John.

Do ya know who you're talking to? said the phone.

No, said John, although he was starting to get an idea.

It's me. Chub. From the army. Remember?

Well, I'll be buggered!

John grinned and Frankie knew there was still hope for him. She politely left them to talk in private and retreated to her vegie garden to salvage what she could of her heirloom tomatoes.

She had restaked two full rows before John returned her phone. He seemed lost. Lost in a pleasant place for once.

Thanks, he said. That was Chub.

Your friend. I know.

You wouldn't read about it. All these years and he remembers me. Even said he'd been thinkin' about me of late. Finished up with the family property after all. Brother went broke or something.

That's lovely John. Lovely that you managed to chat.

Not sure how he found me.

I wrote, remember? He wrote back with a phone number and I rang. The phone must be in his homestead because he didn't answer the first three or four times I rang during the day. It wasn't until I worked out the time difference that I was able to catch him in the evening. I assume he lives on his own and works all day out on his property.

The effort she had put in seemed lost on John. He nodded absently, taking her detective work for granted. This peeved Frankie, but she bit her tongue and asked. So? What now? A catch up?

Said he wanted me to visit him over there. Dunno how, though. Haven't been out of Melbourne since Adam was a boy ... since the army days, really. Planes, buses ... buying tickets. Too hard.

Do you want to go and visit him?

John thought about this for a moment before dismissing the question.

Too hard. You've no idea.

I do have an idea, John. Buying tickets is not difficult. You have the money, don't you?

I think my cousin Lil is holding a few hundred in my account. But I wouldn't have the foggiest how to go about all this.

Would you like it if I arranged to buy the tickets for you?

John looked at her. She could read fear in his look.

Dunno. I really don't. You're too kind. Thanks anyway, but I don't deserve any of this.

I'll arrange the travel if you want. Yes or no?

John began to back away. Look … I dunno about all this. Can I just have time to take it all on board. You know how it is with me... it's a long way over there. I'll think about it.

Promise?

Promise.

John thanked her again and made his escape to the bungalow.

Chapter 42

The Great Northern Bus pulled up outside Nanderra Post Office and John looked hopefully out the window for Chub. A small collection of weathered-looking locals in wide brimmed hats, a large Indigenous family and several young backpacker-looking types were there to greet the bus, but no Chub. John was last to step down from the air-conditioning into the suffocating heat. Everyone had moved away into some shade except for an old man standing alone and to one side.

The old man looked at John from under his battered Akubra and waved away a few flies. John's attention shifted to a group of people emerging from the Post Office. They were young men in high vis work shirts, still no Chub.

He looked back at the old boy who was still eyeing him. John eyed him back.

It took a moment, but John realised with some embarrassment that he was looking at Chub. How could such an energy-filled, vibrant, fit young man become such a wreck? Pot gutted, florid faced and stooped.

Similar thoughts were running through Chub's mind.

Chub, John mumbled, and they shook, both men beginning to grin. Both men relieved that they weren't the only one to be flattened by their life.

The old bond was soon back.

Brothers in arms. Broken brothers.

Perched in the passenger's seat of Chub's filthy Landcruiser ute, John accepted the first can of beer thrust in his direction and they were barely out of the town limits.

Two hundred kays. One slab trip, proclaimed Chub. Kimberly-cool.

When they arrived at Eumarella, John had the worst case of heartburn he could remember. He didn't normally drink beer, let alone hot beer. Wine was his want. They had been chatting away for over two hours without saying much. Both reluctant to talk about themselves.

John had never been on an outback station before, but he sensed all was not as it should be. Broken machinery surrounded the rusting old workshop in ever more dilapidated rings. The further from the shed, the more wrecked and settled into the red earth each scrap metal candidate became.

No sign of life except a couple of vociferous dogs in a wire mesh enclosure.

Don't see any cattle or horses, John remarked.

Nah. Cattle are out bush and there's not a horse on the place now. Don't have the time for 'em. Do all the mustering with bikes and old four-bees I pick up from the wreckers in Nan. Get a mob of backpackers in if I have to. More hinderance than help half the time.

Chub pulled up beside the homestead veranda where there had once been a lawn. Skeletons of long dead fruit trees ringed the homestead. He fetched John's now dust-covered suitcase from the open ute tray.

Home sweet home. Welcome to Eumarella.

Chub cut up some chops for their dinner and if he was hoping for a drinking companion that night, he was sadly disappointed. John passed out before the sun had set.

More chops for breakfast. The kitchen appeared to be the only occupied living area.

That your woman who rung me? Chub asked out of the blue as he plonked a chipped enamel plate in front of John. This was the first attempt either had made at a personal conversation.

Nah, said John. He began eating his chops, conversation over.

Later, Chub took him for a windmill run in the Landcruiser. John had never seen such desolation, heat and flies.

Aircon in the 'Cruiser gave up last year, said Chub, slowing down as they approached a windmill. Been meaning to fix it but only makes you notice the heat more when you have to get out. Better off without it.

John could see the sense in this and nodded, but the heat was making him wilt. Give him Melbourne any day.

Shit, said Chub when they pulled up at the mill. A few cows were grouped around a dry trough.

Only fixed this bugger last year. Never mind, I'll open the gate into the next paddock. This lot can get a drink there until I get onto fixing this mongrel again. Dad sunk this one back in the fifties. Never put it down deep enough if you ask me. Runs dry and fucks the leathers.

John had no idea what Chub was talking about, but he nodded anyway.

That evening Chub lit a fire under a forty-four gallon drum. It was the same donkey heater set-up old Mick had used over four decades ago. John watched on, feeling useless. He still had no energy.

They showered and cracked the first tinnies. Chub was showing John the solar setup that powered his fridges and lights when a motorbike with a rough sounding motor swung into the homestead. The rider, wearing a wide brimmed hat pushed up at the front by the wind resistance, waved as he rode by toward one of the outbuildings.

Old Donny, explained Chub. Lives 'ere on the pension. Helps me round the place and I keep him in grog and tucker. Doesn't eat much.

Right, said John.

Lives in Mick's old quarters. Mick was our cook when I was growing up.

They began strolling toward the machinery shed, beers in hand, enjoying the cool of the evening.

So what happened to him? This Mick fellow?

Long gone. Left when Eric, me brother, started up with his shenanigans.

Right.

They arrived at the shed and Chub checked the voltage on a battery he was charging.

Part of the solar set up, he said.

John looked around the shed and could only see work that needed doing. Disassembled parts littered every bench top and tyres waiting to have their punctures attended to were leaning against any available bit of wall space.

Tomorrow's jobs, or next week's. Chub waved a weary arm around the shed and made for a grease covered fridge in the back corner decorated with ancient Swan Lager and Emu Bitter stickers. He pulled out a couple more cans and gave John one before crushing the now empty cans they had been drinking from and throwing them in a forty-four with the top cut off. It was nearly full. He raised his can and touched John's in a toast.

Never do today what you can do tomorrow.

He took a deep swig of his beer and then looked glumly at John.

Bullshit, of course. I'd do everything today if I could.

Chub pulled some roo meat out of the fridge and they began strolling toward the dog enclosure.

Dunno how you manage, said John.

I don't. Brother did the right thing walkin' away.

You weren't keen on coming back, last I remember.

No, I wasn't. Workin' on a property near Borroloola after the army when mum contacted me. Place was goin' into receivership, dad dead and Eric had shot through. Turned out the old man was more cunning than any of us had realised. Had a secret back-up stash that he'd been building up for years. Only to be used if those banking bastards ever came knocking on the door, he'd told mum before he went. Trouble was, Eric had run the place so low, the money didn't stretch to re stocking or employing. I was never game to borrow. No security. Battled ever since.

The dogs could see them coming and were throwing themselves at the wire mesh enclosure.

Sit ya mongrels! Roared Chub. Buster, sit! I said sit!

The dogs sat, tongues hanging out. Chub opened the gate and tossed them each a handful of meat.

For the next few days John tailed around after Chub as he went about his various tasks and in the evenings they drank beer, slowly relaxing in each other's company. Neither had set the bar very high so neither felt pressure from the other although John was feeling a mounting pressure from the other side of the continent. Frankie. She hadn't rung but he could hear her voice, growing more insistent by the day. You need to talk about what happened.

It wasn't until the fourth night, when they were sitting around a fire outside Donny's quarters, that the subject came up.

It was Donny who cautiously asked if they had served together.

Yeah, did our bit, said Chub. Dragged our arses through that shit of a place.

Vietnam? asked Donny.

John felt a rush of emotion at the sound of the word. He dropped his gaze to the beer can he was beginning to crunch between his hands. He hoped Chub would hold up their end of the conversation because he didn't trust himself to talk.

Yeah. Bloody Vietnam, said Chub.

There was a silence and Donny, who was well used to silence, tactfully stepped away from the subject. He finished his beer and, to John's relief, stood up and stretched.

That's me for the night fellas, he said.

Donny sloped off to his quarters and left them to their drinking.

Another hour passed without a mention of Vietnam but John could feel a tension building. He'd always accepted fate and perhaps it was time he accepted what was coming. At the back of his mind he knew that Frankie was probably right about the need to talk with Chub and that it might even lead to some relief but he was still terrified to open up the subject. Terrified by his inability to deal with it rationally. Terrified of himself.

Eventually, Chub opened up the subject for him.

You know, Chub said as he passed John another beer, still bugs me, that friendly fire thing. Never shot any noggies in the time we were there but I could've shot one of our own. Gets at me, sometimes.

If Donny's mention of the word Vietnam had set off a tremor in John, then Chub's casual comment was the quake that started the tsunami. John's shoulders began heaving uncontrollably, something he had now experienced countless times over the years. He knew that when this started to happen, he was helpless to control himself and he might as well let his emotions take over. He buried his face in his arm, still clutching his unopened beer. Chub watched in growing consternation.

You ok, mate?

John's next words came from a place he was unfamiliar with. It was as if Frankie was uttering the words for him; it was not him speaking.

You didn't shoot him.

Come again, mate?

I shot Hedley, said John, face still buried.

Chub was totally flummoxed. He didn't know whether he should go to John and comfort him or leave him alone. It must be the grog they had drunk, he reasoned. They'd put away nearly two slabs.

I fuckin' shot him. No one else, it was me.

John began blubbing, dropping his beer can and wrapping his arms over his head like a kid protecting himself from an assailant.

Jeez, mate. Chub rose to his feet, frightened that he was now witnessing some sort of breakdown. They were a long way from help. He moved toward John but stopped short of making physical contact.

You ok? Can I do something?

It was me. Saw him move. Fired and he screamed.

Shit, mate. Chub remained immobilised. I had no idea.

It was some time before John's blubbing eased and he looked up at Chub, firelight reflecting off his tears.

I shot him, mate. Fucked him for good.

Chub felt relief. Not relief from the knowledge that his bullets had not been the ones to hit Hedley, but relief that John had stopped blubbing. Another man crying was more than he could cope with. His relief was so intense that he felt lightheaded, causing him to speak way too flippantly for the occasion.

Didn't fuck 'im, mate. Hedley's doin' alright from what I've heard. Prob'ly done him a favour. With his compo, I mean.

John looked totally confused, wiping away tears, embarrassed at his melt down in front of Chub.

Lives less than a day's drive from here. Take yer over. Been meaning to visit 'im for years.

Hedley's still around?

Last I heard, mate.

John looked back in the fire.

Thought his injuries would've got him by now.

Take yer over.

Thanks, but couldn't face him after what I did. No way.

Suit yourself, mate.

Chub picked up John's unopened beer and handed it back to him.

Better be careful, could be a bit frothed up.

John took the can and held it, still looking into the fire. His mind now a scrambled mess of conflicting thoughts. He'd finally told someone other than his useless father, but now he had to tell Hedley. He simply had to.

Next day, Chub found John an old red-dirt-encrusted Stetson, plonked it on his head and told him that he now looked the part.

Little by little, John found himself becoming of use. Not much use, but a little. Helping Chub lift gear into the Landcruiser, a bit of cooking, even winching Chub down into one of the old round windmill wells in a bosun's chair. Dug by the Chinese, Chub had informed him. Our lot always dug in a rectangle.

One night there was a phone call for him. It was Frankie.

John took the receiver from Chub feeling an unexpected pleasure at the thought she had called him and at the sound of her voice.

She asked how he was.

Oh, you know, he said with a wink to Chub. Old mates, old stories. Few beers. What about you?

This was the first time he had ever inquired after her wellbeing. On the other end, Frankie was taken aback. Surely a sign of improvement in him.

When the conversation was over and John had hung up, he turned to Chub.

You know, mate. Might just take you up on that offer. The one about visiting Hedley.

No worries. I'll see if I can dig up a number for him. Happy Valley. Shit of a place. Blackfeller's paradise from what I hear.

When they were on another fencing run the next day, John asked him what he meant by a blackfeller's paradise.

Paradise for blackfellers, that's what. All bludging on Government grants. Same all over the country. I pay tax and they finish up with it.

You don't think they deserve it? Seem to remember you were going to improve their lot here.

Yeah, I did have plans but there were no blackfellas left here when I returned. Couldn't afford to put any on. Couldn't afford anyone.

Thought you were keen on letting them use their old tribal grounds or something like that. Sure you used to say that.

Things change. Never have anything to do with 'em now. You'll see when we drive out to Hedley's. Make yer own mind up.

John was thinking it was Chub who'd changed, but he said nothing.

Chapter 43

The knot in John's stomach had been no more than a loose granny knot when he and Chub had started on the five hour drive to Hedley's. Now they were almost there, the knot felt like it was binding his whole innards into an ever-tightening ball.

Bloody Abos, he heard Chub say. Would yer look at all this.

Chub skimmed his Landcruiser over a new-looking cattle grid and past an old bullet riddled sign on the righthand side of the road with the words 'Happy Valley' barely discernible under coatings of red dust.

What did that sign say on the left? Chub asked. The other one on your side. Something about a joint project between the government and some Abo mob?

John's mind was fixed on the conversation ahead. How was he even going to broach the subject? What reaction would Hedley have?

Did yer read that sign, mate? Chub repeated.

Sorry. No.

Taxpayer's money everywhere you look. New lookin' solar powered bore over there past the trees. Bet that cost an arm and a leg. Who paid for that?

None of this was registering with John. He hoped Chub didn't start in on Hedley when they arrived.

They got their first view of the homestead when Chub eased his Landcruiser over the same little rise that Hedley, Jane and Frank had stopped at all those years ago. The original asbestos sheeted cottage was still standing with the same lean but surrounding it were multiple dongers with shiny iron roofs. New yards and stables had replaced the old ones and the creek flats were well grassed. The old bush pole living shed had trebled in size and had a near-new roof. There was a cooking fire in one corner and quite a few figures could be seen moving around in its shade. Down at the yards, a group of youths looked like they were being given instructions on horse breaking, most sitting on the rails watching while someone worked a set of long-reins.

A pack of interesting looking dogs bounded out to greet them, led by a particularly savage looking bull terrier-greyhound cross with weepy pink eyes and randomly coloured patching.

Chub pulled up beside an open-topped Landcruiser wrapped in iron bars looking like a refugee from a Mad Max movie.

Bull-basher, explained Chub. Got one m'self. Not in as gooda nick as this one. Mine's just an old Diahatsu.

A tall fit looking fellow ambled out from the shade of the living shed to greet them. His hair greying under a sweat-stained hat and his muscular arms on show outside a sleeveless, check flannelette shirt.

Gerrout! He bellowed at the dogs who retreated a couple of metres. Chub eyed the bull terrier-cross warily as he eased himself out of the Landcruiser.

Forty kay set of jaws, but he won't 'urt yer, said the fellow, holding out a hand to Chub. Alfie.

Chub Jackson. They shook and Chub nodded to John. And this is John Mitchell. Come out to see Hedley.

Oh, righto. Havin' a snooze this time a day but we'll give 'im a boot. Follow me.

As they were walking toward one of the dongers, the fellow turned to Chub.

Don't remember me, do yer.

It was a statement, not a question. Chub looked at him.

Can't say I do.

Born on your run.

Chub held his look, recognition growing.

Frank and Jane? Little Alfie, the eldest?

A grin spread across Chub's face but there was no return grin from Alfie. He mounted a set of steps onto the veranda of one of the dongers and called through the flyscreen door.

Hey, old cuz. Coupla visitors for yer. Can't sleep all day.

After a few moments slow footsteps could be heard and a shadowy form appeared behind the flyscreen.

Who we got here?

The door opened and there stood Hedley, shirtless and bootless, wearing only a pair of grubby jeans, white hair rumpled up like a spinifex roly-poly.

It was the first time John had seen him since soon after he'd lost his arm. The shock of his short stump and distorted Donald Duck tattoo had not been lessened by the years, although the tattoo had faded a little. Hedley grinned.

Chub. Bin expectin' yer.

Chub held his hand out for a shake, but Hedley moved past it, inside and close. He gave Chub a light hug around the ribs with his left arm and stepped back to look at him again.

Good to see yer after all these years.

Likewise, said Chub. Remember John, here?

Yeah, sure do.

Hedley held out his left hand and John reached out awkwardly with his left.

Great to see you again, Hedley, said John, giving Hedley's hand a quick squeeze.

At first, the sight of Hedley's stump had been confronting for John, setting forth little tremors of panic. Now, he found himself relaxing a little in Hedley's calm presence. Hedley's features were surprisingly smooth and he had the serene bearing of an elder.

Have you blokes met my little cousin? Hedley said.

Alfie towered over them all.

Sure have, said Chub. Chip off the old block. Big chip.

Runs the place now, said Hedley.

Put you out to pasture old cuz, Alfie grinned.

Pasture be buggered. Not ready for that by a long shot.

Chub looked up at Alfie.

Sorry to hear about your dad. Passed on a while ago I heard. And mum?

Alfie nodded and shrugged without answering.

All long gone, said Hedley. Mick was the first to go but he helped us get started here. All up there now with the old ones. He motioned up toward the escarpment.

Yeah, well. Better get going, said Alfie. Good to meet youse.

As soon as Alfie had gone, Hedley motioned for Chub and John to take a seat on the veranda.

I'll put a brew on and then take you both for a look-see around the place.

Can't stay too long, said Chub quickly. Gotta get back to town tonight.

Hedley was having none of this.

Rubbish. Stay the night, plenty of room. Too much catchin' up to do.

John looked at Chub, wanting to stay, more time to unload.

Chub was reluctant. Really should get back. Don't like leaving the place for more than a day.

What about Donny? said John.

Chub lifted his battered old hat and itched underneath.

Yeah. Spose … last time old Donny got pissed and forgot to feed the dogs. Forgot to do any fuckin' thing. But alright. Have to get going at sparrows tomorrow, though.

After they had been shown over a few of the dongers and had a look at one of the new solar bore pumps, Hedley took his guests over toward the yards. John's mind was nervously on the past, waiting for the right time to broach the subject of Vietnam. Maybe in the evening.

Tell me, said Hedley, how many head you run over there now, Chub?

No more'n a thousand right now. Been sellin' 'em off while the prices are high.

Hedley looked surprised but said nothing.

What about you? said Chub.

Full capacity and more. 'Bout two thousand.

How'd yer build up the place like this? Bit of help?

Hedley knew what Chub was getting at but shot back a straight answer.

Bit lately, but all hard yakka, really. No other way to describe it. Kept costs down early and built up slow.

Borrow?

Nah, stuck to me budget. Puttin' down the early bores nearly busted me but it paid off in the end. Lifted the carrying capacity of the joint out of sight.

When they reached the yards, the young would-be stockmen were taking it in turns to long-rein a nervous looking bay with a white blaze. Their tutor, a tough looking middle-aged woman, was speaking to them in Wadjarri. Her soft tones belying her looks.

That's Nola, said Hedley leaning on the rails. Alfie's sister. Bin runnin' kids through here for forty years. Keeps 'em off the streets for a while.

Free labour, Chub grunted.

Could call it that but some of 'em need a lot of looking after. Specially of late. Drugged-up city kids, some of 'em.

Surely the government must help you out there, John leant on the rails next to Hedley. You're doing their work for them.

Got a grant to build the dongers. Only took 'em about fifty years to pitch in. Better late than never, I spose.

Well, good on you, said John.

After Chub's 'blackfeller's paradise' comments he had been expecting the worst, but he could only pick up a confident independence about the place.

At dusk the camp kitchen swelled in numbers as workers came in from different parts of the property. There was even a German backpacker, beetroot red from the sun, hands a mess of blisters, but exuberant at his lot.

Vere else on der planet can you get dis sort of experience? he exclaimed to John.

Dinner consisted of roo tail and spuds. All the goats were shot out years ago and now the main problem was wild dogs, according to Hedley. Much harder to shoot.

Chub agreed. Big numbers down my way, he said. Give the newborn calves buggery. No sheep farmers left along the Murchison now. Remember how the neighbours all ran sheep back in your day?

Hedley nodded.

All gone over to cattle now. Shearing sheds all sitting idle for years. Blowin' away in the winds.

Everyone wanted to chat with John, curious to know about Melbourne. Young kids bug-eyed at his attempts to describe the trams and high-rise towers. In recent years, nobody had shown the slightest interest in anything he had to say beyond advice on which supermarkets were good for dumpster diving and which bridges provided the most protection from the weather. When it was time for the swag, John realised Hedley had disappeared and he hadn't had a chance to talk to him about Vietnam.

As he lay in one of the dongers, listening to Chub snore, he kicked himself for missing his chance. He couldn't sleep for thinking about it. He'd have to bail Hedley up in the morning when Chub would be wanting to take off back to his property. Everything would be rushed and besides, how would Hedley react if he dredged it all up right when they were leaving? With no time to think, he might do anything. Neither Hedley nor Chub had even mentioned Vietnam in all their station talk, maybe he should shut-up about it like everyone else.

Chapter 44

Sure enough, Chub was champing at the bit to get going in the early morning.

No time for a cuppa? Hedley asked.

No, sorry, mate, said Chub, already heading for his Landcruiser. Too much to do back home and only old Donny on his own.

Hedley, Alfie and John followed him toward the Landcruiser. John was walking behind Hedley, mind racing. He needed to say something to Hedley. Chub was already opening the driver's door and Alfie's presence was complicating things further.

Thanks for putting us up, he heard Chub say.

John's heart thumped into overdrive. Now or never. He tried to think of his youthful mantra. Fate. Say something, any bloody thing, and leave it to fate. He would accept Hedley's reaction, whatever it was.

Excuse us for a sec, mate, he said apologetically to Alfie as he put his arms around the shoulders of a surprised Hedley and Chub and guided them away from Chub's Landcruiser and away from the confused Alfie.

Sorry about this fellers, but I gotta say something in private.

His mind was becoming surprisingly calm as he guided them to the evil-looking, bar-wrapped, bull-basher Landcruiser. He was going to do this. Hang the consequences.

Both Chub and Hedley were silent. Chub had an inkling as to what was coming and Hedley strangely sensitive to the moment.

John tried to collect his thoughts into plain, ordinary words. But now all he could think about was the recoil of his rifle and Hedley's screams. He had to grip one of the bull-basher's side-bars while he pulled himself together again.

Hedley, he said.

Hedley waited but no words followed from John.

John gasped in a lungful of air as he found himself patting the spot on his shoulder where the butte of his rifle had been pressed when he fired that day in the rain-soaked jungle.

Chub looked at Hedley, but Hedley didn't return his look, eyes on John, waiting patiently.

The shot, said John, now glaring down in front of himself at the bar he was gripping fiercely.

I fired it. The shot that hit you. It was me.

John swivelled to face Hedley, expecting to see his indigenous features drawn in fury. But he saw only mild curiosity.

Hedley nodded before answering.

That's ok. Don't matter who fired what. All doin' a job.

But it was me! I fired and you screamed. The scream and everything … it all happened at once. I fuckin' shot you mate.

Again, the curious look.

You reckon? Forward scout, weren't yer?

John nodded, now too drained to form words that weren't in the script he had hurriedly written for himself.

Then you'd a been carryin' an Armalite, wouldn't yer?

John nodded again. What was Hedley saying?

Then it wasn't your bullet hit me. Couldn't 've been.

John knew what he knew. It was, he said weakly. Heard you scream.

Nah, said Hedley firmly. Docs at Vampire reckon I'd a still had an arm if I'd been hit by an Armalite. Angle it hit and all that. Bullet hit me was fired by an SLR No question.

John closed his eyes and Chub thought he may have been about to faint. He made a move forward to support John, but John gripped the Landcruiser bar again and opened his eyes.

Could've even been fired by one of my section, Hedley went on. We had two newbies didn't know up from down. Anyway, doesn't matter. We were all in there tryin' to do what they trained us to do.

All three men were now leaning on the bull-basher. Alfie was on his way back to the camp kitchen. Not his business. Left the old fellers to themselves.

Did the docs pull the bullet outa you? said Chub.

Nah, went right through … but they were pullin' bits and pieces out of us diggers day and night. They knew their stuff. I was shot by an SLR They reckon there was no question about it. An SLR did the damage.

Could've been me, said Chub. I had an SLR

Hedley turned on Chub, showing his first hint of aggression.

Mate, are you deaf? It doesn't matter! They trained us up to do a job and we were all tryin' our best to do that job. Somebody up the ranks stuffed up and put us in the same area. That poor bugger, or those poor buggers, prob'ly know it and had to live with it ever since. But even them fellers are not to blame ... we were in a war ... bullets flyin' round ...

Hedley's voice trailed off as he noticed John beginning to slump. Both he and Chub made a grab for him but John crumpled silently into the red dust beside the Landcruiser's front wheel. His heart rate off the Richter scale but blood not getting where it should.

Waves of nausea, regret and relief were quickly being replaced by rage and hysteria. The legs that wouldn't support him began threshing wildly, trying to run but only rearranging the ground surface mosaic, small quartz pebbles and innocent ants being swept sideways.

He began thumping the ground with the fleshy side of his right fist, smashing the enemy his whole life had become. Smash it to pieces. But the red earth and quartz pebbles wouldn't smash and the side of his fist turned to blood.

Easy, mate. Easy. Chub grabbed John's fist before it did any more damage to itself while Hedley tried to pin his kicking legs and bucking torso.

For a moment John's fury made him as powerful as any mickey calf Hedley and Chub had tangled with at branding time in the early days, but he soon subsided into a pitiful sobbing and bellowing mess. Just like a calf after the searing branding iron had left its imprint.

Get 'im out of the sun, eh? said Hedley. Inside one of the dongers.

Chub nodded. Both men were stunned, feeling a little like they were back in Vietnam again themselves.

Chub gripped John under the armpits and Hedley slipped his arm under John's feet.

They shuffled across the open ground with Hedley leading the way, walking backwards.

A concerned Alfie was watching from the shade of the camp kitchen with Nola.

Old feller in trouble. Better help.

Nola followed her brother out into the sun. She was the Happy Valley healer.

John woke later. Not from a sleep, but a state of mind.

Among his seething emotions of anger and confusion, remorse and sheer self-pity he felt something else emerging. Distant at first but slowly seeping up through his senses, switching off one overloaded circuit after another until he became aware that the something was a voice working its way through his insides. He was lying on his back on a bed. His bungalow at Frankie's? Not her voice. Words he couldn't understand. An indigenous voice. Hedley's place. Not his voice though.

He opened his eyes and saw Nola. Her expression timeless, eyes not on him but gazing out through an insect screen door at the ever-present escarpment. Singing, rhythmic, repetitive, dreamy.

The next morning when they were leaving, Chub more impatient than ever to get back to his property, John asked Hedley if there was anything he could do for him? Maybe a gift of some sort. He felt hopelessly indebted to the man. Frustratingly so. If only he was rich or a magician who could conjure up anything Hedley wanted.

Hedley just laughed. Got everythin' I need.

John climbed into the passenger's seat of Chub's Landcruiser.

Hedley was giving Chub a farewell cack-handed handshake through the driver's window when he suddenly looked past Chub across the cabin to John and fixed him with a big grin.

Johnno. Just thought what ya can do for me. He thumped Chub playfully on the chest. Talk this old bastard into takin' on some of the young blokes I've trained up.

Chub responded with a half grin assuming Hedley was joking.

Steady on. Think they're gonna ride round on shanks pony? Don't have horses no more.

That's ok. I'll supply the plant and boys and do all your mustering for free if you let me run cattle on your place. All that good river country goin' to waste.

Chub looked at him to see if he was serious. He was. Chub shrugged awkwardly.

Dunno. Wouldn't want to mix breeds and I've got no fences down there now. Flood took 'em out twenty year ago.

No matter. My young blokes'll re-fence.

Chub pursed his lips and ummed and ahhed for a bit.

Pay yer good agistment. Besides, Frank's kids'll die and never see their country again way things are goin'.

Chub looked long and hard at Hedley. He was aware John was an interested spectator to all this and there was a dormant sense of right and wrong playing out inside him.

Dunno about this, he said.

Chub, I'll pay agistment, do yer mustering for you and re-fence that river paddock which'll up the value of yer run. What more can I do, mate?

Chub began wiping dust off the fuel gauge on the Landcruiser's dash with the broad of his thumb while he tried to take all this in. He would have to refuel in town before heading home. He looked up at Hedley again.

Ok if I think on it? Never any good at snap decisions.

Hedley grinned. You think, mate. And you … he looked back at John. You start sleepin' easy. Ok? All that's behind us.

John did sleep. All the way back to Eumarella.

They had a system going. Chub found the broken end of the fence wire, often buried under wind-blown red sand, and pulled it tight. John held it from recoiling while Chub untangled the other end and handed it to John while he carried out the repairs. Simple enough.

At first John had found the forty plus degree heat and ever-present flies debilitating. Leave the fencing pliers or wire strainers on the ground for more than a few minutes and they were too hot to pick up.

How did Chub do this stuff every day on his own? But they had been at it for a week now and somehow John was beginning to find a kind of solace in the repetition.

Just what I do, Chub had said. Kangaroos and emus bust the wires, I fix 'em. Along with every other bloody thing.

Shit, the wire was hot. John tried using his shirt as a kind of a glove. Chub, who had hands of leather, scoffed at the use of gloves. Chub came crawling out from under a mulga bush, having found the other end of the wire. They had been talking politics when he went under the bush, the mine-at-all-costs mentality of the west. Pastoralists last, miners first, Chub had said. Now he seemed to have lost the thread of the conversation. He began forming a figure eight with the length of wire John was holding.

When you booked on that bus, mate? he asked.

John had to think. Soon. Day after tomorrow, maybe. I'll check it out tonight.

Right, no worries. Chub began setting up the wire strainers. So, he said, that wasn't your missus who rang me?

Nah. That was Frankie. Landlady. She's been helping me out.

Right.

Got myself in a bit of a rut. She's been great.

Right. So, never got hitched?

No way. Couldn't deal with meself so what hope dealing with someone else? Know what I mean?

Chub nodded, focused on the wire strainers.

You? John asked.

Hitched? Nah, not me. Went close once, back in the early days. When I'd just taken over here.

Yeah?

German, she was. Most beautiful thing I ever set eyes on. Hitchin' through town, met up in the pub. Give her a few days work and one thing led to another.

And didn't work out?

More than worked out at first. She got me a beauty. Right through the heart, as they say. I wanted to marry her, have kids, the whole lot. And she loved the place. Fired up mum's garden. Planted stuff around the house. All that.

But didn't work out?

Chub shook his head and began levering the wire strainers.

Homesick. Up and left. Predictable, I s'pose when yer look back at it. But that was me. Took the wind right out of me sails. Never game to try that caper again. Woman round a place gives it a shot in the arm. But that'll never happen now.

John took a step back as Chub clipped off the excess ends of wire with his pliers.

Maybe the deal with Hedley might give it a shot in the arm. Thought any more about that?

Chub began packing up the tools. Not really. Place is mine. I'm comfortable enough with things the way they are. Can't say I'm that keen on a bunch of blackfellas runnin' round the place. Never get any peace.

Hedley would look after you.

Sure he would, but once you sign up to these sort of things they don't go away. What happens when Hedley goes? I'm stuck with some leasing arrangement that goes on in perpetuity or whatever the legal people call it. Same as bein' tied to the bank.

Don't think it would add a bit of life to your property? Like Hedley said, it could be good for everyone.

And like I said, there goes my peace and quiet.

Chub slung the tools in the back of the 'Cruiser with a thump and they climbed into the cab.

What about if you signed up to something short term? Like, a year or something. See how it goes.

Dunno, said Chub firing up the diesel motor. Dunno, dunno, dunno.

Chapter 45

Thursday 4th May.

Frankie's electronic diary announced to one and all that she would not be contactable on this day and that all meetings should be scheduled for the following day.

Did she owe this day to him or did she owe this day to herself? She lay in bed pondering this question. He deserved the day for being a wonderful, caring, sweet human being who had provided every one of their shared days with another layer of richness that complemented her own spiritual energy. Sometimes subliminal, often duplicating, but treasured. She deserved the day because it was the day he had bloody-well left her, and she had to cope with the never-ending grief.

It had been three years today since he died. Some days she barely thought of him, busy days or days when her mind was skimming over shiny sun-reflecting pebbles like a mountain creek, babbling to its own tune. But most days he was there, wrapped around her like a cloak, normally light but occasionally heavy. Impeding her.

She instinctively reached for her phone and went to her messages knowing who the caring ones would be, and, sure enough, top of the list, Angela.

Frankie read her loving message, full of her favourite 'Dad' memories and, when Angela wished her little Jordie had been able to hug his grandfather just once, Frankie allowed her tears to flow. The bastard. It wasn't just Frankie he'd left behind.

He wasn't a bastard, of course. The bastards were the board members of James Hardie who knowingly allowed their cancer-causing asbestos product to be sold to an unsuspecting public. But Frankie snapped this thought closed, she knew too much about her own psyche to allow any negativity on this day.

The second message was from Jack's sister, full of her own childhood memories and wanting to catch up on the weekend. The third message, dear reliable Cindy, suggesting she come around and they could play a few tunes together for Jack. Again a few tears flowed.

She would reply to all the messages, but she chose to reply to Cindy's first. Her thumbs skittered over the keys on her phone. 'Yes. Come around this afternoon and bring your guitar.' She needed to share this day with someone other than Jack.

As Frankie talked, she walked. Phone pressed to her ear, sheep-skin slippers wet from the dew. She picked her way around his building material, being careful not to come in contact with the edge of the blue roof sheets still leaning against the bungalow. They could cut into an ankle like a steak knife slicing an over-ripe tomato. She knew.

It was nearly midnight in London and she had been talking with Angela for over an hour. When Jack's condition had really gone downhill, Angela had flown back home to share her father's final weeks, days, hours. She and Frankie had watched his human form change from Jack to a transparent imitation of Jack, like an insect's discarded exoskeleton.

The first part of their phone conversation had been spent remembering that shared time but, healing as it may have been in the longer term, it became too much in the shorter. Angela had complained of having mascara-stained cheeks in a laughing-crying voice. They were now trying to cheer each other up with talk of the present. Life after Jack, life after dad. Little Jordie, Frankie's impending retirement, the things Jack had missed out on. In the end it was Jordie who ended the conversation, waking and bawling for attention.

We always let you cry yourself back to sleep, said Frankie. You'll be at his beck and call forever if you keep picking him up whenever he cries.

Things aren't done that way anymore, mum. At this stage of their development, it's very important not to allow any feelings of neglect.

You survived.

But I was special.

You were.

And so was dad, but life goes on. Anyway … must go, mum. Jordie's not letting up.

It was still another five minutes before their fingers finally found the little red buttons at the bottom of their phones.

That afternoon the autumn sunshine was irresistible, so Cindy and Frankie took their guitars and glasses of champagne out into the backyard.

They picked over some of the old Snoopies tunes for a laugh, chatted and drank.

Conscious of neighbours, they kept their voices and playing to a muted level but there was something uplifting in bouncing off each other, matching notes, timing the harmonies and improvising.

Frankie tried the old Reid Stevens song, 'Like Martians on the Moon' that she had sung at the Station Hotel before visiting Jack in jail, but it brought on tears. She had to stop playing and Cindy put an arm around her.

Oh dear, said Frankie. Too many bubbles. Sorry. I really do have to move on. She looked around her. Trouble is, he's everywhere.

Cindy followed Frankie's sweeping arm gesture.

The building junk. I'll ask Daniel again if he'll collect it. No, I'll *tell* him to collect it, if that's what you want. No asking, I'll demand it.

That would be nice Cind.

But only if you do something for me.

What?

Promise me you'll think about performing together again. We could start out doing open mikes, that sort of thing. Jams.

I promise. But only after I retire.

Which should be soon?

If they ever let me go.

They hugged and began playing again only to be interrupted by the side gate opening and the unexpected form of John appearing, suitcase in hand.

Frankie put her hand to her mouth and looked at Cindy. Oh, no. I forgot to pick up John. I'm sorry, she called to him.

Nothing to be sorry for, said John, joining them. I jumped on the Skybus and a train. Easy.

So, did you enjoy your trip?

Yeah. I did, thanks to you.

Frankie could detect a certain ease in his demeanour that had not been there before. Something must have gone right for him.

You look suntanned, she said. Like you've been on a Mediterranean cruise.

John laughed. Only a chuckle, but again, something new to him.

You could say that, but I didn't see a hell of a lot of ocean out there. Only liquid in large quantities was beer; never drunk so much of the stuff. Quite happy if I never see another drop of it; give me heartburn, it did.

Frankie knew this was a sensitive subject, but she tentatively asked him if he would like to join them in a glass of bubbles.

Nah, nah. Not for me.

What about a play? Cindy asked, indicating the guitar. I heard you were a bass player.

John seemed a little surprised at this offer. Dunno, he said.

You're probably ready for a rest, said Frankie. We can go inside and play where we won't disturb you.

No. No need. I'm not tired. In fact, I might just have a strum. I'll grab that guitar you lent me. Hang on one tick.

A few minutes later, all three were cautiously working their way through a few Beatles songs, John quick to pick up on their rhythm.

Very good, said Cindy, when they had finished. Perhaps he could be our bass player? She smiled at Frankie.

Up to him, said Frankie, not sure if Cindy was serious.

But John was now picking a few blues notes, so intent on his playing that their words hadn't registered with him.

How about we have a go at Boom Boom by the Animals? You girls know that one? Midnight at the Southview Surf Club, we played that.

It was a complete stuff up with John and Frankie playing the wrong chords and Cindy forgetting the words, but they had a laugh. And a laugh was something.

Hedley saw the movement from the corner of his eye. Upwind. The scent may have come first. Wild dog. A black one with white streaks, two more dogs following. They were across the face of the escarpment from where he was standing, heading for the newborn calf he was trying to protect. Down on his arse in a flash and firing. Direct hit, but not a kill, the dog howling in agony. Hedley felt a belt of remorse, his intention had been to fire over the dog and scare it off but somehow his reflexes had worked faster than his brain. He liked dogs, respected them, not like those goats which were good tucker. As the dog's howling intensified, he had a flashback to that moment in the rain-soaked Vietnam jungle when the firing had broken out. He could remember the sound of the bullet hitting him but not the sound of his own screaming, that was the memory that poor bugger John was stuck with.

The howling was now ringing around the escarpment, bouncing off each quartz outcrop, echoing down every crevice into wallaby lairs and into the big cave, stirring the living daylights out of the resting spirits of the old people, out of Frank, Jane and Mick.

Hedley moved quickly over to where the dog had crawled behind a tuft of wind-blown mulga clinging to the rocky slope and fired again. Silence from the dog but its howls were still echoing. He'd stepped over a line with the old people and they were letting him know it and he had to squat down, balance deserting him for a moment.

Should've known better. Shootin' this high up on the escarpment.

He stood up and called out toward the big cave, still some distance away around and further up the cliff face. Me wanguny. Proper sorry fella yuwarrimanha. Then waited fearfully hoping that things would settle down. Eventually they did and he began to relax again. He'd been given a warning. He sat down on a low rock, back to the cave and immediately aunty Jane filled his mind. Maraji. Prob'ly you tellin' me orf, he said to himself. She had given him the only hugs he could remember getting in his boyhood years. Her big encircling arms, her voice, her smell were never far from his thoughts.

He let his gaze wander to the horizon then to the Happy Valley homestead below. The yards, Nola showing a couple of young kids how to saddle up, the new bores and dongers and cattle grazing on the creek flats. The spirits were resting again.

He began to sing, a low resonating mumble of words. A song that he knew came from his father, the father he had never known. A song about country, the country he had been taken from by the white police as a child before he and that country had time to become acquainted with each other. But he sang for this country below and around him, Djujima country. This country had taken him in now and he was singing his thanks.

Donny saw a column of crows spiralling high up into the early morning sky; looked like they were hovering over the old blacks' camp. When he rode up on his stock bike the whole macabre scene was laid out before him; the crows retreating from the sound of his bike,

Chub's 'Cruiser with the driver's door still open, a shotgun laying where it had dropped on the ground and beside it a mutilated body sprawled between two termite riddled mulga doorway posts, all that was left of Frank and Jane's humpy. Chubby Jackson was no more.

Donny turned off the engine and sat on the bike in silent shock for a while. Shock became sadness then wondering what had pushed Chub over the edge. He dismounted and did what he had to do, covering the mess with a few sheets of iron that he dragged out of the surrounding ruin. Why would you choose this junk heap to do yourself in, old mate? He noticed a scrap of paper held down with a stone near where the shotgun had fallen. He removed the stone and picked up the paper which was a hastily scrawled note flecked with Chub's blood. He shook a few ants off the note and read it, then scratched his head and read it again. Bugger me, Hedley Yangaboora. Leavin' the lot to a blackfella.

He scrunched the note up, mounted the bike and rode off toward Nanderra.

Acknowledgements

Thanks: firstly to Reid Stevens, singer songwriter, Vietnam veteran and mate; to Victoria Templeton-Tainsh, cuz and editor extraordinaire; to brother Andy for overseeing all musical references; to Anthony Cooper and Laurie Muller for their insightful comments; to Andrew Ballard for his copy editing; to early readers Bianca Tainsh, Erin Schrauwen and Lachie Tainsh and to the Cusacks for their Melbourne 'backyard'.

This book can be purchased through
all the major online outlets.